# THE PROSPERINE PAPERS

OTHER BOOKS BY JAN CLAUSEN:

*After Touch* (poems), Out & Out Books, 1975
*Waking at the Bottom of the Dark* (poems), Long Haul Press, 1979
*Mother, Sister, Daughter, Lover* (stories), The Crossing Press, 1980
*A Movement of Poets: Thoughts on Poetry and Feminism* (essays),
    Long Haul Press, 1982
*Duration* (poetry and prose), Hanging Loose Press, 1985
*Books & Life* (essays), Ohio State University Press, 1988

# THE PROSPERINE PAPERS

## JAN CLAUSEN

✳ **THE CROSSING PRESS**
FREEDOM, CALIFORNIA 95019

**Library of Congress Cataloging-in-Publication Data**

Clausen, Jan, 1950–
    The prosperine papers / by Jan Clausen
       p.  cm.
      ISBN 0-98594-274-7         ISBN 0-89594-273-9 (pbk.)
      I. Title.
PS3553.L348P7  1988
813'.54—dc19                      88-22834
                                          CIP

*To all my real-life heroines, especially*
*Edna Wright Shannon*
*and*
*Carmen Sanchez*

# ACKNOWLEDGMENTS

I would like to acknowledge the support of the Centrum Foundation in Port Townsend, Washington, which provided a writing residency at the earliest stage of this novel's gestation. During a subsequent, far more labor-intensive phase, the Berkshire Forum afforded invaluable writing time—thanks to Betty and Herman Liveright and Susan Mitchell. Lisa Albrecht gave shelter and encouragement during my trips to the Twin Cities. Bob Stephens was the perfect landlord for a writer seeking peace and quiet in the heart of Brooklyn. Frances Goldin has been an unfailingly perceptive, diligent, and accessible literary agent; Kate Dunn, as always, a sensitive editor. Jen Green of the Women's Press, London, also offered helpful editorial advice. My special thanks are due to Elaine and John Gill for their support of my fiction over many years.

Conversations with several individuals contributed to my perspective on the social drama which figures in this narrative. I would particularly like to thank Meridel LeSueur for urging that I visit the Iron Range, as well as for the inspiration provided by *North Star Country* and the rest of her work. Linda Backiel furnished suggestive details about political repression during World War I. For a sense of atmosphere as much as historical specifics, I relied on a number of written sources. Foremost among these are Carolyn Ashbaugh's *Lucy Parsons: An American Revolutionary*; Paul Avrich's *An American Anarchist: The Life of Volairine de Cleyre*; Kenneth Carley's *The Sioux Uprising of 1862*; Ralph Chaplin's *Wobbly: The Rough-and-Tumble Story of an American Radical*; Melvyn Dubovsky's *We Shall Be All*; Elizabeth Gurley Flynn's *The Rebel Girl*; and Mary Heaton Vorse's journalism and autobiographical writing about the 1916 Iron Range strike. I particularly appreciate having had the opportunity to consult materials at the Iron Range Resource Center in Chisholm, Minnesota, and the Minnesota Historical Society in St. Paul.

*Merely a notion that the tape-recorder*
*should have caught some ghost of us: that tape recorder*
*not merely played but should have listened to us,*
*and could instruct those after us:*
*this we were, this is how we tried to love,*
*and these are the forces they had ranged against us,*
*and these are the forces we had ranged within us,*
*within us and against us, against us and within us.*
                                        —Adrienne Rich

*When you come perhaps cd. help me w/ my papers? Am getting worried if I don't take them in hand soon Lord may call me Home any day now (who knows.). Bless you Merry Xmas be Happy.*

Thus Grandma Rose, in a P.S. to the letter she had begun on the bottom of a Hallmark Christmas card and continued on a neatly-torn half-sheet of onionskin. The economy of paper and the abbreviated style with its scanting of articles and pronouns—as though she were in haste, or in fear of wasting ink—were characteristic. So, nowadays, were the slight incoherence of sentence structure and the wobbly deformity of the cultivated hand that in the second decade of the century had befitted the proud possessor of a State of Minnesota country school teaching certificate.

The mention of God was more surprising. Like nearly all my midwestern relatives, Rose Schlaghoffer was a decided Christian, but a tasteful one, a reserved Methodist who would never dream of crowding her bedroom walls with garish portraits of sloe-eyed Jesuses like rock stars, as my father's side, the Baptists, tend to do. If anything, she went in for sepia prints: the Praying Hands, a Madonna and Child woodcut. Her Christmas card was a secular sleighing scene. As I slipped it back into my briefcase, I smiled at that *getting worried*, which seemed a bit belated since she'd be ninety-one in August. I hoped the note of conventional piety didn't mean she was being brainwashed over there at Fellowship Hill, the "senior residence" she'd recently moved into. The place was run by the Presbyterian Church, and it now occurred to me that a parochial old folks' home might present some of the same drawbacks as a parochial summer camp or kindergarten.

1

If so, I would know all about it soon enough. The plane had left the sunny upper realms and was plunging earthward through a dense, capricious atmosphere. The Twin Cities were socked in. The captain had just turned on the seatbelt sign and announced the evening's forecast, another foot of snow. I congratulated myself on having lugged my new fiberfill coat and winter boots all up and down the warm, drippy hillsides of San Francisco, where the Modern Language Association had been holding its annual convention. I preferred not to give my relatives the satisfaction of appearing unprepared for their atrocious winter, on which Minnesotans pride themselves as Manhattanites do on gridlock.

I was on my way home to New Jersey and Linda and trouble: the flu season, some guilty explanations, the arid grind of a last semester's teaching at a university where I'd been denied tenure. I was coming from stress and infidelity, heartburn and shockingly expensive Scotch, too much stale gossip, paté, and overripe brie ingested standing up, a debilitating round of interviews for unappetizing positions at dowdy provincial colleges. There'd been a major disappointment when Tillie Olsen cancelled a lunch date, and a memorable one night stand with a presenter from a session called "Woman-Identified Themes and Imagery in Some Writing of the Harlem Renaissance." Now, briefly in limbo between two continental extremes, I was dropping out of the sky to pay a duty visit.

Or maybe that would be putting it too harshly. Grandma Rose had been a favorite of mine ever since the summer I was twelve, when my parents had shipped me off for a month in the Old Country (for in fact her Minnesota was to me, who had been raised on the temperate shore of Puget Sound, a sort of internal, domestic equivalent of the Europe of my forebears, as unintelligibly charged with menace and desire as the valley of the Wye or of the Elbe must have seemed to the children of the original immigrants). This had been my first time away from home alone, and I balked and sulked until, Mother confided years later, they nearly didn't send me after all. I recall spending much of the lengthy train trip reading *Jane Eyre*, immersed in the plight of a young orphan oppressed by heartless relatives. It gave me tremendous romantic satisfaction to picture St. Paul as a bleakly sweltering midwestern Lowood.

Twenty-four hours after my arrival I'd not only abandoned my plans for extravagant misery, I'd almost forgotten to be homesick. True, I was unimpressed with Grandpa Eugene, who'd been my favorite when I was

2

ten. Now he had a "nervous" stomach and gall bladder trouble, and was forever swigging Pepto Bismal and pecking away at microscopic, pale meals. He'd been a high school teacher for many years, and I wondered how his students had borne the bland, childish jokes I felt compelled to laugh at. He puttered. He took forever in the bathroom. He sent me running for the Audubon manual every time an unfamiliar bird showed up at the backyard feeder. He was universally described as "such a kind man."

Grandma Rose, on the other hand, I recognized immediately as my sort of person. Grandma was effective. She could drive a nail as straight as my father could, with just as little fuss, and she tatted exquisite borders for napkins and pillow cases. I suppose I must have glimpsed her famed asperity, but undoubtedly she was gentler with me than she'd been with her own children, for it would be years before I saw the point of the standing family joke that it was she and not Grandpa who ought to have been the German.

Her bite and starch suited me. So did her rhubarb cobbler, her homemade pickles and her Graham bread, though at home I was considered a fussy eater. She taught me knit two purl two and passable pie crust—where Mother could barely get me to make my bed—and rewarded me with stories about growing up on the farm near Lake Itasca. "A country fit for a prince, and a man can live like one if he's willing to use a little elbow grease," she quoted her father's saying, while I, still full of Lowood and Jane Eyre and the romance of deprivation, ignored her nostalgia for quilting bees and berrying expeditions in my preference for a few picturesquely grim anecdotes. There had been a late spring following an especially harsh winter when the half-starved family got sick gorging on bitter greens, a year they paid their taxes by selling every drop of milk and ounce of butter they produced, and when Grandma fed the pig a biscuit smeared with the hated Oleo her mother whipped her for it. There'd been frosty dawns she'd lie down in the meadow grass and hug the sleeping cows for warmth.

But my favorite story, and by far the most dramatic, was of how at fifteen she'd gone to high school against her father's wishes. The distance was too great to travel every day, so she'd secretly arranged to scrub floors and wait tables at a roominghouse in town in exchange for bed and board. When she proclaimed her plan Grandpa Bright insisted she was needed

3

at home; Grandma Bright prayed tearfully, as usual. I couldn't get enough of her description of her last morning on the farm, how she'd stood there waiting for the neighbor's wagon in front of the only house she'd ever lived in (which I pictured as an elegant Victorian affair with a wraparound porch and gingerbread trim, though a photograph my mother showed me later revealed it to have been weatherbeaten and lopsided). "I was wearing my best dress, with the rest in a cardboard suitcase. I was shaking, but I was not about to shed tears. I kept telling myself, 'Rose, you have a right to an education.' " The stairstep sisters with the extravagant floral names had wept and wailed, however, and Grandma Bright appeared at the kitchen door in her perpetual apron, a fork in one hand and a bowl of half-beaten eggwhites in the other, when Grandpa Bright came riding up from the fields lashing the tired plow horse.

The patriarch unleashed a torrent of reproaches, topped by one bitter threat. The threshers must be cooked for, the potatoes dug and gathered, and who was to help out when the new baby arrived? If she went to town now, she mustn't think of coming back. "We'll fend without you, hussy, you and your high school education!"

"Father, I am going to town. I have to go," was all the defense she could squeeze out. Her mother opened her mouth, but thought better of it. It wasn't her way to argue when Ezra worked himself up, she'd let him simmer down a little and then have her say. "And the whole time, she kept beating those eggwhites. Of course you can't let them go flat once you've started in. I believe she was still at it when Mr. Tinsley drove up in the spring wagon. To this day I can picture her hand going round— remember how I showed you with the whisk, it's the wrist and not the arm that does the work. She held the bowl high up, so it rested on her stomach. I didn't know when I'd see her again. My sister Ivy was born the following week, and I didn't get word for days."

As soon as Grandma Bright was back on her feet, however, regular communication was established between farm and town, and the scholar-housemaid's drudgery seemed lighter when she could look forward to little packages: a warm winter nightgown, a slice of somebody's birthday cake. By spring Grandpa Bright had relented somewhat and she could go home for Easter, a happy outcome without which, I later understood, I might never have heard the tale; for Grandma Rose had her standards, corsetings strict as the stays her own overweight, harassed mother had

4

seldom bothered with, and along with everyone and everything in her vicinity, the Past was expected to toe an exacting mark. As matters luckily stood, she could afford to think back, to tease me with reminders of ancestral contingency, the old shivery prospect of genetic roads not taken: "And if I hadn't gone to town to attend high school, I likely wouldn't have married Grandpa. Not that anything much happened at the time, but he noticed me. He remembered that later."

"But I wouldn't be me if you hadn't married Grandpa," I'd object on cue, with a child's crass certainty that history happened merely to get to *us*. Not that Grandpa himself seemed so indispensable to the working out of the family destiny, but without him, her life might have been unthinkably altered. I suddenly found myself wishing the humid, desultory after-dinner hours we spent in backyard lawn chairs, evenings full of lemonade and sugar cookies and the reek of bug repellant, of dominoes and croquet and Crazy Eights which we played by made-up rules when we forgot the official ones, of the staking of tomatoes and pea vines, and the almost maddeningly deliberate choreography of Grandpa's lawn sprinkling, might stretch on forever. Never mind that the neighbors had no girls my age (secretly, I despised the breed anyway), or that the TV went on the blink and I missed "The Man from U.N.C.L.E." When my month's stay was up, I begged for an extension.

My interest waned, of course. I entered high adolescence, a time of reflexive loathing for family connections. Yet I never completely lost my affection for Grandma Rose. Years later when I'd discovered the women's movement and was frantically seeking some blood-related heroine I could claim as role model, she was always the one I cast in that position, though I couldn't have stood her life for five minutes, I suppose.

All the same, the coming visit was going to be work. I'd seen her two years earlier, before the move to Fellowship Hill, and I distinctly recalled the peculiar enervation that had descended on me after two or three days of attempting to slow my pace to hers--not to mention the strain of obligatory meals with aunts and uncles who plainly preferred to believe I lived alone, resolutely ignored my mentions of Linda, persisted in speaking of me as an English teacher no matter how many pointed references I made to "my field, American Studies," and in general and at every opportunity made it abundantly clear that in Minnesota's eyes

Dr. Dale McNab was the modern equivalent of an old maid schoolmarm.

Always this gap it was up to *me* to bridge between the heartland that had spawned me and the places I now belonged to.

And now, given the tenure debacle and my discomfiture at being without a job for the next year, I knew it would be more difficult than ever to muster the conventional account of my activities and prospects that the family would tacitly, ruthlessly require. Best foot forward, that was their iron law. Feeling irked yet anticipatory (to Grandmother's house we go!), I set my watch ahead, settled the collar on the rather wrinkled blazer I'd just retrieved from the overhead luggage compartment, and mentally prepared to exchange feminist and cosmopolitan solstice pluralism (my MLA sweetie, for instance, had been celebrating Kwanza) for provincial fixation on Our Savior's birthday.

The plane touched down in gusty arctic twilight, the far prairie of the runway animated by hooded milling figures and manic snowplow activity. The forecast foot of snow was landing on other feet. Funnelled into a tinsel-draped, plastic-decked terminal, I automatically began to scan the frenetic crowd for Aunt Geri's square grey face.

The weather had kept her home, probably. Half expecting to hear a page, I took the down escalator.

But once again I had underestimated native Minnesota grit and Schlaghoffer family feeling. She found me out languishing near a baggage carousel amongst blond holiday hordes.

"Dalie, Dalie! Over here, Dalie!"

I have always detested this childhood diminutive.

Aunt Geraldine is my mother Cecilia's older sister, and like their brother, Eugene, Jr., has never quite managed to break away from the Twin Cities. Or that's how Aunt Leslie, the fourth and youngest sibling, sees it from her vantage point in the Sunbelt. During their four decades of marriage, Geri and Uncle Bert, a sociologist, have lived all over the place, from Mankato to New Delhi, Zurich to DC, but he's back teaching now at his alma mater, my parents' alma mater, everybody's alma mater in that generation, it seems: the "U of M," the provincial and almighty. He supplements his academic income with consulting work. Their large, recently renovated home in St. Anthony Park is only a few blocks away from the narrow three bedroom place where Grandma tended her phlox and zinnias, presided over the punctual installation and removal of storm windows, and painted the rooms herself well into her eighties.

When Aunt Geri got wind of my trip, she informed Grandma I'd be staying with her and Bert (no invitation, just the bald decree), and at first I couldn't see any graceful way out. Not that I minded her particularly, but Uncle Bert I found horribly patronizing, a quality I was reluctant to tolerate, as Mother often implied I should, in charitable deference to his disappointments. These included, evidently, the mysterious mediocrity of his career (he'd been quite the wunderkind when he and Geri married, was expected to author books and father theories) and the equally inexplicable woes that had beset his progeny. One son had drowned in India at an early age: the five children who lived to grow up had so far produced among them three or four divorces, several admissions to psychiatric hospitals and detox clinics, one extended residence in Antelope, Oregon at Rancho Rajneesh, and one conversion to the Church of Scientology.

The pinched and paranoid Scientologist excepted, they seemed like pleasant people, but it was a remarkable fact that not a single one had thus far earned a graduate degree or produced a legitimate baby. My cousin Abbie, the Rajneeshie, had even deprived my aunt and uncle of the consolatory laments of thwarted grandparenthood by mailing home snapshots of a cross-eyed, fatherless infant bundled in scarlet swaddling clothes ("For all the world like a little red Papoose," Grandma reportedly fumed, "thank heavens it isn't my *first* great-grandchild, now wouldn't *that* be something!"). Bruce and his wife Barbie, both "in computers" and a staple of those upbeat year-end letters that come in my parents' Christmas mail, were said to be running the gamut of infertility tests before plunging into the Asian baby market.

In plainly stating all these unflattering facts and arranging them together, I do deliberately what the family traditionally avoids. Each piece of evidence that might tend to point to an unfavorable prognosis for Grandma Rose's lineage is habitually, if not suppressed outright, at least kept strictly segregated from all other such pieces. A second element of the damage control strategy is that bad news is never brutally announced; it's gradually leaked. For instance, the first intelligence of Abbie's pregnancy had traveled by word of mouth among the women. Later, once the blow had been partially absorbed, its less traumatic spinoffs could begin to be reflected in the official record. "Abbie and

7

Mo doing fine, Mo cutting his first tooth!'' might appear on the second page of a breezy letter from Aunt Geri, sandwiched in between reports of Bruce and Barbie's windsurfing vacation and Bert's recent trip to Winter Park, Florida to deliver a talk on the implications of female workforce participation to a convention of retail sales managers. Deep background sources (Mother) would then clue me in that the nickname "Mo" was short for "Motilal."

Held in check by such prudent treatment, my cousins' shortcomings kept modestly to themselves, and failed to provide the company I wanted for my own lonely little scandal, which the family found it easy to ignore since it never resulted in birth, death, or marriage. And yet I rather sympathized with my ne'er-do-well peers. I felt we shared a variously expressed but commonly rooted disinclination to mount starward on the shoulders of our parents according to the ancient plan. A bunch of Bartlebys, we preferred not to.

No wonder we tended to get a bit squashed, especially at family reunions. To switch the metaphor, we puny, aging baby boomers sometimes looked to me, over three bean salad and Rice Krispy-coated drumsticks, like hapless panda infants. Our giant parents kept rolling on top of us and never even noticed. Aunt Geri may be good-hearted, but she still refers to thirty-nine-year-old, twice-divorced Allison and her balding twin Lane as "you kids." I've known her to spoon a soft-boiled egg from its shell into my dish as though I were in grade school.

Thus I'd been relieved when Grandma wrote to say that Fellowship Hill had inaugurated a guest room for out-of-town visitors which she'd be happy to reserve for my stay. As I stood in the hectic baggage claim area tentatively embracing my heavy-boned aunt, I rejoiced: she was only my chauffeur, not my keeper.

On her greyblond hair perched a ruffled green pancake, and lipstick in an unfashionable pink shade lent to her stalwart features a weirdly candied appearance. She wore cotton gloves with pearl buttons on the wrists, and clutched a wicker handbag decorated with cloth flowers. I couldn't imagine where she'd been in such a get-up, and it wasn't until we'd reached the car and she caught a glimpse of herself in the rearview mirror that it occurred to her to explain. Her old sorority, she said, had held a "come as you were" alumni tea, and she'd found the hat and handbag in the attic.

"Mother's pretty worked up about your visit," she went on, gunning the engine. "She called three times this morning, wanting to know what you ate. You're not a vegetarian now, are you? Good, I thought not. That must be Jennifer. I can hardly keep track of what my own kids eat these days, Kurt's gotten on this macrobiotic kick.... Anyway, Mother was planning to serve some sandwiches and things in her room, since the dining room will be closed by the time we get over there. Or did you eat on the plane?"

"I never eat on the plane if I can help it." Though I'd downed two gin and tonics, girding for Fellowship Hill. Grandma was famous for what her sons-in-law satirically termed her "teetotalitarianism."

Aunt Geri kept talking, bore down on thickening darkness, her primly-gloved hands gleaming white on the steering wheel. She'd had to stop off at the cleaners and the cash machine at the bank and pick up some tickets from the travel agent—Bert was flying down to Tucson for two days, leaving first thing in the morning if the airport stayed open. She'd run over to the Fabric Barn as well, to try to match some yarn for Allison, but hadn't been successful. The lube job on the Volvo would have to wait a week or two....

As always it amazed me how she talked, how without the slightest trace of self-consciousness she bared to my critical appraisal the sturdy, unassailably material Schlaghoffer sense of reality, never thinking I might not share it. I didn't, of course, and yet I felt curiously at home. Something about the litany of errands in conjunction with the passive luxury of being ferried through the streets in her Toyota Tercel (though once it would have been a Chevrolet station wagon) felt utterly familiar, like 1962 with JFK in the White House and Mother driving me to an oboe lesson in Seattle.

But we were hurtling through a blizzard, terribly fast it seemed. I kept looking into the windows studded with colored Christmas lights, thinking incongruously, *this is where I come from*. My aunt's nose and chin appeared to me, in the deliberate strobe of widely spaced street lamps, so blunt and permanent they might have adorned Mt. Rushmore. All trace of youthful delicacy was gone, and it would be years yet before the onset of real old age would begin to hone, refine and strip away. Or perhaps that wouldn't happen with Aunt Geri, maybe she'd simply go on thickening. At twenty-one she'd possessed a serviceably pretty face and

9

a figure that hinted at a certain Protestant, repressed voluptuousness, to judge from photographs. She'd resembled Grandma at the same age, except for her lighter coloring, but their looks must have diverged at some later point in life, for Grandma had never been through this coarse-jowled stage, as far as I remembered.

"How was your trip?" Geri got around to asking.

Relieved to have something respectable to report, I began to talk about the convention.

"Oh, conventions," she disparaged. "When the kids were little and I'd go with Bert, I remember thinking it was such a treat to get away, not to have to cook or make beds. Now you couldn't drag me. I've lost my tolerance for the cigarette smoke, so many competing egos and those tacky hotel rooms—"

Heat pooled in my crotch at her mention of hotel rooms, I'd been so sweetly dissolute in one recently. I touched the place on my neck where a purple bruise was fading and wondered if I'd find time this evening to try the phone number I had for Ruta Karlessen. (I ought to call Linda, too, but maybe I'd put it off.) It would make my trip if I could get to see Karlessen, an old lefty who was beginning to receive belated recognition for her writing and feminism. I wanted to interview her for my new research project, an investigation of contacts and influences between Black and white women writers of the Harlem Renaissance and the Depression years.

That reminded me. "Listen, I meant to ask—Grandma wrote me something about wanting help with some papers. Do you know what she's got in mind?"

"Oh, those," Aunt Geri groaned, and offered me a breath mint.

"I mean I saw some of her writing last time I visited. Reminiscences about growing up on the farm and so forth."

"You know she's got scads of papers. I had no idea how many until the house was sold and I had to help her sort through everything. Stuff's in my attic now, some of it—she can't store much at the Hill. I guess she's been scribbling for thirty, forty years."

"Good for her," I defended on principle, though in fact I hadn't been particularly inspired by the pages she'd shown me.

"Well yes, it's terrific and all, but the problem is, she can't seem to finish anything. Every so often she drags her folders out and starts rummaging through umpteen million versions of the time Grandma Bright collected the bounty for shooting the timber wolf, or whatever. Of course Dad used to encourage her a lot. She misses that, with him gone. I did some work with her on it too at one point, trying to get the stuff more organized, but pretty soon she gets tired or feels under the weather, or something else distracts her, and then that's the last of that for another six months."

"What would she like to do with it eventually, do you suppose?"

"I don't know if she knows herself, exactly. I guess she has some notion about a book, but at her age. . . ."

"We might have something printed, just for the family." I felt a sudden affinity for this scheme. Certainly the material she'd shown me had been spoiled by conventional language and sentiment, as the writing of people with something real to say so often is. But what about her stories, what about that unforgettable picture of Grandma Bright, nine months pregnant, doggedly beating her eggwhites, and the string of tearful, unkempt little sisters named Flora and Lily and Daisy, and Grandpa Bright denouncing her for a hussy because she wanted to go to high school? Maybe some of that flavor had survived. Perhaps I could bring it out.

"But wouldn't that cost quite a lot, having a book printed up?" Aunt Geri objected, evincing a peculiar neurosis she shares with my parents, people who've grown used to the idea of owning a second home and vacationing in Europe, yet behave, when faced with an unaccustomed expenditure, as though abruptly stripped of municipal bonds and money market accounts and projected back to the depths of the Depression.

"Not necessarily. I could look into it." It so happened I'd recently started to do some work with a feminist literary magazine, and knew women who did design and typesetting.

"If you have the time, Dale, it's a nice idea," my aunt replied in the tolerant tones of an overworked housewife whose child proposes to cook dinner—a gesture the mother wearily foresees will cost extra effort in the long run. I ignored her and decided to speak to Grandma. Our visit would go more easily, I figured, if we had some explicit project. I rather liked the thought that here was something I could do, a unique contribution I could make to a family that saw me as superfluous.

Exclaiming how all this snow changed the look of things, Aunt Geri hung a dismayingly sharp right and trod on her good brakes. We skidded.

I saw we were in a parking lot. Ahead, streaming with light and low to the ground, modern yet irreproachably conservative in design, stood Fellowship Hill. There was not a hill in sight.

Grandma, even more shrunken and vivid than I remembered, waited for us on a curved couch beside an elaborate creche that dominated the pleasant, high-ceilinged reception area. Her carefully groomed hands, twisted like tree roots, were folded in her lap. She looked exceedingly distinguished and permanently surprised, the latter on account of her vision problems, I decided. Her lips were thin to the vanishing point like the lips of all the Brights, and set in her trademark grimace of endurance, which I knew could be disturbed by a ripple of tart humor. Her forehead was high—patrician, she'd probably hoped as a girl—and above it her famous "naturally curly" hair, almost perfectly white now with one iron grey streak elegantly positioned to one side, had thinned appreciably, but she continued to wear it in the French twist fastened with a tortoiseshell comb and those old-fashioned crinkly hairpins, so much more romantic, it used to seem to me, than my mother's bobby pins. Her cheeks were faintly rouged, possibly with lipstick. Above her grey wool skirt and streamlined orthopedic shoes she had on a "nice" blouse with a cameo pin at the throat. (I *was* an event, then, but this came as no surprise; we've never lived close enough for casual visiting.) Her nose, like mine, still turned up at the tip too much.

I groped for an appropriate phrase or gesture. But, "I'm glad you managed to land in all this snow," were Grandma's first words to me, and I felt let off the hook, given permission to be comfortably superficial. She stood. We hugged, barely, and I learned how slight she was, so light it seemed a careless move might crush her. Despite her erect bearing I towered over her; fifteen years ago, according to photographs, she and Mother and I had been almost the same height. The collapsing planes of her face were webbed with violet shadows, and though her failing eyes still shone with some of their old dark energy, I sensed she was in some entirely new stage, some immense extremity.

Yet she took it calmly, and didn't seem ill, looked as fit as Mother boasted in her letters. It was just that she stood so radically close to death, that elusive celebrity we've all heard about, in whom we're all so interested.

She immediately proposed we have a bite to eat in her room before taking my luggage over to the more distant wing where I'd be sleeping. We made a halting procession, I struggling with my suitcase and glad that Grandma kept stopping at what she considered points of interest.

She seemed quite proud of the setup, and of the fact, which she mentioned more than once, that the Hill had a six-and-a-half year waiting list. (I wondered if she'd conveniently forgotten, or never actually known, that Uncle Gene was supposed to have coughed up ten thousand dollars to get her moved to the top of that list at the point when deteriorating vision and some unexplained dizzy spells had persuaded the family that she shouldn't live alone.) We saw a crafts room, the chapel, and some common living areas furnished with poinsettias and pianos and tropical fish in tanks. Low tables held large-print editions of *Readers Digest* and *TV Guide* and the King James Bible. Grandma scornfully indicated the Bingo Nook: "That's where quite a few of these ladies while away their mornings. I don't care for it." Here and there a sedate foursome played pinochle or canasta, here and there we encountered a cautious pedestrian in the carpeted corridor, but, "Most of them," she explained, if they're not in their rooms, they're attending Dr. Jerebold's lecture on 'African Nativity.' That's the program for this evening, about the famine relief work."

It seemed in most respects an impeccably gilded cage, everything as bright and cheerfully functional as a well-appointed Montessori school. Floodlamps illuminated icy shrubbery and snow-heaped tracts where flowers bloomed in summer. Each side corridor we passed had a posted name like a street sign. ("Some of these elderly people are terribly forgetful.") We turned the corner at Brotherhood Boulevard. I noticed many of the room doors sported elaborate name signs, framed needlework pieces complete with a welcoming message, Bible verse, or proverb. "Ve get too soon old und too late schmart," one philosopher had embroidered. Grandma's door displayed a pretty cross-stitched bit of cloth: no invitation or admonition, just a flower-twined "Rose Bright Schlaghoffer." I'd never known her to use her maiden name, and it oddly reminded me of those ambitious married women's studies types who sign their academic papers with two men's names instead of one.

The room we entered would have had to be called cluttered. Though Grandma still observed the letter of her maxim, dinned into my mother and Geri in their youths, "A place for everything and everything in its place," she now stood in violation of the spirit by possessing, apparently, far too many things for the space available. The walls were crammed with family photographs; I glimpsed my sister Jennifer's baby, the first great-grandchild, ruddy cheek by somber jowl with a blurry tintype of some Bright ancestor. The wall-to-wall carpet was redundant with braided rag rugs. There were clashing quilts on the pillow-heaped bed. Every available surface was laden with doilies, trivets, vases, candy dishes, an ancient flat iron, ivory napkin rings. Much of the stuff was of dubious utility in a "senior residence," and if I did feel the pity of it, that she'd had to compress a lifetime of loving accumulation into this off-white cell, at the same time the jumble seemed unworthy of her. There had been a time, I thought, when she'd have known how to be ruthless, would have opted for style rather than sheer mass.

But she maneuvered deftly through the litter, directing Geri and me to set up a card table, plugging in a clever electric kettle she said Leslie had brought from England. From a drawer she produced a linen tablecloth, only slightly wrinkled, and a few pieces of her precious Haviland china wrapped in yellowing sheets of the St. Paul *Pioneer*. On them, she set out a meal that reminded me a little of those haphazard Sunday suppers we used to compile in my college dormitory. There were shrimp salad sandwiches on bread she said she'd baked in the residents' kitchen, cashews in a fancy cut glass dish, pickles and wilted celery and carrot sticks and olives, Lipton's tea with evaporated milk, and for dessert, kiwi fruit and storebought cookies.

Aunt Geri ate methodically and at length, and talked when she wasn't chewing. Grandma wore the abstracted expression of a meek youngster at a grownups' dinner party, and would only infrequently interject some stray comment at best marginally related to the topic under discussion, which during most of the meal was Bert and Geri's recent trip to Kashmir.

"How about putting on your other hearing aid, Mother?" Aunt Geri at last proposed, loudly enough to command attention.

Grandma shrugged. "It makes such a *clatter*." But after a few minutes she got up and fished in her bureau drawer. With the second device in place, she participated more actively.

"I doubt you need that, Geraldine," she rapped out with a sharp look, as her daughter plucked yet another Fig Newton from the hand-painted plate. It had been my thought as well, yet her severity was shocking. I imagined Aunt Geri blanched, but she bit the cookie and said calmly, "So I hear Dale is going to help you with your papers. Isn't it nice to have an English major in the family?"

"Well I've got to take them in hand. I've made my mind up. I've been looking through a few of the things this week," and with that Grandma lifted the corner of a quilt to reveal the space beneath her box spring packed alarmingly tight with cartons.

We cleared the table, all three of us insisting on partaking of the domestic ritual despite the cramped setting. Grandma won the argument over who would wash dishes. She was used to doing them in the bathroom sink and it was her china, she said.

"After all these years, your grandmother *still* doesn't believe either Cecilia or I are capable of handling breakables, and simply because we once cracked a dish," Aunt Geri protested.

"Dish, she says! My best serving platter!" And they fell to good-humored bickering over a painful incident of fifty-odd years ago that had become famous in the family. I'd often heard Mother describe how she and Aunt Geri, assigned to clear the Thanksgiving table, had dropped the platter with the turkey carcass which they were carrying between them, and thus suffered the unprecedented humiliation of being spanked publicly and sent upstairs in front of all the relatives; how guilty they felt at Christmas when a mere roast chicken appeared, served up on a crockery platter; how Grandma never said another word about what it had meant to her to lose her favorite piece of china, apparently irreplaceable in that Depression year and with Grandpa out of work; and how he'd bought her another platter identical to the broken one with the first pay he received once he'd given in and taken the hated, humiliating job in his uncle's butcher shop. That gift, Mother always said, was an extravagance she never would have sanctioned if consulted, and which meant more to her, apparently, than any other present she'd ever received from him or anyone.

With the dishes put away, we trooped over to my room. Situated near the kitchen on a corridor redolent of steamed cabbage and egg custard, it was labeled with a small brass plate beside the door: HARMONIA P. MELBOURNE GUEST ROOM.

"Wonder who she was," Aunt Geri muttered.

Grandma guessed some Presbyterian, perhaps a missionary.

Inside, the acoustical ceiling tiles, motel-issue drapes, and color television were offset by a magnificent carved four-poster bed, matching chest of drawers, and old-fashioned rocker. "People leave such nice things to the Hill," Grandma explained wistfully. "They encourage bequests, you know. I wish I had something like that bureau left to give."

"And who's this sourpuss?" my aunt inquired. "There's no name on her. I suppose she must be Harmonia P?" She stood before an oval-framed photograph of a middle-aged woman on a horsehair sofa. Despite a severe center part, jutting nose, and prominent front teeth, all of which contrasted a bit peculiarly with her nineteenth-century frills and flounces, I thought she looked a decent type.

Grandma peered. "She looks like a schoolteacher."

"Rather well-dressed for one, wouldn't you say? More like somebody's maiden aunt."

" 'Old Miss Young,' that's what we used to call 'em—women who'd dress like girls half their age."

I didn't like the tone of their speculations, and was relieved when they departed, Grandma promising to come get me for breakfast at eight a.m. I was exhausted, I knew, the minute I closed the door. I brushed and then began to floss my teeth, wandering around the room until I ended up face to face with the photograph.

"Adultery," I pronounced deliberately.

The local patron saint gazed out from her walnut frame, apparently unperturbed.

"Abominations? Crimes against nature? What's your position on the love that dares not speak its name?"

No change in the large, gentle, astigmatic eyes. "All right, Harmonia, I'll take a chance with you, since you claim to be open-minded. I've sinned, I've strayed, I've indulged the lusts of the flesh. . . .

"I mean, the lusts are legitimate and healthy and all, according to our modern point of view—it's the cheating that's the problem. It doesn't matter that it was only one night and I'd smoked a little hash and the woman lives in Boulder, Colorado and we simply impulsively acted on this strong physical thing that probably doesn't mean much. Linda's going to shit a brick when she finds out about it. She's so damned monogamous—"

I stopped right there. How could I possibly explain to a sister from out of the last century why it was that my lover and I were having such

16

a rough time lately? I couldn't exactly account for it myself—though I suspected that the landscape of our discord would be instantaneously recognizable to almost any dyke feminist in the country. Certainly my job difficulties and the recent appearance of Linda's daughter Fiona on the scene had something to do with the problem, but was that all? I lay back on the bed with my Butler Gum Stimulator and tried to make up my mind how to handle the home front.

It was only the second time in a nine-year relationship that this sort of thing had happened. My previous foray into non-monogamy two or three years back had fizzled out quite rapidly when it reached the bed stage, so after a few weeks of heavy scenes and bad vibes between Linda and me the disturbance had blown over. Since then I'd had crushes, but either they hadn't been reciprocated or it had seemed like too much trouble to do anything about them. I'd been preoccupied by the tenure process anyway, and I suppose I hoped I could subsist indefinitely on a mild, sporadic, sublimated buzz, and thus avoid Linda's wrath. (Though she subscribed to an ideal of non-possessiveness, her natural bent was deep monogamy, and much to my irritation she tended to assume that there was something male-identified in the urge for variation.) Lately my restlessness had grown, maybe partly because we hadn't been making love as often as we used to, especially not since Fiona had moved in.

Anyway, I'd leaped without looking, the other night at the MLA, and despite my apprehension I couldn't say I was really sorry. It had felt so great to be in perfect carnal synch like that with a devastating stranger, someone with whom I hadn't built up all those ancient layers of habit and resentment and ambivalence and almost filial tenderness that encrust "relationships." Treecie (Dr. Theresa Brigg-Davis on her nametag) was plump and smooth-skinned, with tiny shells and colored beads woven into her dreadlocks, and round dark-nippled breasts I wanted to suck on all night, though I always said to Linda that I preferred flattish ones. She taught Afro-American and Women's Studies at the University of Colorado, had served on the MLA Commission on the Status of Women (where we'd met casually several years ago), and from what little she mentioned was having some problems with her lover. I'd told myself it was only a one-shot, fluky treat. But now I found myself mentally running over the academic calendar, wondering if she'd attend any meetings in the east before the Berkshire Conference on Women's History in June—she'd be at the Berks, surely? Or maybe there was some way to get her involved in my Black and white women writers project, but I'd have to approach it very carefully. I'd already talked to several Afro-American academics who'd made it clear that their research priorities were not interracial.

I stood and addressed Harmonia again. "Linda will shit a brick," I reiterated.

She wasn't letting me off the hook.

"You're my judge, Harmonia, my ancestral female conscience. Do you really, honestly think she has to know? Provided nothing more happens, what difference does it make?"

There she sat with her buck teeth and her archaic moral standards, no doubt comparing my feeble modern problems to the agonies of women who sweated in childbed for days without medical attention. "Breach birth," I thought I heard. "Placenta previa."

"A good fuck, Harmonia, nothing but a casual good fuck, that's what we call it in this disillusioned, decadent late twentieth century," I protested too much, against my sneaking suspicion that sex as good as that is never completely casual. I'd call Linda tomorrow, I decided. I was much too tired tonight.

Next morning Grandma collected me at the appointed hour, and we proceeded breakfastward, joining a halting pilgrimage. Wheelchairs, walkers, and thick, splay-footed aluminum canes were much in evidence. We would have progressed more rapidly ourselves except that we were held up by numerous salutations, to which Grandma always courteously responded, "Well good morning, and I'd like you to meet my granddaughter. She's teaching English in a university Back East." From the frequency and brevity of these encounters I formed the impression that Rose Schlaghoffer was here in the world of Fellowship Hill, much as she'd been in her old neighborhood, a well-respected, slightly aloof figure for whom common gossipy gregariousness, displays of strong emotion, and the other comfortingly human traits that make for popularity, would have been nearly as unthinkable as public drunkenness.

Passing through a large vestibule that doubled as a wheelchair parking lot, we entered the dining room. It was enormous and staidly vulgar, with a vaulted ceiling and a sweep of windows that displayed a frozen pond, so that the eye was forced to take in large tracts of blue heaven, white earth, pink wall, and maroon carpet. Appalled by the color scheme, I rather approved of a handsome ten-foot fir tree richly decorated with strings of popcorn and cranberries and homemade ornaments. SEEK THE THINGS THAT ARE ABOVE, read a banner overhead.

Grandma nudged me toward a table set for two. Only people with visitors, she confided sotto voice, were allowed this much seclusion. Otherwise you had to "mix." A bulletin tucked under each plate set forth the day's menu and activities schedule; we could look forward to an afternoon discussion on "Seniors in Service," to Tater Tot Casserole and

19

Carrot Coins. I let Grandma show me where to mark down Special K cereal on my menu card. Then a beaming fiftyish man with a skin condition got in front of a microphone.

"Good morning and good fellowship," he boomed.

"Good morning, Dr. Jerebold," scores of pink-faced elders obediently chorused back.

Dr. Jerebold broadcast a rambling, improvised grace, making due mention of "the miracle of the season," "this sparkling, crisp day," "the delicious waffles Mrs. Bandy, our fine nutritionist, has selected for our breakfast and dear Mrs. Kabrowski has prepared," and "Our Savior's message of hope for all mankind." As he closed with the standard, quaint "in Jesus' name, Amen," I sneaked a look at Grandma, but she sat with bowed head and clasped hands, in her posture not a trace of criticism. Probably in her mind Dr. Jerebold was simply a feature of the place, an infelicitous detail like the pink walls which she was prepared to put up with since she was forced to compromise. Of course she'd hated to leave her own beloved home, but took no little consolation from the knowledge that Fellowship Hill was solid quality. After all, wasn't it populated almost exclusively by that aristocracy to which she'd aspired almost all her life, the native, intensely respectable Protestant middle class? It was indeed—and she, Rose Schlaghoffer, was *in*. I remembered Mother's tales of how anxious she'd been to smarten up her wardrobe before making the big move.

Attendants now advanced, dispensing beverages from carts. They were thick-ankled, sturdy, blond or greyheaded, wearing hair nets and nurses' shoes. Not one brown skin in the room, I suddenly realized, not even among the help. Behind me the residents at the larger tables conversed with appetite. "Susan Strangpin in the room next to me—ever since Mrs. Dice passed away in the fall, you know—well, she had that Lydia Bledke for a neighbor on the other side of her and the two of them didn't get on. My, no! Well Lydia, you see, was really not right, and she used to sit in there humming and rocking—what was it Susan said she hummed? 'Pack Up Your Troubles in Your Old Kit Bag,' over and over she'd hum that, and she couldn't carry a tune to save her life. Now Susan is musical, not that this is an excuse—when Lydia had that stroke in the bathtub and was crying out for help, Susan heard but wouldn't call the desk, out of plain spite! I suppose she didn't think it was anything serious."

"Gab, gab, gab," Grandma pronounced with caustic humor. Evidently she was wearing both hearing aids.

But she was taciturn this morning, and I liked the convivial talk. I liked, too, that the talkers were mostly women. When they spoke of men and marriage, they seemed to hark back to a far distant era, almost as though they were feeling, "Well, that was in my youth, a necessary stage." Looking around, I noticed that the tables were largely sex-segregated, a phenomenon that couldn't be accounted for entirely by the predominance of women, since there were all-male tables too.

As though following my thoughts, Grandma nudged me and inquired, "See that flashy fellow with all the white hair?"

She indicated a wiry, florid man several tables removed from us, distinguished by a prominent Adam's apple and an emphatically checked sport coat. "That's Mr. Luckenbill, Arnie Luckenbill."

"Not a favorite, I take it?"

"He fancies himself quite the ladykiller. Well, he better not try with me. He won't get to first base."

"But what makes you think—?"

"He's contrived to sit at my table three times this week. That's the way he starts out when he takes an interest in you. Oh, he's got very smooth manners, not like that other fellow, that Leo what's-his-name, who'd put butter on celery and stick a finger in his soup! But if he thinks he'll get me to sew his buttons on, he's got another think coming! Make him cups of bouillon and arrange his heating pad . . . ."

"That's what you think he's after?"

" 'Mrs. Schlaghoffer,' he wheedles, 'do you object if I call you Rose? I've always thought Rose was such a *poetic* name,' and lets his fingers do the walking." Bony hand on my shoulder, she illustrated. "He's an operator. That's the word for him. Claims to have been an inventor. Well, I'd like to know what he's invented! I happen to know he worked for Fuller Brush. He'd better stay away from my door with his cheesy free samples, I'll send him packing!"

I murmured my sympathy and chewed my prunes and drank several cups of the scalding, weak coffee, silently composing a parody WASP blues which no one in miles could have appreciated:

> *Pack your samples and go, Fuller Brush papa,*
> *Don't need your brush to keep my bottle clean. . . .*

21

Grandma ate about half a waffle, printed the rim of her teacup with scarlet lipstick, and slipped the leftover sugar packets and jelly and syrup portion-control containers into her black purse. Then we started back to her room.

On the way we overtook a plump, drab, cheerful woman who was introduced to me as Phoebe Childs, a former neighbor of Grandma's in St. Anthony Park. The skin lay deeply pleated across her cheeks, but her forehead was almost smooth, her brown hair only lightly mixed with grey. Phoebe marvelled a good deal at the prosaic information that Cecilia's daughter had become a college teacher. She positively glowed when Grandma spoke about her papers. "Have you seen them?" she demanded. "She's got such boxes full. I don't know how she did it, I simply wouldn't have the patience. Years and years, it's like that petit point, just like that petit point some of the women do. Give me a good-sized pair of knitting needles and some good heavy yarn and I'll knit a decent sweater, but that fine work that takes so many months. . .well I've got to be able to see the end of things."

Grandma stood chatting for longer than I'd expected. After we took our leave she explained to me that Phoebe's husband and only son had both had Huntington's disease. She'd spent a total of nearly thirty years nursing first one and then the other. The boy had finally taken his own life. "You know, they get so they can't control their motions at all. They were forever falling down. Robert must have tumbled down the cellar steps five or six times, and almost always broke a leg.

"How she stood it I can't think. Somehow you learn to cope. I do remember when I took my first writing class, the one at the Senior Center, the teacher had been talking to us about how writing can help a person who has had a tragedy. I mentioned this to Phoebe—she'd been widowed for years by then—but she said she figured she'd lived through it once."

Back in her room, Grandma wanted to go shopping. She didn't like to take the bus by herself, she said, not when it was icy out, but now that I was here—

"But what about your papers!" Everything took so long. The morning was half gone, and I was only here for two days.

"Oh, I thought we could see to those this afternoon, if I feel up to it. I was going to go shopping with Geraldine last week, but something came up."

So we bundled into coats and scarves and gloves, she found her wooden cane, and we waited ten minutes in the breath-stopping cold for a bus which took us to a nearby shopping center. There we spent a solid two hours locating hand cream, emery boards, Scotch tape, a precise, apparently rare shade of green thread, and a rarer variety of Campbell's soup she particularly favored.

By the time we got back to the Hill, she'd wilted visibly, and said I should go to lunch while she lay down. "I'm like this now sometimes. I feel—spongy, like. I just run out of steam for no reason at all."

Of course I thought her exhaustion had been quite predictable, but felt relieved to be dismissed, having "run out of steam" myself. I hunted through the halls until I found a pay phone from which to call Ruta Karlessen. I could take a taxi out to wherever she lived, I thought, eager for an excuse to escape for a few hours. I felt out of patience with the quirks of the old-old. (Ruta, thank goodness, was a decade Grandma's junior.) But there was no answer, and I went to lunch instead. I looked for Phoebe Childs, but didn't find her, and after Turkey Tetrazzini I went pack to my room and lay down.

A peremptory rapping woke me. Grandma was at the door. She looked impatient when I opened, as though I'd stood her up.

"Feeling better?" I groggily inquired.

"Much better, thank you. I heated a little soup and ate half a Mars bar. I thought it was time we got going on those papers."

Resigned, I accompanied her back to her room. She did seem rejuvenated, and in a few minutes was displaying astonishing strength and flexibility as she hauled her boxes out from underneath the bed. She left the lifting to me, and I felt a twinge in my back. I'd have to call my chiropractor the minute I got home.

"What sort of help did you have in mind?" I thought it was time to ask.

"Well, I suppose the first thing would be to sort everything out, you know, to see what's usable and what still needs more work. I do wish I'd kept up with that class I enrolled in over at the Y a couple years back. I took the spring term and continued in the fall. Then when it came Christmas, I got so tied up sending out cards and making gifts and fruitcake and what-have-you, I guess I stopped going. Oh, and my eyes got so I didn't like to drive. The young woman who ran that class was very encouraging, and she gave us, you know, all sorts of useful tips about getting material published."

Published—oh perilous word! So there it was.

"Eugene, you know, was such a help to me, and I always felt he knew what he was talking about, having more education. He claimed to find my stories at least as interesting as most of what's been printed about the early farming life."

"I always loved your stories," I said sincerely, wishing I could turn her over to a competent oral history project.

"Here, start with this box. These are from that writing class."

So I had to begin reading:

> ### SPRING COMES TO THE NORTHLAND
> *The farmhouse bubbled with excitement on the day the ice went out. For weeks the buds had been swelling on the trees. Now spring was truly here. "Mother, can I start sewing my summer dress?" ten-year-old Flora begged. . . .*

It was exactly the type of thing I'd been shown on my last visit. Not the worst apprentice writing I'd read, by any means, but bland with careful grammar and conventionalized emotion. In the margins I could follow the pencilled comments of the MFA manqué who'd inspired the performance. "Strong description here. Good active verbs." "How about varying the pace with a few lines of dialogue?" "See if you can't go back and work in some foreshadowing to prepare your reader for this development."

Grandma took up the newspaper and a magnifying glass and read in disciplined silence. It was fifteen minutes or so before she ventured, "So, what's the verdict?"

The hopeful inquiry came at a bad moment, for I'd just finished the story of the slaughter of her pet goose, a narrative whose grim, angular progression, inexorable as an old English ballad, had made a deep impression on me when I heard it as a child. Of course she'd gone and wrecked it, planed off the hard edges and added a lot of sentimental drivel.

"Interesting, very interesting. You *have* written a lot."

She smiled shyly. She really was ambitious.

"But then, we'd best remember, quantity never makes up for quality,"

24

she rapped out the next minute, reminding me she was sharp as a tack, as well.

I asked to see the other boxes. "Oh, that other isn't much, she disparaged. "We did a great deal of polishing in my writing class." But she looked as though prepared to be persuaded that even her rough drafts were of passing interest.

I sat there with her folders while twilight closed in, until she said it was time to go to supper. After the first half hour I grew increasingly absorbed. The sequence was familiar from graduate school, where I'd perfected my handy if rather embarrassing knack for adjusting my sights to the scale of my material, so that rather than yawn and doodle in my carrel, rather than find increasingly frequent excuses to duck out for cups of coffee, cigarettes, and diet pills as most of my friends did, with the passing hours I grew keener on the scent, quicker to detect the flash of the tiniest nugget amid the tons of sand I sifted.

Grandma's stuff had an archaeological fascination. She'd accreted it in layers. The successive drafts of what she called "chapters" apparently represented widely disparate dates of composition, and while by no means all of the stock sentiment and uninspired language could be blamed on her writing teachers, still in general it appeared that the earlier the work, the greater the freedom from objectionable "polish," which replaced her native blend of awkwardness and grace with uniform mediocrity.

Here and there I found a really striking passage. Often these were physical descriptions, concerned with weather or plants or the details of farming, cooking, and household routines. One paragraph was a prose poem on the flat iron. To some of them there clung a subtle affective shading that seemed to be the closest Grandma ever got to overcoming her native reticence, her instinct to skirt strong feeling and whatever smacked of gossip—"no *emotions* but in things" might almost have been her motto. Of course she never wrote about, for instance, the sentiments she must have entertained when, as a young teenager already charged with half the housework, she witnessed the arrival of yet another infant Bright.

At the bottom of the last box I examined, I discovered a small pile of jumbled, fragmentary sheets, written out in longhand and really not much more than notes, which in their aptness of detail struck me as conveying a more immediate sense of that ancient lost world than anything

I'd seen earlier. There were lists of Grandma Bright's sayings, sketchy descriptions of games Grandma and Flora played with the other sisters, summaries of Norwegian and Finnish superstition as encountered among the neighbors. There was amusing material on the rivalries among several local Protestant denominations. I learned that Seventh Day Adventists are forbidden pork, that Grandma Bright used to describe what she considered an excessive racket as sounding like "Niagara Falls with a steam whistle on it," that Grandma Rose had been scared by a fairy story about a malevolent grandfather clock capable of bringing to pass any evil wish pronounced at the time it struck twelve.

By suppertime I'd definitely decided to help the author out. We'd discuss it before I left, I thought, looking forward to her pleasure and, probably, surprise—for I doubted she'd really expected anyone to take her writing seriously.

A conversation at dinner disabused me of this naive assessment. On the way to the dining room we'd run into Phoebe Childs, who accepted the invitation to sit with us. Phoebe bore on her chest a phalanx of little pins representing Santa's sleigh and his eight tiny reindeer.

"And how's it coming?" she cried, remembering. "Are you getting all those papers sorted out?"

I said I thought we were making definite progress.

"Dale seems to find some merit in my *book*." Grandma's modest tone practically offset the bold inflation of the closing noun.

"Oh my, isn't that nice. How marvelous if you could find someone to publish Rose's book," Phoebe echoed, turning innocent eyes on me. "I do admire your grandma's way with words. She's read a few of her chapters aloud to me, and I'm anxious to hear more. It certainly ought to be available to the public, and how nice for the family! Do you really suppose one of those New York publishers might consent to print it up?"

I tried to explain the vagaries of the trade. Grandma backed me up at several crucial points; fortunately, her teachers had prepared her somewhat for the notion, shocking to her inexperienced friend, that not every citizen of this democracy who manages to amass a sheaf of typed, consecutively numbered pages is constitutionally entitled to have a bound volume displayed for sale at the local Waldenbooks.

"You need one of these—what they call an agent," Grandma elucidated.

26

Undaunted, Phoebe asked if I knew any.

"Not really," I lied. Thanks to their stubborn unwillingness to notice my private life, the Minnesota tribe were conveniently unaware that I happened to share my home with one of the four or five top feminist literary agents in the country. "Anyway, those people usually won't get involved unless they're quite sure of making money." Grandma's face fell. She was really into this, and I thought I'd better put things in perspective. "With Grandma's material, which certainly deserves to be available, I think we'd do best to see about having something printed for the family and friends. Of course people here at the Hill could purchase copies."

"Isn't that what they call that vain—vainglorious—?"

"No, Grandma. You're thinking of vanity presses."

"Vanity!" Phoebe piped up. "What a notion, at our age!"

"Vanity publishing is when you pay a company a certain sum to act as your publisher. This would be *self*-publishing, which is quite a bit different. Plenty of highly respected writers do it."

"Well, you know more about it, I suppose," Grandma sulkily assented, plainly unconvinced. "I only thought a professor and so forth...."

My reputation on the line, I hated to disappoint her. "Another thing we might consider would be to try submitting short selections to a few literary magazines." It had crossed my mind in the course of the afternoon that some of her notes and brief descriptions might, if properly arranged, find a place in one or two feminist journals in which I'd published or had connections.

She perked up instantly, was off and running. "Eugene always urged me to try *Reader's Digest*. You know, they used to have that column every month, I believe it was called "My Most Astounding Personality" or something like that...no, thanks, I think I'll wait. Didn't I see Butter Brickle ice cream on the menu?"

The kitchen help was offering dishes of stewed plums.

"I'll have ice cream too, please," Phoebe said. "Be sure and let them know a senior citizen wrote it. Just mention your age. That might help to spark their interest. Was it you, or Maryann was telling me how books by older people have been in the news lately?"

I did my best to warn them that *Reader's Digest* was out of my league.

"Beggars can't be choosers, I guess," Grandma sniffed.

"Oh but Rose," Phoebe urged, "just seeing your name in print!"

I excused myself to go try and call home. To my relief Linda had the machine on. I left a message saying I'd call tomorrow. Then I hunted up an 800 number that permitted me to charge a dozen American Beauty roses to be delivered to Dr. Brigg-Davis at her office address, on the assumption that she'd go there to pick up her mail. I told them to write "Happy New Year" on the card and leave it unsigned.

Next morning Grandma and I buckled down right after breakfast. Not that I was exactly in the mood. I felt lousy, for one thing. I'd had insomnia, and my back and neck hurt; evidently I'd done more damage than I thought, lifting boxes yesterday. Grandma, too, announced she'd slept poorly and complained of a shooting pain in her right side, but nevertheless was full of nervous energy. She seemed to have decided to make the most of my offer of help, however short it fell of her initial expectations.

So we sat in facing chairs in her warm, crowded room. Beyond the window glittered another frigid, cloudless day. Our knees almost touched. Manila folders were heaped around us. I was deciding what to xerox and take home with me. She, unfortunately, increasingly displayed the indecisive tendency that Aunt Geri had prophesied. She fed a growing stack on the table beside her, muttering that this or that item "needed work" and sighing over the additional material she said she still had to complete—for what purpose she didn't mention, and I didn't ask. It was fairly obvious to me that she hadn't entirely abandoned her notion of a commercially published book.

"You've got plenty here that's fine the way it is," I tried to point out. The truth was, the uncut diamonds I'd unearthed yesterday appeared substantially smaller and rather less promising in the glaring morning light reflected off still-untrampled snowbanks. Suppose I'd allowed my literary judgment to be led astray by my feelings for the author? Suppose I couldn't get the editors I knew to print anything after all? Not that I'd promised, of course, but I'd gotten her hopes up. And it wasn't as though I could palm the stuff off on some crappy NOW bulletin in Hackensack or Mahwah. For Grandma Rose, a class act or nothing.

"If you really are thinking of doing some new writing," I went on, "what I'd most like to see would be that story about the day you left home to go to high school. I think that and the one about slaughtering the goose had the most effect on me of any of your stories."

"Well I think the goose is around here someplace."

"I know it is, I read it yesterday. But it wasn't quite like I remembered," I couldn't help adding.

She bristled. "What I wrote was exactly how it happened."

"Yes. But there's different ways of saying what happened."

She didn't pursue it then, and I figured either she'd decided the philosophical implications of my statement were too deep for her, or she'd taken real offense at the implied criticism. But half an hour later, when I'd forgotten the whole thing, she demanded uneasily, "What was it you thought was the matter about that goose business?"

"Mostly the tone, I think. I remember when you told it, it was all very straightforward, matter-of-fact. I understood how you felt about that goose, partly because it had a human name—Letty, was that it?—and because you described how you and the goose would play. There was that story about how it saved you from a whipping, remember, when you hadn't done some chore, and your mother came after you with the switch and it ran at her and pecked her till she laughed and let you go. Then you described the preparations for killing it, how your father sharpened the ax blade and so on, and told you to call the goose as if you were going to feed it, but you wouldn't. You ran upstairs so as not to hear the sound."

"But the teacher said to put our feelings in."

A pedagogue who, I thought uncharitably, clearly ought to have been strung up at the crossroads as a warning to all such well-intentioned malefactors. "From what I've seen of your writing, I think you have a knack for making people visualize things the way you saw them—like a picture, you know. When you sit down to write, try to concentrate on those pictures. Why, I've never forgotten that description of yours of the time you left home, with your father bullying and blustering, and your mother beating eggwhites, and that row of shabby, tearful little kids."

Grandma stiffened. "Shabby? Who said anyone was *shabby*?"

Too late, I recalled it was Mother and not she who'd told me they used to make the younger children's dresses from flour sacking.

"Or *bullying*? My father never raised a hand."

The Past was closing ranks. She was of it, and not I.

"But you had to go against him to get your education."

"They needed me at home. He was right about that. There weren't any boys, except for Joey, and he was little. We always had enough. We ate well, being farmers. The girls were neatly dressed. Of course there was sometimes not a lot of cash money, and Mother and I had to sew out of what we had. In any case, whatever we wore was clean, and everybody washed every morning and had their hair combed and braided. I used to do what they call that French braiding on some of them, Flora and Lily mostly, and Daisy who had such pretty yellow hair when she was little.

"I remember one time the teacher came to visit. She would visit around the various homes in the district during the course of a school term. After she'd been to our house, she said she was so impressed because everyone had his own place at table and took it quietly—there wasn't a lot of bickering and shoving like you'd see in many large families.

"I recall she stroked my hair and called me 'little mother.' I would have been about twelve then. I believe that's when I made up my mind I wanted to be a teacher. She had such a soft, refined speaking voice."

Grandma subsided, her defensive irritability forgotten, along with my advice. I went on leafing through her folders, thinking about Treecie. My mind kept gravitating to certain details of our tryst.

"But I really ought to write about Prosperine," she continued thoughtfully. A stillness hung about the statement.

"Prosperine?" I supposed she meant a town, maybe the one where she'd taught her first school and had the famous run-in with the religious madman who maintained the alphabet was a sin before God.

"Prosperine Munkers. You've heard me speak of her."

"No, Grandma, I don't think so."

"My chum from Normal School? But surely. . .well, your mother or Geraldine would know. Geri was nearly named for her, in fact. Her father had a grocery business in Bemidji. I boarded with the family for a time, when I was at Normal School there. Eventually we taught in neighboring districts. At one point we were even going to go set ourselves up in Chicago, and I don't know what-all."

"Really? I never heard that."

"A bunch of foolishness," she pronounced so savagely that of course I broke down and inquired why she said so, though I wasn't in the mood to be prying stories out of her.

"A couple of girls. What could we have done?"

"What did you want to do?"

"Oh, Prosperine had some notion about newspaper work. Imagine, a little country girl like that, straight out of the jack pine woods. Of course she'd had a different upbringing from mine. Bemidji was quite a little place in those years." She pronounced it "Bemidja." "And her mother came from money, years back. I'm sure I don't know how I would have managed. I guess I'd've taken in sewing, or hired out to cook in a boardinghouse, anything to get enough to live on while I studied to pass the State of Illinois teacher's examination.

"But Prosperine. She used to talk of Europe. New York or Paris, that was her idea. She made up her mind to study languages, but she couldn't locate anyone to teach her French, so she studied German with the farmers instead. I guess she made some progress at it too. She was a flighty little thing, highly impractical, but yet she could be so obstinate at times.

"She might have done something nowadays, I suppose, what with this woman's lib.

"Her family, I remember, had a little terrier dog she'd named Potiphar. That impressed me, that peculiar dog's name, and a piano they had, made out of some kind of beautiful blond wood, and an oriental carpet. Of course her mother had inherited those pieces. She came from Baltimore. Her people were supposed to have owned slaves." She said this as though impressed with the distinction. "Not that the Munkers themselves were well off. But to me, you know, coming from the farm, it was quite a novelty to see so much boughten stuff, crackers and sardines and store cheese, white sugar and Ivory soap. Mrs. Munkers kept potted plants, that seemed so elegant.

"Mr. Munkers was known to have been a Single Taxer. He used to subscribe to a freethinking magazine."

"What happened to Prosperine?" I blurted, completely attentive now, instinctively feeling I'd found something.

"She died young, very young. A real tragic thing. Took sick in that severe influenza we had, when was it, just after they signed the Armistice. Of course there'd been so many dead in that period. I was married to Eugene, we'd moved down here to the Cities, and had quite a time of it ourselves, what with the war. I don't know if you're aware of it, but there was a fair amount of feeling against the German-Americans in this area, and even though he and several cousins went off to serve—well, you can imagine how I felt with him over there, and I walked out my door one fine morning and found 'Kaiser-lover' in yellow paint on the front steps."

"But Prosperine? Where was she when she died?"

"It was months before I learned what had become of her. Oh, I knew she'd been staying up on the Iron Range, around Hibbing, you know. And of course I realized something was amiss when her letters stopped coming. She used to write me pretty regular.

"I don't know all about it, but evidently she'd got herself mixed up in some socialistic business."

Socialistic business? It sounded better and better. "She must have been—why, still in her early twenties."

"That's right. We were only three months apart in age. My birthday fell on the twenty-fifth of August, hers on the twentieth of November. I never fail to think of it, even to this day, when November comes around.

"Her mother finally wrote me what had happened, that's how I found out. She left for the Range immediately she heard Prosperine was ill. Distracted with the worry, she had a premonition. Found her up there staying in some freezing lean-to, with newspapers under the bedquilts and ice in the slop bucket. By that time it was too late to do anything. Had to lay her out herself, with the help of a Finnish neighbor.

"She wrote that Prosperine'd got so thin it was pitiful. Not that she'd ever been stout, she was always wiry. Of course she wasn't taking proper care of herself. Had nicotine stains on her fingers, she was smoking that much, and women didn't smoke in those days the way they do now."

"You must have been upset."

"Yes, it was a blow. But they were such peculiar times—oh, I can't describe it. Not like the Second War, either. Maybe it was just we weren't so used to all the unsettlement. The worry of the boys being overseas, and Eugene of course, though thankfully he came back with all his arms and legs. And then the German business, and all that talk about the

33

Reds. . . .

"But I never did feel easy about Prosperine, after she got to know that Frank Stuberfield."

"Who was he?"

"A newspaperman. She'd met him in Chicago when we first went down there."

"When you—but I thought you said—?"

"Oh yes, I was actually there for a little time. But Flora fell off a ladder and broke her collarbone and her arm in three places, and I was called home suddenly. Everything changed, then. Your grandpa and I began dating—well, we called it something else in those days. We were practically engaged, and when the war came on we decided to be married. He felt it might be better to wait till he came home, but I wouldn't hear of it. I put my foot down."

I'd heard this romantic story any number of times, how Grandma'd sworn she'd rather be his widow or his nurse than any other man's wife. "And the newspaperman? Did Prosperine get work?"

"Oh yes, I believe she wrote some articles for one of these little papers. There wasn't much of a living in it though. I recall a clipping she sent me—it was about these, what they used to call the Wobblies. I don't guess we have them anymore, it seems like such a long time since I heard anything about them."

"The IWW, the Industrial Workers of the World," I supplied.

"My mother had a saying, don't hide your lantern underneath a bushel, and I felt that's about what Prosperine was doing, traveling around, sleeping in strange houses. The bugs! I remember she wrote me about bedbugs, and catching lice from the dirty little children.

"And yet, goodness knows where she'd've fit in. She didn't have the temperament for housekeeping, and even though she used to go around and write up all the farmers' meetings, I don't believe she possessed any more practical notion of farming, really, than the banker's daughter in Bemidji did, who asked me once how come the farmers in the Dakotas that were losing their shirts on wheat didn't switch to dairying. Possibly if she'd had a chance to attend college—but anything that family had went for her brother Garret, who wasn't cut out for school unfortunately. All he cared to think about was Ford automobiles. Matter of fact, he eventually started up one of the first taxi firms here in St. Paul, and made a go of

34

it too.

"Prosperine was a fair teacher but she got to hate the work. For a while I was afraid she was interested in this Frank fellow, though he was a good fifteen years older than her, and married besides, and drank, and used such language! But he helped her get into the newspaper field. Quite a time after she died, I visited up in Bemidji, and Proppie's— Prosperine's—mother gave me a cardboard box full of her diaries, and some mementoes and things. I still have a locket with some of her hair in it. As far as that goes, I've got a photograph. Would you like me to look and see if I can find it? If you'd just reach me out that last box from underneath the bed. I'm afraid it's shoved back under there quite a ways."

I complied, despite the twinges in my back. This carton was smaller than those I'd lifted yesterday, but every ounce as heavy. Dustballs clung to it.

"Just a few old notebooks and things."

A few indeed. There must have been two dozen, as I saw when she rummaged through and stacked some around her on the floor—everything from old-fashioned school exercise books to spiral-bound steno pads. Finally she selected a small, fattish volume with a tattered leather cover. "My Diary" was embossed in curlicued gold on the front.

"You kept a diary!" What wouldn't I give to see it? And here instead she was feeding me all that writing class stuff.

"Oh, there was quite a fad for diaries at one time. Half the girls in the Normal School had 'em," she replied casually, leafing through the volume, so that I caught a glimpse of unlined pages closely covered in perfectly even rows of faded ink: penmanship that to my era represents a feat as gratuitous and legendary as the lady-like trick of sitting straight-spined for hours without touching one's chair back.

Having found what she was looking for, she passed the book to me. "There. We would have been about eighteen at the time. I believe a friend of Garret Munkers took it."

The photograph was pasted to an otherwise blank page, though a diary entry began on the one facing it. The two friends stood on the verge of a ragged line of trees, a swaybacked barn for backdrop. Their arms were linked, Rose's wrist through her shorter companion's elbow. Prosperine slouched with her hands in the pockets of a short jacket. Rose was a dark-eyed, nearly mature beauty, her hair swept proudly "up," full

35

breasts and trim waist not especially flattered by the peculiar, amphibious clothing of the immediate prewar period, when women had more or less emerged from the nineteenth century's billowing fabrics, yet not quite begun decisively to inhabit the streamlined fashions of the twentieth. She inclined toward her friend with a heavy-lidded glance that might or might not have been meant as parody.

Prosperine, however, glared straight out at the camera, her small pale eyes shaded by a brimmed cap. She'd clamped a stalk of grass between her teeth, her jaw set in such a way as to emphasize the extraordinary distance from her wide cheekbones to her pointed chin. Except for the skirt and the colorless, wispy braid that snaked limply across one shoulder, I thought she might have passed for a Polish-American farm lad—a rather dissolute child of agriculture, whose circled eyes and slumped stance and something else I couldn't quite define conspired to produce the debauched appearance healthy teenagers often have.

PROSPERINE AND I, "THE FARMER TAKES A WIFE," was printed in block capitals beneath. SEPTEMBER, 1913. HUBBARD COUNTY, MINN.

"That's quite a picture," I remarked inadequately.

"Oh, we were cutting up, the day that was taken. We'd been fooling around with Garret and an older friend of his, another town fellow who had the use of a camera—actually, I think he was interested in me, and wanted to impress me, I suppose. Prosperine was chewing on a stalk of timothy, and we started kidding her about looking like a hayseed, and she snatched up Garrett's cap and jacket and put them on. She said we'd pose as the farmer and his wife—just for a joke, you know, because she'd heard me declare many's the time I didn't mean to marry a farmer. Not that I'd got anything against them, it was just I'd made up my mind to try another sort of life.

"I remember we started singing "The Farmer in the Dell," and then that fellow, who was quite a smart aleck, and not the sort I would have ever been serious about, said she ought to be the cheese instead. 'The cheese stands alone,' in other words. I guess he was sore because here he'd come courting, and he thought she was in the way. I knew he'd hurt her feelings, but she didn't show it outwardly.

"It wasn't that she couldn't have had boyfriends of her own, but she seemed to scare them off. For one thing, she never would take the slightest pains with her appearance. She bit her nails something dreadful, and she'd think nothing of going out in a dress or a coat with a tear in it, or a button missing. Then she was smart as a whip. I was at the head of the class too, we generally vied for first place, but you see, she could have beat me every time if she'd applied herself steady. She wasted a lot of time scribbling poetry, mooning about the woods and the back roads when she should have been studying.

"She'd a mind, Prosperine. But she hadn't got the stick-to-it-iveness. A person who truly wants to better himself has got to be consistent. How does the saying go? 'Genius is one percent inspiration and ninety-nine percent perspiration.' "

She chuckled at the hoary formula. I studied the photograph. Beside it on the right-hand page, I was able to make out the first few lines of her diary entry. *P. and I made up our quarrel. We each apologized. I fixed a batch of fudge for a peace offering, and received a poem where she calls me Rosamund and a supply of licorice to last the month. Sweet girl!!*

I sat there, paralyzed with interest. I didn't know what to do. I wanted to keep on reading in the worst way, of course, but I didn't have the nerve. I needed time to think. Surely I could get around her somehow, with the proper strategy.

"Do you ever reread your diaries?" I asked.

Grandma reached over with surprising agility and, scooping the book from my lap, clapped it shut. "I suppose I ought to do that," she evaded. "It might refresh my memory about certain things. Luckily my handwriting was clearer back then than it is now. Still I'd have to use the magnifying glass."

"I'd be fascinated to know more about Prosperine."

"Maybe I'll write her up, if I find the time."

"You said you almost named Aunt Geri after her?"

But evidently she was finished with that topic, for instead of answering she wandered off into a long involved account of the circumstances attending my aunt's birth. It had been a difficult delivery, they were thankful the baby lived. "In fact she was a perfectly healthy child. And every one of my four children were quite healthy too, and such a satisfaction to your grandpa and me, and all of them finished up their university degrees, and now Eugene, Jr. is such a well-respected doctor, and the girls all married college men, and had such fine families, and you're a college professor Back East . . . ."

To my amazement, she wept suddenly, fluent tears the likes of which I'd never seen from her. She was quiet but unstinting. The front of her blouse got wet. When she was finished she groped around and found her purse, from which she withdrew a clean, lace-edged handkerchief. She dabbed beneath her glasses and softly blew her nose. I noticed as she did this how carefully filed into perfect ovals her fingernails were, on the tips of her liver-splotched, purple-veined hands. The small diamond that had been a gift from my grandfather twenty years ago on their golden anniversary swung loose on its crooked finger, but a swollen knuckle saved it from falling off.

Then she began to explain and excuse herself. "I'm sorry, Dale, I don't know what got into me. The years . . . the years . . . Eugene and the children . . . I've had a fortunate life, I know that."

I would have hugged her, but I thought she might dislike it. My family has always dispensed touch sparingly, as though it were potent medication, like penicillin better not over-prescribed. I cupped a hand over one of hers instead. She caught it and clung with an almost painful grip.

"Was it sad for you, talking about your friend?"

Grandma stared at me, perplexed. She blew her nose again. "Oh, no, nothing like that. Whyever should it be? Prosperine and I were chums, I couldn't forget that, but we'd gone our separate ways by the time she passed on, and anyhow, it was all so long ago."


Late that afternoon Aunt Geri called with an offer to drive me to the airport for my early-morning flight. She suggested I spend the night at her place, and by this time I was sufficiently worn down by Fellowship Hill's exacting tedium to be glad of the invitation. After supper I hastily packed my things under the penetrating eye of Harmonia P. Melbourne, who looked a lot less sympathetic than she had on first acquaintance. Tonight her mien was stern enough to hint she wouldn't feel out of place driving her buggy around the countryside, a Bible and sawed-off shotgun in her lap, fomenting temperance sentiment. Possibly she divined the evening I was planning: a Scotch-on-the-rocks or two from Uncle Bert's well-stocked liquor cabinet, then early to bed to savor my memories of Treecie one last time before I had to face the music back home.

38

"Judge not," I quoted at her. "Ever heard that one?"

"In my day. . .," I fancied she retorted.

I ignored her and finished packing, adding to the contents of my briefcase a thick sheaf of photocopied pages from Grandma's manuscript. I'd promised to send some editorial suggestions for the collection we planned on printing, and also to select material for submission to magazines.

Aunt Geri came to get me around eight. Grandma and I parted almost casually. Evidently she had no better idea than I what to say or do about the unpalatable fact that she might die before we saw one another again.

"I'll come back soon," I promised, without being asked. It seemed quite possible to me that I really might, particularly since a scheme involving that carton of diaries and the tale of Prosperine Munkers, with her penchant for cross-dressing and her "socialistic" leanings, had begun to hatch in some remote corner of my brain.

"Next time," I added banteringly, "I want a better look at that last box of yours, the one with all the notebooks."

"What, and read my secrets?" she cried, with coquettish humor— then swung around and added pungently, "When I'm gone, the postman can read 'em, I suppose, or Mrs. Busybody down the block."

I winced, it came so close to my own speculation.

Once installed at my aunt's I asked to use the telephone, and finally managed to reach Ruta Karlessen, who was friendly and urged me to get in touch with her the next time I was in the Twin Cities. Then I tackled Linda, who was also home this time.

"Sweetie, I've missed you," she said right away.

"I've missed you too," I gave the countersign—somehow, hearing the warmth in her voice, nearly believing my own fib. She seemed to be trying to make up for some sharp words we'd exchanged the last time we talked (which had been shortly before I'd spent the night with Treecie), and though I'd already made up my mind I wasn't going to say anything long distance about what had happened, now I almost wanted to confess, just for the company. Linda was my best friend, we talked everything over. That running conversation—a sort of higher gossip, gloss on life's contingencies—kept us going when even eros was in the doldrums. We were always two smart women figuring out the world. It seemed strange to be keeping secrets.

"I wish you were home already. The bed is cold."

"I'll be home this time tomorrow. Anyway, I thought you had your work to keep you warm," I said, only half joking. Her literary agency had been booming since the summer, and there'd been plenty of nights when I'd fallen asleep before she left her desk out in the office she'd converted from a double garage.

"I've worked so bloody hard I'm cross-eyed. I just want to relax. Actually, I've started fantasizing about going away. Alix and Deb stopped by. They were talking about the Cayman Islands again."

The intimate note began to make me nervous. "You know I'm pretty much stuck, for the semester anyway. And there's Fiona."

Linda dropped it for the time being. "On a more immediate topic, suppose we just spend tomorrow evening at home after all? I'll cook. We could rent some silly movie or something."

"And your daughter?"

"Going to a New Year's Eve party. We debated it for days. She finally promised she'd take a cab and be home by two, so I said she could go."

"In other words there'll be a knock-down-drag-out fight around three or four when she comes waltzing in. Great way to start the year off," I grumbled, recalling too well some other evenings in past months when we'd taken advantage of Fiona's absence to make love in the old peaceful silence of the empty house, *our* house, the place we'd made together. After, though, instead of falling asleep peacefully together in the old way, we'd lain tensely side by side, waiting to know had she gotten home all right and by the appointed hour. Linda always said I should just go to sleep, but I hated to let her keep her vigil by herself. It would have made me feel even more shut off from this new preoccupation of hers than I did already. So I lay awake, boiling with resentment.

I had difficulty understanding Linda's attitude. She and Fiona fought a lot, which was almost inevitable given Fiona's constant challenges— irksome, so far, more than frightening—to adult authority. Linda complained loudly when these clashes occurred, threw up her hands and said she simply wasn't cut out for the job, but I always felt that underneath it all she was almost boasting of her difficulties, was bursting with pride that this brat in fifty dollar jeans was flesh of her flesh. That would have made more sense to me if Fiona had been a cute, difficult three or four year old instead of fifteen, but I supposed the explanation lay in the fact that the two of them had lived apart for so many years. Maybe my lover was just suffering from delayed maternal instinct.

I thought I got through the rest of the conversation pretty well, but after saying good night I felt nervous at the thought of spending the evening home alone with Linda. I still wasn't sure what I was going to say or not say. Linda and I had never actually promised to tell each other *everything*. In fact, I recalled a conversation we'd had à propos of friends who were in the throes of nonmonogamy in which she'd mentioned that she'd prefer not to hear about brief encounters. (Though how remote the very possibility had seemed at the time!—which must have been at least five years ago, because the interchange had taken place in the kitchen of our Upper West Side apartment, before we'd moved to Jersey. What could we have been thinking of, what children had we been, that such threats to our coupledom had seemed remote, theoretical, something only other people, unhappy people, had to face?) At this point, when there seemed no reason to think that what had happened at the MLA would have lasting repercussions, I felt it boiled down to a practical issue: could I get away with *not* telling her? Could I act innocent? Could I avoid thinking of Treecie at inconvenient moments?

I decided the answer was probably yes, but the whole thing would be a lot easier if we didn't have to be alone like that right away, especially given that Linda seemed to be (why now? I thought; she'd been so distant lately) in a cozy, romantic mood.

Aunt Geri offered me decaf or Diet Pepsi, and I didn't have the nerve to ask for alcohol. It's just not done—by women, anyway—in our family, where adults drink wine with dinner "for the taste." I accepted the decaf and, after a decent interval of smalltalk, escaped bedward. But instead of indulging in what a flippant friend of mine calls "digitally assisted fantasizing" about my new flame, I lay awake thinking about home and what had happened with the old one.

When I first met Linda Sprague she'd been an adjunct at the college where I was then teaching. She was completely inaccessible, evidently— the fact that I bothered to notice illustrates how strongly and quickly I was attracted to her. She'd already had a lesbian relationship with her M.A. thesis adviser, but I didn't know that when I disdained her at women's studies program meetings (she was married and teaching mostly basic composition). Femmy, femmy, who needs it, I said to myself. She was a year older than I and slightly taller, especially in the high-heeled boots she liked to wear, with glossy thick brown hair she would shortly whack off—it's since grown long again and quite grey—spread out over her narrow shoulders. She looked good in tight jeans, and in fact once confessed (much later, of course, in the revisionist era accompanying the feminist sexuality debate) that she'd loved to wear bikinis before her Caesarean, that she'd always been ashamed of her too-long chin and her too-heavy eyebrows—she came from an old Philadelphia family where such things were noticed. I, who've got that German look from the Schlaghoffer side, a face a bit too much like a boiled potato, and am chronically a few pounds overweight, have always assumed my brains made up for it.

When she came out for me, left her husband and all the trimmings, I was so high for months I thought I could never feel dissatisfied with anything again. I'd wanted her so much through our confusing months of courtship, and had been so sure how it would end with me losing her; though I'd never have admitted it back in those days of new, unexamined pride, I guess I hadn't believed deep down that what we had could possibly weigh in the balance against the straight world's blandishments. Her leaving Fiona, incidentally, had nothing to do with me; it was something she decided on and worked out with Michael, her soon-to-be-ex. She was angry and ambitious, and felt she'd done her share. Michael was one of those decent, wimpy fathers, rather afraid of his emotional wife, I think, and glad to have something small and needy to hang onto.

After Linda and I had been together for a while, we agreed that when we'd first met part of the attraction for each of us had been our view of the other as ever so slightly vulnerable, in need of our protection. I for one continued to feel that way about her for a long time, though I quickly learned how competent and fearless she was in almost anything she took on. Those were heady days when we were first together: we were building a world, and not just our own private one, but the large, important world of lesbian-feminism, that made a context for our passion. For several years we were both heavily involved in women's studies, but without a Ph.D. she had a hard time getting a satisfactory teaching appointment, and eventually she ditched her half-finished dissertation and against much prudent advice began her literary agency. She was like that, much more daring than I was when it came to taking risks for what she wanted. When we decided we wanted to get out of Manhattan, even though her income was still undependable she didn't hesitate to sink a small inheritance into the down payment on the New Jersey house.

That place could certainly never have happened for me without Linda, or at any rate not nearly so quickly and satisfactorily. Sometimes I wondered if it was because she'd been married that she was so good at all those adult things like balancing a checkbook and buying furniture. She just kept telling me it wasn't any more difficult to understand the terms of a mortgage than to figure out what goes into a decent publishing contract. I never quite believed her till we'd closed on a three-bedroom home in Plainfield, on the express bus line so we wouldn't feel too cut off from the city. (Goodness knows why I, a child of middle-class privilege, who'd grown up on a spacious lakefront lot with bamboo and rhododendron landscaping, should have marveled at a working fireplace, a yard with real dirt—but the fact is, I think I'd always pictured myself spending the rest of my life in rent-stabilized apartments, with strips of plaster hanging from the ceiling and tons of books in cartons and mismatched plates and chipped mugs on the cupboard shelves.)

At first I wasn't thrilled to rejoin the suburban scene, but Plainfield was surprisingly integrated both racially and in terms of the number of gay and lesbian households, really light years away from the suburbs of my childhood. I rapidly succumbed to its attractions. Linda presented me with a how-to carpentry book for my thirty-fifth birthday, and before I knew it I'd built a deck out back and was sitting on it drinking a beer, typing a course outline and looking up every so often to admire the snowpeas pushing through the topsoil. Things were finally showing signs of getting comfortable, I thought. Perhaps when I had the tenure business out of the way, I'd take some time to begin work on a book I'd had the idea for years ago, but had never gotten around to what with the whirl of politics and teaching, Linda's career change, and fixing up the house.

And then I began to get hints that the tenure process wasn't going as smoothly as I'd anticipated. Suddenly my friends were telling me that I'd better try harder, better not make waves, better cultivate so-and-so, better be better than anyone in sight, because the political climate was becoming more reactionary by the minute and they'd already tenured a dyke in my department. Suddenly my enemies, bland pricks who'd never dared oppose me openly in curriculum committee meetings, felt free to sidle up to me and insinuate that in the mid-eighties feminist scholarship was "no longer exactly on the cutting edge." Suddenly my rivals, two or three straight women with considerably less teaching experience than I had, only one of whom even called herself a feminist, were giving me guilty smiles in the parking lot and a wide berth in the faculty lounge.

At first I had trouble believing matters were all that serious. There wasn't a doubt in my mind that I *deserved* tenure, dammit. My scholarly work was solid (though too radical, of course), I took my classroom preparation more seriously than most, and students seemed eager enough to sign up for my classes (though popularity with them, my supporters reminded me, might actually do more harm than good). Finally the danger signals were unmistakable, and I panicked and spent six or eight months scrambling around trying to exert some influence over what in retrospect appears to have been an inexorable process. Then I waited, miserable and full of hope, nursing a lingering virus and my sense of outrage—for a dark and muddy week in late winter when I learned in quick succession that I'd been denied tenure and that Fiona proposed to move in with us as soon as school let out in Boston.

Fiona and I had always gotten along fine. It had been easy to be patient and entertaining when she was younger and would visit us for weekends or a summer month or two. Linda sometimes fantasized about having her live with us, but she seemed happily settled in with Michael, and our lives were too busy and unpredictable for it to have made sense to try to alter the arrangement. Now Michael's second wife had recently had a baby, and Fiona had this and probably some other, less obvious reasons for picking up the phone one evening and informing my lover, "I want to live with you, I want us to reconnect. I'd hate to go away to college without the chance to really get to know *my own mother.*"

Linda was thrilled with the proposal, so enthusiastic in fact that it was hard to be around her with my own disappointment so fresh. From her point of view the timing was good; her career was thriving and we had plenty of room. I was too shell-shocked to think matters through very clearly, and anyway, did I have a choice? I knew enough about her ambivalence over not having raised her daughter to realize that to voice major objections now would be unpardonable. Afterwards it occurred to me that at least we could have put off the move until fall, but by then it was too late.

Fiona arrived on a beautiful day at the end of June in the parental station wagon, accompanied by her father, stepmother, and the nursing baby. Michael deposited in the upstairs front bedroom her state of the art stereo and tape deck, record collection, skis, tennis racket, and Benetton wardrobe, and departed—with, I imagined, something of the relieved air that must have appeared on Hansel's and Gretel's father's face when he ditched them in the forest. It became obvious within the first week that she wasn't going to settle in without a lot of testing, and while Linda in her newfound zest for mothering feigned to take this in stride, I had no similar incentive. So far as I was concerned, things had been better without Fiona, and I was too worn down and depressed to be able to conceal that conviction all the time, or to obey the admonition of the couple therapist Linda and I resorted to, who told us to "*work* at being a family." I did nothing of the kind, just subsisted from day to day with Linda complaining she felt caught in the middle and resentful that I wasn't giving her more support, and Fiona circling, eager to draw blood, sometimes from her mother but more often from me. (She specialized in subtle homophobia.) Soon I began to spend more and more time avoiding the house when I knew she'd be around.

Such was the happy home I'd be returning to tomorrow. Things would work out eventually, I figured—after you've been together as long as Linda and I had, so long that you've stopped knowing anyone who's been together longer, you tend to assume you'll survive anything—but I did wish that Fiona would disappear for a few months, that Linda and I could agree on how to handle her, that Linda and perhaps I myself hadn't internalized such old-fashioned standards of sexual fidelity, that winter were over instead of just beginning. Finally I escaped into visions of Treecie, and slept until the alarm detonated in the December morning dark.

Uncle Bert, who'd flown in from Tucson quite late the night before, was up for breakfast at six-thirty, typically talkative, displaying even in decline what looked like more than his fair share of that poisonous, innocent engineering vigor that brought forth the mechanical reaper and polio vaccine, blazed the Soo Canal through the cholera-ridden north, and set the IDS tower for a sign in Minneapolis' sky. He quoted Wallace Stevens and Jürgen Habermas over his Cheerios, and regaled us with a short analysis of the socio-economic factors which were "driving," as he put it, the Southwest's booming convenience store industry.

On the way to the airport, it occurred to me to ask Aunt Geri what she knew about Prosperine Munkers.

"Oh, the friend Mother taught with. The one who died so young?"

"Did she ever mention you were nearly named for her?"

"What? Not that I can remember. Is that what she told you? Every so often lately she seems to come up with some story we've never heard before. Hard to tell how accurately she's recalling these things."

"I thought you might know why she decided against it."

Aunt Geri shrugged. "Who wouldn't think twice before saddling a kid with an offbeat name like that?"

It was a diamond of a day, a day made out of light, that amazing light of winter in cold northern climates, completely divorced from heat. The plane took off on time, separating quickly from the flat white world, the Siamese twin cities that are one metropolis, and share the Mississippi like a cardiac artery. Bulbous water towers reared above the suburbs, then stands of evergreens showed up as black patches on the open countryside. I remembered a passage from *Gatsby*, something about trains, the trains running back in the snow and deep cold of Nick Carraway's midwestern youth—nothing I could remember too precisely, but I knew it was one of those three or four items college-educated Minnesotans like to quote to demonstrate to themselves as much as easterners that the North Star state figures in world literature. I thought how brief had been the age of railroads, and marveled again, as I had so frequently while writing my dissertation, at the strangeness of our distance from the Past, whose inhabitants are, after all, our kin. I felt the old ambition to close that gap.

When I returned six months later, everything was different. For one thing, I arrived by car this trip, which made my destination seem more real, more particular and strange, moored stubbornly in time, than those facile cities whipped out of the continent's hat by the airlines, our quotidian magicians. I planned to stay for a couple of months, and I'd made the solo trek across the farm states with the back seat of my middle-aged Datsun stuffed full of books and clothes, fifty bucks' worth of coke—a parting gift from a student who'd had a crush on me—in a plastic baggie secreted beneath the floor mat, and most of the trunk taken up by a Leading Edge PC and letter quality printer.

It was summer now, another country altogether. As I looped through the clean, lake-studded metropolis on that first evening, a warm one of rare low humidity, I found the lately snow-bound streets sunk under a new green spell. Driving those boulevards felt like burrowing into a hedge, with the difference that this growth was so various: broad sycamore leaf, pine needle, generic shrub, flowering porch vine, the sleekly achieved lawns replete with white-blond children. Once, needing to consult the map, I pulled the car over in a little park and smoked half a joint I had in the glove compartment. Then I grew doubly attentive to the minute articulations of light and shade that hung in each great-branched maple, and amused myself awhile tracing corridors in the labyrinth of foliage that crowned a wooded hillside.

Even in the Northeast it had often occurred to me that neither our bodies nor our consciousnesses are adequately geared to be whirled so rapidly through the stunning shifts of temperature and plant growth decreed for a northern twelvemonth. Here in Minnesota on the last day

47

of June, beneath trees that had all but completed their swift transit from May's variegation of mixed species to the darker, more uniform hues of high summer, I enjoyed a subtle thrill, like science fiction, in thinking how lately this flowering territory had been a blasted Gulag. But then I was spoiled, and too imaginative, a product of mild Seattle. If the ancestral Brights, Schlaghoffers, and McNabs had all thrived in this radical climate, no doubt it was by virtue of their strict literal outlook. *They* never questioned forty below zero, or a hundred and three in the shade.

My life had changed too, though I didn't clearly know it yet: changed by virtue of the fact that the bad period, the novel awfulness of which had so preoccupied me at the end of the year, had stretched itself out imperceptibly until discomfort had begun to seem like the natural state of things. I'd gotten so accustomed to tension between Linda and me that I ignored it as much as possible, tending to assume that our relationship would improve if I could only get settled in a halfway decent job. Throughout the spring I stayed away from home a lot, spending time with friends, running around to interviews; Linda focused on Fiona and the agency business.

I hadn't told her about Treecie, and for several months that seemed like the right choice. Treecie and I exchanged letters and occasional phone calls, but the mail came to my office and I paid the phone bill and everything went smoothly until late February, when she came to New York for a conference. We spent a night at a friend's apartment in Manhattan, and Linda found out about it. Of course she was completely furious—about the deception, she claimed, more than the affair itself, though I had my doubts that full disclosure would have placated her. Her indignant accusations only hardened my position: I refused to be locked up in a sexual jail. We were on pretty shaky ground for a number of weeks, and though we said nothing directly to Fiona, she noticed, naturally. There's nothing quite like waking in the morning after a night of close combat with the woman you love—waking puffy-eyed, headachey, hung-over-feeling, as if strong negative emotions were controlled substances— and descending to the kitchen to encounter a Walkman-wired fifteen-year-old who clutches a pop-up waffle which she dunks nonchalantly into the maple syrup pitcher while she cheerfully inquires, "You and Mom were up late—you screwing or arguing?"

"Lesbians don't screw," I'd told her once, before I wised up.

Then I got a long letter from Treecie explaining that she and her lover had decided to be monogamous, that they wanted a family, that both were planning to begin insemination within the next few months in hopes of giving birth around the same time, and that therefore she was going to be too busy taking care of various projects she hoped to complete before becoming a mother to be able to help me out with my research. She wished me all the luck and hoped we'd meet again at some point when she was able to be more active in academic matters. I was stung, but relieved as well. It was difficult to feel that a night or two every few months was worth the daily battle I'd been waging. Linda made me promise I wouldn't ever sleep with anybody else without letting her know about it (*"especially* with AIDS out there," she emphasized, lending a convenient veneer of rationality to her requirement), and we patched things up somehow.

For a while it even seemed that all the fireworks had helped clear the air. We had one good time over Easter weekend, when we went away to a gay guesthouse at the beach and ate lobster and made love three nights running, but we came home to discover that Fiona, who'd been up in Boston visiting her father, had been in a car full of kids who'd been stopped by the police; the driver had been charged with drunk driving. Of course a family free-for-all ensued, sucking Linda into weeks of heavy drama and many calls to Boston. She ignored my point that the satisfying uproar was probably just what Fiona had been after. I was pissed as hell, she was worried and upset, and our sex life was out the window again.

As far as the job search went, my luck couldn't have been worse. Early on, sure I was bound to find something more attractive, I'd passed up an opening in American history at a local community college. I'd also had to turn down a job I really wanted badly, a tenure track position at UC Santa Cruz, because Linda vetoed it. We actually talked out in some detail the possibility of moving. She already had quite a few California contacts, and might have continued to handle some of her northeast authors from the Bay area, but in the end she decided it wouldn't be fair to Fiona.

I was angry at having to make yet another sacrifice—wasn't it enough that the kid was wrecking my home life, did she have to mess up my career as well?—and briefly considered going out there alone. Linda got very upset when I suggested that. She didn't see, she told me, how the relationship would survive such a heavy separation, especially considering all the strains it had been under recently. I said that since nothing else seemed to be working, I thought maybe the separation would actually do us good. But of course I had doubts of my own, and was grudgingly glad to have her hold me and tell me she needed me at home, that she knew how awful the past year had been for me, that she wanted to help take care of me, too, until things got better. There was a night when we lay in bed and cried for hours. Something softened between us, and I said I wouldn't go. As the months wore on, however, and no work materialized, it was hard not to feel resentful when I remembered the missed opportunity.

Meanwhile, I was trapped in the pedestrian nightmare of finishing out the semester. I began avoiding my colleagues, dreading almost as much the expressions of sympathy I received from friends as I did the perfunctory or over-elaborate condolences from people I figured were glad to see me go. I was increasingly impatient with my students, bored with the curriculum. I couldn't wait to have the whole thing over with, yet dreaded June and unemployment. Linda had gotten the idea that we ought to rent a summer place on Long Beach Island, a vacation community north of Atlantic City where her family had gone when she was little. She was often volatile in her fantasies, at one moment dire in her apprehension that our dyad was on the rocks, the next optimistic that even the shaky troika could get along famously in a flimsy-walled cottage miles from the helpful buffers of work and social life. She said we could have people come out on the weekends (though many of our friends were scattering for Europe or the Cape, white water rafting trips or Central American language study programs or women's studies institutes). I think she pictured Fiona roasting wienies on the beach. "Don't you think you owe your mom a little quality time, toots?" she cajoled the pouting maiden.

Fiona came back with her favorite British adjective, "Ma, the Jersey Shore is *grotty*."

I myself was feeling leery about the plan, and when I happened to hear from a grad school friend of mine who taught at Carlton that his lover was trying to rent out a cabin on the St. Croix River a short drive from the Twin Cities, my sudden envy of the person who might live there—alone—gave me an inspiration. The more I thought it over, the more I felt convinced that I desperately needed some time out from all the pressure, family pressure included. Why not this place, as well as any other? Renting it would be a somewhat arbitrary act, but that attracted

50

me, caught as I was in the tentacles of choices made long ago.

Spending two months away from Linda seemed like a radical move, since she and I had usually vacationed together, and had never been apart for so long, but the risk here, unlike that of taking the Santa Cruz job, appeared comfortably limited. Being near the Twin Cities, I thought, I'd have the seclusion I wanted without being too isolated. I could see Ruta Karlessen and Grandma, check out that Prosperine business, and maybe cultivate some contacts at the University of Minnesota, where I might want to apply in a year or two if I hadn't found permanent work. (I was still waiting to hear about a couple of New York area openings for fall that had come up at the last minute. I'd decided to try to ignore the situation for the time being; if necessary, Linda could support me for a semester, just as I'd done for her when she was starting out as an agent— though I hated the idea of depending on her now.) In a way I suppose I was secretly intrigued with the symmetry of this return to my ancestral home, and hoped Minnesota might have some special experience in store for me, some magical surprise, which would change my life without too much exertion on my part.

I figured Linda wouldn't like it, and I was right. At first she said it was very threatening to have me go off alone after such a difficult year. Also, she wasn't happy about parenting Fiona all by herself (though I frankly couldn't see what I was contributing). We had several more sessions with the couple therapist, and eventually she came around to the view that I had to have some time for myself. "Dale isn't rejecting *you*," the therapist beamed. "Ultimately, her meeting her own needs in this way will probably strengthen what the two of you have together."

In the end she decided she felt all right about taking the beach place alone with Fiona for a month. We agreed we'd talk as often as we wanted on the phone; even if it did get expensive, the contact was important. And we started to make a few plans for fall. Somehow the process of hashing all this out seemed to improve the atmosphere, and even Fiona mellowed appreciably, recognizing our anniversary with a joking card and a batch of homemade brownies.

Linda and I made love the night before I left, and in the morning she got up with me very early and fixed bacon and eggs. As we lingered in the shadowy kitchen, held by a combination of anxiety at the coming separation and enjoyment of the moment's romantic intimacy, I assured

51

her once again that I wouldn't sleep with anyone without first letting her know. "Though honestly," I added, repeating things I'd said before, "I really can't picture wanting to anytime soon. Number one, I'm looking forward to being with you again, and I don't want you furious at me. Number two, I need peace and quiet, not more complications. I need to slow down—you know, have space to *think*. Read books for a change. Lie in the sun, start relating to my body, lose this weight I've gained being so stressed out all year—"

"I'm enamored of every pound." She kept her tone light. "But how about cutting back a little on the booze?"

It was the age of Just Say No and twelve-step programs. It seemed that half the world was in recovery from something, half the lesbian-feminist world especially. And Linda happened to be one of those people who falls asleep after more than one beer—all of which tended, I felt, to skew her view of my drinking. Still, I knew she had a point, and didn't want to argue; we'd exchanged some heated words on the subject once or twice in the past.

I smiled and took her roughly in my arms, in a parodied butch stance that was an ancient game between us. " 'Lips that touch liquor shall never touch mine'? I hear and obey." We kissed.

A few minutes later she stood in the driveway, her bathrobe clutched around her against the early chill. The posture accentuated a slight stoop she had, which I suddenly saw quite clearly would increase as she aged. This and her large bare feet and the wispy greying hair framing her completely familiar face made her look so vulnerable to me that I wanted to stop the car and go back to hold her again. I felt how startlingly much time had gone by since we'd become lovers, and how lucky we were, how inexplicably lucky, to have lasted when so many couples that we knew had broken up. Parting like this, even for months, we didn't really have to miss each other so much, because we had the improbable luxury of the future.


Afraid of too much lack of structure in my life, I'd made some definite plans for my time at the cabin. I was hoping to get through a draft of at least part of my paper on Black and white women writers, and perhaps do some more research for it. I had a date to see Ruta Karlessen. I also planned to devote time to Grandma's writing. In recent letters (I heard

52

from her more frequently now) she seemed increasingly enthusiastic about the plan to have a small book printed.

Her budding career was doing surprisingly well. Already the editors of two well-established feminist journals had responded positively to the prose mosaics I'd created by carefully juxtaposing some of her brief, informal jottings. Philliss Dix of *Woman's Estate*, the more scholarly of the two rags, had even been enthusiastic enough to slip something into an issue called "Generations of Sisterhood" which she'd been about to send to the typesetter, and I had some copies with me in the car. *Arco Iris*, where I was on the editorial board, would publish another piece in the fall/winter issue.

That alone was impressive progress, but there was more. The minute I'd firmed up my summer plans, I'd gotten busy and set up two readings for Grandma. One, which she already knew about, would be at Fellowship Hill, a variant on the slide shows, concerts, and worship services with which the more energetic and accomplished among the residents sometimes entertained a captive audience of peers. The second, which I'd saved for a surprise, I considered a real coup. It was a date at a literary bookstore whose proprietors I'd talked into letting her fill a gap in their "New Authors" series. I planned to pack the place with every able-bodied relative, friend, and former neighbor of hers that I could dig up. I looked forward to watching her rise to the occasion of the minor stardom I'd arranged.

The morning following my arrival I spent getting settled. Though it couldn't have been called a wilderness retreat, I found the cabin to my liking. It had the rustic, musty atmosphere of a family summer home built in the early fifties, and copies of *Fag Rag* and *Leather Man* in the bathroom. The neighboring cabins were screened from view, birds and trees abounded, and the wiring seemed able to handle my computer. Following a swim in the wide, pebble-bottomed river, which was reached by a short, steep path dipping through evergreens, I showered, dressed, and drove into St. Paul. I had some shopping to do, but first I wanted to stop by Fellowship Hill, greet my protegée, and let her see her name in print for the first time. The new *Woman's Estate* had come out so recently that I was sure she wouldn't yet have received her contributor's copies.

She didn't meet me in the lobby as before, but let me find my own way through the airy, flower-bordered corridors to "Brotherhood Boulevard." After we kissed I inspected her carefully, for she'd been hospitalized in February with a bad flu. I thought she looked the same as I remembered, or a shade thinner, maybe, but with that same air of curiously robust frailty, as though she might keep on this way for decades, matter-of-factly going about her business with one foot in the other world.

She made tea, and I got out the magazine. She examined it more critically than I'd anticipated, using the magnifying glass. As for the accompanying graphics, attractive old photographs of farm buildings and equipment, she objected that some of them weren't authentic: the barn design was from back East, she thought; and then of course her father never had a combine, which was used in wheat country. "And what's this?" She pointed to the heading. " 'Eat the Devil'—where did they get that?"

"Well, it's just the title we—the editor and I—picked out from your own text." Actually, I'd preferred another, rather less suggestive phrase, but had bowed to the wishes of "The Godmother," as Philliss Dix is sometimes known in women's studies circles. She founded *Woman's Estate* way back in 1970, and she runs a tight ship.

Grandma still looked dubious, so I added, "Don't you remember? You wrote that your mother used to have a saying, 'Might as well eat the Devil as drink his broth.' "

"Oh, of course I remember *that*. But which chapter is this? I can't keep track."

Her confusion bothered me. We'd been over this already. "You see, it's not really a chapter. If you remember, I wrote to you that I was going to pull together some short descriptive passages you had. For instance, here's the part about sayings and proverbs. Then there's that neighbor with the pie plant. It makes it almost like what you might call a prose poem."

"Well, I don't guess too many are liable to see it," she concluded ambiguously.

"Oh, don't be so pessimistic." I was getting a bit impatient. "Look, I'm sorry the type is a problem for you. I guess you'll need a copy in large type when you do your reading here."

"The Fellowship Night? I don't know. I got to thinking, maybe it isn't such a good idea."

54

"Reading from the magazine? But you're published now, you've got to promote yourself," I suggested humorously. "If you read from the magazine, they'll all want to buy copies."

"No, no, I meant . . . getting up there, making a spectacle of myself in front of all of them like that. I guess I better not."

"But Grandma!" I couldn't believe it.

"There'd only be a lot of talk come of it, a lot of backbiting gossip. You don't know how prying some of them can be."

"But this has been scheduled for over a month now."

"And envious, if they think you've got something, anything they lack. I don't know why they don't realize Rome wasn't built sitting in an easy chair all day, or playing bingo like they do, or fooling around that crafts room. Why, I'd never get a morsel of work completed if I took it to the crafts room, the amount of chatter that goes on.

"Anyway, I never forget Mrs. Drake, the doctor's wife, you know. She's the one I worked for when I attended Normal School, and I got so many pointers that stood me in good stead after I was married. How to set a table just so, how to write a nice invitation. I always remember how she once disapproved a dress I'd borrowed, of Flora's, a yellow dress with puffy sleeves that she considered loud. 'A woman of refinement avoids needlessly drawing attention to herself,' that was her motto."

"But Grandma, you've got something to *say* to these people."

"When my book comes out, I guess we'll see about it."

I cast about for a more constructive line of argument. "What does Phoebe Childs say?"

"Oh, well, Phoebe." But it looked like I'd guessed right. "Phoebe thinks I ought to do it," she conceded reluctantly.

"Don't hide your lantern underneath a bushel."

She glanced at me, surprised. It *was* a neat trick—turning her own quote against her. Taking advantage of her momentary disarray, I broke the news about the bookstore. She appeared slightly dazed at the mere idea, but didn't reject it out of hand; possibly she objected less to appearing before strangers than to performing for the gossips of the Hill. Her, "Oh, I don't know what I'd wear, I got such a bad berry stain on that nice beige dress I wore for my ninetieth," amounted, I thought, almost to an acceptance. I made a mental note to ask Aunt Geri to use her influence. Calling her up was a duty I really couldn't avoid much longer, though

I knew it could only lead to a tedious family get-together which possibly no one else looked forward to any more than I did. Probably I'd even have to endure Uncle Gene and Aunt Judy, who (my sister had reported after a recent visit) displayed on their Cadillac-sized refrigerator an 8 x 10 glossy of Ronnie and Nancy, signed in one corner by the movie star himself in token of his deep appreciation for their help with the re-election effort.

I thought I'd done enough for one afternoon, and we settled down to second cups of tea and crumbly snickerdoodles which Grandma had been hoarding in a fruitcake tin between leaves of wax paper (she disdained plastic wrap).

"I baked these in our community kitchen a week or two ago. I thought I'd make some fresh yesterday, since you were coming, and then I didn't feel up to it . . . but they don't get stale, snickerdoodles, if the air doesn't get at 'em." Her taste buds must be faltering, for they certainly tasted stale. But she chatted pleasantly—the Hill, the family—and referred to her health very little, and then with great refinement. It was a restraint I appreciated since I'd visited Grandma Gladys in Milwaukee only two days before. Eighty-six and still with her own microwave, my father's mother had centered her conversation on kidneys, bowels, bone marrow, liver, potassium, copper, electrolytes, CAT scans—and Jesus Christ, of course, Who Died For Us.

In making my summer plans I'd devoted some thought to the explanations I might be called on to furnish. My nearness to Grandma Rose would, it seemed to me, provide all sorts of opportunities for her to delve into my questionable past and uncertain future, ask questions that hadn't arisen when our contacts were brief. My jobless state, I thought, might especially bother her. But she was behaving now as though her presence, or her papers, were ample motive for my visit. She showed minimal curiosity about the rest of my life, and though she inquired politely about my research, which I'd mentioned in a letter, she introduced an unrelated topic before I could reply.

This solipsism was, it seemed to me, perhaps the result of a necessary triage policy. With shrinking resources and so very much past to manage, maybe the only thing to do at a certain point was to throw in the towel and let the present run itself. You couldn't keep your grandkids in fresh snickerdoodles forever; no more could you ensure eternally that the family toed the mark—though perhaps there'd always be flareups, moments of supreme exertion in which you displayed some of the old fire, as in the case of the great grandchild, Motilal. And I was no heathen unwed mother, just a spinster out of work.

As I was preparing to leave, Grandma inquired almost sharply whether I'd made much progress on "getting the book ready." As I was reminding her that we needed to do some work on it together, Phoebe Childs knocked and was admitted. She appeared badly flustered.

"Rose, it's happened again. He's *been* there."

"Did he take anything?" Grandma demanded.

"Nothing valuable, that I noticed. I came straight over. Oh, a piece of peanut brittle I had laying on the shelf. But he rummaged through my bureau. Everything's a jumble. My slips, underthings. It's terrible."

"But Phoebe. How *could* you forget to lock your door again?" Grandma upbraided.

"I was late for my hair appointment." Phoebe hung her head.

"Tie a string around your finger next time. I suppose I better come have a look. Did you report it at the front desk?"

"Not yet I didn't. Of course they won't believe me."

I stood by, mystified, as Grandma got up and located her purse. She never left her room without it, even for a few minutes. I think she'd have felt undressed.

"Can I do something?"

"No Dale, you may as well wait here. I don't think we'll be long. Poking his nose into other people's things, I hope he gets it caught in a door someday! Serve him right, the old goat! Plaguing the life out of us!" And with this cryptic imprecation, the two of them bustled off. Weary and wanting a drink (and I ought to call Linda to say I'd safely arrived), I was trapped in a holding pattern till they got back. I sat bolt upright in the fancy new recliner that Grandma rarely permitted to recline and looked to see if she had any interesting books in her tiny library.

Just as I'd expected, the pickings were slim, though I was glad *My Antonia* roosted there with the James Michener and Edna Ferber and *Reader's Digest* condensed volumes. Everything was in hardback, even Arthur Hailey. She possessed a popular history of the state, the Betty Crocker cookbook, a thirty-year-old, two-volume encyclopedia, and a Bible in modern English.

And then I stumbled on it, flanked by *The Thornbirds* and *All Things Wise and Wonderful*. Possibly I'd passed over it several times without noticing, because the spine was blank, but finally that worn binding registered. I knew what it was before my fingers touched it, knew I'd find MY DIARY in flaking gold on the cover.

I easily found the snapshot of Prosperine with Grandma. And if my ribcage constricted, making it hard to breathe, certainly this was less because there was anything especially questionable in my picking up an artifact which had, after all, been left out in plain view, than on account of the theory I'd nursed since my last visit. Like a hard little blackberry seed in the space between two molars, that astonishing caption, "The Farmer Takes a Wife," had stuck in some crack in my brain. I kept going over it. Likewise I'd pondered the fact that my pragmatic relative had been prepared to move to Chicago with this eccentric girlfriend who called her "Rosamund" and wanted to live in Europe.

Prosperine looked even dykier than I remembered.

Nerving myself with the thought that I'd hear Grandma and Phoebe at the door when they returned, and could certainly move a lot faster than they would, I paged hurriedly through the volume. The clues (to what?) would be in minutiae.

It seemed an unremarkable enough schoolgirl diary. There were agonies and rapture over marks, and complacent references to attentions from young men whom Grandma clearly didn't care for. There were patches of self-centered adolescent metaphysics ("Is this Planet any the better because Rose Bright is on it?"). There were touchingly precise observations on etiquette ("To Beryl's for Sun. dinner. Mother instructed Amy Beryl's sister never to lay knife handle on table with blade resting on rim of plate—all of knife must rest on plate. Was glad I hadn't done this, as they sometimes do at home."). Then Daisy had run away from the farm, seeking refuge with Grandma in Bemidji. At fifteen, this hotblooded sister was in love with a "river pig." I sensed that Grandma was divided between her relish of the drama and her prudent nervousness lest the family reputation be stained by the muddy morals of a North Woods logging camp.

Daisy was, I vaguely recalled, the sister who'd ended up running a boarding house out in the Dakotas. Possibly she was also the one who'd been shot by a crazy husband. . . . All at once the door swung open, more silently than I'd anticipated, and I quickly jammed the diary back onto the shelf. Too late, as Grandma and her friend entered, I saw an envelope fall to the floor. It had slipped from between the volume's final pages.

I had the presence of mind then to stand up and move in front of the incriminating evidence, hiding it—or so I hoped—without actually stepping on it. If I could only keep Grandma from noticing (her restricted vision was in my favor just as surely as her inbred neatness, sonar capable of homing in on the smallest flyspeck on a just-mopped floor, was against) maybe I'd get a chance to retrieve it unobtrusively.

"Mission accomplished?" I inquired.

"Mmmph." Grandma rolled her shoulders in an incoherent mixture of distress and indignation.

"Now Rose," Phoebe soothed. "I think she's more worked up about it than I am," she appealed to me, "even though it was *my* room."

"It's not as though he hasn't gotten in *here* before."

"What's going on? Please enlighten me. Who's *he* and what exactly did *he* do?"

"Well, we're pretty sure it's one of the residents."

"We're more than pretty sure, we're positive!"

"Wanders into ladies' rooms when they forget to lock their doors, rummages around, gets into private things. Oh, it's happened to two or three of 'em besides Rose and me."

"Steps ought to be taken, that's what. He ought to be *expelled*," Grandma fairly hissed. "Let him live in a hotel for all I care, where the police will see to him and his trespassing."

"You see, when Rose and I report this to the staff, they only look at us like we're talking through our hat. They say they'll look into it, but they haven't done anything. Of course, so many of 'em here are so forgetful, I suppose they just figure we don't remember where we put our things. I'd like to know why I'd want to turn my drawers upside down like that! They must think we're demented!" Phoebe looked as though she might cry.

"So," I interrupted, "who's your suspect?"

"Arnie Luckenbill," Grandma pounced. "The same one that used to pester the daylights out of me."

"What makes you so sure he's the one? What motive could he have?" Their distress bothered me, though at the same time I was wondering how I was going to divert their attention long enough to pick up that envelope.

"Revenge," Grandma proclaimed.

"We're not sure," Phoebe admitted. "But Anna Crotter saw him lurking around their wing, where he had no business being whatsoever, just before Elva Sorensen's room was gotten into."

"And he'd been making up to Elva not long before that. You see, he takes offense when his advances are rejected. Why, he used to come right up behind my chair in the dining room, and stand there, and stare—I could feel his *look* just creeping on the nape of my neck," Grandma shuddered. "One time I said something, and Mrs. Osborn says—Mrs. Osborn is one of our social workers—'Oh, but Mrs. Schlaghoffer, you've found yourself a male admirer! I think you ought to feel flattered!' Well, *I didn't*."

"Let's don't get all worked up," Phoebe urged. "Don't you think it would be better if we all sat down and had some hot tea?"

"Probably scheming to make us think we've lost our marbles!"

"You two have some tea," I said uneasily, riveted to the spot. "It's a drive back to the cabin. I'd better get going soon."

"Why, what's this?" said Grandma. "Can I have dropped something?"

She stooped, but I beat her to it. "Oh, that must have fallen out of one of my folders," I improvised, snatching up the envelope. "I was glancing at some work while the two of you were gone." And with an aplomb born of chagrin, I shoved it into my backpack, glimpsing as I did so the minute, faded writing on the tissue-thin paper.

Grandma looked surprised, but let it go. She couldn't have seen much but a white blur.

I made an impulsive stop in the industrial outskirts for a cheeseburger and Coke, during which nostalgic repast I slipped the letter out and glanced at the signature. *PM*, it said. I read a line or two, then put it away. This was going to be good, I could tell, and I thought I'd just as soon have something to look forward to later in the evening. For some reason it felt a little lonely to be going back to that empty cabin.

Once home, I headed for the river. There I found a seat on a mossy rock where I could slap bugs and watch the water go by. The northern dusk lingered a long time. After a while I searched the rough shore for some flat skipping stones. I was out of practice, but didn't do too badly. I'd never been as good as the camp counselor who taught me. Kris. She used to manage six or seven skips.

Jesus, I hadn't thought of that in years. "I light the light of love; WoHeLo means love," all that fake Indian shit they lay on Campfire Girls, that I'd thrown myself into because of her, weeping at fire circles with devotional fervor. To my everlasting regret she wasn't actually my own counselor, though she taught my advanced swimming level, the Steelheads. On the last night of camp the Steelheads chased her with kelp whips, forced her down on the sand, shoved S'Mores in her laughing mouth.

Once I came swimming up from beneath the dock and there she was sitting on the edge, her dangling legs spread wide, dark cunt hair fringing the crotch of her tight Spandex suit. I could get damp right now just running that film by. At the time I'd felt embarrassed (for one thing, you never saw anything like that on the other counselors) and simultaneously confirmed in my resolve to be a counselor myself when I got old enough. After lights out, when all the other girls were fiddling with their hair rollers and zit cream and passing bags of Fritos and listening to a contraband transistor radio with as much excited precaution as though we'd been behind the Iron curtain and the Beatles were the Voice of America and swapping whispered lore about hickeys and hardons, I'd lie there feigning sleep, my thighs squeezed tight together, weaving complicated tales which featured Kris as heroine. I hated and feared my cabinmates, their giggly group power, the cultivated female incompetence which prevented most of them from making Steelheads—but I still imagined I wanted to be a counselor.

I'd dug all this up in my coming out group, of course, then shelved it for another fifteen years. And suddenly, skipping stones in Minnesota, I was drowning in that summer. I could smell the Sea & Ski.

It was not an easy beach, or conventionally pretty. The salt Puget Sound water was fraught with jellyfish, the freezing plunge a threat even in sunny weather. The waveless surface rocked, hiding slime fronds underneath. The land was greyish green, the sky often overcast. Kris made us do our laps even when it rained.

$B$ack in the cabin, I gave Linda a quick call. Everything seemed to be okay at home. Then I opened a beer, lay down on the sagging couch, and, enfolded in the comforting night hum of crickets and distant motors, I read Prosperine's letter.

*20 March 1915*

*Rosetta Mia,*

*(Really I should ask Alma for the proper German tonguetwister to salute you with, to impress you with my progress, but somehow I can't imagine addressing you in that heavy, blunt language.)*

*Nothing much has happened since I wrote you last. Winter drears and drags till I could scream—but you know all about* that. *Twenty below this morning, I'm sick of root vegetables. I feel stupid with cold, too—Mrs. Jett won't burn enough wood in the parlor heater. The field from my window is all pock-marked, scabby with scrub growth rising up through the snow, not smooth and romantic at all. Beyond is a little rise, and then the evergreens shut off the horizon, which is too bad. When I can get a great gulp of open sky, I sometimes feel like a human being—for a minute!*

*Oh, I do long to sneak off to an island of FREEDOM somewhere. What is freedom you ask (always so practical). Definition: FREEDOM is the liberty to say Damn if I stub my toe read anything I please come and go at will leave my shoes off in the house—and lie in bed till nine or ten on Sunday morning without some prune-faced Christian frowning judgement on me when I beg off preaching service another week (I've* been only once this month, I'm running out of excuses). And then the woman had the gall to hint perhaps I would care to take on a Sunday school class—*after a week's drudging with my pupils!* I am afraid of what lurid deed may shortly be committed with a poker, a crochet hook, or even a darning needle, if spring holds off much longer.

Oh, yes, and freedom includes a blooming Rosebud—is it really only ten days since I shared your lumpy mattress—how you snored, my farmer's daughter! Not that I cared for sleep. I always feel I want to stay awake, when we've only one night in the month to share everything.

Mrs. Jett has let me know, "quite frankly," as she says, that although she considers my conduct and opinions ill becoming to "an educated Christian, dedicated to forming the minds of our community youth," she feels duty bound to treat me with civility as long as I board here. So she saves her tongue lashings for the hired girl. Poor Minnie, she's so slow that sometimes I get fed to the teeth with her myself, though I try not to show it. She fawns on me like a puppy, wants me to help her improve her reading in my "spare time." Owing to family troubles she never really got out of the First Reader. She'd like to be able to follow recipes, she says. She confided in me that she's considering marriage to a fellow named Barney Muscle, and added sadly she "never can stiffen bread to Mrs. Jett's satisfaction," as though that were a point in favor of the engagement. I guess she's about sixteen. She calls me "teacher" like the children do. I long ago gave up trying to make them say Miss Munkers, though it sets my teeth on edge hearing that "teach, teach, teacher," all day long. I suppose it would be worse being mother to a brood, always having some youngster with a runny nose tugging at skirt or apron.

This reminds me, Mrs. Jett found some papers in my room (she was dusting, she pretends, though I very much doubt it since I'm of course in the habit of sweeping up myself) and was scandalized nearly to apoplexy by some article about the Birth Control agitation. A Mrs. Sanger, who I believe has actually made available some practical method of family limitation as well as tracts on the subject, has been jailed. A Miss Emma Goldman, a well-known Jewish Anarchist, has been going about giving lectures, and may be arrested as well. I admire their courage and fortitude, though if I were given the chance to travel and meet interesting people, I think I should be more selfish, and not wish to risk being cooped up in prison! Mrs. Jett's typical comment was that no respectable woman would allow such matters to be discussed in her presence, let alone mount the lecture platform to sully the minds of others.

Let me know what you think of this topic, my Rosalie.

I've nearly made up my mind to wipe the dust of this school district off my shoes at the end of the spring term and never come back, whether I get a better place in the fall or no. That's how much I hate and despise it here, though goodness only knows how we're to get money for Chicago so quick. Perhaps Aunt Ellen will die and leave me something! I made the older pupils read part of the long Walter Whitman poem and copy it out for memorization, and Winifred Lepka's mother sent a note by her next week demanding a halt to "immorul licensus" reading matter, as she spelt it, and threatening to complain to the School Board. Well, let her (but of course she won't bother and most of the children couldn't understand the poetry anyway, they wondered who the "I" was and said they couldn't see how he could be all over America and watch everything happening at once). But just think, no more Mrs. Jett and I'll go on the streets of Bemidji and auction my virtue to the highest bidder—or do you think it might fetch more in one of the logging camps?

Oh dear Primrose please don't look so shocked, you see I'm simply in one of those cross impossible moods I get in sometimes. Remember you once told me I looked sour enough to curdle milk?

The thaw will come one of these days—then we'll live in mud.

Do you feel sorry for your pupils? I often do for mine. They try about as hard as they can, and it's not their fault they make such slow progress, small boys blear-eyed with getting up twice in the night to check the ewes during lambing, and then they are so frequently kept home altogether to help with various chores—twelve-year-old girls out for weeks when mother's new baby comes. Some of the laborers children bring nothing but doughy bread in their lunch pails, and probably ate no better than that for breakfast. One girl about ten asked me yesterday whether the Kaiser and his army were farther than Duluth. A whole family of four stopped coming when the weather got too cold. The oldest told me their father had got "a eatin' cancer" on his leg that was keeping him from work, and they had no money to purchase the necessary winter things. Their struggles hold a kind of fascination for me.

The truth is Chicago isn't half far enough, though Mrs. Jett always speaks as though it were Sodom and Gomorrah and Gay Paree and the

64

*Black Hole of Calcutta all in one. London or Paris would be my ideal goal—or Berlin possibly, with my German. Of course this war will be concluded soon, and then it really might be something to aim for, though I know you will roll your eyes and gnash your teeth and stomp your pretty foot, my skeptical Rosina. (Mrs. Jett, by the way, hints that insofar as our national duty lies in opposing the Hun and his barbarities, etc. etc., that it would be much more suitable for me to take up some language other than German. Alma the other day was close to tears because Buck had been taunted by a group of boys who bid him go fight for the krauts.)*

*I know it's wrong, but sometimes I can't help thinking Europe must be rather thrilling just now. Did I ever tell you I had a relative who was a child at New Ulm during the Sioux rising there. He had a gruesome story about watching the settlers come crawling over the prairie, trailing their mangled bowels. The Indians claimed they'd been purposely issued tainted meat from the government. There is history and horror, and drama and poetry for you. Some on my mother's side saw Sherman's march to the sea. Rose, do you ever think about the past, how strange it all is, and the strange people in it—does it have a separate meaning all its own that we can't guess, or are the same things just repeated over and over in slightly different form?*

*It seems to me modern Minnesota has been nothing but mud and snow and endless stumps to be jerked out of the ground so the land can be planted, and men hacking down trees and women bearing children— so much brute life. (Remember, we always used to talk and say there must be "more"—I wonder, do you and I mean the same thing by that?) The talk from the men I always used to hear when I was little and would sit behind the stove in the store doing my school lessons (Mother tried to keep me away from there, she thought I'd hear something I oughtn't I suppose, which only made me listen harder naturally)—so much of it was methods and measurements. Plough so many acres in so many days using this coulter—you know that kind of talk. And their wives would be full of buttons and biases and did the jelly jell. Surely there must be other things to think of than getting so much hay to the acre, or having success with such-and-such recipe for lemon layer cake?*

*Do many besides us ever miss the "more"?*

*When I was little Mother bought a book from a peddler,* Foreign Lands with Illustrations, *you must have seen it on the shelf behind the rubber plant. I used to lie on the sofa with my feet up and pore over that volume for hours. The picture of the Mohammedan holy man in his lacy minaret is stamped forever on my brain, likewise the woolly long-necked llama of South America. I think I actually believed I should get to see all that for myself one day, in the natural course of things. And then I would read Jack London, and picture myself the "hero." And here I am nineteen years old already, and have been twice out of the state.*

*Oh, news from home is that Garrett proceeds with his notion of a livery business. He talks of locating in Mankato. I guess he'll start with horses and branch into the automobile side as fast as he can.*

*When we get to Chicago I'm more and more determined to try for some type of newspaper work. If I had a foothold in journalism, there might be a chance to write other things as well. I only wish it could be Greenwich Village instead. Have you read of Greenwich Village, in Manhattan? All the people with fresh ideas seem to be thronging there.*

*Sometimes I feel quite hopeful, thinking interesting times are coming and I'm bound to be in on them if I just keep my eyes "peeled" and don't lose my nerve. Others, I get frantic, feeling the world is passing me by, and then I'm liable to fall into one of those bottomless black moods. And you, my tender pink and white Rosette—how do you stay on such an even keel? You help me get my balance.*

*How much simpler if I'd only been a boy. (And how awfully depressing to catch myself echoing a complaint that has probably been on feminine lips since the world began—you know how I despise any unoriginality.) Alter a few minor anatomical features and I could carry you off to Chicago—slip a ring on your finger and nobody would say boo not even Mrs. Jett. The Hindoos say we are born many times over, so maybe I'll switch off in my next life. Don't you think I'd make a plausible male, with a little practice?*

*You never mind being a girl much, do you? Yet you are better at many boy things than I am—managing a team, or any sort of farm stuff.*

*You simply mustn't change your mind about our plan, not now. Your family aren't relying on you this year anyway, and after we're settled you'll be in a better position to do things for the younger children. Flora and Daisy are perfectly able to help your mother out—and why shouldn't they, after all the years you've borne the brunt of it! Just keep it firmly in mind, if you were leaving to be married, they'd be in exactly the same boat,*

*and nobody would object. You have a right to make your own way, and
don't you suppose I have a rightful claim on your friendship as well?*

*I consider your promise binding.*

*Don't be jealous, but Alma seems to like me. She held me close about
the waist and kissed me very warmly, I thought, following the lesson.
(We spent an entire hour discussing hog butchering in German—ugh!)
She's a plump little bird of a girl, with such nicely waving brown-gold
hair, thick and crispy, combed back from her high forehead. But you
needn't worry about her usurping so much as one iota of your place in
my affections—unless of course you do anything to make me very
aggravated. (She doesn't think about the "more.")*

*Here's Mrs. Jett—breakfast—a whiff of burnt oatmeal—Minne must
have scorched the pot again. Oh how I despise our sex sometimes. And
the whole horrid day to be gotten through. Did I mention we've a plague
of head lice?*

*Think how we talked that night, and I braved your thorns.*

*Your everlastingly devoted,*

    *PM*


In the minute, blocky hand that had been Prosperine's—a curious
mixture of self-effacement and self-assertion, I've often thought—this
lengthy message fit onto three sheets of tissue-thin stationery, closely
written on both sides. I got quite a rush reading it the first time. I felt
as though I were opening an hermetically sealed tomb and touching the
fresh, dead things that hadn't been handled in a thousand years—that were,
because they had no continuous history, in some weird sense almost
contemporary. This headstrong, hungry daughter, this baby butch
schoolmarm, this would-be Jack London hero in ankle-length skirts,
seemed to be speaking to me directly. Of course Grandma had probably
glanced over her dead friend's message-in-a-bottle in recent years; still,
I could be quite sure of being its first new reader.

When I read it to Linda over the phone, I was pleased that she seemed
to find it almost as extraordinary as I did, though she reacted skeptically
when I mentioned my intuition that there might be a book in this
Prosperine business.

"But you don't even know for sure that there's more material," she
objected.

"Grandma said something about diaries."

"That's not a lot to go on."

A week went by, and I kept her up to date on my frustrated efforts to return the letter without Grandma's knowledge. On two successive visits I'd never been left alone in the room long enough to risk replacing it.

"Do you think she knows it's gone?"

"I seriously doubt it. If she did, she'd only blame her memory."

My slight uneasiness on this score aside, Grandma and I were getting along well, I thought. With some help from Phoebe, we were preparing for her readings. She wanted to be rehearsed in the use of a microphone, so the three of us went down to the carpeted common room with rows of chairs and a movable lectern, and held a practice session. Phoebe played the part of audience. Her dark head bobbed in the back row like a cork on a sea of folding chairs. At first Grandma was unnerved at being unable to tell from the sound of her own voice whether the microphone was working, but soon she caught on, and claimed there was nothing to it. Rather than practice with her own writing, though, she gave us a few paragraphs from a *Protestant Life*, something about preaching Christ's message of meekness in today's Rambo world. She'd go over what she was actually going to read in her own room, she said. She didn't like to tip her hand where anyone might eavesdrop. "They talk among themselves," she reminded us.

"Oh Rose," Phoebe put in, uncharacteristically disputatious. "Why bother about them? People always talk. They always have and always will. What of it? She didn't, however, question Grandma's plain opinion that the pair of them represented a local aristocracy of breeding and good sense. It was like her to accept in her friend a complete lack of her own humility.

"Or else that Mr. Luckenbill is liable to show up. That would be just like him, to come in and sit there grinning, getting me all flustered. You couldn't ask him to leave, this being a public area."

"Whatever happened to him? Have there been more incidents?"

"Well, we thought there was one, anyway, when Olive Toth was missing her brooch for three days, but it turned out she'd simply stuck it in the bathroom cabinet by mistake. But we did speak to Dr. Jerebold, and he *says* he's going to look into what happened to Phoebe and all. I don't know, I seem to be missing something else myself, but I can't

68

be sure, my memory has gotten so unreliable." Grandma's sharp glance as she said this—or it looked sharp to me—reminded me about Prosperine's letter, and I felt a twinge of concern. But she didn't dwell on it, and for the time being I dismissed the remark.

After we finished the microphone practice and discussed what Grandma should wear—a subject that really seemed to worry her more than any other aspect of her public debut as a writer—I took her and Phoebe out to lunch. She picked the restaurant. It was a chain called Best of the Wurst and served "German" food. The waitresses wore dirndl skirts with embroidered suspenders, and ours greeted us with a "Guten Tag" when she brought the menus.

When the orders arrived, Phoebe bowed her head, and Grandma followed her example. Softly, the former repeated the old grace, "Lord, bless these gifts to our use and ourselves to thy service, Amen."

"You can get a very reasonable lunch here, and they keep the place clean," Grandma observed. "Of course in the evening they attract a more raucous type of crowd. I tell Geraldine I don't care to come then. It's a shame they feel they have got to serve liquor."

"Well, I suppose most places today think they can't make enough without," Phoebe theorized.

Neither one of them ate enough of the wiener schnitzel to keep a carnivorous bird going, though Phoebe did slightly better than her friend and afterwards ordered a towering "Viennese" pastry—the menu, and the motif, veered alarmingly, with fake lederhosen on the busboys and posters on the walls advertising Fassbinder films.

"I *like* ethnic food," Phoebe said in the car. "Chuck never did, even when he had his health. He was steak and potatoes, roast beef and gravy."

"Eugene avoided German cooking. I never knew why. He was fond of chop suey and wonton soup, though. And when pizza first became popular, he used to go for that, despite his poor digestion. He was foolish that way. I never could understand why a person would persist in eating a dish that had him reaching for the bicarb an hour afterwards." This frank speech surprised me. It was most unlike Grandma to voice casual criticism of her family in front of an outsider, and showed, I thought, how much she'd unbent with Phoebe.

I saw the two of them back to their rooms, then drove home to my river. Aside from the visits to Grandma, I was leading an almost completely unstructured existence. Most mornings after I had some coffee I'd put on my bathing suit and lug a plastic lounge chair down to the stony shore. I often spent the better part of the day there, ostensibly taking notes on some of the books I'd brought along for my Black and white women writers piece or writing in my journal, but in fact more often dozing, daydreaming, watching the breeze riffle the willow branches that trailed in the golden water. Each morning I was surprised at how easily I seemed able to slip into this meandering, unmotivated routine, as though the river's example were contagious.

Sun and water, however, were feeble analgesics. Late in the day they wore off like Valium. I grew restless with inaction, some vague guilt of time misspent—a mood that on several occasions got me into bar clothes and headed for Minneapolis. The first place I tried was all women and mostly Black. The killingly handsome butches wore glossy loafers and sharply creased men's slacks and pinky rings with their initials in them; they whipped out gold cigarette lighters to accommodate their sweet, gussied-up fems. Nobody looked at me, and I left after one beer. A few nights later I tried a mixed gay bar, two-thirds men, shockingly blond. The women were under thirty, dressed for success, and looked straight as women in lipstick and skirts always do to me. In my tight white jeans and tan I felt out of date and out of place. All I'd wanted was a flirtatious conversation, maybe a slow dance or two, a nostalgic taste of the bars of my early coming out phase: those theaters of stylized sex, stage for our glad defiance. But not even vodka and orange juice would jog my memory. I felt as though my failures were emblazoned on my forehead, and found myself almost wishing I'd taken the Santa Cruz job. The excursion ended ignominiously with me returning home early and retiring to bed accompanied by a pint of mocha almond fudge ice cream and a stack of old (how quaint they seemed already!) suck-me-fuck-me-fist-me magazines, courtesy of my landlord.

Such were my typical pursuits in the first two weeks of my stay. Following the lunch at Best of the Wurst, however, I felt I'd better bestir myself and do something about the letter I'd made off with. Grandma, I recalled, had hinted that something might have been taken from her room, and though I had no way of knowing what she had in mind, I naturally didn't want to contribute to her agitation over Arnie Luckenbill, or let her worry needlessly about her memory.

There was no easy way out, evidently. I'd have to admit my transgression and hand the stolen goods over. I wasn't pleased to have gotten myself into such an absurdly sticky situation, since it now seemed to me I could perfectly well have been straightforward about the fact that I was glancing at the diary in the first place; after all, what could she have said? But what was done was done, and I'd have to take my medicine.

First of all, however, I copied Prosperine's letter out by hand. I did this partly because I wasn't sure the faded ink would photocopy legibly, but also I think because of a completely irrational feeling that bringing in a xerox machine would somehow transform what had been nothing more than a slightly discreditable accident into something bordering on criminal conspiracy. And I didn't want to let that letter go. Already Grandma's long-dead friend had awakened in me a strong covetous impulse, as though through her testimony I hoped to grasp, to possess permanently, a bit of the real past, the mysterious ground in which the present, *my* present, had germinated. I told myself that if Grandma seemed really disturbed at what I'd done, I could always destroy the copy.

As it turned out, she actually hadn't noticed that the letter was gone; it was a March of Dimes can she'd missed, which had been sitting on her bureau. It took me quite a bit of embarrassing repetition to get her to understand what I was apologizing for. Even when she did, she looked perplexed, and wondered why I hadn't simply asked to see the diary. At last she set her mouth and shook her head slightly. "Well, Dale, I wouldn't have thought you'd read other people's mail," was all she said, but it stung like old-fashioned antiseptic.

Nevertheless, I took comfort in the fact that she would have let me read the letter if I'd asked, and made use of the opportunity to press my suit a little. I said that even this early, casual piece of writing showed unmistakable signs of talent. I told her I wanted to look up the newspaper Prosperine had worked for; it might turn out that her letters were of some real historical interest. I reminded her that she'd spoken of having a box of Prosperine's diaries. "If you could possibly let me have a look at those—I mean, I could do it more or less at the same time as I'm helping you edit your own stuff."

She looked mollified at the mention of her "book." "Well, I'd have to look around and think where those diaries could be, if I didn't throw them out. Not that I'd have wanted to do that, but I had to get rid of so much when the house was sold. There was a World Book Encyclopedia set, one of the early ones, that was worth quite a sum, and I had to let it go for a nominal price, and so many wool clothes—I always planned to use 'em for braided rugs, but I never got the time, and there wasn't room to store them anymore."

"Couldn't they be around here somewhere?" I persisted, thinking she was like a wily old bird, hopping the opposite way from where her nest was hidden. "Do you still have all those boxes underneath the bed?"

"Oh, not there, no. Those are all family things."

Politely, I waited.

"I'm tired out now. I guess I'll take a nap."

I felt properly rebuked. I hadn't been there half an hour. She hadn't even offered me tea. She sat on the edge of the bed and removed her wedge heels, revealing slender gnarled feet in sheer hosiery with opaque reinforcements at heel and toe. "Nylons"—a sexy item to me for some reason. Probably they were actually modern Sup-Hose, vastly improved over the thick brownish tights old women used to wear.

I prepared to leave, but she said, "Well, Dale, I don't know that I can fall asleep right away. Maybe you'd be good enough to read the news to me. I used to do that for your grandfather every afternoon. He liked to keep up with things, even when he'd got so weak."

I was glad to be pardoned—if she meant to pardon me—and took the neatly folded copy of the *Pioneer* that she pointed out. She lay down on top of the quilt and, complaining of a chill from the air conditioning, covered her legs with a light crocheted blanket. She massaged her temples, then stretched out flat, almost rigid, with her arms at her sides. Her purplish, pleated eyelids closed deep in the shadowed sockets. It was startling how fast the look of life drained away, once she lay still. Her flat chest swelled and sank almost imperceptibly. I hesitated to disturb her, but she said in her normal voice, "You may read now."

I thought she'd want to hear the local news, but instead she chose a story on the financial page about the takeover craze on Wall Street, full of the romance of junk bonds and poison pills, and largely incomprehensible to me. She followed this with a gory and equally convoluted dispatch form Beirut, then something on Star Wars, and I understood with sudden admiration that she really was trying to "keep up," just as Grandpa had.

"My," she murmured, after the last item, "wouldn't it be something if they could get that space shield to work? We wouldn't have to worry about those frightful atom bombs. Now, that's enough of that. Can you find the garden column?"

At last she said she thought she really could take nap now, and apologized so for being poor company that I really felt my offense was forgotten as well as forgiven, and that I needn't destroy my copy of the letter. Just before I left she quietly remarked, à propos of nothing in particular, "There's a young woman here who works on the grounds, doing landscaping. Funny job for a woman. She's quite attractive though—not *mannish* in the least. For some reason she always makes me think of Proppie."

Irked and amused, I took my leave, wondering mightily how she privately classified me. I don't carry a purse. I don't wear earrings. I'm one of that sisterhood who, in winter's shapeless garments, gets almost used to hearing "sir" in restaurants.

$A$t the time I met Ruta Karlessen, her fame was in transition. Over the years she'd built up, so I gathered, a sort of rusty, dingy, localized renown: people still remembered that in the Sixties she used to trail around in a robe like a priest's cassock, leading groups of students out into the woods where they'd all drop mescaline and invoke the Life Force, and more recently her dramatic readings of her own and others' work had become standard fare at radical rallies and fundraisers. Now, however, in her early eighties, she was beginning to receive some national attention for the first time in decades. Several masters' theses and doctoral dissertations were already underway, and her journalism from the Depression years and the Spanish Civil War was once more available. But her undoubted masterpiece, the novel *Mabel Hunneger* (which I'd heard about but not yet actually read at the time of our first encounter) had been out of print for a quarter-century, and the feminist free-for-all was still in the opening stages.

Have you ever seen a picture of a Pacific Northwest beach a hundred years ago, with an entire Coast Salish village turning out to divvy up a whale carcass? That's how they strike me sometimes, these female Masters in our midst: they're beached leviathans, we adore them for their blubber. Doesn't everyone and her sister want a hunk of Adrienne, a slice of the true Tillie? If I'd been really on the ball, I guess I might have arranged to tape an interview with Ruta, edit an authorized collection of critical essays on her work, maybe even get a peek at her notebooks and early drafts (which, by the way, I heard the other day some straight married lady from Stanford has sunk her delicate incisors into). As a matter of fact, all these possibilities crossed my mind. In another, more self-confident and energetic year, I might well have pursued them, and by now could have been in the first rank of Karlessen experts, well-positioned for a shot at writing her biography when she departs this vale of ink and microfilm.

As things turned out, my stake in her legend has been relaxed and amateur, and I've been able to observe with fairly detached interest her ascent to her current celebrity status. Actually, there are considerable gaps in what I know about her that I wouldn't mind seeing filled in when and if that definitive biography gets written, which I hope is no time soon. The events of her life following the fairly well-known European period (dips into the rarefied, aesthetic lesbian circles of Paris in the Twenties, followed by increasing politicization and then her journey to Spain) are especially hard to pin down, since, as is the case with many such gnarled and layered characters, her revelations often seem to serve a larger privacy. Obviously she's always been gregarious, but it's a trait which doesn't cancel out her essential isolation. She's the type of loner to dwell in the thick of humanity, bound to attract notice and relishing the fact. Yet when she returned to the U.S. in poor health following the fall of Madrid, she didn't settle on the East Coast as would have seemed logical, but moved back to Minnesota, where she'd spent part of her childhood.

She subsisted on God knows what, struggled with her writing, mysteriously acquired her only son. (I've never found anyone who has the faintest idea who the father was.) She attended all the union picnics, and later Ban the Bomb marches. In time she would do support for Wounded Knee. I once heard her claim, presumably in jest, that she'd invented the slogan "Think Globally—Act Locally," but it looked to me as though she'd beaten McCarthy to it, buried herself alive before the blacklist could do her in, and I wondered what permanent injury the Spanish war—or was it the Spanish love which she so frequently referred to?—had inflicted on her.

In the decade following 1948 she published almost nothing. In '59 she surfaced with *Mabel Hunneger*, which is supposedly based in part on the life of a cousin of hers who grew up on an isolated South Dakota farm dominated by a rigid Lutheran stepfather. Mabel's relationship with her friend Lottie Karpfoos, a clerk in a Woolworth's, is infused with a sensual and emotional intensity that undoubtedly had something to do with the book's lukewarm reception when it first appeared. It sold a few thousand copies before going out of print.

Genius is the capriciously-blooming flower of a hardy little weed. Minus this novel, arguably the most remarkable fictional portrait we possess of white Midwestern working-class women in this century, Ruta's life story, for all its interest, comes off as yet another saga of thwarted female creativity. Yet Ruta herself never appeared to set great store by her masterpiece in the years it was out of print. Now that it's receiving a lot of attention, she's proud of it, of course, and I recently heard her give an absolutely stunning reading of that stark chapter "The Night Shift," in which Mabel's little son is crippled in a fire that breaks out in their rooms while his mother is at her factory job. However, she still maintains she wants to be remembered for her journalism and her "Spanish" sonnets, a lengthy sequence of conventional love poems—conventional, that is, except for their lesbian theme—which have just been issued by a gay press after nearly a half-century in the drawer.

On the day of that first meeting, I got up earlier than usual in order to be sure of making it to Ruta's by noon. In her note she'd suggested I come for lunch, and provided a hand-drawn map with detailed driving instructions. Her place, which she called "The Farm," turned out to be a modest acreage a short drive southeast of the Minneapolis city limits, in a suburb still uneasily clinging to its agricultural roots like a loose tooth getting ready to fall out. To the north, a tract sprawled, decades old and gracelessly aging on exposed concrete foundations. Further south the earth flattened; streamlined silos stood up to be counted against a horizon grey with heat. It was not yet noon and already the car seat was sticky behind my back and under my thighs.

Ruta's dwelling was a rusty pink mobile home set well back from the road. In the front yard a sentinel elm reared, enormous and battle-scarred, with several withered limbs. Parked at an odd angle in the gravel drive was an old boat of a Ford with a smashed fender and bumper stickers announcing I SUPPORT LOCAL P-9 and UFF DA! NORVEGIAN DRIVER. An ambitious stand of corn and beans and squash had been fenced with chicken wire. From somewhere out back came the furious barking of many dogs, lending credence to the sign advertising Malamute puppies which I'd passed on my way in.

I rang the bell. The dogs barked tirelessly. I rang and knocked for good measure. At last Ruta appeared, noiseless in house slippers. She filled up the doorframe, a raw heap of old woman, taller than I and far heavier than I'd guessed from the photographs I'd seen, so broad indeed that I thought of some of Grandma's sisters: cheerful Lily the farmer's wife, with flesh puddled around her ankles, or dour depressing Iris, widowed early, who'd toiled for thirty years dishing up the same liver and onions from the selfsame steam table in the Stockholm Cafeteria in Hibbing, and died without having set foot outside the state. ("Think of gaining all that weight on *cafeteria* food!" my mother always shuddered.) These were the ne'er do wells among the Bright sisters; their having "let themselves go" seemed all mixed up with social status. The successes, like Grandma, somehow kept their figures despite the "Bright hips"— and it seemed entirely natural, according to the family's conception of cosmic/cosmetic justice, that the youngest, fabulous Amaryllis, who'd married an Upshott, was thinner than all the rest.

Ruta Karlessen, however, was no slouch. Though her bare arms jiggled as Lily's used to do, she sported a western string tie with a turquoise clasp at the throat. When she gripped my hand so hard the sharp rings marked me, I felt I was in the presence of some monumental power, like a female Pope or Speaker of the House.

"Come in," she boomed, holding the screen door. "It's hot out there, I know. I made some lemonade—real lemons, boiled sugar water. I can't stand that phony stuff that comes in cans." She turned, and I saw that the yellow-white hair, raked loosely back in what I at first had taken to be a modified DA, actually culminated in a wispy bun at the back of her wide neck.

Inside was unbelievable disorder, a whiff of cheese and ripening catbox, a welter of books and papers, steno pads and pots and pans and canning jars. I noted a colander and a hammer and an egg beater on the couch, a toaster and double boiler on a bookshelf. The few chairs were occupied by stacks of newspapers. Herbs and onions hung from twine strung across the ceiling. A table was piled high with jumbled garments, some in children's sizes. The walls—I continued my survey while lemonade was being poured—boasted framed photographs and torn posters, some Kokoschka and Klimt prints, a Mexican ceramic mask and a primly stitched sampler: DO I CONTRADICT MYSELF? VERY WELL THEN I CONTRADICT MYSELF, (I AM LARGE, I CONTAIN MULTITUDES.).

Like any normal hostess defending her housekeeping, Ruta vaguely apologized for the lack of seating and mentioned that the clothing on the table was destined for Nicaragua. "I agreed to help out with a material aid campaign. I figure it's the least I can do. When I came back I had all kinds of good intentions of doing solidarity work, but other things are always taking up my time." As she spoke she was arranging Ritz crackers on a plate and getting plastic containers out of the refrigerator.

"Oh, you've been there, have you? What did you think?"

"Well, I'm afraid I can't say I was quite so enthused as some of the young people seem to be, when they come back from their work brigades. I was only there ten days, just long enough to get the runs. It's a brave little place, of course, a brave little battered place." She slammed the door on the old Frigidaire, seeming to relegate such courage to the margins of history.

"I don't know, the dreadful poverty—not that I haven't seen suffering, of course. But all those children begging, packs of them, so aggressive. Well, why not, we've been robbing them blind for over a hundred years!

"And the walls riddled with bullet holes, and those pathetic teenage soldiers, and the barefoot mothers all worn out with child-bearing. As I say, I've seen slaughter, I've seen poverty aplenty. Spain was hell on earth. I've seen Appalachia, of course, and the Dustbowl in the Thirties. However, in Nicaragua one got the feeling...one *saw* what under-development *meant*. They're like spun sugar in a downpour, those Sandinistas. They don't stand much chance."

"But, barring an invasion—" I objected. Her implication, I felt, was that we'd come down considerably in the world, from an age of gold to an age of brass—or plastic. Sheer loyalty to my times obliged me to contradict her, though actually, come to think of it, I hadn't followed Central America very closely, or paid that much attention to anything else political recently, either.

She wasn't listening. "If we'd stopped them in Spain, you see, we might have halted fascism. We might have prevented the Second War altogether." She paused and noticed the food she'd gotten out. "But you're hungry, aren't you? Let's eat outside. There's no place to sit down in here anyway, and the electric fan only stirs up the hot air. We can sit out under that elm tree in the shade, maybe catch a puff of breeze.

"Poor old scraggly thing, that tree ought to have been done for a

78

long time ago—Dutch elm disease—but her life force is strong. She struggles on, year by year. One of these days I'll simply have to cut her down. I don't know what I'll do without my shade tree.

"Don't misunderstand me. I support Nicaragua. Objectively, it's the frontline. I understand that.

"Harry—that's my son—Harry calls me sentimental. He's always threatening to bring over his chain saw. He grew up hearing nothing but scientific socialism, I'm afraid. Yet he's turned out completely apolitical."

We sat there sweating under the doomed she-elm, and drank the real lemonade, which was very good, and ate cold fried chicken and macaroni salad. Ruta reminisced about old acquaintances: Djuna Barnes ("pretentious female"), Frida Kahlo, Floyd Van Arp. Kahlo and she, I'd heard, were supposed to have been lovers—was that in Europe or California, and hadn't I read some anecdote somewhere about a drunken brawl between Ruta and Diego Rivera?—but I gleaned nothing of substance on this mesmerizing topic. Instead I learned much more than I cared to know about the life of Van Arp, her former neighbor, a farmer from a conservative pioneer family who had been radicalized somehow in the conservative Twenties. He'd been active in the Farm Holiday protests of the following decade. He had a fine platform voice, Ruta said, and always used to read the Declaration of Independence to the crowds at rallies and picnics. He'd been red baited in the Forties and Fifties, shunned by the neighborhood. In recent years he'd had a struggle to keep his land, and had gotten no help from family. (A son was a Lincoln-Mercury dealer in Eau Claire, a daughter a television evangelist.) He'd tried to organize against the encroaching developers, but last year had finally given up and sold out to some millionaire who was building a subdivision.

"Money enough to die on, that's what he got. He moved down to Phoenix and six months later he was flat on his back in an ICU with tubes and wires sprouting out of him like eyes on a seed potato. That's Floyd Van Arp—an American original, yet in a sense an Everyman. I thought I'd like to write it sometime, maybe do it as a play. Put the old man right up there on center stage, maybe sitting upright in a rocking chair, but wired and hooked to monitors and IV's, all the death machinery beeping and bleating around him, while the story of his past unfolds on either side. At the end he'd rise like a Greek chorus of one and make his comment on the action. What do you think?"

I smiled, though I thought it sounded fairly deadly.

"There's a radical theater group in St. Paul that's eager for me to do it. But it will have to wait a year or two. You know, I'm writing about Spain."

In fact, I'd heard a rumor to that effect. To scuttle Floyd Van Arp, I asked, "Is it true you were in Barcelona at the same time as Orwell?"

"*That* self-righteous little posturer," she snapped. "No, that's an honor I'm afraid I can't claim." It had been a stupid question I realized, and probably everybody asked it. Still, I was taken aback at her vehemence. She'd been aligned with the CP during the Spanish period of course, but had gone her own way long since.

After a minute she said more mildly, "You have to understand I was stuck in Madrid for most of those thirteen months. I was coordinating a relief effort and doing some journalism on the side. They did everything they could to keep a woman from getting near the fighting. There was a regular little colony of American females there, Lincoln Brigade wives a lot of them. They used to cry their eyes out in my cubbyhole, those wives.

"But you see, if one was different...in one's desire...this complicated matters, don't you know."

She squinted delicately out at the horizon. The elm's spotty shade was shifting, and the sun was in her eyes. My god, woman, I thought, don't get coy on me now. As if everyone didn't know already—everyone, at any rate, who's ever seen that Berenice Abbott shot of you with your shirtsleeves rolled, the one on the postcard. Besides, who do you think *I* am, anyway?

"There was a Spanish girl," she added.

Of course there was, I thought. There's always a Spanish girl.

"She was La Pasionaria's niece."

"Are you writing about her?"

"I'm trying to."

"We need this, you realize. We need these stories."

Her faded blue eyes darkened a shade; she seemed to recognize me. "I'm sorry, Dale. Isn't that silly of me! These bad habits of...not saying things out loud...grow on you, you know. It happened the same way with people in the Party."

I was dying to hear more. Had Ruta been *in* the Party? Nothing I'd

80

heard or read had indicated a definite answer, one way or the other. And what a butch fatale she'd been—La Pasionaria's niece, indeed!

But an old red pickup came grinding up the drive, raising a thick cloud of dust and spoiling my chances for followup questions. The driver, a taciturn woman with terrifically hairy legs in Bermuda shorts, was introduced as Ann: "She's been helping me keep the garden under control." Ruta fortified her with iced tea and ginger snaps, and protested a good deal about the heat, but Ann trotted off to hoe the beans anyway. At the time I assumed she'd been hired for the task, but later found out she was part of an informal volunteer corps of Ruta Karlessen fans, most of them women under forty-five (though one couldn't discount the occasional gay male poet or bearded socialist food coop manager) who weeded her vegetables, photocopied manuscripts, ran to the post office on half an hour's notice, carted her Malamutes to the veterinarian, and kept her in marijuana and men's magazines.

Even in the shade, the heat was now punishing, and the purple-topped field grass barely stirred in an occasional puff of breeze. I was aware of having eaten too much chicken too fast, but roused myself enough to mention the purpose of my visit.

"Ah, yes, your research. I must hear about that. Refresh my memory—it's on what, exactly?"

A bit self-conscious at her magisterial tone, I began outlining my notion that there might have been connections worth exploring between Black and white women writers of the Twenties and Thirties, connections of a different depth or texture from those that obtained between their male counterparts. Almost immediately Ruta interrupted me with an anecdote I didn't care for much, about watching Zora Neale Hurston dance on a tabletop at a party up in Harlem. "It was dark as Egypt in the room, you couldn't see much but her tossing purple skirt and flashing teeth. Every so often she'd shout something out—I had trouble understanding the dialect. Langston Hughes was there as well, I think, with that very handsome tall young fellow—what was his name?—that followed him around—or maybe that was later?"

This wasn't exactly what I'd had in mind. "What I'd like to do, if it's okay with you, would be to come back another time with a list of specific questions. Not a formal interview, exactly, but some structure might be helpful."

"Of course, of course." Ruta beamed amiably. Producing an engraved cigarette case, she asked if I'd care to "turn on." "Home grown," she added proudly. "I call it 'North Star Gold.' "

I was going to refuse; I felt slightly depressed as well as drowsy, and grass sometimes made me anxious unless I'd had a few drinks. But then I noticed how the shadows were lengthening, and gratefully realized that the waste expanse of ebbing energy, dull regrets, and creeping angst which I identify with mid-afternoon wasn't going to last forever. I knew from experience that after five o'clock, when it got too late to rescue the ruined day, my prospects would appear to improve dramatically, and my brain would be flooded by dancing endorphins. I could mosey back to Minneapolis, have a drink somewhere, anticipate night's promises and threats. I'd heard something about a dance at the gay and lesbian center, and had brought a clean shirt with me, just in case.

Besides, while I'd supped with most of the senior dignitaries of feminist literature (the "highnesses," as Linda liked to say), and had even slept with several years ago, I'd never gotten stoned with the likes of Ruta Karlessen—whose Sixties archaism "turn on" charmed me no end. Imagine dropping acid with Gertrude Stein, or doing some lines with Radclyffe Hall!

I inhaled, held my breath, and passed the joint back to Ruta, who pinched it jauntily between forefinger and thumb. She'd put on dark glasses and looked like a state trooper.

The stuff was stronger than I'd expected of "North Star Gold."

"So tell me about yourself," Ruta commanded. "The young fascinate me...your view of the world...how you manage your love lives, for instance. Have you got a 'friend'? Are you non-monogamous? Or celibate, perhaps?—I mustn't forget that option!"

*All of the above* was on the tip of my tongue, but I trotted out Linda and Fiona.

"A family! Why, isn't that nice. Yes, I know quite a number of young women hereabouts are eager to have children. Soon the community will be one gigantic nursery." She didn't look as though she exactly relished the prospect.

"I've tried with Fiona," I admitted, "but so far anyway, it doesn't seem to work at all. Every time I make an effort she shoots me down. I'll take home pizza for dinner, with all the stuff she likes on it, and she'll look at the box and groan, 'Scarlucci, the most *retarded* pizza in New Jersey.' Thanks to her I can sit in my own home and listen to heterosexist remarks I wouldn't tolerate from a stranger on a bus.

"Linda assures me she's really a seething mass of insecurities. She says I shouldn't be fooled by aggressive grooming and a superficial command of brand names. Fiona's friends wear braces on their teeth, but all the girls use hair remover on what they call 'the bikini line.' Some of them have their *own* VCR's, to go with their own TV's. They do their homework to Talking Heads and Depeche Mode, Run-DMC and the Boston Philharmonic. They write book reports for English class on anorexic little novels about rich teenage faggot coke addicts who rape young girls out of existential pique. They discuss 'sexual ethics' in gym class. They know what they want to be when they grow up, for Christ's sake! Fiona plans on entertainment law, though she also wants to study Spanish and Swahili as a backup, in case she decides she'd rather, as she puts it, 'get into hunger in the Third World.' "

Ruta smiled at my indignation. "But you have your relationship."

"Right," I shrugged, suddenly longing to come clean.

She made it easy for me. "You haven't found...well, anything cloying in the exclusivity, after nine years?"

I guess I must have blushed as I owned up to Treecie. "It was kind of weird," I boasted. "I suppose that's what's popularly known as 'just a physical attraction'—the way our bodies just seemed to belong together."

"Ah, it's good when it's like that, isn't it?" she reminisced. (Enchanted, I perceived we were talking butch to butch.) "And isn't it interesting how *bed* is so often the crux of things? In my experience, when one satisfied a woman—well, of course I mean when she satisfied one, as well—all the rest would tend to fall into place.

"That was part of the tragedy with Pia—my Spanish friend, you know. On top of the war, and history, and all that. This awful Catholic culture, a millennium of repression, the hatred and loathing of the flesh— she had a strong sensual streak, but they'd gotten to her early. Those prohibitions seep into the marrow.

"But when I was young, what a wicked thing I was! I had a boy cousin in New York, you see, about a year younger than I. We used to ogle women in the streets, analyze their good points. He was so hesitant with girls I couldn't stand it. I'd coach him but he'd rarely follow my advice. 'Did you feel her up?' I'd ask, when he came home.

"Those girls must have gone crazy, waiting for him to make a move. I'd learned through a process of trial and error myself, and thought he ought to take a little initiative. I got pretty far with some of my own little friends. Of course I understood *their* pleasure, better than any boy of that age, I daresay. I can remember once being in the bushes in Central Park with some hot little thing, and having her push my wet hand away, and whisper in my ear she was afraid to get in trouble. I never knew if she'd actually forgotten, or was that ignorant!"

To my dismay, I felt a faint erotic tug. Could I blame it on the dope? Not bloody likely. I hoped Ruta didn't know about it; I wasn't at all sure that I wanted to be turned on by her sudden, sexy shift from coy to coarse.

I thought of a joke Linda might have appreciated: "Two butches, what could we *do* together?" All the same, I felt relieved when Ann came charging from the garden, hoe in hand, with some news about the corn. When she went back to work I thought it best to change the subject, and told Ruta about the letter of Prosperine's and my fascination with her papers.

"Prosperine Munkers," she mused, "that name does ring a bell. It's so unusual, there can't have been two of 'em. It was a peculiar custom, the way parents in those days used to make up girls' names simply by tacking 'ine' onto anything. I even knew an Alfredine once...but Prosperine, Prosperine, where have I heard that? The Wobblies, you say?"

"According to Grandma."

Ruta sat for a moment in concentrated thought. "*Solidarity,*" she announced decisively. "You know, the Wob paper. Or it might have been *The Industrial Worker*. But I'd suggest you try *Solidarity*. At the start of the war that would have been, before the crackdown."

"Then Prosperine was important!" I exclaimed.

"Well, she evidently had a certain place in the organization. She was quite young, I take it, and it was no small thing for a woman to make her way in that masculine outfit. Gurley managed it—Elizabeth Flynn—but she was a queen bee. Later on, in her Party years, there was a good deal of resentment of her on the part of some people because—"

"Did you *meet* Prosperine?" I interrupted. "Is that possible?"

"Oh, I wouldn't remember. I only went once with my father to Chicago, where they had their headquarters, the last summer I spent in the Midwest. I only remember the godawful heat, and being put out because Bill Haywood talked down to me, I thought—he kept calling me 'Missy' when I wanted to be 'Fellow-Worker.' I was intrigued by the colorful terms the men used, and later when I was back in New York, I'd read *Solidarity* when I could get a copy, before it was suppressed. . . .That must have been where I came across this Prosperine's byline."

"I'll look in the library," I said, wanting to ask a great many more questions, glad I'd have all summer.

"There comes Stacy," Ruta added. I gazed off in the direction where her swollen finger pointed and saw a churlish-looking young woman in a tube top and cutoffs pushing a child in a stroller with a sunshade, while at the same time dragging behind her a supermarket shopping cart. She wore high, teetery sandals, smoked a cigarette, and paused every so often to rearrange her scanty outfit, all of which gave her bumpy progress along the shoulder some of the fascination of an ant's exertions in hauling a massive crumb.

Ruta waved, called out, "Hello, Stacy. I've got the papers for you."

"I'll stop on the way back," Stacy yelled, hardly looking at us.

"Lives with her parents up the road," Ruta explained. "She had a Canadian boyfriend who went back to Saskatoon. You know what she's doing with that cart? She goes out collecting people's old newspapers. Turns 'em in to some recycling outfit, makes a little pocket money that way. They're getting food stamps. Tough life for a kid like that."

I started to say I thought I ought to get going, but didn't say it loud enough.

"When Harry was a baby we were so fuckin' poor, I used to push his carriage through the snow a mile each way to get a loaf of day-old bread for fifteen cents. . .I believe I might have gotten further with my writing, but I hadn't the ruthlessness of the great male authors. . .my book about Spain is called *Did We Count*? It only poses the question, which can't be answered yet. Time is the problem now, that's what keeps me up nights. Do we have time enough? My God, we didn't think of that in the Nineteen Thirties, we thought about Hitler. I've been reading about this hole in the ozone. . .I used to be enamored of male systems. . .China, of course, too, has been a terrific disappointment. . .South Africa, that's the place now. The future is there, and with the women too, a Black girl

85

of fifteen...It can't be stopped now, what's going to happen there, no matter how bloody and terrible some of it will have to be...That's such a male notion anyway, isn't it? Prediction and control, the basis of Marxism, 'scientific socialism' as we always used to say. Suppose one just let go, sank into the endless ooze? The original muck of things, the *female* universe. That would be the Life Force in its purest manifestation. And it *is* terrifying...Be plankton in an ocean of contradictions, molecules in the primordial protoplasm! Democratic centralism was too limiting a concept, it was that more than anything that finished the Party here... They called me an anarchist, an anarchist, *me*! I did go back to Spain after Franco kicked off. I visited Pia. She was living in a hideous modern apartment complex on the outskirts of Madrid. It was a strange meeting. In the Fifties she'd had a breakdown. She'd converted, become intensely religious. All those years...it's probably simply incomprehensible to someone your age. We hardly talked. What can you say? We didn't need to, it was all there. Yet we were *old women*, you see...that was the strangeness of it. I felt *she* shouldn't have aged, the beloved doesn't age...We ate olives, and drank to the Life Force, to Spanish democracy. What does that mean, I thought, *Spanish democracy*? The words might have been nonsense syllables. I kissed her on the mouth when we said goodbye. Of course we knew we would almost certainly not meet again—in this life, she'd say. After, in the airport, I blacked out. I thought it was death, I'd never fainted before."

Of course all of this couldn't have literally have emerged, toothpastelike, in one unbroken ribbon, but that was the effect as I remembered it—as I was reconstructing it already on the drive back to the river. I was relieved to get away, and had decided to skip the dance. Ever since that odd erotic moment I'd been feeling slightly claustrophobic. But suddenly, in the stifling hot car, it seemed to me that the visit had been highly significant, that I'd been privileged to touch some corner of history. I was in a rush to get back to the cabin and write it all down in my journal.

A few days later, when I got a call from my old friend Bonnie who lived in Chicago and knew Ruta slightly, I was quite indigent at her flippancy. "How *is* old 'Life Force' Karlessen, anyway?" she chuckled. "Did she bend your ear about her Spanish love affair?"

On the day after I met Ruta, Grandma had her reading at the Hill. It went off more or less to everyone's satisfaction. Aunt Geri and I were there. So was Uncle Gene's wife Judy, with her laugh like a nervous colt's whinny. Uncle Gene himself, along with Uncle Bert and the relevant cousins, had promised to go to the bookstore reading instead, since the Fellowship Hill event took place in the afternoon. At least two-thirds of maybe forty chairs were filled, which made a respectable showing, and Grandma looked stiff but sweet in her high-necked beige dress, though she'd fretted that it was really a *fall* outfit.

She managed the microphone with only slight awkwardness, and with the aid of her magnifying glass read several "chapters" in a clear, tense monotone. She might have been more chatty and anecdotal, I thought, but the formal setup with the lectern didn't really encourage that. I felt it had been a good practice session, anyway. The response from her peers was polite, no more; but then enthusiasm was hardly to be expected from ancient Minnesotans. Most lingered afterwards for cookies and a fruit juice punch, spiked with gingerale and garnished with orange slices. After a while I did notice several residents sidling up to Grandma, and, as they engaged her in an absorbing conversation, moved closer to hear what they had to say about her writing.

"Would they give you dips and chips and little sandwiches and things? Deviled ham with the crusts cut off?" one woman was saying. I listened a moment longer and realized she was simply interested in the procedure for reserving the lecture room.

Arnie Luckenbill was present, but left without attempting to speak to Grandma. "I *hope* Rose didn't notice," Phoebe whispered, standing on tiptoe to reach my ear. "She gets so worked up." On the other hand, Dr. Jerebold himself came over to offer his congratulations.

"Dr. J. seems to think I gave a good performance," our author mentioned as we walked her and Phoebe back to their wing. Her tone modestly hinted at unreported superlatives, and I felt a sudden pang of identification. Grandma had been a firstborn daughter like me, always eager to shine in the eyes of authority, actually far more comfortable and confident in the classroom than in the wilderness of the schoolyard. What happens to such a child when she's outlived all her teachers?

"Why don't you stop in for a minute?" she unexpectedly suggested. "I've got something I was meaning to show Dale."

Geri, Judy, Phoebe, and I crowded into the room. From a square white cardboard box on her dresser top, the kind in which bracelets and earrings are sold, Grandma removed a tarnished silver oval strung on a silver chain. On its surface was engraved a delicate pattern of intertwined leaves and flowers. She pressed it into my hand. It was heavier than it looked.

"A locket," Phoebe knew before the rest of us.

"Here, I'll open it." Grandma fumbled for the clasp. I tried to help, but didn't understand the mechanism. At last her cramped fingers touched the right place, and the tiny hinge swung back.

"Your friend Prosperine gave me that." There was the merest note of irony in her tone. "It was an old Munkers family heirloom. She removed the other picture and put her own in. That photograph was taken when she graduated from Normal School, I think. The border is a braid of her own hair.

"I ran across it the other day when I was cleaning," she added, implausibly. I strongly suspected she'd looked for it on purpose, a fact I felt boded well for my investigative efforts. There were two powerful impulses at work here, it seemed: one secretive, the other revelatory.

The sepia image lay under a curved lid of glass, framed by a minutely braided lock of pallid hair. Immediately I recognized the same broad forehead, arched blond eyebrows, and steady gaze I knew from the other photo of Prosperine I'd seen. But here she looked almost tender, almost vulnerable, with wisps of hair escaping the confinement of a young lady's special-occasion hairdo. Her mouth was wide and soft, with a full lower lip. Her androgynous bloom made me think of those beardless naked boys one sees laurel-crowned in the work of certain German photographers.

"She gave me that when I went away to teach my first school. She didn't teach immediately herself, you know. She thought it would interfere with her reading and poetry. She stayed home for a term and helped out in a drugstore."

"Just look how that's braided!" Aunt Geri admired. "How did she manage that? The work is so fine!"

"Attractive gal. Who was she?" Aunt Judy, as usual, sounded as though she felt left out. It was common knowledge that Grandma had never completely accepted her, never judged her quite good enough to be joined to our family, though her father had made a bundle with five bowling alleys. *He's Catholic, and he drinks*, was her immortal comment.

"My friend Prosperine. We were inseparable." Grandma uttered the melodramatic adjective without emphasis, making it sound like quiet fact.

"She seems to have been a bit of a firebrand, a radical and socialist. Isn't that what you told me, Grandma?" I interjected, provocative on purpose. She seemed happy about her successful debut and Dr. Jerebold's praise, and I thought this might be the time to get her talking. Besides, I felt an impulse to stir things up a little. I thought of what Ruta had said about *Solidarity*, but of course that would have meant nothing to this bunch.

"Prosperine and Grandma," I continued, "ran away to Chicago when they got fed up with teaching school. They lived together for a winter there. Grandma might have stayed—Aunt Geri, just think! She wouldn't have married Grandpa, and where would that leave us?"

Grandma was unamused by my fantasies. "*Prosperine* disliked teaching," she corrected.

Phoebe professed astonishment at learning that Rose had once resided so far away.

"It was quite a time to have been in Chicago. It was shortly before we entered World War I. The city was a national hub for labor organizing. The famous Big Bill Haywood ran the IWW office there. Did you ever hear him speak, Grandma, or Elizabeth Gurley Flynn, the 'Rebel Girl'? Emma Goldman may have lectured too, that winter. You were in fast company!"

"Well, I don't know if I recall any of those, specifically." Nor did

89

she, evidently, possess the least conception of their notoriety, for she sounded vaguely sorry to have missed them. "Anyway, we didn't go out much. I had a job in a book bindery, low pay and long hours. Proppie was just getting acquainted with this fellow Stuberfield, that ran the newspaper. You'd go over to his place and his wife Mary—he had a wife, for a wonder—would've cooked up some stew or spaghetti in a wash boiler. She'd start it in the morning, let it simmer on the back of the stove till suppertime, and whoever came by would get a plate of that. Men would come that were out of work—and she was raising three youngsters.

"I remember how she let them run around the icy floors in the middle of January in their stocking feet. Of course the socks always had big holes in 'em. You'd see some strapping fellows sitting there, sopping up the food with big hunks of bread, washing it down with coffee. Those little pitchers used to hang on every word, of course—and some of those words weren't fit for man or beast! Mary did the best she could in her own way, I guess. She had a lot to put up with.

"I do remember one fellow though that had a Jewish name. He was quite the gentleman and never swore. The most he'd ever say was 'gee fuzz,' or, 'what in Sam Hill.' But he had his oddities, like all the rest of them. Always wore a bright red shirt and black suspenders and a flowing black tie."

"Were they Wobblies? IWW's?" I was charmed.

"Oh, I wouldn't know. A few might've been, though later Prosperine decided the crowd at Stuberfield's was just a 'phony bunch of pampered college boys,' she said. This was after she took up with that real fringe element."

"What would they talk about? Do you remember?"

"The rights of labor, all that kind of stuff. Most of them were pretty bitter against the war, though one fellow raised a ruckus by insisting we ought to get into it. They wanted him put out, but Mary wouldn't stand for it. She said there was free speech, in her place.

"I didn't see any real harm in most of their talk. I guess I just thought they were like young fellows anywhere, even the boys I used to know up around the farm. You didn't take their remarks too seriously. Those IWW's, though—people said later they used to set fire to the fields of crops and wreck the farmers' combines. Later on the government had to deport a lot of the subversives that were foreign-born."

"Did Prosperine go to meetings, or anything like that?"

"I don't remember. Not much, I guess. Oh, I remember once there was a big memorial service, like, for some fellow that died—well, he got himself shot, out west someplace. Proppie—Prosperine—was determined to go to that. I didn't want anything to do with it. I knew there'd be a crowd, a lot of shoving, and standing in the cold, and I always was afraid of the policemen on horseback."

"What was the man's name? Frank Little?" I guessed. Though he'd been lynched later on, during the war, it seemed to me.

"I don't know. It was around Thanksgiving time. It was all in the papers the next day."

"Joe Hill?"

But Grandma wasn't sure, and it wasn't important to her.

Phoebe wanted to know why she hadn't stayed in Chicago. I was surprised at a wistful note in her inquiry, a hint that she herself wouldn't have been in such a rush to abandon the bright lights.

"Oh, it wasn't much. I didn't care for it. All those miles of ugly buildings, and pavement everywhere. It made you feel there were too many people in the world, to see everybody living all cramped up like that. Even if you found a little open space to grow geraniums or a few vegetables, the soil wasn't decent. And the stockyards! Even in freezing weather you could smell 'em.

"Besides, I wasn't trained for anything but teaching, and it wasn't easy to get the certificate."

"But it must have been an adventure," her friend insisted, "at that age, and coming from the country. All the cars and stores and theaters and things."

"It was quite an adventure raising four children," Grandma retorted.

"Well of course for a Christian, anything in life is an adventure," Phoebe agreed, and I thought of how she'd spent all those years watching her menfolk die off. At the same time, I wondered whether Grandma's decision to leave Chicago had really been as simple and straightforward as she made it sound. Not that the final result, marriage, wasn't completely predictable; impossible, surely, to imagine her learning to enjoy the company of men who swore casually, or women who let their children run around in socks with holes—let alone consorting with a "real fringe element."

Yet she *had* gone to Chicago in the first place, which meant she'd wanted something. Maybe there'd been ambitions and sympathies she'd suppressed? Maybe she'd even been in love a little, not just swayed by "Proppie's" passion.

Aunt Judy said she was going. She and Gene were having a couple of doctors and their wives over for a cookout, and she needed to stop at the store and get the charcoal grill lit. Aunt Geri thought she'd better start supper, too. I decided to accompany them out to the parking lot. I didn't want to push too much in one day.

We all complimented Grandma on her performance as we left. Aunt Geri said she still had a few people on her list to call, to make sure they knew the bookstore reading was coming up. At Phoebe's suggestion, she agreed to check with Dr. Jerebold's office about whether the mini-bus could be made available to transport Hill residents who wanted to attend.

Recalling a line from Prosperine's letter ("I consider your promise *binding*"), I tried a final probe. "By the way, what was Prosperine's reaction when you . . . didn't like Chicago?"

Plucky Grandma hesitated, then lied through upper and lower plates. "Oh well, I guess at first she felt a little disappointed."

To my frustration, none of the local libraries turned out to have *Solidarity* in their reference collections. Evidently I'd have to visit Chicago one day soon if I wanted to track it down. Luckily, I could stay with my friend Bonnie and get some minor research for the Black and white women writers project out of the way as well.

Actually, I welcomed the thought of an excursion. Living alone out at the cabin was proving harder than I'd expected. Though many days brought quiet, perfect moments in which I felt that I was getting exactly what I'd come for—when I spotted a rainbow set above the far river bank, when I inhaled the hot pine needle smell on the brief path down to the water, when I stood shivering beneath a thick swarm of stars and remembered how, as a child, I used to love to watch the same indelible display from the depths of my sleeping bag—I had to admit that the isolation was difficult for me. Often I fell prey to that nagging sense of sin—or, not to be melodramatic, let us merely say an absence of that synthetic, secularized grace which even atheists depend on, known as self-esteem—that tends to afflict me precisely in those moments when

I've planned to savor an earned liberty from duties and daily schedules. This time it was worse than usual, because no matter how many times I reminded myself that the vacation was deserved, I couldn't dismiss my anxiety about not having a job.

I missed the phone's discreet cricket chirp, which at home had seemed to harass me unmercifully. 1 talked regularly to Linda, occasionally to Bonnie, and racked up more of a bill than I'd intended, calling others around the country. But many of my friends were vacationing beyond the range of phones, and anyway I was in that shrunken frame of mind in which only the reassurance of being sought after will do. Paradoxically, on the other hand, I tended to retreat from local society. If a neighbor stopped to chat, as happened several times a week (my thoughtful landlord had commended me to the attention of a pair of friendly faggots, ex-New Yorkers, who were staying up the road), or if I had to endure a visit from the septic tank man, the strain of conversation seemed excessive.

After my unsuccessful visits to the bars, I tried a women's "coffeehouse" I'd seen advertised. Enormous signs at the entrance spelled out in lurid detail the rationale for the establishment's stringent drug-free, alcohol-free, chem-free, and sugar-free politics and policies. Even decaf, it appeared, was banned from the premises. Uneasily remembering the fact that I hadn't yet cut down on my drinking very much—not that Prohibition struck me as any viable solution!—I ordered a cup of tea made from boiled twigs. On one side of me four or five women were planning a canoe trip; on the other a tall, flat-chested blond with a nose ring, her hair in a crewcut relieved by two skinny braids sprouting above one ear, was assessing the prospects for the upcoming Michigan Women's Music Festival. She mentioned a number of musicians, none of whom I'd heard of, and explained she might volunteer to do security. "But only if I can take my clothes off. I'm not into this fuckin' fascist prude trip."

Behind me two women were discussing co-dependency. One admitted she'd found herself taking inappropriate responsibility, not only for her lover's allergies, but for the woman's aging cat's incontinence.

"That stuff's real important, but I'm getting into shame," I heard from her companion.

"Oh, yeah, for sure. I really need a shame group—maybe after softball season."

"If that's Lesbian Nation, I'm emigrating," I told Linda later.

She laughed and advised me to lighten up. "They're doing their thing, sweetheart. Let them have their fun."

"It's just that their *thing* seems so fucking insular. Is this what's taken the place of politics? They even turned some woman away at the door because she was wearing patchouli oil."

"What? I don't get it."

"I guess it's a chemical. Some people are allergic. This very nice, naive baby dyke explained it all to me. We got to talking, and she told me she grew up in the area, went to the U, came out in the women's studies program, and worked in a bookstore collective. Now she's graduated and has a job with the AIDS hotline. She's never lived in the United States!"

"Now you *are* going off the deep end, Dale. Isn't that the space we've worked for? People have to have the freedom to do silly things. You sound like Grandma McNab, haranguing the children about how many miles you used to walk to school in winter!"

Linda's laughter irritated me. I thought about how, around the time we'd met, I'd volunteered to do speaking engagements as an out lesbian. I'd arrange myself like an insect on a pin in front of student audiences, exposed to all their offensive ignorance and sporadic hostility. The question and answer sessions gave rise to some priceless anecdotes, and soon I developed a parody presentation that became a standing joke. *Well, I get up bright and early every morning, hop into my lavender underwear, put on my boots, stick my dildo in my pocket, slick back my hair with Crisco, and head for the women's bar.*

Linda hadn't done those speaking gigs. "I just wonder," I said, "if they know anything at all about recent history. I mean, would this kid be familiar with 'The Woman-Identified Woman'? Would she know who the Daughters of Bilitis were? Has she read Pat Parker—or even Judy Grahn?"

"Yeah, sure, in some women's studies class. What's the matter, love? Are you upset about something?"

"Just a little lonely, I guess. How about your flying out for two or three days? I know you'd love the cabin."

"I really wish I could, but I don't see how. There's so much work I have to finish up, and you know Fiona and I are leaving for the beach in two weeks."

"I thought you were taking work along."

"I am, but of course there's stuff I have to see to here."

"Price of success."

"I guess."

"Don't knock it. But look, next summer let's do it differently, okay? I miss you too much."

"I miss you too. But it's only till September."

"Haven't met any devastating authors, have you?"

"Oh, at least one a week," she said gaily.

"And were you devastated?"

Ordinarily she would have played along, but now she said, "Sweetheart, it's midnight here, I ought to get off...tell me, though, how's your work going?"

"Not too badly, I guess. The last couple of days have been crazy. Lillian called me Tuesday in high dudgeon—NWSA nonsense, nothing serious, really, but you know how she can be. Like a jerk I got involved. It's meant a lot of telephoning."

I disliked admitting how gratified I'd been to receive an appeal from the head of the program committee for the following year's National Women's Studies Association conference. At least I wasn't completely forgotten by the world. Contrary to the voluptuous fantasies of throwing myself into work in a fertile solitude which I'd entertained when I rented the cabin, I found that the very absence of pressures and distractions—combined, of course, with my general listlessness—seemed to make it hard for me to buckle down. I'd gone back for a not particularly informative interview with Ruta, had spent some time in the library looking at microfilm of two literary magazines from the 1920's which were relevant to my project, and had even managed a few pages of very rough draft, but it wasn't much to show for the time involved.

I'd also checked out four or five histories which covered the First World War era in Minnesota and mentioned the Wobblies. I wanted to have the period in focus at the point when I got my hands on the Prosperine material. And certainly it was easier and more pleasant to doze on a towel down by the river, rousing myself now and then to skim a chapter, than to sit at my computer screen up in the darkened cabin. I decided lying fallow for a few weeks might not be a bad thing, if only I could squelch my uneasiness at taking, for once, the path of least resistance.

As I watched the river, soothed by its effortless life, I found that memories surfaced more and more frequently, sharp as stakes and with the earth of deep childhood still clinging to them. Memories, I say, but if that implies plot then I really mean simply pictures, images. This was the fossil remnant of early life, indelible imprint on a just-hatched, eager consciousness. Most of it was mundane, pedestrian—except for the uncanny clarity of detail, that fascinating trick the mind knows of delivering the past intact somehow, a whole time-demolished time poignantly reconstituted. (The pictures seemed to comfort me, but I couldn't have said how, or explained why it was that I needed comforting.)

Drowsing down by the river once, I had a sort of numinous vision of those light-weight, nickel-sized metal discs—aluminum, I suppose—that my sister Jenny and I used to call "money." They were to be found scattered around construction sites at a certain stage in the building process, and with Father we went to many construction sites. Sometimes we'd go to inspect one of the buildings his architectural firm had designed; other times he was merely satisfying his curiosity, for he took a detached professional interest in even the tackiest tract housing. As he strode around jotting figures in a little spiral notebook, Jenny and I would hop on the studs that made a see-through floor, enveloped in the familiar grammar of the house, whose parts of speech were creosote and sawdust, cedar shakes, chalky sheetrock, and the itchy pink cotton candy filling of fiberglass insulation. There was a scale of values here that verged on morality, which we acquired by osmosis and never thought peculiar: fake leaded glass was suspicious as platinum blonde hair, asbestos siding a scandal akin to plagiarism.

We kids collected the "money" avidly, our imaginations fired by the analogy to cash. We did the same with sand dollars at the beach, blackberries that grew in the surviving strip of Douglas fir second growth that began fifty feet from the redwood deck. The thrill of *finding* was inexplicable as the charge of feeling that lights up certain dreams—though wasn't the world at large a beckoning place, then? Mashed potatoes, God—all vivid, glistening.

Who remembers? All beloved colors swallowed up in adolescence's monotone self-centeredness.

There are racier scenes from that bleak period. A cramped, mildewy kitchen, architecturally unredeemed. At the two-burner stove stands a sturdy young woman of perhaps twenty-one. It's Seattle, not my suburb of Mercer Island but the metropolis itself—just off the Av in the University District. The woman is frying bacon. It is late afternoon. Her sandy hair hangs in sexy disarray. She's wearing a terrycloth bathrobe and an old pair of men's slippers, too large for her flat white feet. A red-gold stubble mists her thick calves. Kai. She's a "fringie chick" (this is still before hippie times) whom I met recently through VISTA tutoring. My parents are uneasy at her advanced age, and obviously wish she didn't live in the notorious U District. If she were male they'd never, ever let me come over here alone, even though they claim to respect my ability to make mature decisions, but as matters stand they can't very well object. I claim we talk about philosophy, and display a copy of *Existential Man* which I've borrowed from her shelf. (In fact, she hasn't read it. She doesn't read. She plays the dulcimer, and sings in coffeehouses.) I don't mention her cockroaches, the first I've ever seen, and I certainly don't report, except to my top secret diary, our clumsy, exigent caresses (*mutual masturbation*, I set down pedantically), or the proud surprise of coming the first time, an event my reading in the standard novelists has prepared me to think has something to do with men.

Between Kai and me, the pretense that this is simply a casual bohemian experiment. Perhaps for her it is. She has an "old man," a small-time dealer on the Av, who crashes here sometimes, lays half a lid on her, a foil-wrapped nugget of black, sticky hash, or a handful of Dexedrine caps like candy kisses. "IwannaFUCKYOUBABE," is his boisterous salutation when he shows up after a long day on the job, dawdling in the chilly rain in front of the post office, ducking into the Coffee Corral for a cup of hot chocolate and another few cigarettes. He probably doesn't mean it. He's a heavy speed freak. Kai claims he'd starve to death if she didn't make him eat once in a while.

My parents find my hidden diary. They're completely horrified. Nothing like this has ever happened to anyone they know. They send me to a shrink and put me under house arrest. It's hell. It doesn't matter. I read *Existential Man*, gain fifteen pounds, and make a 4.0 average for my entire senior year, knowing all the time I've got my exit visa, my early admissions acceptance to a college Back East. Once I get out of Mercer Island, I'm never coming back.

It didn't even occur to me to go down on her. It would have seemed too dirty, would have shocked us both, I think.

Around the third week in July, the inevitable happened: a family gathering was proposed which I couldn't very well avoid. It didn't sound too bad, though, just an innocuous female lunch. I'd gotten past the dreaded Fourth unscathed. The cookout this year had been at Uncle Gene's, and I heard afterwards all about the goings on. Aunt Judy's dessert had been a devil's food cake with satiny seven-minute icing studded with tiny American flags, accompanied by some concoction of ice cream or sherbert balls in red, white, and blue, arranged in a design to spell out U.S.A. HURRAH #1. (Grandma, who'd always liked the Betty Crocker cookbook with its iconographic foods, admired the flags but thought that *blue* dessert was going too far.)

What I hadn't been told, but supposed from past experience, was that while the Schlaghofer females would prudently have shunned what is known as "politics," Uncle Bert had probably needled Gene and Judy until they confessed their most obtuse Republican superstitions, which he then proceeded gleefully to bury beneath a crushing heap of statistics and expert analysis. Nimble-witted, sarcastic, reined in by Aunt Geri, he was capable of doing so without raising his voice. It was his brother-in-law who might speak louder, get pinker in the face, and tug at the tuft of fuzz on the front of his squared-off skull. He and his wife would agree after the guests had left that of course Bert was handy with the liberal mumbo-jumbo (why shouldn't he be, he got paid to know that stuff), but he still hadn't explained how throwing money at poverty had solved anything.

But now Aunt Leslie was coming to town for a few days, and some sort of reunion was obviously in order. Grandma proposed treating Geri, Leslie, my cousin Allison, and me to lunch. It was too bad, she said,

98

that Cecilia wasn't here; we could have made it a real mother-daughter thing. She left the arrangements up to Aunt Geri, who thought we might as well go to Best of the Wurst, since that was handy to the Hill and Grandma liked it.

On the day of the lunch, the telephone woke me. I must have snagged it by about the dozenth ring. It was Aunt Geri, who, when she heard my groggy voice, apologized for disturbing me in a tone which almost concealed her surprise and disapproval that a relative of hers should be abed at 9:30 on a weekday. She was just about to leave the house, she explained, in order to run over to the Hill; she and Leslie were supposed to take Grandma shopping for a new dress to wear to her Friday reading at the bookstore. She'd been trying to call me since yesterday afternoon. (I'd dined with my gay neighbors, which was why she hadn't reached me.) Our lunch spot had been switched, and the guest list rearranged: Aunt Amaryllis would be joining us.

Apparently Les ("she keeps in touch with Aunt A., you know") had called my great aunt and, mostly as a formality, invited her to our little get-together. Surprisingly, Aunt A. had accepted. She sounded sincerely eager to see everyone. "You too, Dale—oh yes, she remembers you! 'Cecilia's oldest girl, the reader!' she said." Since it wouldn't do to ask an eighty-three-year-old woman dependent on cabs to trek out to a mall in a St. Paul suburb (here Aunt Geri's logic was perfunctory, since Amaryllis could easily have afforded a taxi to International Falls if we'd decided to lunch there), they'd selected someplace closer in. The six of us were to meet at 12:45 in the lobby of a new corporate highrise in Minneapolis which had a rooftop restaurant. "It'll be a good deal dressier than the mall, I thought I'd better warn you."

"Dressy" means a dress, I perceived resentfully. Even when I was up for tenure I'd mostly refused to wear the things, and I certainly hadn't brought one to Minnesota.

"Was the switch okay with Grandma?" I asked.

"Oh, well, you know. She went along with it. She hasn't seen Amaryllis in quite some time." My aunt sighed. Then she hesitated, and for a moment I thought she was going to allow herself to complain to me. But she pulled herself together, and didn't.

I hung up, got up, made a forced march to the kitchen, and took a diet Coke from the small refrigerator, experiencing through my fog the

99

odd little thrill of freedom that still came over me in the mornings when I realized there was no Linda around to criticize my breakfast habits. I missed my lover, but rarely before noon. I went out to the porch and downed a couple of Tylenol; while talking about everything on earth except AIDS, my neighbors and I had consumed too many Margaritas, and when, inevitably, we *did* talk about it, we'd had a few more.

I thought about the new development. From what I knew, Aunt Geri had always taken a harder line on Amaryllis than my younger aunt had—had been more on Grandma's side, as it were—and this would account for some of her obvious irritation. Leslie, as she'd said, was the one who kept in touch. Not that this mild, infrequent contact amounted to any flagrant disloyalty, yet with her cultivated Western breeziness—perhaps with her easy money, left mysteriously intact by her too-casual divorce?— Les failed to uphold a tradition of resentment. Add to that the fact that Grandma could be expected to signal her displeasure in some oblique fashion that would further burden her oldest daughter and chief lieutenant: for instance, by sabotaging the shopping trip, complaining of stomach pains or vetoing all the dresses. Grandma was no ascetic, for all her frugality, and would not be likely graciously to suffer the unwelcome change in plans, especially since it was occasioned by this specific sister.

Yet Geri had gone along. I supposed she concurred with Les that the two old ladies ought to be encouraged to get together. ("At their ages, after all," people say, as though proximity of death should exorcise all comfortable, long-savored pettiness.) Rose and Amaryllis were the last remaining flowers from that prodigious Bright hothouse, except for Violet way up in Anchorage, and Lily, who was in a nursing home in Faribault.

There was another point on which it seemed my two aunts agreed, and this was that no matter what one thought of Amaryllis, it was out of the question to ask an Upshott-by-marriage to lunch in a shopping mall wiener schnitzel franchise. Even Grandma might have said so, if you got right down to it. They were snobs, these democrats. They upheld the hierarchies.

As far as I knew, there'd never been a dramatic rupture between Grandma and Aunt A. In fact, it would have been completely out of character for either one of them to have told the other off. Even to say that there was a strong undercurrent of rivalry seems the wrong way to put it—as though apples could be rivalrous with mangoes. Grandma had prevailed through her tenacity, of course, and her achievement sounded meager in summary. She was Rose Bright Schlaghoffer; that couldn't be summarized. With Aunt A., it was more a matter of luck and flare. Not only, improbably, had she become a professional singer (what kind I couldn't pin down to my satisfaction; they always said she used to sing in "clubs"), but she'd somehow used this career as a springboard to a truly astonishing marriage.

Though you could look at it from the opposite angle, too. What had Grandma shown if not audacity in insisting on going to high school? She'd carved a path for the sisters who came after. And really the most remarkable thing of all about Aunt A. wasn't necessarily how far she'd traveled, but how conventionally she'd construed her ultimate destination. The girl who'd squished manure between her calloused toes, skimmed flies from the milk jar, and flirted with sweaty threshers—and the young woman who, I suspected, earned her first real money belting ballads in speakeasies—had been yoked to Timothy Upshott for forty-six years. It was the feat of a provincial Wallis Simpson.

Not that the late Uncle Tim had been an interesting Upshott. He'd borne no responsibility whatever for the stupendous success of his father's uncle's business, the Ideal Northwestern Mining Corporation. Nobody even knew if Amaryllis had literally married a millionaire. But the central, mesmerizing fact about Uncle Tim, fabulous as legends of buried pirate treasure, was that he *hadn't had to work*, as do all other men. He'd had a job all right, but he didn't have to have it. "He doesn't *have* to work, he's independently wealthy," was what the family repeated, almost in a whisper, as though the statement conveyed some real notion of his life and character, of which in fact they were as ignorant as if he'd been a monk in a Capuchin monastery.

"My Aunt Amaryllis is marrying Mr. Upshott. He's filthy rich, my Aunt Flora says." So Mother had blabbed to the neighbors, c. 1930, and had been rewarded by one of Grandma's rare formal spankings when she learned of the leak from officious Geraldine. Soon afterward, the girls invented a game they played more obsessively than Monopoly in those early Depression years: "playing Aunt A.," it came to be called simply, and required them to imagine every sort of weird luxury and excess, much of it having to do with food and drink, such as Pepsi Cola showers, with bars of fudge instead of soap.

Understand: Aunt A. had honeymooned in Cannes. Grandma had motored east as far as Cincinnati, once.

When you put it in those terms, it's easier to imagine the acute strain that must have developed between the sisters at the worst of the Depression, when Grandpa lost his job. Mother was sure that not only would he and Grandma have refused to ask for help, but would have refused any Amaryllis might have offered. He'd gone to work in the butcher shop, instead. And the kids had scavenged Heinz catsup bottle caps, worth a little something for the aluminum.

I'd met Aunt Amaryllis twice that I recalled. The first time I must have been nine or ten. It was on one of those ritual, every-other-summer "trips to Minnesota" that involved three days of driving in the Chevy station wagon, drives that seemed the best and worst of family times, with extremes of camaraderie and loathing succeeding one another as the western miles flew by. One minute it was morning, the car windows were rolled down but the air still had a hint of nighttime crispness, Father's freckled left arm was resting on the ledge getting burned, and all six of us were singing something western and optimistic, like "Roll On, Columbia," or else maybe something western and nostalgic, like "Red River Valley." Then suddenly the boys were scuffling, and Jenny would act so babyish and spoiled, whining and holding her nose when we stopped to peer into the Volcanic Boiling Sulfur Mud Pots, or claiming she was carsick.

And sooner or later, Father would lose his temper and bellow at all of us to STOP BICKERING, adding, to try and pass it off as a joke, "before I bonk your measly heads together, before I toss you from here to breakfast." And I'd clam up for the next thirty miles, refusing even to answer direct questions, because I was so mad, because it wasn't *my* fault. But then, unpredictably (possibly because we'd caught our first glimpse of the Grand Tetons, or were going to stop for a voluptuously swirled vanilla soft ice cream cone coated with brittle chocolate, through the tip of which the melting sweetness could be sucked) the trip would turn fun and thrilling once again. The back seat would forget its differences, and launch into singing "One Hundred Beer Bottles Hanging on the Wall." We'd sing all the way down to zero and the front seat would let us.

On the trip when I met Aunt A. for the first time, there was a family reunion, an ambitious all-day picnic in Como Park, the sort of gathering

102

where children have to have explained to them over and over the definition of second and third cousin, and grownups debate the meaning of "once removed." It was an orgy of homemade baked beans and homemade pies, "moldy" salads as we called them, and "scratch" cakes. Aunt Flora ("Great" Aunt Flora, as I finally understood) was there, bringing a plastic vat of her famous homemade doughnuts. Sad, scary Aunt Iris had taken the bus down from Hibbing. Aunt Amaryllis was there for an hour or so, a quiet tall lady, not so old as the other great aunts. She impressed me on account of her beautiful, strange name and the enormous rich German chocolate cake she contributed. Everybody gobbled it right down, but after she left Grandma remarked (as though objectively) that she'd forgotten to take the bakery price tag off the box. Epler's, it said, which was St. Paul's most exclusive bakery; but that couldn't make up for the fact that the cake was store-bought.

My second glimpse of Amaryllis was on my solo visit at age twelve. Grandma and I met her in a department store tearoom. I understood pretty well who she was by that time, thanks to Mother's stories, and might have paid more attention to the encounter if I hadn't been reading *Exodus* in a fat paperback edition I'd borrowed from my cousin Allison. Probably it was my absorption in this tome, an intellectual brat's *Forever Amber*, which caused Aunt A. to remember me as a bookworm. (Few scenes in literature are so vivid to me as the one where Ari Ben Canaan slides Kitty's nightgown off her shoulder and kisses her tit in that hotel room in—is it Haifa?) Grandma couldn't have been pleased to see me nursing a book on my lap, returning to it the minute the chicken salad had been dispensed with, but she didn't interfere. The Mediterranean landscapes of Cyprus and Palestine got superimposed on the pastel draperies and tablecloths of that Minneapolis tearoom, and the notorious Aunt A. was just a gloved lady in a suit—who smoked, however; I noticed that much. It was certainly not something the other great aunts did.

As for the time I referred to her as a rich bitch, that must have been the summer following my sophomore year at Swarthmore, when I'd told my parents I was dropping out. They panicked at the news (completely needlessly, since it turned out I re-enrolled spring semester, having located what I was looking for during my brief sojourn in a Philadelphia commune, a practicing dyke who'd prove Kai hadn't been a fluke). To placate them, I reluctantly agreed to go along on yet another Minnesota pilgrimage. I remember debating the domino theory, strategic hamlets, and my plunging career prospects all the way across the plains states, defiantly flashing my FREE HUEY NEWTON button at puzzled desk clerks in Best Western Motels.

I'm not sure what prompted my crack about Aunt A., but I think the scene was a St. Paul dining table, with my grandparents and some aunts and uncles and cousins present. Rich bitch, I pronounced, and Mother flinched and glared. Grandpa only blinked, bewildered, but Grandma appeared so improbably dignified and deaf that she obviously must have heard. Wimpy Jennifer clapped her knuckles to her incisors, while a cousin or two smirked. Uncle Bert, who must have been used to this sort of thing from his own children, had the wit to brandish old Bob Dylan at me, like the Devil quoting scripture.

"Don't criticize what you can't understand, young lady."

Did I remind him of what Mother Jones had to say about ladies? It's entirely possible. "I was only putting into words exactly what everybody else in this hypocritical family has been thinking to themselves and whispering for years," I hotly maintained later, behind the bedroom door at Grandma's. Mother, Jenny, and I were getting undressed. "Anyway, do you have any idea what a bunch of pigs Ideal Northwestern is? I read about them when I did my history paper. Notorious union busters."

Poor mother wasn't thinking of history. Her back turned, she tugged at her panty girdle. "Just do me *one* favor. Don't use *that kind of language* in front of *my folks*."

Come to think of it, I suppose I obliged. In any event, of course I was kept carefully away from Aunt A. on that trip. Then there'd been no more visits until I was nearly thirty.

But here, now, was the coda, an unexpected chance to witness something of how matters had turned out between the estranged sisters. I thought it would be fun to call Mother afterwards and tell her all about it. Then I remembered that she wasn't in the country. She and my father had just left for China, on an architects' tour his firm had organized.

I drained the Coke and went to assess my clothing crisis. After some deliberation I settled on a pair of lightweight cotton pants and a madras shirt that didn't look too wrinkled. I couldn't wear the shirt tucked in, though, or the pants would be too snug. I'd gained several pounds in recent weeks, apparently.

It occurred to me Allison was somebody else I hadn't set eyes on in years, maybe not since the time she'd come through New York and slept on my couch on East Seventh Street. She'd been macrobiotic and working for McGovern. I hoped she wasn't still as skinny as I remembered.

Amaryllis, bless her heart, was wearing a pantsuit. It was impeccably tailored, but that didn't matter. Stooped, she was still as tall as any in our party. She looked as though she could have been Grandma's daughter, but of course she was only entering her eighties, and they'd reached a stage in life where a gap of a few years can make more difference than it has at any time since adolescence.

Joining the rest of us beside the elevators, she bent to kiss her sister, then shook hands like a politician until she came to Aunt Leslie, who received a peck on her gorgeously tanned cheek.

"Up we go." Grandma reasserted pre-eminence.

The restaurant was wistfully pretentious. With its bold view and provincial-continental menu, it reminded me a bit of the revolving restaurant atop the Space Needle, that quaintly futuristic white elephant bequeathed to Seattle by its World's Fair, where in the mid-Sixties we'd been taken several times, Jennifer and I, to shudder at *escargots* among the entrees.

"Is that like eating *slugs*?" we invariably demanded.

Allison was seated next to me, so gaunt her bones protruded. Maliciously, I hoped she suffered from one of those trendy revolting eating disorders, but the truth was she didn't exactly look unhealthy. She just gave off an air of exaggerated languor that I found totally incomprehensible in a modern female who presumably had to earn a living. In a denim smock, she looked faintly bohemian, faintly pre-Rafaelite. She had grubby fingernails and a strong vertical crease between her eyebrows. She kept lifting her thick salt and pepper braid from her neck with a long, pale hand, as though its weight were insupportable.

Amaryllis coolly ordered a glass of white wine.

"Make that two," said Leslie.

I gratefully made it three, and my cousin made it four. Only Aunt Geri struck by Grandma, who ordered her usual. We were on our best behavior, and nobody cracked a smile, not even when the waitress asked

105

what a Shirley Temple was.

Though Geri and Leslie had thoughtfully steered their mother and aunt into facing chairs to minimize hearing problems, after a few conventional remarks concerning health and weather their conversation flagged. Then Leslie and Allison, who'd telegraphed with a shrug their common opinion of the menu, launched into an authoritative discussion of food. My aunt, it appeared, had become an expert on Southwest regional cookery during her years in Santa Fe. My cousin had a job in a gourmet takeout shop, and contemplated opening her own food business. (The last I'd heard, she'd been in early childhood education.) Aunt Geri chimed in every so often, free-associatively scattering anecdotes in which crockpot, Cuisinart, or microwave played starring roles. She'd majored in "home ec" once upon a time, and despite her years in India and Southern California, she probably wouldn't have recognized *garam masala* or *tomatillos* if they'd bitten her.

Lunch showed up, bland dabs on vast, elegant plates. Amaryllis turned to me. "And Dale, what are *you* up to these days? Still teaching college? Rose always has such a nice report of you."

"I'm job hunting at the moment, actually," I nearly shouted, wanting to make sure she got it the first time. "I was denied tenure at my last school."

"They're unbelievably tough on young people in academia today," Aunt Geri excused me. "Nothing like when Bert was starting out."

I said nothing, though I reflected indignantly that in the first place I was hardly "starting out," and in the second that few if any male academics have to contend with having their bibliographies labeled "ideological" and "shrill" (don't ask me how a book list can raise its voice), or their behavior on curriculum committees "hostile" and "abrasive" when they say what they think.

"Any promising leads?" Amaryllis wanted to know.

To my surprise, Grandma spoke up and took the heat off me. "Dale is helping me with my writing this summer," she announced. "She's got some of my stuff printed up in a women's magazine already. We're making up a book, if I can only find the time. It isn't easy, what with so many activities going on at the Hill. Last week we had our Crafts Fair, and tomorrow's the Founders Brunch. Then I've promised to help Phoebe with the Homeless Clothing Drive, and Friday we've got some kind of

106

politician coming to speak to us about this new crock stuff that's turning all these youngsters into dope fiends."

"Crack," Aunt Geri suggested, but Grandma didn't hear.

"But Rose, how simply marvelous!" Amaryllis praised. "An author in the family! When will we see the book?"

Grandma sniffed and recited, ungraciously I thought, "There's many a slip between cup and lip." But I knew she'd wanted her sister to hear about her achievements, so I announced the upcoming reading. Amaryllis promised to try to come.

"And I want ten copies when the book is out...say, did you write about Bugs Donnelly?"

Amaryllis' teasing tone and Grandma's brusque negative made the rest of us burn to know who Bugs Donnelly was.

"Oh, Rose acquired a beau at one point that was considered kind of fast by our folks. One time he showed up out at the place in the middle of the night, tipsy I presume, with a wagonload of cronies and strumming a guitar. It was harvest season too, the threshers were coming in the morning, and there they went serenading and waking the whole house. Pa was that put out, he set the dogs on 'em."

"I never encouraged Bugs," Grandma wanted us to know.

"Oh, that reminds me," I put in, "looking at Grandma's papers has got me interested in an old friend of hers named Prosperine Munkers. You know, I've done a little research—I didn't tell you about this, Grandma—and I've found out that Prosperine is supposed to have had a story in Margaret Anderson's *Little Review*, a very influential literary magazine of its day." I'd found the item in an index on my last library visit, though unluckily the microfilm of the volume and number it listed had been missing.

"Prosperine...I remember her, of course," Amaryllis mused.

"You do?" This obvious possibility hadn't occurred to me.

"When I was little she used to come and visit sometimes, with Rose. She brought us children things. Licorice whips. That was a great treat—well, her father kept a store. I remember thinking how lovely that must be, to have crackers and boughten bread and soda pop, anything you wanted. Then later, when I went to St. Paul to stay with Rose—before you were born, Geraldine—"

"Yes, I've seen a snapshot in Mother's albums somewhere. The two

107

of you sitting on the porch steps. You lived there about a year."

"A little under. I was attending high school then."

"And I was expecting you," Grandma informed her grizzled daughter. "Your brother was quite a handful, and this way we thought Amaryllis could help me out, you see."

"I wanted to live in the Cities. This was my big chance." The former au pair smiled, ruefully I thought. I was intrigued at the hint that it might have been Grandma herself who provided her sister with the opportunity that eventually led to her precipitous rise in the world.

"Anyway, I remember Prosperine visiting us then—in the wintertime, I think. It seems to me she was living in Chicago? She wore her hair bobbed real short and smoked at the dining table. I wasn't accustomed to anything like that, I suppose that's why it stuck in my mind. And then, Rose, the two of you got into some sort of dispute. You were quite put out. I believe it was over the war, something about the war."

Grandma affected not to hear, it seemed to me.

"That doesn't ring a bell? I can see it so plainly."

"Prosperine—*did things*—" her old friend angrily conceded. The sentence trailed off ambiguously while we sat there waiting to hear what things she did.

"Well, she did go too far, I suppose. Wasn't she mixed up with a radical protest bunch? Strikes of some type, or was it the votes for women bit?" Receiving no answer, Amaryllis paused and lit a Vantage 100. My aunts eyed the far-off pastry cart. Allison, spoiled child, had left half her shrimp curry.

"I'm sure that's how it happened. We were sitting in the kitchen, you and I and she and Gene, Jr.—his father wasn't home. It's such a peculiar thing, how certain scenes like this come back to me so sharp and clear, and other things I know happened I simply can't picture. My mind's like a checkerboard with half the squares blanked out.

"You and I were feeding little Gene, or trying to; I suppose he was two or three then, and had a mind of his own. And you and Prosperine were discussing some fellow you'd known in Normal School, that had come back from Europe, from the war, you know, with his lungs all eaten out from poison gas. He strangled slowly, according to Prosperine, like drowning on dry land.

" 'That s.o.b. of a war,' she says, with such bitterness in her voice.

I couldn't understand what got her so worked up. She didn't say 's.o.b.,' though, she said the words right out. You objected, and it went on from there."

A small perception detonated, derailing the conversation. "Wait a minute," I cried, "Grandma, I thought you said Prosperine died in 1918."

"Why yes, in that awful influenza we had then. Sometimes you'd go into the stores downtown and the clerks would be wearing hospital masks. People wore them on the streetcars."

"But Aunt Geri, when were you born?"

"March 1, 1922."

"So how could Prosperine have died in the flu epidemic, if she visited when Grandma was pregnant with you?"

The minute this was out, I felt I'd pounced too hard. Bewilderment was written on two very old faces, though it disappeared from Grandma's in short order, replaced by an air of executive command.

"Well, I guess you're remembering some other time," she informed her puzzled sister.

"But I'm as sure as sure can be. I can see how the kitchen looked, with those curtains you made with the little green checks. I even remember what Gene had to eat."

"Amaryllis, really, after all this time!"

"Tapioca pudding, so there."

In a minute, I thought, they'll be sticking out their tongues at one another.

"Maybe this was some other friend of mine."

"You didn't have two friends like Prosperine Munkers."

This was true, I was positive—a strong point for Amaryllis. But it couldn't be proven, and Grandma clung to that. "I guess I remember when my best friend passed away. Possibly Prosperine may have come to visit us up at the farm sometime before Eugene and I were married, and that's what you remember."

"And talked about the poison gas and all?"

"Well, why not? We were married during the war. And you've gotten that visit all mixed up with something else that happened when you stayed with us on Taylor Street."

"Nonsense. I'm sure I'm right. I distinctly recall, one of the reasons you were so unhappy with her was on account of Eugene, his sacrifice

109

you know. 'Let the men that fought talk about the war like that. They're the ones that have got the right, not the people who stayed home,' I remember you telling her in no uncertain terms."

"She died a few weeks after the Armistice," Grandma stubbornly recited. She went on to repeat the story I'd heard before, about the cold room ("with water frozen in a basin") and the Finnish neighbor who prepared the body. "She washed the clothes Proppie had been wearing, and ironed them, and put them back on once she'd washed the body, because the poor thing hadn't got another set good enough to be buried in."

It interested me that she chose to emphasize this stark, almost brutal physical aspect. It wasn't at all what I'd normally have expected from her, and certainly not as mealtime conversation. I felt she was competing with Amaryllis' impressive details: the green checked curtains, the tapioca pudding.

"Who knows what a talented girl like Prosperine. . . but she was reckless. There was no telling her to be careful."

"You didn't have to be careless to die of that flu," I reasoned.

"But she didn't," insisted Grandma's little sister. "She had to've lived till '21 at least. I'd swear on a stack of Bibles."

"Who's asking you to swear on a stack of anything!" Aunt Les sounded alarmed. Certainly the controversy was getting out of hand. "No point fussing. How about dessert? I'm in a chocolate mood today, myself."

"Some of that yummy mousse," Aunt Geri concurred brightly. "How about you, Mother? I hope you saved room."

I found my aunts' ploys embarrassing to watch, as though they dangled some bauble in front of crabby infants. But Grandma didn't even notice, as she pursued her train of thought.

"Mrs. Munkers said you couldn't conceive how pitiful it was, her lying cold like that in that freezing cold room." She glanced at Amaryllis, competitively I noted, as though the pathos of it bolstered her position. " 'Be thankful,' the poor woman told me afterwards, 'be thankful if you as a mother never have to know what it is to lose your child.' And I always have been thankful."

A small silence ensued, during which it occurred to me that Aunt Geri hadn't been so fortunate. I was six or seven when my cousin Geoffrey had drowned, almost exactly Geoff's age, in fact, and at first this distant tragedy—it had happened in India—struck me as an apocalyptic revelation, a detail that unmasked the smiling world. For a week I nursed the lonely, dirty secret: in the midst of life, we are in death. I sobbed in private, moped in public, and told my mother I had a stomach ache, a sore throat, an ear ache, anything I could think of so long as it hid the truth.

But death has never been popular in our tribe. Among us then it had the reputation of cropping up in badly-regulated families, like diarrhea in an underdeveloped country, or bedbugs where the sheets are changed infrequently. We expected to succeed, and mortality smacked of failure; *we* were solid citizens, and death somehow wasn't, quite. McNabs and Schlaghoffers kicked the bucket too, of course, but only, we liked to think, when they were ready to go. After the first sharp flurry of dismay, the sorrow of Geoff's death had been hushed up much as scandal might have been. I'd allowed myself to be lulled by the grownups' apparent confidence that nothing so awful could happen more than once.

Noticing the silence at the table, I looked up to see that Grandma was in tears. She tried to speak, perhaps to explain herself, but the single word that emerged was "Prosperine." Desolate and unglamorously exposed with her glasses off, she snuffled and ransacked her purse for a handkerchief.

"Here, use my hanky," Amaryllis urged. "Oh Rose, don't think I haven't realized the friend she was to you. 'Them girls is thick as pea soup the second day,' remember how Mrs. Franklin put it like that one time, when Prosperine had been and paid a visit? That got you 'up on your high horse,' Ma said."

"The busybody, what business of hers was it!"

The two old women drew apart from us; drew around themselves the Past's magic chalk circle. Presumably it was precisely to encourage this sort of communication that we'd exerted ourselves to bring the two of them together: this moment, for example, when Amaryllis inquired, "Didja ever think it would turn out like this?"—meaning, apparently, life, while indicating with a broad gesture the bent river and flattened country, the conventionally impressive urban vista blocked out beneath us, edges softened in the haze. (Her hand trailing cigarette smoke lent her, I realized, a misleading patina of the intellectual, the sophisticated, the New Yorky— or was it those Lillian Hellman eyes?) "Remember that hammock we used to have out back, made out of bedsprings, strung under the Norway pine? Joe and I used to lie out there sometimes and guess what the clouds were shaped like, and I used to ask him, will it always be like this? I looked up to him so, all the time we were growing up, my big brother, poor Joey...oh my goodness, don't let me forget to keep an eye on the time. I've got a hair appointment."

"I feel so bad to think of arguing with Prosperine, you know," Grandma rejoined, clearly talking to herself. "I did feel she carried things too far, but I know she meant well. You might say she was the best friend I ever had, apart from Gene, of course. We both tried to pretend afterwards, but it never was the same."

"Afterwards?"

"It broke my heart when she—"

"When she what, dear?"

Grandma gripped the bony hands her sister held out across the crumb-strewn taupe linen.

"I don't know. When she carried on like that. When she stayed up there on the Range, and wouldn't write. She didn't attend the wedding, either, you know."

"Girls get married all the time," Amaryllis consoled.

"Of course girls get married!"

"Well, then."

Grandma halted for a minute, dabbed at her eyes with Amaryllis' handkerchief, stretched her shortened spine a little to face up to sorrow. "Proppie and I," she declared "told each other everything."

"Ruth and Naomi."

"Oh, you remember that too, do you? They started that at Normal School, calling us that. We used to go everywhere together. Right now I can't recall which one of us was supposed to be which. Of course everything was different later on, she started reading those offbeat authors and went off on a tangent. But when I first boarded with the Munkers in Bemidji, the pair of us was just like a couple of frisky young heifers— you know how Pa used to turn the heifers into that riverfront strip, and they'd wander through the woods like free spirits? Then once they'd come fresh they'd have to stick near the barn. They had their duties then, oh my."

The two pairs of hands were still entwined, and the two gazes met, though Grandma, without her glasses, must have been staring at the void. "I wonder," she insisted, as though for the first time, "would Proppie have gotten married after all, supposing she'd lived?"

112

Amaryllis withdrew her hands; it was time to be reasonable. "What on earth could you have done different?" she demanded.

Chin up. "Not a thing that I can see."

"Of course not."

"Eugene and I thought the world of one another. I couldn't have asked for a finer life than I had with him and the children." But she recited it flatly, a slightly boring true story. There was none of the feeling there'd been in the wintertime, when she'd said the same to me.

"There wasn't a man alive that could have cared for you more, Mother," Aunt Leslie affirmed. "Oh boy," she added, "here comes dessert!"

Bristling with accessible satisfactions, the pastry cart trundled up. Still Grandma wasn't to be diverted. "I suppose I thought then. . .when Eugene and I became engaged, and I saw how she took it and all, I suppose I must have thought. . .you see, I knew in my heart of hearts that it would never be the same again, between us. But I must have felt as though I could get another, somehow."

"Another *what*, Rose?" Amaryllis look perturbed. Was she getting claustrophobic, trapped in the past like that?

"Another friend, another time like that, another feeling similar. But I did not. I always felt some other way."

"That chocolate cheesecake looks outrageous," Aunt Geri trilled.

"Things never come round again, do they?"

"We're old," said Amaryllis, not answering the question.

"I think I know what you mean, Grandma," I blurted. I wanted to tell her someone was listening. But I spoke too softly and she didn't seem to hear.

"Are those hazelnuts in the tart?" Aunt Leslie asked the waitress.

"Nothing for me, thanks. I'm full," said Allison.

Later, while our companions were in the restroom, Geri assured me that she thought everything had gone well, considering. I expressed some unease at having stirred up that old business about Prosperine, but she discounted my worries. She thought it was absolutely the healthiest thing for seniors to be encouraged to vent their feelings about the past. She added that Allison needed a ride to Mendota Heights, where she had an eye doctor appointment, and was I possibly. . . .?

It was out of my way, but I said I'd drop her off.

Allison folded her long pale legs with the rather knobby knees underneath my dashboard, and with a twinge of surprising affection I realized that this was the same anatomy on which she'd trotted, cantered, and galloped the afternoons away, the summer I was ten and she was eleven and she'd stooped to share her horse obsession with me. She explained she was going to the doctor for some sort of irritation in her right eye, probably just a tiny scratch which her contact lens had aggravated. Naturally I'd looked forward to a post mortem on the lunch, once our elders were out of earshot, but she seemed content to deride the restaurant. "Clichés," she fumed, "clichés, clichés, clichés. Not even *well-executed* clichés, and yet the place is packed."

I smiled. "We almost went to Best of the Wurst, you know."

Allison thought that at least a restaurant like that was up front about its motives. She herself wanted to open up a little specialty food place, where she could be completely creative. "You know, if I feel like doing Afghani one day, I do Afghani. If I feel like sushi or Jewish deli, I do that. But I want to get some more training first. There's a South Indian cook I might apprentice to, and this incredible woman French pastry chef." On the other hand, she might want to have a baby. After years of therapy, and now that she was with Basil (whoever he was; it was the first I'd heard his name), she finally felt she could be there for a kid. And she knew it would mean a lot to her parents, after what they'd been through with Abbie and Motilal, and now the disappointment of Bruce and Barbie not being able to get pregnant.

When was it, I wondered, that men started getting pregnant too? I had the impression that sometime a few years back when I wasn't looking, heterosexual couples started reproducing this way, in startling defiance of biological precedent. I figured she was going to ask me whether I'd ever wanted kids, and felt slighted when she didn't. I thought I ought to mention Linda and Fiona as casually as she'd mentioned Basil, but it seemed like too much effort. I thought of that horsey summer, when I'd been such a nonentity, ignored by all the older cousins, unwilling to be relegated to the younger crowd that included my own sister and baby brothers, and therefore in thrall to *her* narrow fantasy life. She refused to take the slightest interest in the plots of the Narnia series I was then absorbed in, though I was convinced that Aslan was far superior, in personality if not in looks, to any golden palomino.

To change the subject, I referred to Prosperine.

"That group she belonged to, the Wobblies—didn't they used to run some kind of religious commune, back east somewhere?"

Allison was thinking of the Shakers. I did what I could to dispel such staggering ignorance, and she, seeming completely unembarrassed, observed that my description of the IWW's iconoclastic tactics "sounded sort of like the Sixties." I explained I had some idea that there might be material for a book in the Prosperine story, and she suggested I ask her mother whether I could take a look in the attic. Probably even Grandma herself had forgotten what was in the boxes she had stored up there.

We arrived at the eye doctor's. "Thanks a million," said Allison. "You know, we must get together." She actually sounded as though she meant it, and to my surprise I found I felt grateful for her warmth.

"You know, I keep wondering just when you're going to break down and officially come out to all those people," was Linda's long distance comment.

"I'm not here to *work*," I objected. We'd had this argument before. Once in a bitter hour I'd even suggested that it was only because she'd taken up being queer so late in life that she'd been anxious to come out to distant cousins. "I'll tell them if it comes up," I said now. "All my *real* family knows. How often do I see these people, anyway?"

"It's just that you seem to resent their not knowing so much. How can you blame them, entirely, if you won't even tell them?"

"Oh, bullshit. They don't know because they don't want to know. I've mentioned you a number of times as the woman I live with, but they never acknowledge it. Whereas all Allison has to do is slip the name of her boyfriend into the conversation." I knew Linda had at least half a point, but I hated it when she got into one of these directive moods.

I was making a sandwich the following afternoon when the cabin phone rang. It was Aunt Geri, calling from the hospital. Naturally I immediately thought of Grandma, but the patient, it turned out, was my cousin. She'd gone to the emergency room early that morning after being kept up most of the night by sharp pain in her right eye, which the doctor she'd seen yesterday had assured her would be fine. He'd sent her home and told her not to wear her contacts for a week. Now she was running a dreadfully high fever. There was talk of intensive care. Of course Geri felt she should stay right there at the hospital for the time being; the problem was that she was expecting a couple of important phone calls. One was from Bert, who was out of town and hadn't heard about the crisis. She was awfully sorry to impose, but did I think I might possibly be able to drive over to her place and "hold down the fort?"

Having seen Allison in perfect health so recently, I had a hard time grasping the gravity of the situation. But Geri sounded really frightened, and of course I said I'd go. I gathered some books, a change of underwear, a handful of the tacky little plaque-defeating appliances which my periodontist had forbidden me to live without, and hopped into my car.

Aunt Geri's was a recently-painted two-story house with modern storm windows, set in the middle of a block of similarly groomed homes surrounded by well-clipped, rather narrow yards. I parked in the driveway beneath the magnificent shade tree that caused such a flurry of leaf collecting every fall. I'd been told where to find a key to the back door, hidden in a crack in the fence. I let myself in and wandered around the place, enjoying a privileged sense of discovery, as though I were an archaeologist deflowering a tomb, or maybe just a high school babysitter enjoying the run of someone else's mother's house once the kiddies were asleep. The rooms with their dark woodwork and light fabrics were in reasonable order, but full to bursting with *stuff*: heaps of folded material and spools of thread and dress patterns on the twin beds in the back bedroom upstairs where Aunt Geri kept her sewing machine open and at the ready: voluminous cupboards in the remodelled kitchen full to bursting with double boilers, egg poachers, angelfood cake forms, pastry tubes, gelatin molds, potato ricers, meat thermometers—mute, faithful objects that had, most of them, followed my aunt halfway around the world. Old-fashioned granite pans lay side by side with Tupperware and Teflon. I knew it at a glance, had got it all by heart in my mother's house, years and years ago. I even anticipated the stiff cleaning rag, made of a piece of white bedsheet frugally recycled, that hung in the crook of the pipe beneath the bathroom sink next to the can of Bon Ami cleanser; and in the upstairs hall a Van Gogh reproduction, that buxom young woman beside the vase of flowers. The same print had hung in our dining room throughout my childhood, only back then the woman had looked old to me.

Next to the telephone in the breakfast nook, I found a note pad with a pencil-jotted list. It went something like:

> deposit
> buttons
> vacuum
> Mother
> Merrill Lynch
> tire sale at Sears
> gift of tongues
> <u>wide</u> masking tape
> RSVP Sheila
> League of Women Voters
> Nuc. winter
> detergent
> Eng. muffins
> Lurch vet. appt.

"Nuc. winter," I decided, might be a problem the League of Women Voters had taken up, but "gift of tongues" was a complete mystery. The last item pertained to the ancient basset hound, nearly blind and deaf, whom my cousin Bruce had adopted when he was already in college, shortly before embarking on the career path that had culminated in his acquiring an Akita named DOS. There'd been some wild oats sown along the way, though, and at one point my aunt had taken Lurch back as a meritorious if burdensome pensioner, deserving of some stability and peace. I looked for him and found him out back, a vegetative furry heap in the shade of a picnic table. When Geri called I'd have to ask what to feed him, and whether he was getting any medication.

I kicked my sandals off and pursued my research, deliciously barefoot on the cool linoleum and shaggy wall-to-wall carpet. I checked out the ice cream flavors in the closet-sized freezer, leafed though sociological journals and copies of *McCall's*. The phone rang once: the piping, self-confident voice of a neighbor child selling pecan clusters to finance a vacation Bible school trip. It rang again and it was Grandma. "Would you please just let Geri know when she comes back that I think we'd better go and exchange that dress we bought yesterday. There's something peculiar about the cut. I noticed it when I tried it on just now, and Phoebe agrees with me. There was a blue dress we saw that might suit. I think they're open till 7:00."

I tried to suggest that my aunt might be tied up. I didn't think I should mention the hospital.

Grandma answered, sounding aggrieved, that in that case, since Geri had her volunteer work tomorrow, she guessed she'd have to wear the old beige that wasn't even really a summer dress, and that people had seen already.

"Wear?"

"To that business tomorrow."

I'd forgotten: the bookstore reading. I heard myself promise I'd figure out a way to make sure she got over to the shopping center the following afternoon.

Which meant, I realized as I hung up, that another whole day would be wasted on family business. "Blood is thicker than water" wasn't a proposition I'd ever taken very seriously, but now, for the first time since turning twenty-one, I began to wish for an anticoagulant.

"Too damn much spinning!" I said aloud. This alluded to a joke Linda and I had. When we'd first moved to New Jersey we'd been introduced to a circle of earnest feminists who had a combination Mary Daly study group and volleyball team they called the Spinsters. They used to talk about the "web of life" a lot, and regarded our sex as uniquely anointed to take charge of its preservation. One of them had once greeted me in the supermarket by inquiring, with a perfectly straight face, "So how's the spinning going?" Linda and I poked enormous fun at them; of course we objected to their blatant substitution of sedentary secretion for old-fashioned goals like daycare. Still, we wouldn't have disputed that the social fabric would disintegrate in a week without women's invisible labor. Now, here at the silent and mysterious source of the countless sticky threads which Aunt Geri was forever casting into the void, I was emphatically reminded to what extent a woman is both spider and fly. This spinster had better watch it, I told myself, if she doesn't want to fritter away her summer tending other people's webs.

Then I remembered the attic.

I knew right away I was going to go up there. If Prosperine's papers, or some of them, were stored directly above my head, as both Allison and Grandma had suggested at different times, it was about as farfetched to ask me to spend the night alone in the house without taking a peek at them as it would have been to have expected Proppie herself never to have attempted anything beyond a cool sororal kiss in all those times she shared a bed with her Rosebud. Nevertheless, I sat there in the breakfast nook weighing the pros and cons. I didn't even budge when Lurch showed up. Exuding a dense doggy smell, he flopped down beneath the table and half-heartedly licked my toes.

Of course I hadn't forgotten Grandma's asperity on the unhappy occasion when I'd been convicted of reading "other people's mail." And if it weren't for the need to avoid alarming her, which prevented me from explaining what I was doing in this house, I could phone the Hill and ask for her okay. As it was, of course, I'd leave everything as I found it, and she'd never know. If a tree falls in the forest and no one hears. . . . Besides, I had no reason to think that she wouldn't show me everything eventually, anyway, if I played my cards right.

Unless.

There was a possible hitch I'd thought about before, and which was part of the reason why I was trying to proceed carefully. Suppose there were something very explicit in those papers, something Grandma would have obvious and strong motives for keeping secret? In that case, persuasion wouldn't work. I'd simply have to be patient and hope that on the inevitable day when that Past she'd so anxiously guarded had taken her home to its cold and private bosom, the papers would still be intact and available to me. At least, I reasoned, if I could get a look at some of them now, I'd have the small advantage of understanding what if anything she might want to hide.

What it came down to finally was that I was the only person capable of evaluating the merits of those papers—and capable of rescuing them, supposing they deserved it. I decided that if Aunt Geri spent the night at the hospital, I'd regard it as a sign and proceed with my clandestine research. Otherwise, once Grandma's bookstore reading was out of the way and she'd had a day or two to rest, I'd broach the matter with her directly.

I spent the waning afternoon relaying telephone messages. Uncle Bert finally called from Ottawa and left a number where Aunt Geri could get in touch with him. My aunt herself called several times, and in the early evening gave her final report of the day. Things seemed to be going better with Allison, whose fever was down, but she thought she'd better spend the night, just in case. Did I suppose I could possibly meet Bert's early morning plane and drop him off at the hospital? Cabs were impossible to get at rush hour, or she wouldn't even ask.

I promised to pick him up, jotted down the flight number, and had the presence of mind to add that I'd be going to bed early. Then I poured another Scotch (Aunt Geri had said to make myself at home) and headed for the stairs.

The rest of the night had a kind of dreamlike drift to it, from the mundane to the super-real, the incidental to the fated. My search started prosaically enough. While a visitor to the lower regions of the house might have supposed that Aunt Geri was holding her own in her Thirty Years' War with the detritus of family life, the attic seemed to forecast her ultimate defeat. After the hot day, the packed space was a sweatbox. I poked around at random, wishing for a flashlight, feeling more and more discouraged. After a sticky half hour I was about to give up. Then I stumbled on a stack of Campbell's soup cartons, and noticed that one of them said "MOTHER" on the side.

They hadn't even been taped shut. I rifled them one by one, shuffling through stacks of high school yearbooks and folders of recipes and wedding announcements clipped from newspapers and nested flower pots cupping sewing machine attachments and misshapen clay objects bearing children's palm prints, until I found three shoeboxes tied up with twine.

Calmly—I felt no need to hurry now—I worked the first knot loose. And there were the mortal remains of my Prosperine, all right: envelope after envelope addressed to Grandma in that minute yet vehement handwriting. Quickly I spread them out on a dusty square of floorboards beneath a moth-besieged bulb, careful to arrange them in such a way as to be able to replace them precisely as I'd found them. Then, realizing that the dim, stuffy quarters wouldn't be bearable for long, I carefully packed everything up again and carried the shoeboxes down to the guest bedroom.

I made a pot of coffee and sat up till after three. After the first hour I felt invincible. Here was not only good writing, but a devastating plot. If there were diaries besides, I was sure I could do a book: *The Prosperine Reader*, I titled it tentatively. Of course I'd use the best of the journalism, and maybe that *Little Review* story, if it turned out to be any good. Womanpress, Inc. might do it, or even one of the better university presses; here I counted on Linda. When I went to Chicago I could also ask my friend Bonnie for advice. She had great connections, and could be really generous when she got enthusiastic. And then there was Ruta, whose name on a foreword would be a great selling point—though here I'd have to be careful, given her eccentricity.

After I'd skimmed everything once, I was still too keyed up to sleep, and spent another hour copying out a few of the most interesting letters in the speedwriting I'd often used in grad school. That way, I thought, I'd have something to show people right away. Then, exhausted but still speedy, I carefully replaced everything in the attic, set the alarm, and got into bed. I fell asleep mapping out my introductory essay, which would provide a biographical context as well as an historical overview, and should, I thought, discuss not only movements on the Left, but the women's rights movement and such social phenomena as the emergence of the "new woman" as a background to Prosperine's development.

I still have the copies of those letters in my files:

*Virginia, Minnesota*
*July 27, 1916 (Tuesday)*

*Dearest Rose,*
*I arrived safely two evenings ago, after a jolting sooty ride. I am afraid the Duluth & Iron Range RR Co. is better suited to moving quantities of ore as efficiently as possible, than frailer human cargo. (Thirty open cars every day going down to the docks at Duluth, all this past spring before the strike put a stop to it.) I'm writing at what is truly the first chance I've had. I got off the train about 9 p.m. and had to go trudging about, suitcase in hand, looking for a "flop." Luckily the streets are well paved and lighted. Finally found a small cheap hotel and boardinghouse run by a little Italian lady with lots of black hair—tremendous rat & mother-of-pearl combs. The room is fairly clean though you wouldn't like the flies. Signs everywhere, in three languages, forbid smoking and chewing indoors. Mrs. Perletti looked at me queerly but asked no questions, to my relief. After Frank's words of caution I thought it best to say nothing of my business. You never know who sides with the Oliver Mining Co.*
*I was up first thing in the morning, guzzled some weak coffee and ran over to strike headquarters to see if I could get to talk to some of the organizers. Too late, I found out—they had all gone off to various towns and locations, as they call the outlying settlements, where strike meetings were planned. I spoke to three or four trammers, the lowest*

grade of labor. Conversation was difficult due to their scanty command of English. They were Slovenian, if I understood correctly. The one who spoke most fluently complained bitterly of the "rushing" work he said they do in the open pits. "A man slave for the Oliver ten-fifteen years, be finish, be all use up like a machine that rust clear through. Then the Oliver say, throw this fellow on the junkheap. Got plenty strong young fellow come take his place. Show me a man of 35, 40, been working these mines from his young years that is good for anything. I bet even the Devil in Hell pay better wages, and pay them twice a month!" (That is one of the strike demands, paydays twice a month.)

I spent the rest of the morning looking the town over, saw the modern school building of which the residents are very proud, and the two-story brick Socialist Opera House, with the red flag flying above it. I got chatting with a fellow named Booth who offered to drive me around to see some mine workings and locations. Of course I wondered what to do—he is not a strike supporter in any active sense, and works in a brewery—but I am dead set on "getting the story" and so anxious to show Frank what I'm capable of, so finally I said yes. (I made up some yarn about working for a paper in Bemidji, that wanted to print a series of articles about the eastern part of the state.) We were out all day today, driving around in the brewery truck. Booth didn't give much trouble and I'm glad I went with him, he only pouted a bit when I wouldn't let him buy my dinner, and Mrs. Perletti was sitting on the porch crocheting when I came in and looked at me sideways, and then I daren't even have a quiet smoke in my room, after refraining all day out of the need to appear of spotless moral character in front of my escort. But I will be moving on to some of the locations in a day or two, I hope, and get away from his attentions and her scrutiny!

It is stark strange country, this Mesaba, like a desert decreed by men. In places, coming out, we passed through stands of pine & fir that told how the whole landscape must have been in the wilderness state of only a few years back, but most of it has been logged off just like the forests around Bemidji. There have been some bad fires in recent years. It is gently rolling country and must have been quite pleasant. Now it seems so exposed, with the pits everywhere, and blackened stumps, and the great manmade hills or mesas of red ore and dark earth, rearing up haphazardly. It rouses a peculiar mixture of feelings in me, pity for the

123

spoiled earth, and pride in the industry and ingenuity that have wrought such drastic changes. You get the idea someday this whole territory will be one blind gaping hole. Yet there's an undeniable grandeur in the scale and ambition of the thing. Booth took me to a pit near Eveleth that hasn't yet shut down, where I watched one of the snorting, rearing steam shovels do its work. Three or four men could have ridden in the scoop. I'm told several of the towns have already been moved—the nearby pits were played out and the ore beneath the streets and homes was wanted. This, it seems, is the other face of our nation's smiling, bustling progress—tucked away up here in Northern Minnesota where most of the farmers, villagers, and inhabitants of our tidy cities scarcely imagine what goes to feed their ravening Steel Hunger.

The strike seems highly successful thus far, as two-thirds of the men are said to be out. They are demanding the eight-hour day, minimum pay $3 per day underground ($3.50 in wet places) and $2.75 on the surface. (I have heard several of the "blacks," as they term Slovenians, Roumanians, Croats, etc., relate how they frequently must work below in the dripping damp, returning home at the end of a shift soaked to the skin through several layers of protective clothing—imagine that, in the breathless airless heat of the underground workings, for 10 or more hours.) The chief object however is to do away with the so-called contract system, where a miner's wage is set according to the hardness of the ore, the man then being paid at that rate according to the quantity he produces. The men complain that rates are lowered if they hit a softer vein (though not raised in the opposite case), making the amount to be anticipated in the pay envelope completely unpredictable—of course it often turns out far lower than expected. They are also charged by the company for a variety of small expenses which are seldom explained to anybody's satisfaction. Even worse, under this capricious system the mine captains have waxed fat and become petty tyrants most of whom expect bribes from those miners who would secure advantageous "ground." There have also been reports of straw bosses making advances to the wives of men under them.

The strike began quite spontaneously at the beginning of this month. There had not been much prior union activity, and although a number of organizers from the IWW have arrived in recent weeks at the request of the strikers and are doing a brisk trade in their red membership cards, there is no demand for union recognition or a formal contract, these being counter to IWW policy. Everywhere the Finns are active, they have their own Socialist paper and Finn Halls in most towns, but there is actually quite a fantastic jumble of nationalities, more like Chicago than my idea of my pokey home state. In order to prepare my first piece for Stand (which you can see I have been rehearsing in this letter) I have to tackle certain boring questions of interest to Frank, such as why the Western Federation of Miners has not played the active role in this strike which they did in '07, and the effects on the Range of relations amongst the Socialist Party, the IWW, and the AF of L. I also want to talk to some of the miners' wives, get the strike from their point of view. I read in the papers that they played a large role in the march from location to location, that called the strikers out. Some pushed their baby buggies over those primitive roads.

I arrived here too late to attend the funeral services for the striker John Alar, who was killed last Thursday following a strike parade through Hibbing. Apparently the gun thugs came right into his house and shot him in the back. I have read several newspaper accounts of the funeral procession, headed by a large banner carried by four women clad in white, which read: MURDERED BY OLIVER GUNMEN. No priest would consent to conduct the services, but the Finnish Socialist Band was on hand to play the funeral music. Mr. Alar leaves a wife and three kiddies. So the valiant warriors of the Steel Trust (must be some valiant warriors among 'em, though the deputies I've seen look like miserable drunken curs) pursue their sacred mission to uphold the Law and protect defenseless Capital from being trampled upon by Labor.

I am completely fagged out, but must do an hour or two on my piece for Frank before I can think of sleep. Forgive me for confining myself so much to the news here. I think of you very often, but so much is going on.

Here's a kiss from your devoted

Prosperine (who misses her daily petting
        "something fierce")


June 30

Dear Darling Rosa,

I have just come back from a tour of some locations, the scattered *settlements adjacent to mine workings where many of the men live with their families. I got a fellow from the strike headquarters here to take me. In contrast to Virginia with its wide boulevards and blazing electric lights, these places present a picture of total desolation, the dwellings being tar-paper shacks or shanties patched together from scrap-wood and scrap-metal, all cobbled up with boulders, stumps, rubbish—nothing you could properly call streets—and tiny garden plots with beans and cabbages. Chickens, children—pigs and goats, even—wander listlessly about. On the way we saw a horse carcass some little distance from the roadside, that had plainly been lying there two or three days, judging from the smell.*

*One of the chief torments for the miners' wives in most of these spots is the eternal problem of water, which frequently is to be had only from a single "company" pump at some distance from their homes. Thus under even the best circumstances securing the day's supply requires considerable heavy labor, and you can imagine what washday must be, especially for a woman with five or six children. They say that since the first men went out earlier in the month, they have frequently been threatened with having their access to the pumps cut off, and in some cases the deputies have molested them to such an extent that they dare not go for water in groups of less than half a dozen. Of course they have set out buckets and wash-boilers to catch any rainfall, but so far there has been none beyond a few thunder-showers. Their scraggy garden patches barely limp along. Still some of them invest great care in small improvements, such as a sprig of ivy or geranium nursed in a tin can on a window ledge. Most places appear quite clean and tidy, especially considering the circumstances I've described. (Such, alas, was not the case with our overnight lodging, a home in a little settlement of perhaps 40 families—oh, the frightful bedbugs! I never knew such a strong stench of vermin, worse than the bites I think. Ugh! In the morning we were given breakfast—fried cornmeal mush, fat pork, watery coffee—I ate with difficulty—yet I'm sure it was the best the poor woman could contrive. "Oh, goody, meat," her little girl said, as though she hadn't seen any recently.)*

*Many of the women still cover their hair with kerchiefs, and thread gold wire through the ears of the tiniest baby girls. Their English is generally worse than the men's, but they seem anxious to adjust to their* new country. I wonder what life was like in the places they came from. Explaining the strike to me, one Slovenian woman said, "I want to wear hat to church like American lady do." Being a "dratted female" I am thrown together with the "ladies" more often than I care to be. Not that I disdain their company but I am mindful of the need to be out where the men are, getting the strike story. I am so anxious Frank should think well of my articles.

Mama of course is frantic for my safety, sends piteous letters beseeching me to avoid situations with "rough, disorderly men" (by which she means workers naturally—I wish she could see the Law's representatives around here—it is said some of the deputies were actually let out of jail in Duluth and shipped to the Range for the purpose). It is the bane of my existence, being shunted among the women, with Mama like a millstone around my neck.

This time though I really think I have come closer to escaping. I feel perfectly fit, all those little aches and pains I complained of in the winter seem to have disappeared. Perhaps it's because I finally— hurrah!—feel I am doing something. If only I could see you every day I think I would be perfectly happy, but I comfort myself with the knowledge that we won't be separated long. Please let me know you miss me too—I thought your last letter was a little dry and cold, or was that only my imagination? Remember, I'm used to regular petting now. Sometimes I lie on my bed in the little room, and close my eyes, and imagine I feel your beautiful hand softly stroking my hair.

I was glad to hear you are keeping up with your review of science and mathematics. For your Chicago certification, those subjects are essential. Here are some vocabulary words I ran across recently, and jotted down for you to add to your list, though up here where unbroken English is such a rarity I'm becoming more appreciative of Frank's saying that the most powerful speech is often the simplest. "We didn't get this country by somebody not fighting for it!" That was one of the most eloquent statements I have heard since coming here, spoken in a strike meeting by an IWW organizer. It was something to hear how the men cheered, and drummed with their rough boots on the wooden floor. Anyway, the words: plangent, ubiquitous, tumescent, bucolic, coruscating, visceral—all adjectives, this time. As for reading-matter (though you did not ask), if you have even a scrap of spare time and can come by a copy,

127

*I heartily recommend the autobiography of the Russian, Peter Kropotkin, also his book* The Conquest of Bread. *There is also a volume by our own Emma Goldman,* Anarchism and Other Essays, *which I had just begun when I left Chicago. Miss Goldman is the editor of* Mother Earth, *a very interesting magazine. You might look up the* Iconoclast, *the Minn. socialist paper, or the* Appeal to Reason, *out of Kansas. (And that is only a drop in the bucket, as I've found out by reading as widely and diligently as I can manage in the "radical" press. Frank says if I want to make the grade I have got to understand the ins and outs of all the "isms"— anarchism, socialism, trade unionism, syndicalism—not to mention the Wobblies, who appear to be sort of a mixture. Then of course there are the suffrage crusaders, the Non-Partisan League, the pacifists, vegetarians, educational reformers, Mexican revolutionists and Eurythmics practitioners—much more interesting than Baptists, Methodists, Presbyterians, and Catholics—and all equally certain they have charted the high road to heaven!*

*Dear girl, I picture you in the summer-kitchen, amidst a flurry of housewifely duties, a trifle harassed, supremely competent. How sweet you look with flour on your hands!—and barley beards and little sisters clinging about your skirts. I wish I had you here in this bleak Mesaba country.*

*I kiss your fragrant petals, one by one,*
*Prosperine*


*Biwabik, Minn.*
*July 4, 1916*


*Dearest Rose,*
*And a glorious Fourth to you—if it means anything.*
*I saw a man shot dead yesterday, gunned down off the seat of a soda pop delivery wagon. I had got a ride up here to this little place from my home base in Virginia early in the morning with some members of the strike committee. There was to be a Biwabik strike meeting in the afternoon. The gathering began shortly after lunch and went on for some hours. A major concern was the continuing harassment being offered by the Oliver Mining Co. henchmen—pardon me, the deputies. Communication was sometimes hampered by the usual language problems—*

128

they translated amongst themselves but it often became next to impossible for me to follow what was going on, especially when some of the men became heated in their indignation at the Oliver. All in all it was a spirited confab, though by now having been to a half a dozen such, I can testify that one's sitting-down equipment undergoes a severe test as the hours wear on.

Many wives were in attendance, and most had brought their kids. When the young ones got too restless an older girl with three long braids down her back took them over in a corner of the hall and somehow bewitched them into proper meeting behavior. Nothing could be done about the cranky babies, though sometimes their mothers would take them out back hoping for a breath of air. Weather has been frightfully hot this week.

The meeting broke up late in the afternoon. After I had taken the chance to speak for a few minutes with one of the leaders among the miners, I started back home with Mrs. Vlasic, at whose house I'm putting up for the time being. I was glad to go—had been up half the night scribbling my piece for Frank and on top of that had just got my monthly nuisance, more painful than usual. We had gone a little distance from the hall when we heard a commotion nearby and cut through an alley to investigate the cause. We found a few bystanders gathered in front of one of the single-story wood-frame houses that are set only about 10 feet apart with weeds and trash in profusion between. A man shouted that some deputies had gone in without a warrant and were mistreating the occupants. I could hear a woman screaming inside, but couldn't tell if the words were English. Then came a burst of shots, not very loud—for a moment I thought they might have been fire-crackers. Mrs. Vlasic instinctively ducked back into the alley with her children. I just as instinctively had my pencil out and was about to plunge forward when I heard a final crack and a man fell backward off a pop delivery wagon that stood in front of the house. He fell straight and heavy, like a sack of grain, and lay there unmoving.

There was an awful pause, like the moment in a bad dream when you try to call for help and not a sound comes out. Then shouting and commotion, more men running up. I looked back in the alley and there stood poor Mrs. Vlasic with her four children about her, clutching the two youngest—she had actually covered up their heads with her apron, *and was pressing their faces into her broad stomach, so they shouldn't see I guess. The look on her face then was—how would I describe it? It wasn't fear, completely. There was a kind of sureness too: she was bound to protect those youngsters somehow. They were bawling their heads off, probably more frightened at being smothered like that than at the shooting. I saw her home, a five minutes' walk, attempting to explain what I thought had happened in the simplest English terms. "So now begin the killing," she pronounced at last, in a tone of grave acceptance, almost as though witnessing the unfolding of some inevitable and long-foreseen drama. (Later her husband told me the family were living in Colorado at the time when all those miners' wives and children were butchered in Ludlow by the Rockefeller gang.)*

*With Mrs. Vlasic safely settled, I returned to the shooting scene. The crowd had at least tripled. The pop man's body had already been carried off into a neighboring house. There was a splash of blood in the street, not much larger than a saucer. The horse stood waiting, still hitched to the wagon, oblivious of its master's permanent departure, while the hot sun glinted temptingly off the crated bottles, golden, ruby, grape. I saw a couple of scruffy boys trying to filch a pop or two each, and reflected that in the past weeks of this strike there cannot have been much ready cash for such indulgences in the homes of either the miners or small merchants hereabouts. But even in that uproar some solid citizen took notice, and put a stop to it. Property rights, you know!*

*Several more loads of deputies arrived, and at last the sheriff's own more luxurious auto came screeching up, with an especially foul-looking plug-ugly glued to the running board. When the "authorities" had mustered sufficient reinforcements they brought out their prisoners—none too gently, but without flagrant abuse before that sullen crowd. Two of the men shouted something in their language—I believe they are Montenegran. The woman of the house—her name is Masonovich—was removed along with them, her baby in her arms. She walked proud and silent. Her face made me think I would not have liked to be the one to take her into custody. Just before they put her into the waiting car she turned suddenly and held up a blood-drenched handkerchief like a signal to the crowd.*

*It is said that the deputies went in to arrest this woman's husband and several boarders on the pretext of a liquor violation, and she gave objection. One deputy lost his life in the ensuing fracas, evidently hit by a stray bullet from a comrade's gun. The Montenegrans are all charged in this death though they had no firearms. Moreover, a number of IWW's are now in jail at Duluth, accused of "inciting to murder" on account of their eloquent speeches supporting the strike effort. For this they are liable as accessories and may get a life sentence, though most were nowhere near Biwabik at the time. Of course no one has been charged in the murder of the pop man, Thomas Ladvalla. He was a strike sympathizer!*

*I keep seeing his homely middle-aged face, his unusually small ears, the blue cap that remained on his head as he fell from the wagon.*

*"But this here is still the U.S. of A.," as one of the miners I spoke with this morning reasoned hopefully. "We get justice same as born Americans."*

*Others, less naive, clearly realize that Biwabik, Aurora, Virginia, Eveleth—all these little Range towns—are further off than Siberia so far as most Americans are concerned, and might as well be ruled over by the Czar and his Cossacks, as by the Oliver. Despite their brave determination I think even the leaders are beginning to feel their isolation keenly. The Duluth merchants are cutting off the credit to local businesses. The Oliver is squelching public marches and protests as far as possible. Still the men are firm in their belief that a little publicity would work wonders for their cause. Their welcome, when they learn I am a "newspaper lady," and from Chicago, sometimes leaves me quite embarrassed. I'm thankful they can't see Frank hard at it in his shirtsleeves in the* Stand *office, the editor-in-chief helping set up type.*

*As a girl alone I am a definite oddity, so much so that one matron positively refused to believe I didn't have a husband hidden away somewhere. Particularly on the "locations" you see hardly any unmarried women, what work there is in the way of taking in boarders, laundry, sewing, etc., being monopolized by the miners' wives. One Wobbly organizer acted downright sniffy at being faced with a five foot tall female reporter, looked me up and down and drawled, "*Stand—*oh, the Socialist paper." I informed him Frank considers himself part of the left-wing. He seemed amused, which I didn't like, but gave the interview. (Part of what they have got against* Stand, *it seems, is that it is backed by a, what somebody called "capitalist dilettante"—though what Hiram Crump's*

131

*character has got to do with Frank's editing or the paper's contents, I am at a loss to comprehend.) With so many in jail following the events of yesterday, I think I shall make my way to Duluth as soon as possible, on the hope of interviewing some of the IWW's, the Montenegran miners—and most of all that remarkable looking woman, Mrs. Masonovich. I hope she speaks English.*

*Of course, perhaps the sheriff will not allow interviews, but I'll get them if there's a way on earth to do it. It seems almost selfish to be thinking of my own career at such a time, but Frank did tell me before I left that if I managed to get something "hot" he might be able to have it reprinted in some of the Eastern papers. I would not do it unless I thought it would help the cause, too.*

*To think how I pined for Europe, last year! I never would have believed I could learn so much right here in my home state. But then, how little most Americans know of their own country. I am ashamed to think how sheltered and ignorant an up-bringing I had, in so many ways. And terrible as conditions are here, it is exciting, too, to witness these people who have decided they will no longer put up with sub-human treatment, who begin to know the strength the down-trodden may possess when once they band* together. *How I wish I could show you all I've seen in the past week. Mrs. Vlasic, for instance, so sternly,* calmly *waiting in the alley, shielding her children from looking upon death.*

*I suppose by your silence on the subject you have finally determined to spend the rest of the summer at your folks'. With Flora not yet mended, and your mother's operation, I guess it is for the best, though I should have thought you would be at all pains to avoid another canning season(!) At this writing I can't say with certainty when I shall return to Chicago, which makes me less insistent, I admit.* But Rose, mind you, no later than September. *I am firmly resigned to taking a drudge-job (anything, so long as it is not more door-to-door corsets) so that even if we are forced to "jungle up" at Peg's for another few weeks, it will only be for that short time. ("Jungle up," I'll have you know, is "Wob" talk—I'm beginning to pick up a smattering.) I am satisfied that things can go more smoothly than last year. I promise I won't foist that Radical Book Shop crowd on you again! I admit a few of them were a bit rough-cut. You needn't see the S.'s, if you'd rather—though even if you do not go for Frank, I wish you would admit Mary's good qualities. The great thing*

132

is, to have a home—*you shall cook to your heart's content—I promise to learn how to make three or four things besides spaghetti and walnut fudge. You shall go to night school, study like the dickens, be a bona fide Chicago teacher in no time. We'll read together in the evenings, like the old days—next summer go for picnics in Luna Park. We shall be living proof that a husband and children are quite superfluous to a modern woman's happiness.*

*Incidentally, what do you mean, miss, allowing a pleasant young man to free your team from the embarrassment of a muddy ditch? (So long as he was a farmer, I rest easy, knowing your sentiments toward the breed.)*

*What do you make of all this racket about "Preparedness Day"? I was reading of it in the Duluth papers. Do you really think it is possible we will let ourselves be dragged into all that bloody business. How far away it seems! Yet it's as real to millions and millions over there, as preposterous and real, as that poor fellow Ladvalla shot off the wagon yesterday. Don't you think there is such a mystery about the lost? to be cut off like that, utterly senselessly—to lose your life delivering a few dollars' worth of soda pop. At least a Joe Hill knows why he dies.*

*There is a song the Wobblies sing, that contains the words, "We have been nought—we shall be all." To be nought—that's what I mean—that's what seems unbearable. Those lines are almost like religion to me.*

*But now I'm afraid I really must admit I am chattering shamelessly in order to postpone saying good night to you, dear girl. (Whom I picture in the martial guise you will shortly assume: wooden spoon in hand, how masterfully you preside over the summer-kitchen full of boiling kettles and frenzied troops! Through the clouds of steam I think I faintly make out the frothy jell, hear the terrible word "pectin"—watch your sisters carry out with fantastic synchrony their various duties of chopping, mincing, straining, picking over, stirring, pouring—while keeping up a good supply of small wood in the wood-box—but weren't you destined for higher service, General Bright?) I kiss your soft hands, which not all the "putting up" in the North Star State can spoil.*

*And what were you up to on this roasting Fourth? Did you take Joey and the little girls out to see the fire-works? There was not much celebration attempted in Biwabik, though some of the mothers made lemonade and did other little things for their "American" children. I* spent the afternoon here at Mrs. Vlasic's writing my piece for Frank, or trying to, all the time the oldest boy, a tyke about eight or nine, was out on the porch playing a noisy monotonous game of "deputies and strikers" with "carbines" he and a couple of friends had fashioned from kindling.

I know it's uphill work, but would you please mention the facts I have written to anyone you think might be gotten to send a letter of protest to General Burnquist? His actions have been terrible thus far, all on the Steel Trust side. Of course farmers won't want to take much interest in the lot of a few foreign-born miners. Then they'll holler when their own ox is gored.

Good night, dearest friend. How I wish we could talk. I am sure a great many things must have happened to you, too, over these last weeks. Everything could be so much more simply explained, if only we had an hour or two together.

Continue to write me at the Virginia address.

Tender kisses from your
    "fellow"
        Prosperine


Virginia, Minn.
July 14, 1916

My Wild English Rose,

I am so sorry that a Stink-bug wormed his way into the nice dish of wild raspberries and cream which you prepared for Mr. Schlaghoffer's refreshment when he came to discuss hay prices with your father. Even sorrier he had the misfortune to bite down!

But I cannot lie to you, my fairest one—perhaps I had better admit that I am not so very sorry, after all. I told you already that I consider eligible young men have no business whatever dawdling about your neighborhood. And Schlaghoffer, with his "two years of college" and his mild un-German aspect. . . is almost eligible. Still I admit an insect of that hideous description does seem rather cruel & unusual punishment.

Remember in Bemidji that first year, when I got a frog and put it in the lunch you prepared for the Basket Social, and it sprung out at Elmer Pease? Feels to me like a million years ago.

I am still working on my plan to travel to Duluth. I require the

134

*assistance of the IWW's who are now arriving in increasing numbers, despatched by their national office in Chicago. A Strike Bulletin is being prepared, various publicity, protest, and relief measures are being discussed, and of course there is much to be done for the defense of those arrested. The latter is in the hands of Elizabeth Gurley Flynn—"Gurley" she's called in Chicago, though up here it is amusing to hear them all say "Mrs. Flynn." I heard her speak last November at the great memorial meeting I attended that was held when they buried Joe Hill, who was shot out in Utah. (I'm sure you remember—we quarrelled—you wouldn't come.) I thought her less impressive in person than on the lecture platform. People speak of her beauty, but only her fine blue eyes seemed exceptional to me. She was tired, I suppose. I found her rather abrupt, but she didn't condescend. She promised to do what she could to help me get an interview. That cheers me up, even though I'm beginning to worry about Frank—writes he doesn't know how long he can keep me up here, etc. I will stay without any pay if necessary, but I am sure if I can just get to Duluth and send some good copy he'll come around.*

*I do not want to leave with this strike hanging in the balance. I feel so strongly for, and with, these people.*

*You have not said what you think of the conditions and circumstances I described to you in my most recent letters. I'm burning to know your opinion. Do you still feel, as you once flung at me, that I am "riding a hobbyhorse"?* Don't be afraid to tell me. *We shan't quarrel. I know full well by now that what draws us to one another is deeper than mere political sympathies. You are my* friend.

*More soon, when I hear definitely about Duluth.*

   *Ever your devoted,*
     *Fellow-Worker (so the "Wobs" address each other—I think*
     *it is quaint, and charming, like Quakers saying "Thee")*
      *Prosperine*
      Forget-me-not


*September 2, 1916*

*Rose,*
  *Got back late from work on the Strike Bulletin and found your letter waiting. I could not sleep but didn't dare light the precious kerosene or*

even move around for fear of waking others. Now it's almost morning and I can see to write this.

Of course I dimly guessed. I shouldn't be surprised, but I never let myself know, can you understand that? It is curious what I'm feeling, if it were happening to anyone else I've little doubt I'd find it very interesting. You see, I am so used to you being the one I tell my life to, that even now when I've lost you irrevocably, still I'm so used to having that very "you" to describe my experience to, that even this I have to tell you, even for the last time. It is a loss, Rose, as final as death to me.

I can't help this bitterness gnawing, gnawing at my vitals. I feel fooled, Rose. You want the life of a normal woman. Remember how it was for your mother, or mine? Is that what you want?

I hate him—still it's not the poor fellow's fault, if he reaches up to pick the ripe fruit off the tree. Well, I will "take it like a man" I suppose. There is little else I can do. But the world doesn't look the same to me, Rose, on the morning of this news, as it did yesterday.

I always had the aspiration of being completely truthful, soul-naked, with at least one person out of all on this earth. Even though I could see that at times I embarrassed or made you uneasy with my confidences, and even though I could not always be completely frank with you about every thing, still I approached my ideal with you as with no one else. Now that is finished.

Du lieber Gott, as Alma used to say.

Don't misunderstand me. I always knew in my heart of hearts that you would marry eventually. I have deluded myself, but not to that extent. I could see you would want to be "Mrs." somebody or other, and have a house like other people, and a garden, and children. But I hoped we'd have a few years, you see. I told myself you'd come back to Chicago in the fall, and we'd find a flat and live just like we planned. Now I'm numb, dry. I feel somehow as though I'd fallen into one of those enormous cracks that splits the hearts of glaciers. Your stiff, artificial phrase running through my head all night, "Eugene Schlaghoffer and I have come to care for one another a great deal...."

And all the times you let me so close. Yet never did I ever utter three simple and true syllables—because I thought you might not like it. I was afraid my love would scare you off, as though you were a wild thing I'd found feeding in the forest.

136

*And perhaps, despite my caution I did scare you off anyway. I thought of that last night too, I thought of a lot of things. I know it's made you uneasy, me being up here all summer championing the cause of the "garlic-eating" foreigners. You were too polite to say so, but you don't really understand. Deep down in your turnip-fed soul, you farmer's daughter, you, you really do believe it's the fault of working folks, each man and woman individually, if they slave away their lives and end up as they usually do with nothing but broken backs and broken spirits-- their fault, I mean, not because they have not banded together and fought for their rights, but for failing to be smart enough, work hard enough, get lucky enough—each for himself, and devil take the hindmost. You think like America thinks, in other words. I don't. But all the same, we needn't have parted, simply on account of a difference in views. Take Mary Stuberfield and Frank—I don't believe she gives a fig for politics, yet she feeds that crazy bunch he brings home out of the goodness of her heart, because she likes "the boys" and because he is her husband. (Mary is a* wife. *You will understand* that.)*

*And in Chicago sooner or later I'm sure you'd have met some decent fellow, maybe even one of Frank's parlor socialist cronies, the sort that's no longer quite so young and has got himself a cushy office job and goes to meetings after hours. That way we could have seen one another, and you'd have been in with people who at least knew something of what is going on in the wide world. Now you'll bury yourself alive up there in the woods, you and hubby will start a family as soon as possible of course—so many tender little balls-and-chains dragging at your heels. You're finished, Rose. This is it. Your life is over. Your biggest excitement will be the baby's croup. You'll fret over the Sunday roast, and whether you put the proper amount of blueing in with the white laundry. . . .*

*I think of the mother of four of the kids I taught at my last school, who told me quite proudly how she used to go down to the bank every year at the beginning of January and get the clerk to give her the old calendar when they put the new one up. She would cut out the colored illustration and pin it on the wall, so the children would grow up looking at "pitchers" and be improved thereby. You'll be a cut above that of course, but the same general principle. I can see you with an upright piano, sheet music spread out which no one ever plays, or maybe a hundred dollar phonograph. I'd have the phonograph, more practical*

137

*I think.*

*No, I won't show up for the wedding, thank you.* I hate and despise the man, can you understand? *Not for* who *he is, which is not of the slightest concern to me and I'm sure he's a perfectly nice, hard-working boy, not too stupid either or you wouldn't have him—but for* what *he is, a male creature capable of bestowing on you with barely a lift of his eyebrow and a crook of his little finger that position which means everything to you, and which I never could,* because I'm a girl.

*You, Rose, I can never hate. But I can't forgive you either. I hate this thing you're doing, that you would trade your soul and body both for such a commonplace mess of pottage as that—why, the lowliest street-walker only sells half of what you sell.*

*Bitter, intemperate words. If pressed, you'll say you "love" him. You even have the brass to hint to me that perhaps I ought to try it myself. That would tie things up for you in a nice neat little parcel, wouldn't it, if I'd only get a man? I find myself wondering how it was exactly that I came to care for you and nobody else. It's a question I can't answer. You know because I've told you that before you such friends as I had were almost always boys. Girls seemed silly, the things they talked about. Your knowledge of farm life attracted me, the toughness you hid under your soft looks. It impressed me that you were capable of driving a bundle team. I began to feel with you like I felt when I was small and read some book and fell in love with it. I never could believe there would be another to enchant me in that way.*

*I remember when we first started Normal School and you were boarding at our place, how I would stand behind your chair when you were seated, and feel every tiniest hair-thin nerve in my body alert and quivering with the* need *to rest my hands on your two slim shoulders just so, and press my lips ever so lightly to the nape of your neck, where the wispy hairs escape from their confinement despite all your efforts. There was a day I didn't dare, and then a day I did. I swear a thousand Eugene Schlaghoffers can never give you the passion—yes,* I dare *to call it that— which thrilled through me then.*

*But you'll mother nations—with* him. *That mustn't be forgotten. Your great-grandchildren will thank me, for stepping quietly aside.*

*Even now, heaven help me, I imagine that these words are a disfiguring acid, I imagine flinging them into your face. Would* he *have*

138

you then, with your spoiled looks? But that's enough, I'll stop. I know how you hate "scenes." I'm trembling and trembling as I write, till I can scarcely shape the words. And I've got to go out directly to help nurse a woman who was beaten by the deputies, several days ago. She lost the child she was carrying. But she'll be all right. She says the roughing up she got was no worse than what she's had from her husband more than once, when he'd drunk too much whiskey.

I ache inside, Rose. My womb aches with this, as a woman's must when she loses her child. The waste of it appalls me, like the look in the eyes of some of the youngsters on the locations, the ones with hacking coughs who've been living too long on split peas and soda crackers.

Maybe when we're both old and gray and don't care anymore, we'll meet and speak calmly of the past. You may as well keep the locket, and my letters—if they mean anything.

Prosperine Munkers

**D**ragged by the alarm too early the next morning from a dream in which Prosperine was playing pool with Ruta Karlessen in an old-fashioned beauty parlor (one of the faces sternly helmeted by the dryers belonged to Grandma Rose), I rushed out to the airport. There I waited, bleary-eyed, for over an hour. Uncle Bert's plane had been delayed in Chicago by mechanical difficulties. At last he strode through the gate, a tall, rumpled figure, attaché case in hand. It was the way his ears stuck out that made him look like an old kid, I realized consciously for the first time in all the years I'd known him.

"Hello, I'm so sorry, what rotten luck," I said, planting a dutiful kiss on his stubbled cheek.

He flashed a crooked grin. "I am not a happy camper."

He insisted on driving my car, saying he knew the way better, and though I resented the paternalism, I acquiesced in this emergency. When we finally reached the hospital, I accompanied him upstairs. We found Aunt Geri at the nurses' station, looking reasonably composed for a woman of sixty-five who'd spent the night on rock-hard naugahyde. Her hair was flattened and slightly greasy, her features puffy with fatigue, but she had on fresh red lipstick, her badge of competence. Allison had stabilized, she told us. They'd be having more specialists in to look her over, but it appeared fairly certain that she was battling a massive systemic infection of a type that occasionally occurs in users of long-wear contact lenses.

My uncle at first hooted at the notion that a dangerous illness could stem from a trivial eye irritation. He spoke as though he blamed my aunt for the diagnosis. Finally, as she plied him with medical terms, he subsided into muttered threats of litigation.

"Let's get Allison on her feet first," Aunt Geri suggested reasonably, and I thought in how many doctors' waiting rooms and lawyers' suites and morticians' panelled offices she must have humored him, over the decades.

We discussed what to do about Grandma. I agreed to chauffeur her around. I wasn't likely to get much else done, anyway, in my exhausted state. Happily, those letters in the attic were like a sweet romantic secret. I could forget my weariness by resorting secretly to last night's memories, taking sips of the nectar of my honeyed expectations. (Now was not the time, I told myself, to worry about how I was going to get permission to publish my find. The material was smashing; there had to be a way.)

Aunt Geri promised to try to come to Grandma's reading. Of course I urged her not to think of it, to go home and get some sleep, but privately I hoped she'd show up. Her presence, I knew, would reassure Grandma, and now that I had a better idea of what was at stake with the papers, I was more anxious than ever for this event to go well.

As it turned out, she made it, dashing into the Giants in the Earth Book Emporium exactly at the scheduled starting time. Grandma, who'd been eyeing the door nervously, seemed to relax when she saw her daughter, and calmly allowed herself to be installed in a carved wooden chair, a glass of water within easy reach. She had on the new dress she'd selected that afternoon in my company, electric blue and with an odd swatch of toga-like drapery pinned at one shoulder. On her bosom bloomed an orchid; I'd thought of everything. The bearded, ponytailed proprietor uttered a few hearty words of welcome. I followed with a short introduction, and then Grandma was on. She read to an audience of thirty or so, perhaps half of them strangers. Faithful Phoebe was there, and Amaryllis sat in the first row, what I took to be diamonds winking on her flat spotted wrist. There were several cousins I hadn't seen in twenty years, including Scott with his busty Mormon fiancée, and of course his parents, Uncle Gene and Aunt Judy. Judy had whispered to me before sitting down that they'd bought flowers to present to Grandma afterwards.

Grandma managed her magnifying glass more gracefully this time. She read from *Woman's Estate*, two selections of about ten minutes each which I'd marked off with an orange felt-tipped pen so she wouldn't get lost. After the first segment she wandered a bit, told a lengthy anecdote,

141

and then, just when I was afraid she'd really get off the track, meandered gracefully back to the prepared material. The audience, which had begun by listening respectfully, seemed to warm to her as she went along, and by the time she'd rather uncertainly closed the magazine and sat there looking bewildered amid vigorous applause, I knew we'd pulled it off. I stood and announced that Mrs. Schlaghoffer would now take questions and comments.

There were two or three questions about her working methods, which she answered seriously, and then came a pause which lasted so long that I was about to suggest we adjourn for coffee and cookies and more informal discussion, when a dark-haired woman spoke from the back of the room. "Mrs. Schlaghoffer?"

"Yes?" Grandma chirped, straining up expectantly.

"I speak as an Indian woman." The voice was hesitant, barely audible. I glanced at Grandma, who looked blank, and though I'd have preferred to disappear at that moment—I sensed instantly that there was going to be trouble—I responsibly suggested that the speaker come up front.

She advanced until she stood beside the front row of chairs. I noticed she was wearing a nurse's uniform.

"I speak as an Indian," she repeated hoarsely, but louder this time. "I wanted you to know. It's pretty difficult for me to be saying all this. I came tonight because I'm a poet, and I heard about this series. Mrs. Schlaghoffer, I liked your presentation. . ."

"Thank you," Grandma graciously conceded, misinterpreting. I was having trouble breathing. *What is it?* I thought.

". . . I liked what you read, because you had a lot of very vivid images, pictures that made me feel like I was right there in the middle of some of the scenes you were writing about. That part about the orioles' nests, I liked that especially. But then all of a sudden I heard something that shocked me, I mean to me this just seemed completely out of the blue, so vicious and cruel—and I'm, like, hey, what's going on here?

"It was when you told that story about the neighbor girl that had the rag doll with a wig she claimed was made from what you called 'a real Indian scalp,' from one of the people they hanged in 1862. The way you put it, it could just as well have been some old piece of skunk fur you'd picked up in the woods."

She stopped. Grandma still looked puzzled. I couldn't be absolutely sure she'd heard, though the woman had spoken very directly to her, and her voice had strengthened as she went along. The audience had been listening, sure enough. You could tell by the expressions of studied unavailability, like the faces of New York City subway riders when a double amputee in a wheelchair rattles a cup.

"I mean, I'm thinking, these are *my* people! So this is how the whites look at us! Of course I'm not that dumb, I mean I know that's how they think, but you know, the funny thing is, you never really get used to it."

"Well, maybe I misspoke," Grandma muttered sullenly, and I wondered how on earth she'd hit on that verb.

Her accuser stood silent. She and Grandma were about the same height. I felt I should do something, save someone from someone else, but I hesitated while my relative rattled on, uncharacteristically loquacious. "To tell the truth, I never put a lot of stock in that neighbor girl's nonsense, anyway. Most likely it was just a tall tale, like some others she told. Youngsters sometimes make things up to impress their playmates. Actually, there was quite a few Indians left in our area when I was growing up, and we always got along with 'em just fine. I remember sometimes you'd see the squaws coming into town," (*shut up*, I prayed, *just shut the fuck up*) "to get supplies, I guess, a couple of them sitting on straw in the wagon box, and the old chief driving.

"I remember he chewed tobacco, and could spit so he'd hit a quarter on the sidewalk at six paces. Some of the store clerks would put quarters out just to watch him do it, and then he'd get to keep the quarter, you see. . . ." Mercifully she trailed off, but felt the need to add, "About that hanging business, I wouldn't know. I wasn't born yet. I'm an old lady," she brightened, "but not *that* old."

Relieved laughter exploded quietly. Still the woman didn't move. She held us there. "Never mind," she finally said tears and fury in her voice. "Why don't you just go home and read some history, all of you!"

I had to do something, I felt even more strongly. "Thank you for your comment," I shouted idiotically at her retreating back. In spite of everything, I felt loyalty to Grandma. Then I heard the bookstore owner suggesting we continue what he called this "dialogue" over refreshments. He even remembered to remind the audience to buy copies of *Woman's Estate*, but I no longer cared. As I sprinted for the door, I glimpsed a proudly beaming Phoebe, and Uncle Gene advancing with a bouquet of yellow roses.

I emerged on the street just in time to see Grandma's challenger disappear around a corner.

"Excuse me," I hollered, "just a minute, please stop!" When I caught up with her, I instinctively put my hand out and touched her lightly on the arm. "I'm sorry, please listen, don't run away."

She flinched, but I'd stopped her. "Don't touch me," she blurted, and for a split second, I felt, unbearably, that she was frightened of me, I mean physically afraid. Her wary eyes were green, I saw by the street light, and despite my shame I felt a twinge of curiosity.

She was MS. DECOTEAUX, according to her hospital I.D. tag.

"My name's Dale McNab," I began, completely forgetting I'd been introduced at the start of the reading.

"The woman's granddaughter."

"That's right, I'm afraid—I mean, at this particular moment I don't feel particularly proud of the fact. You were absolutely right in what you said, and I just wanted you to hear that *someone* in the room understood, anyway. I know it took guts to say what you said, because I've been in situations like the one you were in, I mean not exactly like it, of course, but sort of comparable, trying to explain my oppression to people who don't get it.

"I'm sorry about what Grandma said. I know she didn't mean to be so racist"—I knew I shouldn't be defending her, but it was happening anyway, my words tumbling all over themselves and uncontrollable— "but it *was* incredibly racist, obviously. Actually, it's weird, I've never heard her tell that story either. I guess it must have sort of occurred to her right there on the spot."

"If you knew all that, why didn't you back me up?"

"Well, I ought to have said something," I admitted, feeling that somehow, somewhere, there was a good reason why I hadn't, but aware that whatever it was, it wouldn't mean anything to her.

"Listen," she instructed. "Maybe you'll learn something."

I obeyed her while we stood in the humid night, the joyful punks of Hennepin Avenue streaming by: a Black kid in a Mohawk haircut licking a tall ice cream cone, blond girls in modishly ripped T-shirts. She started with the Sioux Rebellion of 1862. I heard how the government

144

had squeezed and starved the tribes to make them sign away their land; how the people had had to beg for rancid meat; how some who'd argued against the armed rising had joined in when they couldn't stop it; how the men had been hunted down, those who'd fought and those who hadn't, and condemned by a kangaroo court (some of them sentenced in the place of others for whom they were mistaken); how they'd chanted their death chants as the dozens of gallows were being constructed; how Chief Little Crow, who escaped the mass hanging, was murdered by settlers the following year, scalped, and his mutilated body buried in a dung-heap.

She quoted infant mortality statistics and fetal alcohol syndrome statistics and figures on TB and malnutrition. She told me about the White Earth reservation, where they'd been whittling away at the Chippewas' land for over a century, taking it piecemeal for back taxes.

I kept wanting to stop her and tell her I knew all this, say the magic words to persuade her I was really on her side. But the truth was, although I prided myself on being pretty good on Afro-American and Puerto Rican history, when it came to Native Americans I didn't really know specifics.

"I'll speak to Grandma," I promised.

"Oh, I wouldn't bother, you won't change her mind." She seemed to sag a little, like a stern and lofty oracle coming out of her trance and revealed to be an ordinary woman with a wide, pretty mouth and too little chin. I suddenly realized that she was much younger than I. "Look, I'm going home, if you don't mind. I've had a rotten day, two cardiac arrests we managed to pull through and one old guy who bought it on my shift. I probably shouldn't have tried to come this evening."

"Well, good night, then," I said helplessly. "Look, do you mind just telling me your name? I'd like to know your name, at least."

"Sharon. My name's Sharon."

"Next time I'll try to do better."

"Don't *try*. This is not about *you*. Can't you people ever get that through your heads—that it's *not* all about *you*?"

I walked back to the bookstore as slowly as I could, sweat streaming between my breasts. I felt like a jerk, a dead tired jerk. Certainly I wasn't in any mood either to congratulate Grandma or to try to raise her consciousness. What bothered me most of all was the realization that I hadn't registered anything amiss about the scalp anecdote, which had come in the middle of her off-the-cuff remarks. Not that I'd have approved of it

145

if I'd stopped to think, of course, but it was typical of someone of that vintage, and I hadn't paid it any mind. It certainly hadn't occurred to me that there'd be anybody present who'd be personally offended.

And Treecie—how depressing. I was thinking of Treecie. A woman of color who hadn't called me racist.

Which only proved, of course, what a racist dog I was.

I found Grandma still enthroned in the carved chair, her roses on her lap. She was autographing magazines, and I could see she was composing elaborate messages, taking a long time with each one. Geri and Amaryllis were halfway across the room, chatting with Phoebe and several other Hill residents. Gene and Judy stood in a little knot of fans, Gene with his dense look of a polled Hereford chewing his cud. After a minute he swallowed, then spoke.

"We've really got to hand it to you, Dale, organizing all this. It was a real special evening, didn't you think, Jude? Except for that gal at the end there. That was the one sour note."

I was furious. "I thought she had a point."

"Oh, for crying out loud," Aunt Judy said.

"Kinda thin-skinned, if you ask me."

Grandma waited until she'd placed a deliberate period at the end of her snaky sentence of dedication. Then she raised her pen and glared indignantly at me. "That pale little thing!" she sniffed. "Huh, some Indian!"

The following night I called Linda and eagerly read her parts of the letters I'd copied at Aunt Geri's. She said she agreed that they were fascinating, and that a book was beginning to seem more and more feasible, but she sounded a little distant, not so enthusiastic as I'd hoped. I did my best to swallow my disappointment. I knew she was preoccupied with work, and would probably seem out of sorts and withdrawn until she was safely settled in the beach house and had gotten a few days' rest. Fiona, she mentioned, was being a pain in the ass too, persistently bemoaning the injustice that she hadn't been allowed to attend some super-expensive camp where "all" (in fact, three) of her friends would be in August.

What really set me off, and derailed the conversation, was the reaction I got to my account of Grandma's reading. True, Linda groaned at the scalp anecdote, but she didn't seem to understand why I was still feeling upset about the whole thing. She commented that Sharon Decoteaux sounded "pretty sensitive."

"You sound just like my Republican uncle. *He* called her 'thin-skinned.' "

She took offense at the comparison, of course. "There's a world of difference between 'thin-skinned' and 'sensitive,' " she maintained. " 'Thin-skinned' is critical. 'Sensitive' is descriptive. I'm not suggesting there's something *wrong* with her reaction, I'm just not sure most people would have felt the same way, *and* I see no reason why you should be taking it all on yourself. It's not your fault what Grandma Rose said."

"But I should have supported Sharon. She was right about that."

"But you were thinking about your grandma's feelings, too. Nobody

147

likes to be slammed out of the blue like that. She grew up in a different milieu, too, remember."

"Yeah, a *milieu* where it was cool to shit on Indians," I said, though I recognized a pattern that had sometimes led us into unpleasant arguments. It wasn't that I was much of an activist, or even paid attention to political issues (aside from feminist and gay ones) on any consistent basis. But I'd done time in the antiwar movement in the early Seventies. By her own admission, Linda had spent those years preoccupied mostly with Fiona, the narrative structure of Beowulf, and the restoration of the eighteenth-century farmhouse she and Michael had owned upstate, and I sometimes felt that she adopted too cheerfully pragmatic an approach to life in a world of large injustices.

Now she pointed out that we were sliding into one of the destructive spirals that our therapist had advised us to interrupt; we were to come back to the conversation at a less emotionally charged moment. She suggested that she wait and call me from the beach. I agreed, ignoring her faintly martyred tone—as though she hadn't chosen the pressure she was under! After I hung up I felt unhappy to think that now we wouldn't talk for over a week. But I planned to be in Chicago; the time would pass quickly. We really needed to take time to go away together more in the coming year, I decided.

I then dialed Bonnie, whom I could usually count on to cheer me up, at least when she wasn't involved in some crisis of her own. She sounded fine, though she claimed to be depressed about a recently soured romance. She said I definitely should come and stay with her. We could sit around her apartment and gripe or go out and paint the town.

"The former, please," I said. "I'm unemployed, remember."

"Just talking will be a treat. I haven't been seeing anybody lately, just working and getting stoned. Hey, we could do a dinner."

We'd cooked as recreation in grad school, when we were on stipends and couldn't afford to go out very often. Usually we'd smoke a joint or two first. Bonnie had always been a pothead, and I enjoyed turning on with her. Then we'd open a bottle of some decent, cheap California wine and sip it as we worked. Bonnie did all the planning and more elaborate maneuvers, while I acted as sous-chef. Sometimes, particularly when by coincidence we were both in love or lust at once, we'd share the resultant feast with guests. But usually the most memorable part of the evening was the leisurely, rambunctious cooking-and-talking session, which veered delightfully from intellectual to raunchy. We got along so well that at some point neither one of us had been able to resist the logical conclusion that we ought to become lovers. But after one or two uninspired attempts, romantic as dissertation research, we'd had the sense to put the relationship back on the old comradely footing.

"I know what," I offered. "I'll bring this coke I've been saving. I never feel like doing it alone, and I want to use it up while I'm out here. Linda's so rigid about that kind of thing."

"Perfecto," said Bonnie. "Absolutely. I haven't had any in ages. My source moved away, and I must be chickenshit because I haven't even tried to find another one. This puritan age is undermining my character."

I hadn't seen her in two or three years, hadn't been to Chicago since she'd bought the fancy, messy two-bedroom condo where she now welcomed me. When she opened the door, instead of the familiar, naturally frizzy brown halo framing her elongated face I saw a helmet of red spikes. "You're all pointy!" I exclaimed. She had on black pointy-rimmed glasses, and those popular, ugly black high-topped shoes with pointed toes—and lipstick. "God," I added, "you make me feel old," though come to think of it, it was only at a distance that she would have looked twenty-five. Up close I could see that she was acquiring sags and creases at least as fast as I was.

"Oh, this," she said. "Don't worry, it's all surface. I found my first two grey *pubic* hairs last week. Now why should that bother me? The ones on my head didn't, before I dyed it—which, by the way, is just an experiment."

We did the coke that first night. She thought it was cut with speed. I wasn't enough of a connoisseur to know, and didn't care that much about the high anyway. Mostly I just wanted to feel that thrilling sense of grownup intimacy that belongs to long-term friendships, and which I associate especially with women like Bonnie with whom I first experienced it. Unfortunately, though, the minute we'd snorted the stuff she launched into a detailed description of her plans for a graduate seminar on Julia Kristeva. She was given to intellectual enthusiasms, and this was evidently a new one, so I listened with a politeness which the drug facilitated, not liking to admit that my mind glazes over every time I hear the word "deconstruct." ("It's just a tool," she insisted earnestly.

149

"Deconstruction is a tool that feminists can use, just like we use computers.")

After a while she remembered to ask how I was feeling about the whole tenure thing, now that it was over.

"Lousy," I admitted. Recently I'd been congratulating myself on my success in adopting a philosophical approach, but the helpless, degrading envy I was suddenly experiencing in her presence exposed that myth for what it was. Bonnie had tenure.

"At least you have a lover. You have a *family*."

The wistful note surprised me. How could I explain the facts of life to someone who spent her time hanging out with a pack of Marxist semiologists?

"Lovers come and go," I pointed out. "Tenure is permanent."

It came out sounding more serious than I'd intended. Bonnie raised her eyebrows above her black glasses rims. "You're unhappy with Linda."

"No. Not unhappy. Well, I mean there've been moments. . . it's just been a rotten time, that's all. I feel so displaced. If I had a job, it would be a lot easier to work the rest out."

"Sometimes you have to begin where you are," she said, but I didn't believe she knew anything about it.

The second night we cooked, drinking Scotch from a bottle I'd brought. I told all about my short affair with Treecie, in the clinical detail Bonnie encouraged when she'd had a few drinks. Later I got down to the war stories, like the one about the student who'd been cautioned against getting "too close" to me by her faculty adviser (who happened to be on my tenure committee), and the other one about how I never officially learned the committee's decision because somehow they forgot to send me the letter.

When I woke next morning I could recall sobbing over a half-eaten meal, but had absolutely no memory of how the conversation had ended or when I'd gone to sleep. When I finally got up I found Bonnie in the kitchen. She offered me coffee and asked how I felt.

"Shit, my eyeballs seem to be lined with ground glass."

"You were really going at it last night." She peered at me in a way I resented. "Poor kid, you've been through the wars, haven't you? Listen to me, Dale, you can't internalize this shit. You're a good teacher, a fine writer, and you've got it in you to make an important contribution to feminist scholarship. It would be simply obscene if you let this damage you." In her bathrobe and with her spikes still flattened by sleep, Bonnie looked severe and drawn—a mother or older sister. In the past I'd usually been the one to give the pep talks, and now I was irked and grateful at the same time.

That afternoon, still feeling shaky, I pulled myself together and began my library research. Over the next few days I located some useful material on one obscure Black Chicago woman writer I'd been interested in. But the real excitement came in what I found on Prosperine. First of all, there turned out to be not one but two *Little Review* stories, the second of which had appeared in 1920—which strongly supported, though of course it didn't prove, the notion that Prosperine had lived later than Grandma claimed. Then, though I couldn't find *Stand* (a conscientious librarian discovered that it was available on microfilm in a labor collection in southern California), I did get to see the *Solidarity* material. I found pieces on the recruitment of agricultural workers into the "One Big Union," the role of women in the Finnish Socialist movement, the situation on the Iron Range a year after the strike, the tarring and feathering of South Dakota farmers active in the cooperative moment known as the Nonpartisan League (or "Hun Partisan League," as patriotic wags would have it), and a tongue-in-cheek item called "How to Ride a Side-Door Pullman."

For the most part, these articles were competently written in the frequently bombastic style of the rest of the publication, which was enlivened with a great deal of corrosive satire at the expense of "plutocrats" and "scissorbills." The treatment of the Finnish women, however, was sober, sympathetic, and implicitly feminist, and would be a perfect complement to the *Stand* interview with Mrs. Masonovich which Prosperine had planned to write—if in fact such a piece existed. The "side-door Pullman" item was a delightful satire, in effect a woman's-eye-view debunking of the Wobblies' masculinist cult of hobo life. Its conceit was a deadpan gender neutrality, and it began with instructions on what to wear to hop a fast freight ("Trousers, as skirts and petticoats are apt to become entangled with hooks, couplings, and other obstacles"). It definitely belonged in *The Prosperine Reader*.

The two *Little Review* stories would go in, as well. The first, entitled "Water" and set on the Iron Range, was a three-page interior monologue

151

in which a striking miner's wife considered the problems she would face in attempting to get her day's supply of the precious resource from the company pump. The second, "Marjorie," was a much longer and more ambitious piece about a prostitute who'd worked in a meat-packing plant until she discovered she could "go with gentlemen" instead. Though less successful overall than "Water," I found it memorable for its evocation of the feverish atmosphere of a large Midwestern city during the First World War, as well as its approach to its heroine's profession, which it treated with exactly Marjorie's own blend of frankness and euphemism.

I was elated at these discoveries, and got into a hassle with Bonnie, who unexpectedly took the position that the last thing I needed at this point in my career was to take on editing the writing of some obscure lez rabble-rouser who'd died before completing any mature work. If I were going to get involved with anything that would drain energy from the all-important job search, it at least ought to look good on my C.V.

"Good to who?" I demanded, ungrammatical on purpose. "Fuck, man, I'm going to be forty any day. I'll be jumping through hoops for the rest of my life at this rate. I'm a dyke," I glared, "that's the fundamental problem. Whatever I do, it's never going to look good to *them*."

Bonnie, injured, pointed out that she was gay, too, and accused me of harboring a more radical than thou attitude; also of being defeatist. I made a rude remark about some people's preference for texts over real life, and in a matter of minutes we each felt completely misunderstood.

We patched things up before I left, of course, but as I headed back to the Cities I still felt bad about it. In the sweltering car between Black River Falls and Eau Claire, Wisconsin, I made the mistake of smoking part of a joint Bonnie had given me as a peace offering, and got paranoid on top of my depression. I was never going to find a decent job. No publisher would want the *Reader*. How were Linda and I going to work things out if I couldn't even spend a couple of days with an old friend without the whole thing blowing up in my face?

Hoping for some reassurance, I tried to call Linda at the beach the minute I reached the cabin. Receiving no answer, I dialed Ruta next, and she lifted my spirits somewhat by inviting me over to talk about my discoveries. She promised to try to locate several people—she thought she knew of three or four that were still alive—who were veterans of the IWW's Chicago operation. Maybe I'd even be lucky enough to find someone who would remember Prosperine.

Wanting to get some notion of how the land lay before speaking to Grandma, I called Aunt Geri next. I learned that Allison was better, though she might be hospitalized for another few weeks. She reported that Grandma was thrilled by how well the bookstore reading had gone, one sign of which was the fact that she grumbled about the attention she was receiving because of it. Though only six or eight Hill residents had actually been present, apparently the word had gotten out, and now people who in the past had never even bothered to say hello in the halls were practically mobbing her in the dining room, requesting autographed copies of *Woman's Estate*.

"We want to thank you so much," Geri added, evidently feeling she spoke for the family at large. "This means so much to Grandma, we think it's just tremendous. And the way you've been working with her on that book of hers—"

Seeing how my stock had risen, I took the chance to do a little lobbying. As best I could, I explained the importance of the writing of Prosperine's that I'd found in Chicago, and my hopes for getting access to the papers in Grandma's possession. My aunt casually promised to do anything she could to help.

After hanging up, I got to wondering, as I had from time to time since conceiving of the *Reader*, just exactly how I'd handle the romance. I couldn't really imagine censoring anything, not even if censorship turned out to be Grandma's precondition for allowing the papers to be published. It would be like cooperating in my own oppression. If that was where I was going to end up anyway, I might as well have kissed the right asses and gotten tenure.

On the other hand, while Grandma was alive, even supposing she agreed to publication, how could I possibly write freely about her and Prosperine, as I'd imagined doing in my introduction?

*While she was alive*, it kept coming down to that. There didn't seem to be any way around the unattractive fact that whatever I did, whether it was to pursue the book project vigorously or to lie low and wait for a more auspicious time, would be done with the thought in mind that she was nearly ninety-one.

Yet it wasn't as though my stake were purely personal or selfish. Since reading the letters in Geri's attic I'd begun to feel more strongly what I'd sensed with my first look at that extraordinary snapshot Grandma had shown me in the winter: Prosperine had had "something to say," as those who don't so frequently like to put it. Against all the odds, because I'd happened to come along, her message-in-a-bottle might have a chance to circulate. Didn't I have a responsibility which extended beyond Grandma, to a future of female readers? I also felt a strong if less rationally defensible obligation to the past, to the fiercely hungry baby dyke my heroine had been. She was more my foremother, in a certain sense, than any relative I could trace, and if the record she'd left were to vanish just now, after having come down to me against all the odds, what hope was there for all the rest of us? Wasn't my discovery potentially too significant simply to allow the material to languish indefinitely in cartons, subject to any sort of mishap, while it became less likely every day that I'd be able to get in touch with those few surviving souls who still remembered the author? I decided I'd simply have to go ahead as I'd planned, approach the dragon's lair respectfully, and request to view the treasure.

After all these stark reflections, it came as a relief to hear how like her normal self the dragon sounded on the phone. She complained vigorously of the exhaustion she'd experienced following her performance at Giants in the Earth. It had "laid her out" for several days, she said, but she was feeling okay now, and I should come over after lunch. That way I could bring a stack of her magazines, which she could autograph before dinnertime in order to be able to hand them out in the dining room. She wanted to ask me, too, what I thought she ought to do in those cases where people asked her to write something in their copies, yet she didn't know them well enough to be able to think of anything much to say. Did I know how big-name authors handled this problem?

I'd actually planned on having a quiet afternoon and visiting her within the next few days. However, I promised to come at two o'clock and bring magazines.

When I approached her door, I saw it was ajar, and was surprised to hear a man's voice coming from inside. I knocked. Grandma called, "Come in."

Much to my amazement, Arnie Luckenbill was installed in her recliner. He had it tipped back comfortably, too. Grandma had the rocker, and Phoebe Childs a straight chair. The middle of the room was filled up with feet.

Phoebe made the required introductions; as much as I'd heard about Arnie, I'd never actually met him. She seemed her usual cheerful self, but Grandma looked perturbed. I deposited my armful of *Woman's Estates* and sat on the edge of the bed.

Arnie was wearing a raspberry-colored bow tie. "So you're the gal," he said, conversationally.

I didn't think an answer was required.

"We were talking about you just a few minutes ago," Phoebe explained. "Mr. Luckenbill wanted to purchase a copy of Rose's writing, and now you've come, he can take it away with him."

If this was a hint, Arnie ignored it. "I'm a great admirer of your grandmother's," he assured me. "She has a way with words. Fine lady, too. Yep, a fine lady."

"You were telling us something," Grandma drily observed.

"That's right, I was just in the middle of explaining a job I had once, working as an efficiency expert for a manufacturing outfit. They made ball bearings. I had to go around to all the different plants, and figure out how long the different operations took versus what they ought to take. Eighty percent of it was pure psychology. You'd go into a new place, you'd have to butter up the foreman, because the foreman, see, right off the bat he's your worst enemy, and he's got to be your friend if the thing's gonna fly. I mean you walk through that front door, before you shake his hand he's thinking, who's this bird in a blue serge suit with a stopwatch in his pocket, spying for the higher-ups, thinks I can't run my own shop? It'd always be some big old ugly buzzard too, you'd think they picked 'em for looks as well as disposition.

"But *I* was going to love 'em. Be on *their* side. I used to use some old tricks from a Dale Carnegie course I took. One of the best was to tell the guy I needed *his* help to figure out what to do—sound him out, you know, get his ideas for improvements—though half the time he wouldn't come up with anything I couldn't have figured out myself after about half an hour in the plant. And right away, see, he's interested, because probably I was the first one to come in from outside that ever bothered to ask his advice.

"So I'd keep that up for two or three days and I'd be in his drawers. I could do whatever I wanted with him then. I used to have a boss who'd laugh about it. He'd call me up: 'Hey, Lucky, you in his drawers yet?' "

155

Phoebe nodded politely. I glanced at Grandma, who looked as though she had a stomach ache. Shit, I thought, he's wrecked it, I can't talk to her now. But I couldn't help enjoying the scene.

"I've worked a lot of funny places in my life. Learned something every time. Worked as a USDA chicken grader, after I retired from Fuller Brush. You ought to've seen the chickens they'd try to sneak past us—cancer, lung diseases, the whole shebang. Never eat a chicken gizzard, that's my best advice."

"My word," Phoebe shuddered, "don't tell us about *that*—they've got chicken on tonight's menu, too!"

Arnie stayed for perhaps another ten minutes, then left with his autographed *Woman's Estate* rolled under his arm. (Grandma, I noticed, was catching on fast; she'd only signed her name beside the date.)

"I'm surprised to find *him* here," I commented, meaning here in Grandma's room, but thinking that his presence anywhere at the Hill was a matter to marvel over. "A real live wire, isn't he?"

Grandma didn't answer. She had risen from her rocker, bent over, and was grimly tugging at the lever on the side of the recliner, trying to return it to its customary upright position.

"You mean she hasn't heard?" demanded Phoebe. "You didn't tell her, Rose?"

Grandma said crossly, "We only just found out."

It seemed that a resident named Lucy Zema—a shy, retiring woman, the last person you'd spot as being a troublemaker—had been exposed as the individual who took things from people's rooms. Rumors were flying about how Dr. Jerebold's office was going to handle the situation. Occasionally, in the past, incorrigible cases had been sent away; but so far Lucy had merely been warned. Luckenbill, evidently, was innocent as milk.

Grandma felt that didn't mean they had to have him in their *rooms*.

"You were the one who invited him in."

"What could I have done? *You* brought him here."

"I only felt sorry for him, because we'd judged him so."

Grandma was silent for an ominous interval. She busied herself in the bathroom, gathering up some hand washing she'd had drying there. When she came back with her left arm draped with withered panty hose, her only remark was, "I just don't like to see some people. . .taken in."

I thought Phoebe reddened beneath her light coat of rouge. "Which road did you take driving down to Chicago, Dale?"

After we'd discussed the interstate highway system for a few minutes, she said she'd let us visit, and went off to the crafts room. Grandma seemed to forget her resentment by degrees, as we talked about the response to the *Woman's Estate* piece which her readings had generated. After we'd taken a short stroll down to the end of the hall to watch the gardener working on the chrysanthemum beds, I decided to make my move.

Over tea and Lorna Doones I spread out photocopies of the *Little Review* stories and *Solidarity* articles. "These are for you," I told her.

"To keep?"

"I have others."

Grandma looked wonderingly at each piece, and stroked the pages as though they were in Braille, but didn't take up her magnifying glass, though she read out two or three of the titles. What actually seemed to interest her most was the signature on one of the stories, "P.F. Munkers" instead of "Prosperine." Proppie's middle name was Frances, she said, and she'd tried to sign some compositions with her initials that way, but the teacher made her stop. She thought initials looked more serious, and she swore that when she grew up and wrote books, this was how she would sign them.

"She talked of writing books?"

"Oh, yes! She might have, too, if she hadn't died so young."

Slowly, but in as casual a tone as I could manage, I began to talk about the significance of these pieces. I spoke of the recent move to create a history, not simply of the rich and privileged, but of everyday people. I explained that Prosperine's work fit in perfectly with that. "She *did* write a book," I insisted. "It was a book that could mean something to a lot of Americans."

With a touching air of possessing experience in the field, Grandma intimated that the articles and stories she held in her hand would add up to an awfully slender volume.

"There may be a good deal more published stuff. Remember, I've only begun to research this. There's what appeared in *Stand*, if I can get the microfilm, and there are all sorts of other small magazines and newspapers she could have contributed to. But it's not only that. Grandma,

I have to see her papers. Journals, letters—everything she left. May I? It's important."

"Well I don't see why not," she cut me off, with a joyless alacrity I didn't care for much. "Not that the bulk of it would be what you're after, I guess, just a schoolgirl type of thing. Personal."

"Personal papers can also say a lot—to historians."

Grandma sighed and blinked. I felt my fate was being decided. "Well, I need to sort through all those boxes anyway, only it's tedious work and I tire out so easily. When would you need it by?"

As soon as possible, I told her, and naturally I'd be ready to look at things in stages. I could help her go through cartons, or even do it myself if that would make it easier on her. Perhaps we could agree on an afternoon at the beginning of next week to make a start? We might combine the sorting with work on her own book.

She was a slippery customer, but I pinned her down to Tuesday. Then we sat and talked of other things, such as the fact that my mother would be in Beijing now, and why it wasn't "Peking" any longer (she seemed to fault the Chinese for their confusing new spellings), and how incredible it seemed that children of hers should be quite matter-of-factly shuttling back and forth across the International Dateline. And to think that even when she was growing up, people preparing to travel distances of only several hundred miles would bid goodbye to one another as though separating for life. Her own mother had wept inconsolably when she'd had to leave her childhood home in Iowa to come to Minnesota. Bert, on the other hand, when returning from a conference in Stockholm last month, had hopped over the pole and dipped down in Anchorage for just long enough to meet his sister June for lunch. Then he'd continued on to Seattle and eaten dinner with my parents. Aunt Geri had flown out there to meet him, they'd spent a long weekend, and she and my mother had gone to Nordstrom's and gotten some fantastic bargains on shoes. Look at me, for that matter, moving all the way Back East—where did I suppose *my* children were likely to end up?

Caught off guard, I answered sharply. "Grandma, I don't expect to have any."

"Oh, that's right," she answered comfortably, unembarrassed at her lapse. "Of course you haven't married."

"It's nothing to do with marriage. I don't want to be a mother. I've got plenty of other things I want to do in my life."

"Proppie was like that. Said she didn't care for children. She was always so different from other girls...mind, Dale, you don't do anything you'll regret."

I was struck by the somber note of admonition, which perhaps was prompted by the thought of her friend's fate, though at the time I only heard a conventional exhortation to be fruitful and multiply. "Even in China," I snapped, "they're only having *one*."

"My, that isn't very many, is it?"

"Well, I suppose it's plenty when they're down with chicken pox, or you have to go out and can't find a sitter."

"Your roommate has a daughter, doesn't she?"

In the worst way, I wanted to tell the truth. "She's not my roommate, Grandma," was the abyss that tempted me. "Linda is the woman I share my life with." I wanted to let her see, and comprehend for the first time, the practiced gesture with which I withdrew my wallet from my back pocket; I wanted to display the snapshots I kept there, evidence of my family of women. And I wanted to explain the reasons why Prosperine and I had always been different from "other girls": that early on, before we could remember, even possibly in the womb, we'd taken one look at our assigned places in life and turned up our noses, decided not to settle; that, though each of us would instinctively have recoiled from any supernatural dispensation which might have offered us the opportunity to switch bodies—let alone destinies—with our clumsy, complacent brothers, still in secret and without directly admitting it even to ourselves, we had somehow determined to become the boy heroes of our own imaginations. Years later, far advanced in hubris, we would stretch out blunt-nailed hands to appropriate that ultimate reward and consolation prize for earthly suffering which the gods have set aside for their spoiled sons: the soft, delicious, yielding love of women.

And still we were women too, and bled every month, and attached ourselves by invisible tendrils and tentacles of feeling to everything around us, everything that moved.

But the papers were at stake, and anything I might have said would have come too close to the danger zone at the heart of Prosperine's and Grandma's friendship. I lied mechanically, "Right, my roommate has a daughter."

159

Shortly afterwards I got up to leave, as I did so reminding her we had a date for Tuesday. She sat gazing out the window at a bright pinwheel flower bed, nervously twisting her crocheting in her lap.

"It seems strange," she murmured, "to a person my age."

I waited. Best confront resistance head on.

"Like a heap of fall leaves to be shuffled through, out in the public street."

"What's like that, Grandma?"

She still looked away. "Oh, nothing, just the notion of going through a person's private papers, as though they were common property. But I suppose that's how they do it nowadays."

She was like a child, I thought, that had to have a splinter out. You pity the kid, but you sterilize the needle.

I said that in a way they *were* common property. "When you think about it, it's probably only an unfortunate accident that Prosperine isn't known as a writer already. We should think of her work as we would the contribution of any important reporter or novelist, something to be enjoyed by everyone."

Grandma turned to me. A helpless, almost beseeching look I'd never seen on her before came into her face, a look so unmistakably though fleetingly expressive of a sense of her own impotence that I wanted to turn away. "Dale," she appealed, "those papers, are you going to *publish* them?"

"Let's cross that bridge when we come to it," I said.

I spent a quiet weekend at the cabin. On Saturday I slept in. When I got up I did a series of yoga exercises which I'd performed faithfully each morning when I first arrived, but had neglected recently. After breakfast I wrote some letters, then changed into my bathing suit and went down to the river. I plunged in immediately, but instead of heading out toward the middle and then swimming against the current, which I often liked to do for the enjoyment of feeling my muscles at work, I drifted down alongside the thicketed bank for a few hundred yards. Here I found a backwater where with very little effort I could remain floating in one spot. Lying on my back in the tepid water, I felt as though I were lying in the center of the earth, while above me in a sky blue-grey with humidity the towering cloud formations mirrored my suspension.

Gradually my thoughts drifted to Sharon Decoteaux and what she'd had to say outside the bookstore on the night of Grandma's reading. It was the first time I'd let myself dwell on the episode since it happened.

I thought of what she'd said about the past, the rising that was put down near New Ulm, and which I now remembered Prosperine had mentioned in a letter. I saw the bloated corpses of Indians and whites nestled together in the prairie hollows, a native woman with her belly ripped, a fair-haired toddler wandering lost all afternoon to lie down in the roadless grasses. I easily pictured the Mankato carpenters whistling as they hammered in the snow to build the gallows where the mass execution of the rebels was held on the day after Christmas, 1862; but I was less sure about the mood of the crowd of settlers who'd gathered to see their notion of justice carried out. Were they sobered by their memories of terror, or flushed and jeering, giddy with victory?

What I could not gauge at all, it seemed to me, was the creeping misery the Indians had faced: watching their horizons squeezed tighter every year, going down to another winter of rancid meat and treaties. How could I understand? I belonged to the winning side. While children of both races who'd survived the conflict must have grown up with the indelible, wordless conviction of possible harm engraved behind their eyes, it was the Sioux who'd been sent to exile in Nebraska. My own hard-working, hopeful forebears, well-satisfied with the course of history, had continued to fan out across the continent, eating out its substance.

All this I seemed to review in detail, yet from some unlikely height, as though from the vantage point of one of those scary satellites capable of photographing a crowbar on the ground on the Kamchatka Peninsula. I floated, and my judgement floated with me (this is not about *you*, Sharon Decoteaux had said). Closing my eyes, I could feel the land mass breathe, its bloody past and terrifying future expressed in the deliberate exhalation of an August afternoon. I could sense the swift trajectory of seasons, counterpoint to history, here in high summer already working down toward February ice-lock—and the half-exhausted, still enormous power of the earth behind my back.

The next morning I got up early, took binoculars and a lunch, and went for a long, marshy, reedy, birdy hike at a state park my neighbors had recommended. On the way back I stopped to buy a bird and plant handbook. For some reason it suddenly seemed important to me to be able to identify the living things around me, and it bothered me most of all not to know the names of trees. When I got home I called Linda at the beach, only the second time we'd spoken since she'd gone on vacation. The first time, things had been fine, but now she sounded out of sorts. Fiona wanted to go to her father's for the last two weeks in August. Authors were bugging her. She had someone visiting right now, in fact, a talented young novelist who'd driven down from the city to discuss a contract and would be staying overnight, so we should probably make this short. We could talk in a day or two.

"Hey, don't put me off. We've hardly talked in two weeks," I complained. "Things were going to be better when you went away, remember?"

In the end we spent an expensive hour or so trying to bicker our way back into one another's good graces, but it never really worked. We seemed out of synch. I was particularly irritated by her reaction to my efforts to get Grandma to show me the Prosperine papers. "Remember," she advised, in what sounded to me like a moralistic tone, "*she* has to be getting something out of this, too."

I pointed out that for one thing, she was receiving plenty of recognition for her own writing, and that for another, Prosperine herself surely wouldn't have wanted to see her life's work held hostage to her friend's bourgeois propriety.

"Oh, don't bother rationalizing. You're in love, why not admit it!" Linda added that she'd only meant that perhaps there was some way in which dealing with the papers could help their custodian come to some sort of resolution about events in her own past. She suggested that I mention to Grandma the possibility of donating the material to a women's or labor history archive. That way it would be protected, but she might be able to retain some control, and not feel it was out "in the public street."

The idea had its merits, but I wasn't in any mood to appreciate them. I felt criticized by Linda, in a way I didn't like. Maybe it was just that there'd been too many edgy conversations recently, but for the first time I was feeling really queasy about the strain our long separation might be putting on the relationship. After I hung up, I tried to reassure myself. I'd be home in a few weeks; we could work it out then.

Later, when the moon came bounding up over the riverbank, a day or two off the full and orange as anything, I restored my equilibrium by taking a flashlightless walk up the gently slanting path that originated in the fringe of trees behind the cabin. Sitting on a stone at the top of a little pasture and gazing out over countryside that looked like the hidden truth of the landscape I knew by day (moonlight could do this anywhere, I thought, even in Manhattan, if it weren't for Con Ed), I realized it was high time to face the issue of what my life was going to look like in the fall.

To my surprise, I didn't feel so bad about the prospects anymore. I'd give myself a year for non-achievement, I decided—let my career lie fallow (sorry about that, Bonnie). Take any kind of adjunct job, or even editing, to bring in enough money; finish up the Black and white writers paper; get as far ahead as I could with Prosperine; use the time to think very deliberately about my next moves. Supposing things went well with Grandma and I got to see the papers, I'd probably need to come back to Minnesota soon anyway, so it would be just as well if I had the flexibility of minimal job commitments.

I also liked the idea of getting politically active again, though I wasn't sure what issue I'd pick. Come to think of it, I wasn't even really sure what organizations were out there anymore. Then of course I ought to start exercising regularly; it was probably the only way I'd ever lose weight. That and drinking less—I was ready to tackle that. . . .What else? Spend more time working in the garden. Plant narcissus and tulips in the backyard border, where they'd look smashing from the dining room, come April. Try one last time to get into Gertrude Stein. Make love with Linda more. . . .It was odd, but even though I still thought of Treecie every so often, my restlessness of a few months ago had largely evaporated. Maybe all I'd needed had been that one brief adventure. Now I just wanted to be in the sack with my familiar old sweetheart, going through the familiar motions, the infinite subtle or bold variations on the classic theme. She could come till we both lost track, I remembered longingly, when her body was in the mood.

The next day I got a letter from Fiona. It was written on a pictorial greeting card with a glossy photograph of a rock formation awash in a sea of desert flowers. "Dear Dale," it began, "I don't know why, but when I saw this exquisite picture I thought of you for some reason." She alluded breezily to her coming visit to her father, during the second week of which they'd be going to the Vineyard, "and my tan will limp along till then, I guess." She *definitely* had to start prepping for the SAT's *the minute* she got home; otherwise she'd miss her chance of getting into the Ivies, and for the career she had in mind a good degree was a must. Last year some of the junior girls had been so nervous they hadn't eaten for weeks, and Akua Shapiro had lost twelve pounds by the day of the test and her clothes just hung on her. For her Sweet Sixteen she wanted to rent a movie that would make the kids think, maybe "The Killing Fields" or something. "Hurry up and come home," the letter closed, "so we can have a reunion of our *intergalactic* family. Luv ya."

"I wonder what Fiona wants now," I said to myself, unable, however, to be entirely cynical about the fact that she'd used the word *family*. Was I foolish to think that she might be mellowing? I indulged in a detailed fantasy of the scene two years hence when Linda and I would deliver her up to a dorm at one of "the Ivies" and she'd introduce me to her new roommates: "This is Mom's and my friend Dale, who's sort of like my second Mom."

I spent a good part of the afternoon shopping for groceries and tidying the cabin. Ruta was coming to dinner. Not that she of all people would expect immaculate surroundings, but it really was time to do something about the mess that I'd allowed to congeal around me. I was in the middle of making pesto sauce—no mean trick without a blender—when I got a call saying her car wouldn't start. I had to drop everything and go pick her up. When I arrived at her trailer she was on the telephone. She was wearing a long skirt and tennis shoes, with an object woven of red and yellow yarn which resembled somebody's daycamp crafts project strung around her neck, but she still looked something like a stevedore as she stood there gesturing indignantly, one foot on a stack of bundled papers. "Em Wok's written *what* in *In These Times*?" I heard her yell.

"Something wrong?" I asked, as she hung up.

She kissed me on the lips before she spoke. "Labor Day rally. The usual. Em Wok's got this feud going with the Latin America-Minnesota People's project, LAMPP—I don't know, something to do with their position on the Peruvian Whosiwhatsis. The one that always makes me think of that scary movie with Jack Nicholson. Glowing? Gleaming? Glittering?"

" 'The Shining'?" I suggested.

"Right, *Shining* Path, that's the one. Sendero Luminoso."

"Wait a minute. I'm confused. Who's Em Wok?' From the name I pictured a female representative of some local Asian-American group.

"MWOC, Minnesota Workplace Organizing Committee. They're Maoists, I think, or maybe Trots. The problem has to do with the FMLN-FDR's opposition to Shining Path, which MWOC supports. The Salvadorans in LAMPP don't want to participate if MWOC is involved, or is even an endorser. It would be fine if MWOC simply dropped out, but they're not about to do that, and some of the peace groups don't want to exclude anybody. On the other hand, without LAMPP the whole thing may fall apart."

"I see," I said, thoroughly confused.

"Now they want me to play the peacemaker. I was supposed to speak at the rally; I get called for all these things. They want a Prehistoric Radical Who Hasn't Given Up—I always think that's why they ask me. There'll be a slough of others, obviously. Native American. Union. Anti-Nuke.

165

This guy from P-9 that got himself busted under Minnesota's dear old criminal syndicalism law. You know about that, of course."

I said I didn't, but thought we'd better get going, considering the state my dinner preparations were in. Ruta had to feed the dogs before we left. I helped her, but it took a long time. After the torrent of verbal energy, the effort simple movements cost her always came as a surprise.

On the drive to the cabin she lectured me nonstop on the history of organized labor in the state of Minnesota. She explained that the criminal syndicalism law had been enacted in 1917 with the express purpose of smashing the Wobblies. It forbade advocacy of so-called "violent" disruptions of industrial production, and had only recently been struck down. One of the leaders of the Hormel strike in Austin had encouraged fellow picketers to resist moving along when told to by police, had been arrested and charged under the statute, and had eventually gotten it declared unconstitutional.

"Why, your Prosperine herself may have been charged under that law! You don't really know what finally happened to her."

"Not for sure, just that she died young."

"She may have died in prison. The jails were chockablock with radicals, you know, those years of the war and after."

When we arrived, I parked her under a pine tree, handed her a glass of wine and the Prosperine photocopies, and went inside to finish making dinner. I felt as though I'd just entrusted some treasured family heirloom to a jeweler for appraisal. Something she found in the first article, however, suggested a thought about the way in which an application of Leninist principles—modified, of course, and applied flexibly—might have strengthened the IWW, which had been hampered by its anarchistic leanings. This in turn brought to mind the opposite abuse encountered in the CPUSA, where democratic centralism had failed miserably, and she hollered through the open window so many observations on these and other points that I was surprised she had time to read anything.

"That story, the long one about the prostitute, isn't that remarkable! Don't you get the feeling Prosperine was really more or less in love with this Marjorie character?" she suggested at dinner.

Her eyes sparkled. I saw what she meant, though it wasn't an angle that had occurred to me before. "She was certainly in love with my grandmother," I confided, and told her about the letters, being vague about where I'd seen them.

"Why, Dale, what a fantastic discovery! You *must* pursue this. It's simply extraordinary!"

The praise delighted me. I felt my face glow with pleasure, like a kid who's gotten A+ on a book report. I told her about my worries as to whether Grandma would cooperate with having a book published. "It isn't even just the sexual thing," I said, "though that's bad enough. Grandma disagrees with how Prosperine led her life. And I think she wants to promote *her* version of the past."

"You're referring to a certain—shall we say petty bourgeois element in your grandmother's thinking?" Ruta paraphrased. "Tread softly, Dale. I suspect she'll come around. You know, the desire to have the truth come out, to leave a valid record—that's extremely compelling as a person ages. It's the last of the *individual* manifestations of the Life Force to be extinguished, very frequently. Don't forget, the word 'testament' is close to 'testimony.' "

Later, after we'd smoked a small joint—I drank another glass of wine, to forestall paranoia—Ruta declared that on the basis of what I'd told her, this Rose Bright Schlaghoffer sounded like someone she'd very much like to meet. "Why don't you bring her to my reading next week? I might even get a chance to chat a bit about Prosperine with her."

"I don't know, do you promise not to use any four-letter words?" I laughed as I said that, but privately I was thinking that the fragile boat of my negotiations might be rocked by the encounter. However, after Ruta good-humoredly criticized what she called my ageism in assuming it was too late for Grandma to shed her puritan attitudes, I jotted down the time and place of the reading, and promised to mention it.

We sat under the trees a long time, slapping bugs and sipping coffee. As stars took up their positions for the night, she began to talk about her childhood, that part of it which had coincided with the first years of the European war, which Woodrow Wilson, the "damned schoolteacher," had promised to keep us out of.

Small bats blacker than the sky above the cabin swooped and dipped in the warm air as she spoke of a strangely split yet not unhappy youth. An only child, she'd lost her mother to tuberculosis in Watertown, South Dakota the same week the Maginot line was breached, and after that had been sent to New York to go to school, where she lived with the dead woman's relatives. These were, I was amazed to learn, German Jews. There had been an aunt whom she adored, unmarried and beautiful, rather under the family thumb, who worked at a settlement house while continuing to live in her father's Upper West Side brownstone with its Irish cook and maid. This interesting aunt occasionally treated her to social gatherings in smoky Greenwich Village basements, and once an affably drunk young man who seemed mature to the stocky child had spun her to ragtime from a scratchy phonograph. His name was Jack Reed, which meant something to her later.

As soon as the spring term was over, she was shipped west ("In a sealed train, like Lenin," she joked), and for several summers rode all over the Dakotas in a Model T Ford with her father Sam, who at the time was organizing for the Nonpartisan League. They would crawl forever, it seemed to Ruta, over scorching country filled with grain a darker color than her braids, farms where fifty years before had been only virgin prairie, and which fifty years hence would be tunnelled for missile silos. Just when it seemed she couldn't endure either the thirst or the monotony another minute (though Sam would get to telling jokes, and then it wasn't so bad), a small shiny speck would bloom on the horizon, at first with maddening slowness, then more and more quickly, until finally it assumed the familiar shape of a grain elevator.

And there in its shadow would be the railroad tracks, the scant handful of buildings people called a town, and the gathering of self-conscious, hopeful farmers, there to hear Henry Karlessen tell, in his powerful, blunt English which kept the faint traces of a Norwegian accent, how in order to save their farms they must get together and own the grain elevators. At night he and Ruta would sleep in the house of the least self-conscious, most hopeful of the men, and if there weren't enough beds sometimes his wife would take Ruta in with her, while her husband and Sam made do with straw ticking. The next day, Ruta would often be left there while her father drove around to call on neighboring farmers, and she'd share the summer improvisations of any children that were present, hunting eggs where the banty hens had hidden them in the grass, climbing a high windmill on a dare from a smirking boy. Though she'd thrived on the heady density of New York, with its multi-ethnic murmur of brutality and courage, its savor of ideas blown all the way from Europe, she'd wanted to be a farmer.

"Jesus," she breathed, "I was in love with the country, then," and I understood she'd made no distinction between the nation and the earth. But I think it was the note of surprise in her low voice, as though she were reviewing a sensation that had been over with so irrevocably so very long ago, that made me brush my eyes surreptitiously in the dark.

"What happened to change things?"

"History," she snapped.

"The war, you mean?

"The war, for one thing. You must have read about it, you're American Studies, aren't you? Things got pretty rough in '17. After Father was made to kneel and kiss the flag at pistol-point in Fargo, I had to spend my summers in the city."

I have a snapshot from Ruta's reading, taken by Phoebe with her Polaroid camera. " 'The Authors,' Rose w/ Ruta Karlessen," is pencilled proudly on the back in the elliptical fashion with which family photographs are often annotated, as though specifics of time and place and relationship could be counted on to last in memory forever.

The distorted colors of the cheap print portray two very old women who stand so close together that their shoulders almost touch, but whose postures and expressions diverge so utterly that it's as though they'd been photographed separately and their images joined by some purely technical trick. Grandma, wearing a blouse in a sedate floral pattern and a tan cotton wraparound skirt, holds fast to her purse and desperately attempts to mollify the ruthless Instamatic with the embalmed half-smile traditionally assumed by the women of our family for picture-taking ceremonies. Her face is wan with forethought. One senses that she cares, cares terribly, what posterity will make of this view of her, and that at the last minute, after all her efforts to arrive at a suitable disposition of her features, she despairs of the verdict and hopelessly holds her breath, awaiting the fatal click with what dignity she can muster.

Ruta, who looks enormous by contrast, sports a bright blue, tie-dyed, dashiki-like tunic; she wears pants underneath, and on her neck and wrists a great deal of bulky jewelry made of natural objects from the earth and ocean. The direction in which she leans appears to suggest that she may have wished to pose with her left arm around her companion's shoulder, and been repelled by an invisible shield of silent disapproval.

Beside poor, frozen Grandma, Ruta naturally appears extraordinarily vivacious, fluid, "in process"—scarcely fixed in place by the clumsy chemicals. No camera will impede her jack-o'-lantern grin. The Life Force throbs in each cell of her burly body. Together, the pair might be fugitives from some corny allegory: Frugality and Bounty, let's say. And who wouldn't prefer the latter, hands down? And yet, on second thought, it seems to me that Bounty's splendid relaxation bespeaks a hidden arrogance. Is she really so indifferent to her reception by the world, or merely less insecure about winning its ultimate approval? (If not now, then later, after the Revolution.) No point whatever in inquiring what early circumstances formed each twig in the direction the tree eventually grew, or whether, indeed, the bent may be innate, not cultivated. Bounty accepts the universe, and I'm happy for her. Yet in Frugality, grim and gaunt and stripped and striving, I detect a hardy, unsung heroism that compels my ambivalent admiration.

"Weren't those *men's* shoes she had on?" was the single disapproving sentence uttered afterwards, in the car.

"I didn't notice, Grandma," I fibbed.

"Was that story she read good, Dale?" Phoebe clamored from the back. "I don't know anything about it, but it seemed to me she wrote about such ugly things."

"She was writing about the Depression," I defended. "How about the poems? What did you think of them?"

"They were sort of hard to follow. But she didn't write those herself, did she?"

"No, those were by a Guatemalan woman."

"How come she had that fellow playing that peculiar instrument, do you suppose? It distracted me so it was hard to understand the words. He did have the oddest hair I've ever seen."

"A regular mare's nest," Grandma grumbled.

Ruta's accompanist had been a young friend of hers from Madison, who'd had waist-length dreads and played a wooden flute.

"And then that part where *she* bobbed up and down and flapped her arms about. . . ." Phoebe seemed to be at a total loss, though I sensed that she would have liked to keep the conversation going as a means of distracting Grandma from her pique.

Grandma's displeasure had several sources, Ruta's eccentric

170

performance perhaps the least of them. I have a second snapshot from the same event, this one of all three women in an ill-assorted row, Ruta and Grandma more less in their earlier attitude, but separated by Phoebe, who's unfortunately caught with her eyes closed. To the far right, just at the margin, a large pink hand beats a hasty retreat. It's so blurred by motion that it's scarcely recognizable, but since I myself took the picture I'm aware that it belongs to none other than Arnie Luckenbill, who during the conversation just described was in the back seat with Phoebe.

"Well, she's a spunky one, that Mrs. Karlessen," he allowed uncertainly. Possibly Grandma's frosty manner had shaken even his self-confidence. I was completely in the dark about what he was doing there with us. All I knew was that when I'd first mentioned the reading and Ruta's invitation, Grandma had been unenthusiastic, but Phoebe had talked her into it. Then, when I'd arrived to pick them up, he'd been there in the lobby beneath a fiddle-leaf fig, his hat on his knees, and Grandma looking daggers.

The event had taken place in the afternoon. It was close to dinnertime when we got back. Arnie and Phoebe went off in separate directions, while I walked Grandma back to Brotherhood Boulevard.

"I guess I'll just lie down," she announced. "I don't feel like any supper."

"Are you sure you shouldn't eat a little something?"

"I have a roll I saved from lunch, if I feel up to eating it." She took off her shoes, lay down on the bed, and arranged the afghan to cover her knees. I didn't think I should let it go at that.

"By the way, how was it that Arnie happened to come along?"

"Don't ask me. It is all Phoebe's doing. She claims to feel sorry for him. Thinks he doesn't get out enough. Would you please hand that Kleenex box over here where I can reach it? But whose fault is that, I'd like to know? He could visit his children, if he got on with 'em."

"What do you think is really going on?"

Grandma, who'd never been in therapy, seemed unequal to the question at first. Her eyes popped open, but she still lay rigid on her back, her arms pinned at her sides beneath the afghan's colorful zigzags, and I wondered if she really could fall asleep like that. "I can see the handwriting on the wall," she announced at last.

"What do you mean?"

"He's sat at our table twice this week already. I've seen him *pawing* her the way he does."

"But you told me yourself he does that. He tried it with you."

"So he did. But Phoebe is naive. She has never really had the opportunity of much experience, you know."

My amusement at her assumption that she herself had enjoyed much more was halted by the distress of her next speech. "What life does a woman like that ever have, anyway? Cooped up with shut-ins. She never had a moment to herself. Her husband used to be the sweetest man, but the sicker he got, he took it out on her. He'd shout and abuse her terribly at times, just terribly, when he became resentful over not being able to get around and do things. I can't see how she stood for it.

"Now I look at her, letting a charlatan like that Luckenbill feed her a line, and I think, Phoebe Childs! You simpleton! There's no fool like an old fool, that's certain!"

Painfully, Grandma struggled to sit on the side of the bed, and glared at me as though I would keep her down. The sudden, self-wounding bitterness of her judgment was carnage I wanted to put a stop to.

"Maybe," I offered, "if she does get...friendlier with him, you could sort of get used to it?"

"Never!" As though physically ill, she hunched over, supporting herself on the heels of her hands, but her voice rang dauntless, harsh. "Phoebe could do it, I suppose, in my shoes. Phoebe is easygoing. My sister Flora used to be like that. Oh, they took advantage of her, too. And not only the men. It is not in *my* nature to tolerate a person I can see through like a glass of tap water! If anything was to happen between Phoebe and that man, why she might as well be over in the Wing, so far as I'm concerned." The Wing was intensive care, where the terminal cases went.

"You may make other friends, too."

Grandma shook her head. I'd compounded my offense. "Phoebe is the one true friend I have got in this place," she maintained stubbornly, and the bleak way she said it made me see that she hid how often the Hill must seem like jail.

She continued more quietly, still in a dry rage, "All the friends Eugene and I knew together are gone, all, all! People we used to share a cottage up on the North Shore with, and all the lovely couples we knew in our church. Louise Kleibermann, that they have had up on the fourth floor of Holy Cross Lutheran for over a year, has deteriorated so she doesn't know her own daughter.

"Parkinson's, diabetes, heart failure. Cancer, here, there, everywhere. 'We think we got it all,' " she mimicked savagely. "Then they keep cutting. There's no end, no end.

"I'm the last of all of them. I've been to all their funerals. I finally stopped saving the obituaries. I wonder sometimes, doesn't God see?"

It was alarmingly bad, I knew, if she invoked the deity, let alone in that tone. I played my part, speaking gently to her, as I thought she expected and as I imagined either of my aunts or Mother would have done in my place: of her long useful life, her admiring descendants, the husband who'd loved her, the active life she still led.

"Active!" she exploded. "How they all love that word! Why a hamster is *active*, that spins a treadmill in a cage! They none of them stop to think what I am active *for*!"

Listening to her, I felt a selfish vertigo, the strangest sinking sensation, to see her turn so hungrily to the past. What had happened to the fiery ambition for her posterity which had always kept her going? It seemed as though she, our progenitor, were revoking her original creative impulse, abandoning the future. She'd dreamed us, I thought— could she so easily undream us?

At the same time, I felt how like a desolate child she was, and since I didn't dare attempt the ways of comforting I'd learned in the ethnic, touchy-feely East—barely dared to stroke the ropy back of her clenched hand—I knew I'd have to do my best with words. There's a tradition in our family of lulling youngsters with true stories; come to think of it, this probably started with Grandma Rose herself, or possibly with her mother. "Tell me a story about when *you* were little," was a request Jenny and I often made of our own mother: for instance, on long car trips, when we had to sit still for smelly home permanents, or when one of us had to wait in the dentist's office. As I sat there wondering what I could say to Grandma, it struck me that there would be a magnificent symmetry in my telling her a story about when I would be an old woman. But I knew such whimsy was alien to her, and it occurred to me to talk about Prosperine instead. So I told her what it had meant to me to read the material she'd shown me recently. (I'd made good progress in the past week, and had even received permission to take a look in Geri's attic, though I hadn't been over there yet.) The moral of my story, subtly drawn I hoped, was that obscure and seemingly futile efforts are capable of bearing unexpected fruit.

Grandma heard me out, and to my relief seemed at least partially distracted from her wrathful, despairing mood. "Isn't it strange," she mused, "how things turn out sometimes? Proppie was so dead set against my marrying, and now here this nonsense should come up about Phoebe. It almost looks like serving me right. Except of course it's two completely different things. I'd be overjoyed to see her with someone suitable."

I was surprised to hear her draw the parallel. "Are you going to tell her how you feel? It might clear the air."

She drew herself up to enunciate what I should have known without asking. "Of course not. It isn't as though it's any of my business." Before she finally lay down to take her nap, she remembered she'd come across a small notebook of Prosperine's that I might want to look at.

I don't remember exactly what writing of Prosperine's Grandma had shown me during that week. I think there were some notes and letters from early in their friendship, and some less personal documents, newspaper clippings and graduation programs. There may also have been an adolescent journal, or possibly that was among the material which I got to see later. None of it was particularly striking, though of course it would be useful as background. The main thing was that now I had my foot in the door. Grandma appeared to have accepted the crucial point that Prosperine's papers were of real significance, and that an outside expert—so long as it was her own granddaughter, at any rate, keeping it all in the family—ought to be allowed to look at them.

The notebook she handed me on the afternoon of Ruta's reading only raised my expectations. For one thing, it was the first of the documents she'd allowed me to take back to the cabin. For another, it turned out to be from an entirely new stratum of what I now thought of metaphorically as "the dig." Rather than containing the journal entries I'd expected, it appeared to be a rather jumbled and casual jotting of dates, lists of objects, and remembered incidents that were somehow reflective of the political climate in the years 1917-19. Evidently it had been compiled after the fact, perhaps as raw material for some sort of memoir or fictional treatment. The last date I located was that of the Centralia massacre in Washington state, on Armistice Day, 1919. I now had the most direct proof I'd turned up so far that she'd survived beyond the flu epidemic.

I copied out her notes on the infamous raid on IWW national headquarters in Chicago, on the same day in September, 1917 when more than a hundred and fifty Wobblies were arrested in a nationwide sweep:

*A young fed. agent, about my own age, cheeks fair and smooth as though he'd never shaved, sat in Big Bill's sacred swivel chair, reading an illustrated magazine and chewing on a sandwich. Asked indignantly what he thought he was doing. He replied that he supposed the I Won't Works could agitate as they pleased, so long as it was peacetime, but by golly now the country had got to buckle down. "You call this honest work you are up to?" I exploded. He told me quite solemnly that he'd had to get out of a warm bed at 2 a.m. that morning and miss his eggs and oatmeal, but was glad to do it for the effort.*

*Entire desks were dropped from the upper floors to W. Madison St. below, creating no little peril to passersby, their contents then rifled and in some cases hauled away in police vans. A sort of carnival atmosphere, almost gay, all sorts of people rushing in and out. Patriotic young ladies from wealthy families enlisted to drive the prisoners from Cook Cty. jail to the arraignment in their fathers' automobiles—nice touch for the scissorbill press. Jim B.'s son, about seven or eight years old, bit the agent who was leading his father away. Drew blood. Agent handcuffed the child, left him tied to a bedpost, where his mother found him an hour or two later, crying hysterically, "The capitalists took pa." Material seized as evidence from office and private homes included: copies of the U.S. Constitution, sheet music, etiquette books, love letters, various household compounds—supposed to be chemicals for making "bombs." Oddly I recall no realistic grasp of catastrophe. Some sense of grievance on my part that out of that number, Gurley was the only female they bothered to arrest.*

There was a terse description of a memorial service held for Frank Little after he was lynched in Butte, Montana, which included just about the only directly personal reference I ran across in the entire notebook: *Maude would not come along and I thought of the Fall of '15 when the world opened up—that splendid bitter Thanksgiving Day when 30,000 of us turned out to say goodbye to Joe Hill, and I thought nothing could ever be the same for me again—and Rose stayed home to sew buttonholes!* Grandma, I realized, had referred to the same incident, though she hadn't been able to remember who it was that had gotten shot.

"Hmmph," said Ruta shrewdly, when I stopped by her place the following afternoon on my way over to the Hill, "so you've struck pay dirt, huh? Congratulations. You're going to have quite an industry going

176

for you there." I'd found her out back. She was just getting ready to feed the dogs, and they yapped demandingly as she wiped her hands on grubby dungarees, then stood thumbing through the notebook.

I'd come expecting praise, and her knowing tone annoyed me. So did the uproar and the distinct possibility that she was going to smudge the pages. But I said what I'd planned to say, anyway. "I'm hoping you might consider doing a preface to the book. It's a ways off, of course, but eventually—"

I'd hoped she'd be flattered, but all she said was, "So your grandma's given her okay, has she?"

"She's let me see a lot of new stuff."

"The book's okay with her?"

"We haven't discussed that yet."

"Come back when you have," she said, handing the notebook back.

I thought she was being picky, but I didn't challenge her. I sat with her while she husked a dishpan full of corn, and afterwards in the car consoled myself with the thought that it was probably nothing personal; she'd mentioned feeling blocked in her work on the "Spanish" book.

I had better luck, I thought, enlisting Phoebe's help. I ran into her at the intersection of Gethsemane Lane and Harmony Boulevard, on my way to Grandma's room. She was carrying a Bible and had strapped to her black patent leather belt a small cassette tape player, the headset of which she removed to let me know that she was on her way to the crafts room, where one of the women was going to demonstrate how to make wall hangings illustrating scriptural passages by gluing seashells onto plywood backing. Though I hadn't thought much about the role she might play, I realized I shouldn't waste this opportunity. So I explained my errand, emphasizing my excitement over recent discoveries and the support they lent to the hope that Prosperine's papers might have historical importance.

"Oh, so that's what Rose has been up to, poking around down in the storage room!" she exclaimed, as though I'd solved a mystery. She explained that residents were allotted one large, lockable cabinet in the basement in which to keep a limited amount of excess property. Once or twice she'd run into Grandma coming from the elevator lugging a shopping bag, and two days ago the social worker had stopped her in the hall to ask if she knew what her friend Mrs. Schlaghoffer was so busy with downstairs—was she getting her fall cleaning out of the way early? Phoebe had felt worried when that happened, since as she said, "*They're* liable to take you aside if they think you're acting strangely, and I know Rose wouldn't cotton to being quizzed."

I realized she was breathing audibly, and leaning for support on one of the sturdy railings that ran along each side of all the Hill's corridors. She was frailer than the jaunty Walkman and aerobic exercise shoes suggested (in her neat, bright dress she looked like a plump, wrinkled Yuppie), and I felt I shouldn't detain her. I got to the point.

"I'd appreciate it if you'd put in a word for me about doing something with those papers as soon as possible. They're really quite valuable."

"Before it's too late." We understood each other. "Of course," she added, "nothing I say *now* is likely to have much influence on her. She's so put out with me, you see."

"Really? But you're her closest friend."

"About Mr. Luckenbill." She sighed and shook her head. "Though it wasn't *my* idea about him coming along the other day. But she blames me anyway."

"That's too bad. Have you talked it over with her?"

Negative head shake. "My mother had a saying, 'Least said, quickest mended.' "

This policy of silence and indirection on which she and Grandma appeared to be cooperating seemed barbarous to me. I wanted to lance the boil.

"I think she's jealous," I observed, producing an uncomprehending look. "I think she's afraid Mr. Luckenbill might be. . .interested. Romantically, you know."

She lowered her eyes to the carpet, maiden-shy. "Oh, he's not thinking of anything like *that*. Besides, I don't see why Rose would want to be jealous. I'm sure I wouldn't be, if it was the other way around. Anyway, I'm sure Rose could attract all sorts of attention, including from Mr. Luckenbill himself, if she cared to be bothered."

It almost seemed as though she were being purposefully obtuse. "Not jealous of *you*, I meant jealous of *him*. Worried that. . .well, you know, that he might sort of come between the two of you or something."

She continued to respond with the sturdy innocence of a turn-of-the-century Viennese housewife informed that Dr. Freud is saying little

178

boys want to murder their fathers and have sex with their mothers. "Oh, I'm sure she couldn't think I'd ever let anything like that happen. Why, Rose is just about the most admirable woman I've known in my life!"

I gave up. "So you'll talk to her. . .about getting things settled with those papers?"

"For all the good it'll do," she promised serenely. And, after demonstrating with great satisfaction how the Walkman headset was specially designed to accommodate her hearing aid, she trudged off to paste seashells.

That afternoon Grandma once again complained of feeling "washed out." I talked the situation and my strategy over with Linda, who was sounding more relaxed and amiable now, and we agreed that I should proceed cautiously. I stayed away from the Hill for a few days after that, to let Phoebe exert whatever influence she could, and to try to avoid the risk of Grandma's feeling pressured by me. I wanted to use the time to go through the things in Geri's attic; I was itching to see the letters once again, and had hopes that a systematic search would turn up more material. But it turned out that my aunt and uncle were taking a week's vacation, so I was frustrated on that score.

Just when I felt I'd waited long enough and was debating my next move, Grandma herself called. This was unexpected, since I was usually the one to call her. Speaking formally, as she would have if we'd been talking long distance (a sacred, because expensive, ritual), she requested my presence at the Hill that afternoon.

"If you like, sure," I said cautiously. "Anything special going on?"

"Oh, just something I would like to talk to you about." Her tone curiously mingled discomfort and command. Obviously she was less than calm about whatever she had in mind, yet just as clearly she felt completely within her rights in thus summoning me.

I arrived quite nervous myself, but determined to be tough. We were going to talk about the Prosperine book today. Ruta was right, I'd decided. The worst she could do would be to say no, which would be a disappointment—but it wouldn't be the end. I could still work on her, still hope to wait her out.

When I opened her door in response to the familiar permission emanating from inside, she was sitting erect in her "reclining" chair, carefully dressed as usual. I wondered what it was that seemed out of place in the picture, then realized that she appeared not to have been doing anything. Was it possible she'd simply sat there idle, waiting for my knock?

"Hello, Grandma. How have you been feeling?"

She looked impatient with all that. "I've been *thinking*," she announced.

"Yes?" I'd sat down facing her before I saw the boxes stacked behind her chair. There were three of them, rather battered, with the names of various brands of liquor emblazoned on their sides.

"I believe it's high time I put things in order," she explained, just as though it were the first time she'd ever come to such a conclusion. "I have a birthday coming up at the end of this month, you know. A birthday has always been a thing to make me think, especially as I got on in years. I had a talk with myself. 'Rose,' I said, 'it is past time you quite shilly-shallying. You are going to be ninety-one. This can't go on forever.' "

Life, did she mean, I wondered? Or procrastination, merely? Whatever she meant, I was beginning to think that I was in for yet another discussion of the prospects for her book.

The next second, hope flared. "I've tried to think what Proppie would have wanted. I've done some soul-searching."

Proppie! I waited.

"I know she would not have liked to have been forgotten."

I nodded as sagely as I knew how, and after a pause ventured, "I'd say she had a very strong urge to be remembered—not just the way friends do, I mean, but to make herself *known*, through everything she wrote."

"Well, I suppose something really ought to be done with those papers." She spoke grimly, her grimness edged with pride; she was, she clearly felt, Doing The Right Thing. "I know you've always taken an interest in her writing," she added, rather as though coming to the conclusion had required extraordinary insight, "so of course you ought to be the one to see to it. The girls will help me with Eugene's letters and things, I guess...then there's my book. We haven't made too much progress on that lately, have we? I don't even have a title! Do you think we should make a plan about finishing that up?"

"Of course we can," I promised. I would have been ready to promise far more in my sudden optimism. In fact, it was mostly her fault that we hadn't proceeded faster with her memoirs. She was highly distractable, and when we did finally sit down to work on a given chapter she invariably produced dozens of alternate versions and tied both of us in knots attempting to incorporate what she considered the indispensable features of each. "I'll work on your book and Prosperine's papers both," I added, to underscore the quid pro quo which it intrigued me to see she now seemed to propose as though it were her original idea. I was still in the dark as to what she was prepared to do, however, and I briefly recalled Linda's suggestion about depositing the journals and letters in some archive or collection. This would be the time to bring it up as a possibility; also, to mention my thoughts about the *Reader*.

But I hesitated, reluctant to close off any options until I had a better idea of what Grandma was leading up to.

"Prosperine and I, you know, didn't always see eye to eye," she volunteered.

I admitted I'd gathered as much.

"She would flaunt her opinions at times, things she knew were liable to shock others. She called that *honesty*. Well, maybe so, but it wasn't always called for, *I* thought. I'll never forget the time her aunt from St. Cloud was visiting, that was married to a Presbyterian minister. Prosperine got to talking about some young woman in the neighborhood that had had a baby without having a husband first. She was going on about what an interesting person this girl was, and how hypocritical of folks it was not to speak to her and so on. Her aunt tried to turn the conversation, and mentioned the atrocities the German side was supposed to be guilty of in Belgium at the time, bayonetting babies and all that sort of thing. Prosperine turns to her as cool as can be and says, 'Why Aunt Jane, I think that's a bunch of malarkey.' Her poor mother was practically in tears, she wanted to stay on the good side of this sister-in-law, but Prosperine ran circles around that woman. Excuse me, Dale, would you mind just reaching me my sweater from the foot of the bed? You don't feel chilly in that getup?"

I was roasting in my tank top, but I handed the sweater over without comment. Old flesh is colder than young flesh, or whatever ambiguous middling category mine currently fell into. For some reason, my excitement of a moment ago was swamped in a wave of purely irrational resentment at the oppressiveness of the place, with its climate control eternally set at hothouse temperatures, and its wraparound garden views planned to provide an illusion of nature for people no longer able to walk around the block, and the insistent gleam and sparkle of its surfaces, those low-maintenance plasters and formicas and linoleums extravagantly prized by women who remember carpet beaters and boiled wash. So many afternoons I'd spent indoors, when I might have been lazing and dreaming down by the river instead; I'd meant to drive up to the North Shore too, and I still hadn't gone, and August was disappearing.

"Everything's here," Grandma proclaimed, struggling with her sweater. "Everything I could find down in storage, anyway. It was a hard haul," she boasted, "to bring it all up. I couldn't lift the boxes, of course, so I used a shopping bag. I have one from Dayton's with reinforced handles. Most places don't make them that sturdy anymore. I made two trips, down and back, for each of those three boxes. Then, you see, I got things emptied out enough to manage the box itself, with a few items in it."

I couldn't quite grasp what she was driving at. "More of your papers?"

"Oh, no. Prosperine's."

"Prosperine's? *All?*"

She shrugged modestly. "I don't really know what-all is in there, you know. I never could seem to get myself to read more than a few pages, even when Mrs. Munkers first gave me the stuff. I put it away and said I'd look into it later, but I always was so busy, I hardly had a moment. Anyway, it was enough to make you dizzy, looking at so many pages crammed with that awful script of hers. I never could see why she couldn't write a neater hand. And now, of course, my eyes wouldn't be up to it."

I needed to know where I stood, and she wasn't helping me. "So you want me to go through them and—?"

"Go through them, yes." She clung to the meaningless phrase. "Go through them, Dale, go through all of them. I don't really understand that sort of thing, you see, but it's your line of work, I'm sure you know what ought to be done with a person's papers. You be the judge." The words tumbled out in awkward spurts, as though she were anxious to get the fatal step behind her, and once again I thought I should speak about the book, or at least mention an archive as a possibility, but too much had just happened, too much was happening, and it was simpler to stick to the matter at hand.

"Did you want me to take those boxes back to the cabin with me?" My own ruthlessness surprised me. I could see she hesitated. "I'd be able to work faster that way."

"Well, I think it's better if they stay over here," she decided. "You'll be coming over soon to work on my book."

I wasn't really disappointed; perhaps I was relieved. Better not to make too much progress too fast. I did ask, though, if I could take a quick look right away, just to get some idea what type of materials we were talking about. She agreed, a bit reluctantly I thought. Possibly she'd hoped to postpone this step until later in the week.

No sooner had I begun than she got up and locked the door. "I just don't want anybody barging in and disturbing your work," she explained. "People who don't live in an antheap like this don't know the value of their privacy."

I couldn't think of much to say that would ease the situation, and proceeded in silence with my task, trying not to look too eager. Prosperine's effects were in complete chaos, not surprising considering how many times the contents of those particular cartons must have been transferred to new receptacles or shuffled around over the half century or so since they'd come into Grandma's possession. Different decades had been half stirred together, or in some cases blended completely, so that there were childhood diaries and school exercise books resting side by side with yellowed newspaper clippings describing the Palmer raids. I recall, for instance, a small article—really half an article; it was torn down the middle—which detailed the arrest of a Nebraska woman under the terms of the Espionage Act, because her neighbors said she mocked the Red Cross, and was heard to mutter, "No soldier ever sees these socks," when asked to help out with a knitting effort. This suggestive fragment nested inside an envelope also containing half a dozen locks of fine, straight hair in shades of blond ranging from ash to dishwater, tied up in grosgrain ribbon. "Prosperine's?" I asked.

Grandma thought so; Proppie always was said to have been an extremely fair child. Mrs. Munkers had probably saved hair clippings over the years, though how they'd gotten in with these things wasn't easy to say, since Mrs. Munkers had sorted everything carefully and had kept all the snapshots.

Actually, she hadn't kept quite all. In the second of the boxes, I turned up three. The first was a large print on stiff cardboard backing of a very young, skinny, overexposed Prosperine in an ankle-length dress with a white sailor collar, standing on a dock and holding up a string of small fish. Then there was a studio portrait of a pretty young brunette, taken in a trompe l'oeil set which made her appear to be seated in a canoe. Her head and shapely neck appeared in a hole that was cut out above a body dressed in fringed buckskin, its arms wielding a paddle to propel the craft across a reedy expanse of lake. She cast a mockingly flirtatious glance at the camera lens, and for some reason hadn't bothered to remove her complicated hat. "Paddling my own canoe—as ever, M," she'd signed on the back. Grandma said she didn't know who this was. Finally, there was a mysterious shot of a Prosperine who appeared twenty years older than the girl on the dock. It had been taken outdoors in front of an unpainted frame structure, barracks-like, over the door of which hung an American flag. She looked gaunt, faded, and desperately unhappy, and was wearing bangs, which didn't suit her in the least. At her side stood several swarthy, also miserable-looking children in badly fitting pants and dresses. On the back somebody had printed just "Vermilion School," no date. I remembered there was a Vermilion Range somewhere up north near the Mesabi, and wondered if these were miners' kids.

There were handmade valentines, concert programs, rough but intriguing sketches of faces and figures: a one-eyed man smoking a pipe, a boy struggling with a loaded wheelbarrow, a woman with a crutch and a vivid, sneering face. A thick packet of newspaper clippings, secured with a rubber band, had been stuffed into a shoebox, and though I didn't dare dismantle them on the spot because they were obviously too fragile and crumbly to withstand much handling, I could see that the ones on the top, at any rate, were Prosperine's articles from *Stand*.

One of the cartons contained mostly letters, hundreds of them, still in their original envelopes. By far the majority were from Prosperine's mother, directed to her at an impressive variety of addresses in three or four states. They smelled faintly of lavender, and the one I opened contained, incredibly, recipes for sponge cake and puff pastry, copied out in elegant script. Beneath this snowdrift, buried at the bottom of the box, were missives in the scattershot typing and self-consciously "proletarian" diction of Frank Stuberfield, writing from the Chicago *Stand* office to his ace reporter up on the Iron Range. A further assortment of handwritings and return addresses tantalized me with the hope of eventually turning up correspondence from some of the famous radicals of the day.

I found the mother lode I'd looked for, the journals and notebooks, in the third and final carton. Here and there I'd already come across a cheap school exercise book with a blue paper cover, "Private Diary" hand-lettered on the front, or a crude small booklet of poems made from loose sheets glued together, but opening up that last box and handling the contents gave me a sense of victorious recognition rare outside of dreams. I didn't have time to do more than glance at a page here and there, but there were manuscripts too, mostly in longhand.

"She didn't throw anything away, did she?" I couldn't believe my luck.

"Oh, Proppie was a packrat," Grandma criticized. "I remember how annoyed she used to get when Mrs. Munkers would disturb the papers in her bedroom, just wanting to dust and straighten up a bit. She would save her exam papers and everything. I always threw mine out at the end of the term."

Though it had so perfectly answered my designs, this paper-hoarding tendency on the part of the young rebel nonetheless surprised me, it seemed so conservative. Certainly it underscored the fact that here was someone who'd lived for and through her writing, and from a very young age.

Grandma pointed out that it was nearly dinnertime, and I reluctantly repacked the boxes and stowed them in a corner. We agreed I'd come back at ten the following morning and work on her book until lunch. Then I'd take another look at the things I'd seen today. (I said to myself I'd try to get her to go out for a while, or else let me work in one of the resident lounges, away from her anxious eye.)

She wanted to walk me as far as the front desk. We were almost at the automatic doors before she managed, "I've been thinking that I might have been wrong, after all, about the year when Proppie passed away. I was so positive it was directly following the Armistice, but Amaryllis has gotten me all turned around. She's positive it was later."

Amaryllis is positive it was later, and now these papers are going to prove it, I thought. Is that what worries you? But why should it matter?

"Are you concerned about...anything she might have written

down?" I asked point blank. "Something you'd like kept private?" Again it was on the tip of my tongue to bring up the business about the book, and still I held back.

"No, I am not concerned," she replied bravely. "I know I can count on your good sense, Cecilia."

I started to say something, but she'd already caught herself. "Cecilia! Just listen to me! I do that with Allison, too, call her Geraldine sometimes. You'd think I was getting senile, but it's been happening for years. I only meant, Dale, I know you wouldn't do. . .anything unwise. Anything to upset the relatives, or hurt the memory of folks that are deceased."

"And of course we'll talk it over," I vowed.

That was too pious, and she called me on it. "Oh, *I* won't be here long. Nobody on my side of the family so far has ever lived to ninety-three." She kissed me calmly on the cheek and told me to be careful driving home.

That night I called Linda at the beach. She was alone; Fiona had just left for Boston. I was still enthusiastic over my discoveries of the day, and it disappointed me to hear her sounding edgy and cool again. When challenged, she quickly became accusatory: I'd left her by herself all summer, she'd had to parent on her own, and now I suddenly expected her to be supportive of all of *my* projects.

Not all of them, I said, only the Prosperine papers. Surely she'd have to agree that a find like this one wasn't an everyday occurrence. Anyway, had she already forgotten that her vacation plans with Fiona had had quite a bit to do with my decision to come out here?

That was her cue to retort that if I'd really welcomed Fiona in the first place, maybe some of the past year's rough spots could have been avoided.

Furious at having my pleasure in the papers spoiled, I ended up suggesting that if that was how she felt, maybe we just shouldn't call each other, perhaps we ought to wait and work things out when I got back. It would only be a couple of weeks now, anyway.

"Here we go. Dale does her withholding butch routine."

"Don't start. You know I hate that role shit."

"So do I," she said meaningfully.

"Fuck it, I'm butch, all right, and you know why? It's because men in gas stations and delis call me 'sir' and 'Mac' and 'pal' when I wear my winter jacket. That's *all*. Don't fucking oppress me more than *they* do."

"How about being focused on your career to the exclusion of the *people* in your life? What do you call that?"

"What do *you* call it?"

"Slightly male-identified."

I was enraged. "Look who's talking! Your career's been going great! If it didn't run like clockwork I bet I'd be hearing plenty about your worries, Ms. Womyn-Identified Wombmoon! What do you know about having half your classes scheduled for early morning and the rest after dinner, or listening to some slimy little bastard impugn your grasp of American literature because you devote a session to Louisa May Alcott and ignore the enduring achievement of William Dean Howells?"

It wasn't good. We didn't even try to make up before hanging up. And despite Linda's caricature of me as the strong, silent, impermeable type, of course I worried, and had a hard time sleeping, and difficulty putting the whole thing out of my mind next morning, when I was due back at the Hill. Nevertheless, I made an effort, and came up with what I thought were some fairly productive editorial suggestions about Grandma's book. By lunchtime I was feeling slightly better.

My patience in going to the dining room and keeping Grandma company through vegetable-beef soup and something billed as a Lo-Fat Turkey 'n Cheese Croissantwich was rewarded when she asked if I'd like to move those boxes into the room next to hers, where I wouldn't have to worry about disturbing her when she lay down for her nap. It was vacant, she explained; the poor woman who'd been in there was "no longer with us," and she'd received permission for me to use it provided I didn't leave anything lying around.

She seemed so calm compared to yesterday that I decided the main problem had been getting the ice broken. Did she believe in Pharaoh's Curse? Was that it? Well, the boxes had been looked into, and the sky hadn't fallen. Now she seemed willing to have me get on with it. She merely requested that if anyone asked me what I was up to, I should just please say I had some work to do, some work connected with my job.

I promised to be discreet, and left her resting comfortably with the afghan loosely tucked around her knees. I rushed to the other room, bolted the door behind me, and practically lunged at the box of journals. *Alone at last!* I thought.

Hastily I arranged the motley collection of volumes in rows on the naked bedsprings (the room was stripped, and even the mattress had been taken away, to have the taint of death cleaned off, I supposed). I began frantically leafing through first one diary and then another, as though

I hoped to grasp the secret of a life in a single afternoon—or, failing that, at least to hit upon a few key explanatory passages.

I was going to say I read ravenously, but that's not strictly accurate; Prosperine's handwriting was so difficult that it was more like an impatient effort to translate from a foreign language I hadn't quite mastered. Possibly she'd attempted to write more legibly in her letters to Grandma, because I couldn't remember having had this much trouble with the ones I'd found in Aunt Geri's attic. Here I had to proceed haltingly, guessing at words according to context, guessing at context too more often than not, for in entries from later years she frequently dropped all pretense of linear narrative. She was not a naive diarist, a slave of plot and incident and every slightest twinge of feeling, but a *writer*, after all—and modernism was in the air. So there were snatches of conversations overheard on the streetcar, experiments in describing the look of things (protest marches, spring trees, the killing floor in a slaughterhouse), rigorous efforts to probe emotional states. I skimmed dreams, diatribes, even one intensely boring experiment in automatic writing which went on for many pages. Her private stories glinted here and there, mixed up with other people's stories. And minutes of political meetings, even a grocery list or two—she seemed to have used her journal for everything. Add to this the gaps in dating, which sometimes made it problematic even to guess at year or locale, and I rapidly concluded that the hit and miss approach wouldn't get me far. Only when I could proceed systematically (which would mean having a typescript prepared at a cost I shuddered to estimate) would I be able to extract from this overwhelming mass of raw material what I hoped would be a presentable version of my heroine, complete with a plausible beginning, middle, and end. In a sense I'd need to become her biographer before I'd have the perspective to edit *The Prosperine Reader*.

Despite the odds, however, I did almost immediately run across one fascinating episode, in a volume written in Chicago shortly after the war ended, probably in the first half of 1919. Embedded in a discouraging record of the worsening fortunes of the Wobbly organization and other effects of the raging anti-Red hysteria of the age was the evidence of Prosperine's intense and evidently tumultous relationship with a young woman named Maude, usually referred to as "M" (the "M," I guessed, of the corny, canoe-paddling photograph). After I'd read a few of the entries dealing with her I became so intrigued—with Prosperine's obsession as much as its object—that I hunted through the endings of all the other journals to see if I could discover how the pair had met. I was unsuccessful there, as well as in my attempt to find out what had happened between them later, though I suspected their affair had ended unhappily when I recalled the objective tone of the *Little Review* story "Marjorie," which I now realized had undoubtedly been inspired by Maude. Prosperine wrote cryptically of her interactions with her friend; typically she'd describe at some length Maude's pleasure in a new outfit, or some sensational aspect of her sordid childhood in a large family with an alcoholic mother and tubercular father. Then she'd append a sentence of emotional summary: "M and I argued in the Loop, I cried from vexation," or, "M in a good mood, rowing on the lake, coco-nut ices, why spoil it?" There was no direct evidence of a physical relationship, or so I thought at first. Then I discovered an odd phrase that seemed to recur every few pages: *M and I*, it read, followed by a curlicue shape which at first reminded me of the symbol for the atom used in textbooks and periodic tables, with its small black nucleus and orbits, but which I soon saw must have been intended for a simple drawing of a flower. *M and I* ✿. I was sure it meant sex. Sometimes it was *M and I* ✿ ✿. I put aside that volume and began searching through the rest, hoping to locate entries from the time when Prosperine and Grandma had lived together in Chicago, to see whether it contained any similar notation.

As I did this, another idea struck me. Yesterday when I'd looked through the box of letters I hadn't found a single one from Grandma to Prosperine—yet she'd said the two of them used to correspond regularly, and I was positive I'd have recognized her handwriting. Could it be she'd gone through and removed all of them before letting me take a look?

All too soon, an insistent knock sounded. I felt like the hapless maiden in "Rumpelstiltskin": morning already, and I'd spun so little gold.

I opened up. Grandma entered briskly, quietly, as though she were just popping into a speakeasy and naturally preferred not to be observed, but on the other hand refused to sneak and skulk.

"Making progress, dear?"

I nodded. "There's an enormous amount of writing here, though. It's going to take some time. . . . My goodness, is it after four already? I'd better get going."

Hurriedly, I began repacking cartons, somehow not wanting to submit to more of her surveillance than was entirely unavoidable. Before I left I remembered to ask if she had any idea why I hadn't found any letters from her to Proppie.

"But why would that matter?" she asked.

"Why would it—?"

"I thought it was *her* writing you were after."

There was a slight caustic edge to the remark that I didn't take time to analyze, but filed away for later consideration—perhaps a subtle implication that I was slighting Grandma's own writing. Or was she laying small traps for me, as I was doing for her? Were we dancing around the question of the romance? "Well, yes, of course her writing is what concerns me, more than letters, I mean. I just wondered if this meant she kept some stuff separate. Maybe there were things her mother didn't give you?

Grandma seemed to take the question seriously. "I believe Proppie may have destroyed them," she concluded, after some reflection. "Yes, I seem to recall her telling me something about it, a year or two later, when we'd patched things up a little. Said she burned the lot in a wood cookstove, up there on the Range."

"*Burned?*" This was unexpected.

"Stood there poking them through the hole in the stovetop, letter by letter, and the lady she was staying with came in and found her like that and thought she must have quarreled with some young man."

"But *why* would she have burned them?" Grandma appeared so completely oblivious of the irony in this interpretation that it seemed safe to ask. I felt sharp dismay at the vision of that destructive kitchen fire, though it had taken place a lifetime ago.

Serenely, as though it had happened to other people, she explained, "As I've mentioned before, Proppie was quite unhappy when Eugene and I decided to be married. She felt I ought to return to Chicago with her, where there were opportunities we both knew very well didn't exist back home. Of course *I* saw it differently." She gave a wry little laugh. "So far as I was concerned, your grandfather was quite an important opportunity, and he was *not* in Chicago!"

"She must have been pretty angry, to burn all your letters."

"Oh, that was Proppie." She shrugged. "She was strong in what she felt. I know she wanted the best for me, and maybe she had a higher opinion of my capabilities than I did myself. I couldn't see going it alone, like some of these career girls."

*She didn't want to go it alone either*, I thought reproachfully. "But afterwards?" I pressed. "I thought you patched things up. Didn't you write to her after that?"

"Well, I don't know what would have become of those letters. You're sure there weren't a few? Of course I didn't write so often after I was married, with a house to keep up. And then Gene, Jr. came along."

"I suppose there could be something I overlooked. I didn't go through that box very carefully."

"Well, why don't you take another look tomorrow? You're coming over, aren't you? There's something I was thinking about, about my own book, while I was lying down. I had the idea of starting off with that chapter where I go away to teach my first school. Then the rest of it could be going back to the beginning—a flashback, don't they call it? I could be riding along, remembering scenes from my childhood. Of course it would mean doing some rewriting, but how would that work, do you think?"

I promised we'd discuss it in the morning, and made my escape. Even though I was heading out of town at the worst of rush hour on one of the hottest days of a Minnesota August, I felt almost euphoric, dazed at my rare luck. The business with Maude, that mysterious little symbol: Maude and I ✿. Didn't you, just. The thought of the two of them in 1919 was faintly but perceptibly a turn-on.

But the main thing was the papers, and their author. Proppie Munkers was real, and she was going to be my girl. (My "industry," too, in Ruta's vulgar formulation.)

Underneath it all, the nagging anxiety about my other girl, Linda, hadn't really subsided. But I kept pushing it down, reminding myself that such were the chores of a mature relationship, shouting at one another and losing sleep and feeling pissed and sad and still having to face the effort of reconciliation. Maybe if I felt energetic I'd give her a call later.

I arrived at the cabin wringing wet, thirsty, eager for the faint breath of coolness I knew would be waiting for me under the pine trees. Even now in the worst of the dog days, the heat my mother's Minnesota stories had made legendary in my childhood somehow didn't seem much worse than August in Plainfield, and certainly couldn't begin to compete for misery with the salty, stinking, claustrophic heat waves I'd survived in New York City. Here, at least, you never felt far away from some leafy, moist resuscitation.

But the winters would be out of the question. So I told myself whenever I started having fantasies about moving to Minnesota.

I entered the shadowy cabin, its battered furniture gilded here and there by the late light that beamed through the screened porch. The comfortable disorder was all mine, welcoming. A bird I thought might be an oriole lit on a young silver birch outside the kitchen window. I gulped a glass of water, poured a quick gin and tonic, peeled off my sweaty shirt and corduroys right there by the kitchen sink, and braced for the daily disillusionment of attempting to insert a size fourteen torso into a size twelve swimsuit. I knew exactly how the river was going to feel: too cool for the first minute, but after that a felicitous temperature that would make me forget the tensions of both heat and cold, let me float about as if skinless yet entirely safe, momentarily loosed from all determinisms, bathed in the same resistless medium the air becomes on a very few perfect June nights.

After my swim I'd cook dinner, eggs again probably—there wasn't much in the house. Then I'd decide exactly what to say to Grandma about the papers when I saw her tomorrow; I definitely needed to formulate some long-range strategy for them which I could lay the groundwork for before heading back to Jersey. After that, if it wasn't too late, I'd give Linda a try.

She beat me to it, calling around nine, just when I was trying to remember how to eat an artichoke heart. I'd discovered the doughty thistle, a recent impulse buy, sitting in the back of the vegetable compartment, and had steamed it to go along with my scrambled eggs and wine. Now its end-bitten leaves littered my plate, the melted butter was congealing, and I'd just realized that Linda usually advised me at this point. It was she who had a passion for artichokes, she in whose company I occasionally ate them, and I'd forgotten what to do with the pulpy grey-green stalk I held between my fingers.

When the phone rang I knew who it was. "Hi, honey," I answered gaily, "you called just in time. Listen, which is the part of an artichoke you're supposed to cut off before you eat the heart?"

She sounded surprised, but told me.

"You're still mad at me."

In a brittle voice she claimed that, no, she wasn't; in fact, she'd called to tell me she was sorry about last night—well, not altogether sorry, that is—she was still disturbed about several statements I'd made, and she especially disagreed with my unwillingness to take any kind of real responsibility for the friction between Fiona and me.

"But there's something else I called about, something I need to discuss with you."

"I'm listening."

"This is difficult, Dale. It's so complicated. I was hoping to put it off until you got home, but now that's not feasible."

It wasn't like her to prepare me. "You slept with somebody."

Her hesitation at the sullen joke pushed all my alarm buttons. "You know we said we wouldn't without telling the other one," she reminded me, hurt.

"So what's going on?"

"Well, I'm very attracted to one of my authors."

An angry weariness beset me. Not that it had to be serious, of course. These things happen, as I knew perfectly well from my own experience. But I hated the idea of the tension it would cause, the endless arguments, the parallels I knew she would draw to my involvement with Treecie. One more thing to deal with. Why *now*? "Okay, let's have some details," I proposed, as evenly as I could manage.

"This woman—her name is Val, Valerie Brink—she's a novelist, quite gifted."

"A dyke?"

"She came out at a girls' boarding school when she was pretty young. I've read her first novel. It's an amazing book. She's got a contract with E.P. Dutton, but her editor left, and it's been sitting in limbo for a year and a half. I'm trying to help her get it away from them."

"How old is she?"

"Twenty-four."

"Jimminy Christmas. Jesus fucking Christ."

"We *haven't* been to bed," Linda reiterated.

"Don't worry, you will."

"Dale, don't. I'm sorry. It just feels like something I need to do right now."

194

"So that's why you called?" I was furious. "To get my *permission*?"

"I called because we said we'd let each other know."

"Know what? You haven't even told me anything. Is this a crush, a mad affair, a physical attraction, a one-night-stand, a 'meaningful relationship'?"

"How can I say right now? I don't know what it means."

"At least give me a clue."

"This is why I didn't want to talk about it yet. Everything's so confused. I hoped by the time you came home I'd have a chance to get things sorted out a little in my own mind. Right now I'm just not in control, all these feelings are surfacing. Dale, I know how hard this is, but I need you to bear with me."

"All right. Let me understand. Something changed to make you decide to call me up tonight. What exactly was it?"

"Things got...things got to a point between Val and me where I felt the need to...act on the attraction."

*Act on the attraction*, how the euphemism galled me. I thought of something else. "Is she there with you now?"

"She's walking on the beach," Linda admitted reluctantly.

"You send her out for a walk on the beach so you can call me up and ask me do I mind if the two of you get it on when she comes back?"

"Oh, Dale, it isn't—"

"I can't fucking believe this! We're supposed to have our little chat and then I hang up and sit around all evening imagining what you're doing?"

"Don't be too self-righteous." Linda's tone shifted from plea to accusation without a transitional stage. "After last spring."

"Last spring."

"Yes, last spring! Of course you always act like that wasn't so important. Well, it hurt me a lot. It hurt our relationship."

"At least you didn't have to lie awake knowing I was probably in bed with somebody else at that very moment."

"At least I'm being honest."

"Gee, thanks. Thank you so much." In my outrage, I was dying to hang up on her, but was held back by subliminal awareness that it was going to be a long night, a night of stark evaluation, and that there was some crucial information I needed to help me get through it. "Just tell

195

me this," was how I phrased it after a long bitter wrangle, "are you in love with her?"

Her reply suggested matters were bad as bad could be. "I'm not even sure I know what *in love* is," she said.

"You understand what I'm asking."

"It's not superficial, all right? I've never been able to be very casual about this sort of thing. But Dale, listen, I want so badly to work this out with you. You know what our relationship means."

With dread I recognized the moment from somewhere, knew I'd surely spoken these words or ones very much like them to an ex-lover, though I didn't remember which one. Fear and sorrow eclipsed my anger for the moment, as I guessed how sincerely, even desperately Linda was hoping her protestations were true, and in exactly how poor a position she was right now to promise anything.

"No, I don't know what it means," I told her. "Look, let's talk later. This isn't getting us anywhere."

"Don't give up on me, Dale. *I love you.* You're the woman I share my life with."

As I sat in silence at the table, my dinner half eaten, I realized I hadn't even gotten a clear picture of who my rival was. All I knew about her was that she was obscenely young, had been to boarding school, and that Linda, who was obviously infatuated but nevertheless would have been unlikely to allow her professional judgment to be completely compromised, thought she could write. Automatically I poured out the last of the wine, and just as automatically went to find my phone book. I wanted to call my old friend Mattie in Oakland, who was my usual adviser in romantic and sexual matters, as Bonnie was in academic ones, and with whom I'd consulted frequently during my affair with Treecie. But Mattie wasn't home, and I resentfully complied with her tactlessly ebullient phone machine tape, which exhorted "Uranians, fricatrices, and muff divers" to leave a message of any length following the tone.

After I'd brooded for an hour and graduated to Scotch, she called me back. "Well, you know these things do happen," she observed sensibly.

"I don't need you to tell me that. It's what I've been saying to myself."

"You don't think she's just getting back at you on some level?"

"Maybe it's partly that. I don't know, she just sounds so *into* the whole thing."

"Well, weren't you into that...what's-her-name?"

"Yes, but—"

"Yes, but what?"

"For one thing, this will be only the third woman Linda has ever slept with. The fourth *person*, counting her ex-husband. So it's like she's sort of missed the whole experimental stage. That worries me; it's going to give this so much power. And then—I mean, there's been so much trouble at this point, I frankly don't know how much more weight the relationship can take. And just when I thought maybe, maybe things would be starting to settle down....I'm just so disappointed," I wailed.

"Give her a little leeway. You might be surprised. Maybe she'll actually be able to get some things figured out by the time you arrive home, just like she said. In the meantime, get some sun, try to enjoy what's left of your vacation—"

"Vacation!" I groaned, "If it ever was that! I just can't imagine putting my life on hold for the next two weeks, knowing what's coming."

"What's the alternative?"

"Go back early, I guess."

Mattie, who's lived through plenty of amorous complications, thought this was a bad idea. She counseled me to establish from the outset that I was acting on my own, not simply responding to Linda in knee-jerk fashion. However, I knew she hadn't spent much time with kids, much less attempted to untangle a snarled love life in the vicinity of a lover's radar-equipped, sarcastic, ravenously self-interested teenager. When it dawned on me what staying on in the cabin would mean—by the time I saw Linda, Fiona would be back from her father's, automatically transforming the problematic triangle into an even more sinister shape, a parallelogram—I knew I had to make a beeline for Plainfield.

"But those papers you're working on?" In a letter written several weeks previously, I'd mentioned Prosperine, and Mattie had been intrigued, as she always was by lesbian rebels and subversives, especially dead ones.

"I guess they'll wait. This is about my *life*. I can always come back here sometime in the fall."

After I hung up, I felt heartened by Mattie's reassurance that the long connection with Linda ought to be trusted—even though it did occur to me that Mattie herself never stayed with anybody more than a year

197

or two. Before the booze finally put me out, I even soared on a little updraft of false exhilaration: now something definite seemed about to happen, in a life that had been in limbo far too long.

I came instantly awake in a sticky grey pre-dawn, aware of the same peculiar double sense I'd noticed the previous night of standing at a distance watching myself cope with an interesting situation. Now, however, my reaction was more one of dread than of expectancy. I had a grinding headache, and hated the thought of packing, but not so much as I hated facing my relatives. I'd have to think of some plausible excuse for picking up and leaving so abruptly, and it seemed like too much of an effort right now. Everything did.

In the end I decided to stay another night. That way I figured I could start driving first thing in the morning, after a full night's sleep, which I might achieve with the help of a pill or two. Instead of packing right away, I might as well go over to the Hill at midmorning, when Grandma expected me, and break the news gently. I knew she'd be disappointed, and I was sorry, but at the same time the difficulty of explaining myself infuriated me. If I were married to a man, obviously, all I'd have to do would be to plead unspecified domestic obligations and I'd be off the hook. Instead, I felt obliged to fabricate some elaborate, suitably spinsterly emergency.

I like to think that, Prosperine or no Prosperine, I'd definitely have wanted to see Grandma before I left, but I can't pretend the papers were completely absent from my thoughts when I drove over to the Hill. Despite my worries, I entertained some vague plan of delivering a parting pep talk about their historical importance. Maybe, depending on Grandma's reaction, I'd briefly raise the possibility of looking around for a collection where they could be safely housed—though in fact, especially now that I'd had a chance to read some of them, I felt I'd much prefer to keep them in the family if I could be sure of having continued access.

I found my relative in unusually high spirits. She was seated at the narrow antique desk which she ordinarily used only when she paid her bills, already leafing through a section of her manuscript. She wore a more colorful blouse than usual, and cherry red lipstick which she'd applied with a firm hand. She announced she was feeling "zippy," and wondered what I thought of "Bright Heritage" as a title for her book.

198

"Or Bright something. A pun on the name, you know."

I felt that this was going to be even harder than I'd anticipated. I remembered a remark Aunt Geri had made recently, which I hadn't paid much attention to at the time, to the effect that Grandma had perked up quite a bit since she'd begun to think her book might actually come out. She lived with such a drastically foreshortened horizon that I knew a postponement, even one of a few months, wouldn't be trivial for her.

It couldn't be helped. I was in extremities myself, a fact I instantly verified by remembering Linda's tone when she said, "I don't know what *in love* is."

"Oh, but you can't leave *now*," Grandma blurted out when she'd heard my tale about an important job interview having come up suddenly. "Just when I thought I was finally making some headway with my writing!"

I'm still unsure why at that point I jettisoned my script and came out to her. I think her disappointment had something to do with it. It made me want to give her something, and the truth was all I had, though of course I knew she wouldn't like it. At the same time, the strain I was under made the habitual pretenses seem suddenly not only intolerable but not very relevant. And mixed in with everything else, perhaps I was gambling that the shock might prod her to candor about Prosperine.

I don't remember what I said, exactly, but I guess I let her know that the job interview, which I didn't have the courage to admit was nonexistent, wasn't my main reason for leaving; I was leaving because Linda and I had some things to work out, and Linda was not my roommate but my lover. As was my duty, I let her hear the word "lesbian," though perhaps not more than once. All the time I was talking, the explanation seemed to be taking forever, and I felt as though there ought to be some sort of pill or injection developed as a means of humanely administering this sort of information to respectable Protestant ninety-year-old ladies. The minute I finished, breathless with stage fright, I thought the opposite—clearly I'd raced through that excruciating spiel much too rapidly for her to have taken it in.

She sat there twisting the diamond on her ring finger, gazing out the window at rows of pink and white phlox, between which painfully perambulated two women of markedly different sizes, but with identically stooped postures and elongated jaws. What an odd thing family resemblance is, I thought.

"We could use some rain," she observed mildly.

So that was it, much worse than bewilderment or bald disapproval: she'd sprinkle it with politeness like quicklime, get it buried in a hurry. I thought of helicopters dropping concrete on Chernobyl, thought of Fiona when I'd first known her, in the midst of a full-blown tantrum dashing off to put on a pair of earmuffs in order to dramatize her imperviousness to unwanted information. I remembered the nasty, sometimes prurient undercurrent of homophobia in my tenure proceedings, just the most recent in along line of situations in which I'd been called upon to play the mature, helpful homo, the understanding lez. Probably Grandma actually figured she was doing me a favor, handling it this way, smoothing over the embarrassment I'd caused, as she might have done if I'd farted at the table, or forgotten and said *damn*.

"Grandma, did you hear me?" I insisted.

"I've got *both* my hearing aids on." An edge to that, she resented being pressed.

"It wasn't easy to say what I just said. If you don't mind, I'd like to hear what you think."

She played for time. "Does Cecilia know?"

"Sure," I said promptly. "She's very supportive, super actually. As a matter of fact, she and Father have stayed with Linda and me when they've come out to visit." Probably, I thought, it was partly because my mother had been a nervous witness to my rapid transit through a number of prior relationships that she was so good about this one. I just hoped things didn't get so bad between Linda and me that she'd have to hear about it.

"I always have wondered how Cecilia felt about it," Grandma mused, "But I figured if it was something she cared to talk about, she'd have brought it up herself. I never thought much of women who stick their noses into their children's affairs."

The implication startled me. "You mean you *knew*?"

"I didn't know a thing," she corrected. "And I never supposed it was any of my business. All I'm saying is, I've got a few wits about me, I hope. Naturally it did occur to me that a smart attractive girl like you would have been married long before this if she'd had any interest in. . .that side of things. Married, or whatever the fashion is these days. When your sister had the baby and I'd still never heard a word from Cecilia about any boyfriends of yours, why I guess that's when I thought, maybe with Dale it's something like it was with that Lucille Pinkney, that lived about a mile from us, up on the farm."

"Who was she?" Through all the layers of discomfort and resentment, the old urge to hear a story from Grandma reasserted itself.

"Why, Lucille Pinkney didn't fancy any of the men in our area, and she could have had plenty of suitors such as they were. She wasn't bad looking, and she was comfortably off, had one of the best pieces of farmland in the county, inherited from her father as his sole surviving child. She used to chew tobacco, and I don't know. . .people gossiped about there having been something. . .out of the ordinary between her and a cousin, a younger girl who drowned in a boating accident. That's as may be, but she could blast stumps to keep up with most of the men farmers. . . .She lived alone with a hired girl for a good number of years. They kept to themselves pretty much. When she died it turned out she'd willed the house, the barn, the land and all the farm things to that little red-haired servant girl."

What the hell, I thought. It's now or never. "It did occur to me that Prosperine might have been—well, a little like Lucille. Like me."

"Oh, no." She was casual, almost airy. "I surely would have known if Proppie'd. . .if there'd been anything like that. We were such dear friends, you see, I was in on all her secrets. Besides, didn't I mention to you how concerned I was at one point about that Frank Stuberfield she met in Chicago, an older, married man? He exercised such an influence over her."

She was good; she knew better than to protest too much. Still, her instantaneous denial didn't necessarily sound to me like the reaction of a person to whom such a thought had never occurred before.

Was it possible, though, that she really didn't know on a conscious level, and never had? That in fact there'd been the explicit intimacies I'd more or less assumed, and that she'd managed to avoid interpreting them in the same light as she did Lucille Pinkney's fondness for chewing tobacco? Such sleight of mind, though astonishing, is commonplace, of course; because a circumstance occurs in their own lives, people frequently feel it can't possibly mean the same thing as if it happened to their neighbors. Or, on the other hand, had she perhaps succeeded, not exactly in forgetting, but rather in rearranging what she knew of the past, remolding it in a less ambiguous, more satisfactory image?

Either way, I thought, it's a tissue of lies, and noticed how peculiar the phrase was, as though such things were rather frail, when in fact they endure forever. I was aware of having ventured out on a limb, and not knowing quite how to get back.

Grandma had her own approach. "Would you care for ice cream before you go?" she asked, as though that were an obvious palliative, under the circumstances.

To please her I agreed, though I hadn't eaten breakfast, and felt I wouldn't have minded skipping lunch and dinner. We took a last slow stroll down the spotless corridors, then sat for twenty minutes in the "café," a few card tables set up beneath hanging plastic ferns in one of the social rooms where the women residents took turns selling simple refreshments to benefit some charity or other. At Grandma's direction I was provided with a paper plate containing a small paper-wrapped brick divided into brown, pink, and white thirds. She herself wanted nothing but weak tea with lemon. She paid the tab in advance with quarters and nickels counted out from her change purse, then sat back to watch me eat.

"Tastes good?"

I nodded; it was flat synthetic stuff. I spooned it up slowly, in lieu of conversation. I knew I ought to be saying all sorts of things—something about the papers, something about having enjoyed our time together this summer, maybe even something gently valedictory about her place in my life, what she'd meant in my childhood. But I felt sluggish and stupid, incapable of effort. Dread about what would happen when I got home to Linda was a background like chronic pain, dulling my reactions.

I thought of asking about Arnie Luckenbill. Grandma couldn't suppress a small triumphant smile when she answered that she guessed she'd cried wolf; the fickle man now appeared to be after someone else, and Phoebe was taking it in stride. "Seems he got wise to the fact he wouldn't be able to wind her around his little finger!" she added, with a trace of her old wrath.

Her tea stood cold in the styrofoam cup, and my paper plate was soggy. It was time I left to pack. "This Linda," she came out with, "is she a professor like you?"

Suddenly I felt like crying. "No," I said, "she's in another field."

"Things are so different today. You asked what I thought. I don't know what to say. So much divorce, and babies out of wedlock, and drugs, drugs, drugs. And now *this*, too, women pairing off with women, and handsome young men with good jobs and everything to live for spreading terrible disease."

I felt indignant, but secure. I was used to the position. "Women have always paired off with women," I pointed out. "Look at Lucille Pinkney."

"That was a different story. *They* didn't flaunt it."

My patience snapped with that. But perhaps I should have known. Mother, for one, had always insisted that Grandma had led a very sheltered life, had no notion of such things, and was probably too old to change.

But now it appeared she wasn't finished; she was struggling with something—not that I cared a fig what it was. Finally, as though it were the result of an algebraic equation she'd laboriously solved, she announced, "Of course we all want you to be happy."

I didn't respond.

"You are, aren't you, Dale? Then I won't say another word."

"It's not a question of being *happy*. I couldn't live any other way."

"Well, perhaps you'll bring your friend along sometime when you come for a visit. I would surely like to meet her. I always like to meet you girls's friends," she declared, and I knew she was thinking of her daughters, repeating something she'd said to them—was making the effort, really for my sake, to speak as a good mother speaks, with gracious tolerance for what cannot be prevented.

I said that Linda was a very fine person, and turned away, crying as discreetly as I could. Almost everything in my life seemed to be askew, and I desperately wanted help from someplace. From *her*? Apparently, preposterous as it was.

She rummaged in her purse until she found a clean, lace-edged handkerchief which she pressed into my hand. "Now, Dale. Is anything the matter?"

"That's okay," I said. "I'm under a certain amount of stress right now. Don't worry, I'll be fine."

"Take care of yourself. That stress can be a hidden killer. They had a program for us, with a nurse and a psychologist, and talked all about it."

I got out of there as gracefully as I could, not remembering until I'd reached the car that I'd forgotten to mention the Prosperine papers. Grandma had walked me to the front desk and embraced me at the door, physically a dry husk or scrap, yet so clear and definite and tenacious in spirit that as I drove away I was able to banish any superstitious uneasiness I might have felt about the shock I'd given her by telling myself she could easily go on for at least another decade.

I felt she'd bestowed her blessing at the last, the way she'd kissed me on both cheeks, though the words she'd pronounced were only those customary in our family when anyone set out on a long car trip: "Drive carefully. Be sure and wear your seatbelt."

The several hells of lesbian divorce are well and widely known. There's the hell of getting dumped and the one of doing the dumping (at times these roles are somewhat arbitrarily assigned). Most of us, by the time we reach our thirties, have witnessed or even directly participated in enough such debacles to suspect what's in the offing when the worm begins to gnaw in earnest at our own rosy domestic apple; yet, females that we are, constitutionally opposed to the harsh ruptures that beset emotional life, we can cling to our feckless hopes for a long time.

Frequently at the beginning of the process comes an isolated moment of stark clarity, which allows us to glimpse as though in a satellite photograph the complete terrain of our suffering and exile. Or the signs may be subtler: a familiar room suddenly looks blurry, as though its walls were being reduced to their naked molecules, space visible between the whirling atoms—and this is an accurate foreboding, for before many months are out the home that contained that room will have ceased to be home for us. Yet still to come are the weary days in the wilderness; we must slog overland to arrive at the disaster, picking our way through fantastic landscapes of rage and reconciliation. And all along the way we reassure ourselves that no two troubled relationships are ever precisely the same, that spontaneous cures are observed occasionally in the deadliest of cancers. And surely, too, the vast archive of previously accumulated experience in these matters must be good for something? Surely we'll be wiser than Jane Doe and Sue Smith, that notorious couple from Westchester NOW who ended up punching each other out on the sidewalk in front of the courtroom where their property dispute had landed them? Maybe if a parting of the ways isn't to be avoided, we can at least turn out like Liz and Mehitabel, that legendary pair who broke up following a fourteen-year relationship and remain the best of friends.

When in fact there's no halting the smashup whose time has come. Down the slippery slope we plunge, frantically pumping the brake, brave smiles glued to our faces. We're "working things out," we say, in couple counseling. Probably even strengthening the relationship in the process.

At the bottom of that hill, it's a lot like history. Over and over, and nobody ever learns.

After all this time, I can still look at how Linda and I broke up in a number of different ways. At times I'm convinced that if Valerie hadn't come along just then, there would have been someone else; Linda would have invented her. That interpretation is grim but heartening in its determinism, which acquits me of responsibility. Then again it occurs to me that perhaps my lover got in over her head—after all, there's something compelling in the role of faithless bitch, a logic and momentum that have been known to run away with the most well-meaning and domestically inclined among us, once we've given in to a stray anarchic urge. When I see it this way, I'm inclined to reproach myself with having given up too easily. Perhaps I simply grew weary, like a mountain climber who, having survived a dangerous fall, spends hours clinging to some crevice in the rock, then suddenly realizes that the immediately attainable cessation of pain is more attractive than the distant hope of survival, and plunges to her destruction. This is tragic, but with tragedy's consolations —high drama and deep meaning.

Then there's the pedestrian, therapeutic view: everything is everybody's fault. I know it could be argued plausibly that we'd begun breaking up a long time before, possibly as early as the moment when Fiona arrived on our New Jersey doorstep with her society girl smile caged behind her gleaming braces, and with all her ferocious needs.

I have a blurred, partial memory of the awful several months when we were engaged (as I bitterly joked to Bonnie) in "deconstructing" the relationship, exposing all its contradictions with a vengeance, stripping it down to the foundations. Some of the vagueness of my recollections must be due to the drinking I was doing at the time, and some, I suspect, to the curtain of numbness that descends in the wake of major disasters. I do know that we had an unusually lovely late summer and early autumn on the east coast that year, sunny and hot yet not too humid, with just enough rainfall to keep the yards from drying out. Our garden, tended by a neighbor during Linda's beach stay, kept producing and producing: glossy purple baby eggplants, pattypan squash, beefsteak tomatoes swollen like fattened capons. Linda and I canned tomatoes and bickered through the steam, yelled as we mixed the batter to make zucchini bread, wept in fury as we sliced even rows of corn kernels off the ear for parboiling and freezing in ziplock bags. Bad as things were, neither one of us could bear to waste the fruits of our most successful garden ever. I'd picked up a couple of adjunct courses in the CUNY system, miserably paid and just for the semester, but they allowed time for domestic strife and meticulous food processing.

We made love furiously, too, those last weeks, trying to prove something. Linda was seeing Valerie, though on a strictly limited schedule which we'd negotiated and in our madness written down. I'd never experienced such intense sexual jealousy before, and was disoriented and humiliated to discover that not even my memories of having been on the opposite side of the equation several times in the past seemed to help me cope now. Valerie and I met once, in the office of Linda's and my couple therapist, who'd suggested that the three of us try coming in together. She was a tall, mild-mannered butch with crisp hair I identified as "auburn" when I saw it—a word from romantic novels. I told my friends she looked as though she might recently have graduated from a boys' military academy. She had an upperclass niceness and defenselessness about her which infuriated me, as did her habit of cracking her knuckles across her knees and some outrageously naive remark she let slip about homeless people. The thought that my lover was risking all our deep, rich past for this shallow child filled me with grief and rage and hate.

Right up until the very last fight we were still saying we had hopes of working things out. But Linda also insisted she couldn't be monogamous at the moment, due to this accident of how she felt about Val, and finally there was no way for me to read that sentiment (especially in someone who'd always been so much on the side of tradition before this) except as a message of departure. Things got to the point where I wasn't even sure anymore whether I really wanted her; I only knew I couldn't bear how she was leaving me, and couldn't stand myself trying to stop her. There came a Tuesday morning after a sleepless Monday night when I caught the express bus to Manhattan and within three hours found myself signing a lease on an outrageously expensive closet of a studio apartment on Hester Street on the Lower East Side.

Grandma was in the hospital at the time. I'd found out from Mother several days before. She'd been feeling weak and dizzy, unable to eat. The doctors suspected a touch of phlebitis as well, but it didn't sound serious, not nearly as bad as the respiratory infection she'd fought off in the winter. Mother didn't seem particularly alarmed, and in the midst of my confusion over what to tell her about Linda and me (in the end, I put off the announcement), I missed some of the details. As my own crisis unfolded, I almost forgot about Grandma.

The day after I rented the apartment, I returned to Jersey late in the evening, thoroughly exhausted. I'd spent the past ten hours dealing with the building super, getting keys made, having a gas leak fixed, and buying curtain rods and dish drainers. Now I'd made up my mind, I was determined to get the hell out of my old life as quickly as possible. When I arrived back at the house I found a note from Linda under a magnet on the refrigerator. It said that Fiona was sleeping over at a friend's. She herself was in her office and would spend the night there on the couch: I wasn't to disturb her. She had some time free in the morning, between eight and ten, which we could use to go over financial matters. My mother had called at four in the afternoon, and would like me to call back as soon as I got in.

Even though I wasn't surprised by the peremptory tone of Linda's note (she'd already shown signs of trying to establish herself as an equally injured party), it naturally rankled, so the last part of the message took a minute to sink in. When it did, I felt worried. I called right away, but kept getting a busy signal.

I finally reached Mother, and she spoke to me in a calm and gentle voice that reminded me I was still somebody's child. Grandma, she said, had died early that morning. A nurse making a routine check of vital signs had discovered she wasn't breathing, and by that time she'd apparently been "gone" long enough to make any effort at resuscitation futile.

Which meant she was cold already, I concluded—not that they'd have put it that way.

Mother added that the doctors didn't seem quite sure what exactly she'd died from. Not that this mattered much to anyone except Uncle

Gene, who kept muttering about professional standards and diagnostic incompetence—which was, she thought, simply his personal way of handling grief. She was just grateful it had happened this way, without a prolonged illness, and was content with the old-fashioned phrase "died of old age." Aunt Geri felt the same way. Geri would feel it most since she'd always been the closest of the children to Grandma, but she was coping the way she usually did, throwing herself into organizing things.

"When's the funeral? I'm flying out," I heard myself announce.

Mother, who'd long ago given up trying to elicit from me the conventional signs and symbols of family fealty which seemed to come much more easily to Jennifer and my brothers, now indicated I shouldn't go to any such lengths. She knew how busy I was, what with my new job. (Such was the completely spurious excuse which I'd used to justify my recent communication lapses.)

"She's *my* grandmother. I'm definitely coming." As I hung up and began dialing the airlines, the sense of loss I felt was all mixed up with anger. They were trying to shut me out, it seemed to me. Linda had shut me out, and I was losing the house too. (We hadn't even discussed whether I should be the one to move out; it had just never occurred to me to handle it any other way.) I'd lost my improvised family, didn't fit in my fated one. I felt orphaned, abandoned—and guiltily aware of my failure to write or call Grandma, except for one birthday card, in the time since I'd left Minnesota.

After I'd located someone to cover my Friday class, I went to my desk and retrieved from a towering pile of unanswered correspondence the last letter I'd received from her. Written in early September, it described the party Aunt Geri had organized at the end of August for her ninety-first birthday. *Very nice, tho of course not such a 'gala' as my 90th. Good cake from Epler's, attractive decoration, pink and red roses. Fruit punch and cookies. Several friends invited, plus relatives. Phoebe gave me a tea cozy she made in crafts class, which fits my teapot to a 'T'! Ha, ha. Write and let me hear what you are doing. You and room-mate.*

Room-mate. I laughed bitterly, then sobbed for half an hour, not bothering to stifle the sound. "Room-mate" was out in the converted garage; I didn't even have the consolation of sharing with her the obscure joke, which seemed to be on me. Had Grandma repressed everything

I'd told her, or was the reference to "room-mate" her oblique acknowledgement? I'd never know now.

That night I lay awake for a long time in the heavy, wide bed that had been Linda's and Michael's, then Linda's and mine, and which I couldn't wait to exchange for a simple, streamlined futon. Dazed by painful changes, my mind wandered, caught in the vast space between secure worlds, rather as I imagined Grandma herself lost and wandering between earth and the hereafter. I told myself there would be excitement in seeing how my next incarnation was going to turn out, but all I could feel was cold, empty fear at the thought of leaving behind every sure point of reference. I had broken up before, but this would be my first divorce. And Grandma's would be the first funeral I'd attended in my adult life.

*She'd said to drive carefully, be sure and buckle up.* They were all like that, weren't they, the Brights and Schlaghoffers, so cautious and hopeful and striving. And what a tinny paradise they'd built with their unceasing toil. Just like the fairytales in which, by way of punishment, the wish wished in ignorance comes true.

*Did Grandma know?* Suppose she *had* known, had detected at some point along the way the futility of it all, the dead end that awaited at the top of the ascent which she'd begun in the yard behind the farmhouse, where like Amaryllis she must often have lain in the hammock made of bedsprings and plotted a way out? Wouldn't *that* make a story?

But then I remembered how contemptuously she'd dismissed Sharon Decoteaux, mocking her light complexion. My relative was of the conquering race, all right.

Before I finally took a second sleeping pill, I'd made up my mind: when I returned from Minnesota, I was going to bring with me the Prosperine papers, or what I could carry of them. And I didn't care how pushy I'd have to be about it.


Mother and I had scheduled our arrival times within half an hour of each other, and were to be met by Aunt Geri at one of the ticket counters. My flight arrived first. I found my aunt waiting. She was scribbling in pencil on a yellow legal pad, trying to finish an obituary, she explained. She looked weary, sad, and dauntless as she recited the details of some complicated misunderstanding involving Dr. Jerebold and another minister, the pastor of Grandma and Grandpa's old church,

Reverend Bartlett Henry. Grandma had been clear that she wanted Reverend Henry to conduct her funeral services, just as he had Grandpa's. But something Uncle Gene had said to Jerebold on the phone just after she died had apparently given him the idea that *he* was being asked. Things had gotten very sticky.

Ordinarily, Aunt Geri said, she wouldn't have had the least hesitation about setting him straight, in a polite way, of course. But he was a peculiar kind of man, with a reputation for touchiness, and Grandma's recent fame as a writer apparently had impressed him. He might take offense at being passed over, especially since there was a long history of rivalry between Grace Methodist, Reverend Henry's church, and First Presbyterian, where he himself had been pastor. The inconvenient fact of the matter was that Uncle Bert had an ailing aunt whom the family was moving heaven and earth to get admitted to the Hill on a priority basis, and it would be a shame to jeopardize that.

Here she interrupted herself, impetuously exclaiming, "My mother is dead! Isn't this absurd? Rose Schlaghoffer has come to a screeching halt after ninety-one years, and here I am worrying about offending an old fart like that Jerebold!" She began to cry, which seemed natural enough; it was the language that unnerved me, it was so out of character.

She was drying her eyes when Mother showed up. It was almost a year since I'd seen her, and she looked older than I'd anticipated, her body subtly thickened, her soft features inundated by wrinkles. I wondered if she'd be looking at me the same way, noticing all my grey hair and the bags under my eyes that no longer disappeared with a good night's sleep.

She hugged me hard, then turned to her sister. The two of them embraced in the cautious yet tender way I expected. They drew back, each groping in her purse for a facial tissue. As they blew their upturned noses and dabbed beneath their bifocals, their movements were so precisely correlated that I remembered two cats I'd once had who'd been litter mates, and used to sit side by side in identical postures, turning their heads in unison as they responded to a sound.

"How was your flight, Cele?"

"Overbooked, like everything these days. That's why we were late, it took them forever to board. They were offering free tickets if you'd switch to another flight, and you know, for a minute I actually considered

211

it. I mean, I caught myself thinking, that ticket is worth hundreds of dollars! Isn't that terrible?"

"Depression babies never change," Aunt Geri laughed. Suddenly the two of them looked rather happy.

After a stop to drop off the obituary, which Mother had edited in the airport parking lot, we drove back to Geri's. Aunt Leslie was sitting at the kitchen table talking to Aunt Judy, who was wearing a new raspberry-colored aerobic exercise outfit and brand name walking shoes, her grey-blonde locks fresh from the hair salon. In the midst of the hellos the phone rang; Aunt Geri took it and announced that Allison was on her way over.

My elders soon arranged themselves around a plate of cookies and started discussing how best to handle Dr. Jerebold. I took my bag upstairs to the guest bedroom, which I was to share with Mother. I should have been glad that the Schlaghoffer sisters were doing their thing, since this made it unnecessary for me to give an accounting of myself, for the time being at least. Instead I felt utterly depressed, and wondered why I'd come. I lay down on the bed with a novel I'd brought along, some sort of detective story with a lesbian heroine, but found I couldn't concentrate enough to follow the plot. When Allison's voice drifted up to me I put the book away and went downstairs again.

My cousin and I ended up taking a walk down quiet residential streets, under the great flaming maples that stirred my heart with the lie of ancient, innocent pioneer Minnesota, the crispness in the air foretelling legendary snows. She told me she was fine, just about recovered, really, though she still got tired out and had to rest every day. She'd had quite a scare of course, but on a certain level the brush with death had been useful for her. Now she felt more ready to make commitments. She and Basil were going to live together, and in a few months when she'd gotten her strength back, she (she said "we") would start trying to get pregnant.

"Good for you," I said, semi-sincerely, forgiving her even the pronoun. She looked to have gained five or ten pounds, and had lost the languid grace that had irritated me back in July.

Before we reached the house again, she volunteered that Grandma had spoken of me the day she'd been admitted to the hospital.

"Oh? What did she say?"

"Something about her 'book,' how pleased she was you were helping her with it. I remember her sort of hinting she hoped you might go ahead and do something with it even if anything happened to her before she got it finished."

"Her literary executor, huh? I'm afraid that's kind of a heavy assignment," I grumbled, glad she'd thought of me, nonetheless. Give me Prosperine, I bargained with the Goddess. Give me Prosperine and I'll finish Grandma's book.

That was a strange day, with all the habits of privacy and industry which normally prevailed in my family's separate households temporarily in abeyance as we huddled together. It almost looked as though the laws of gravity had changed overnight now Grandma was gone, I thought— and wondered whether in fact it was a woman we'd gathered to mourn, or rather some central orienting point, some guiding principle in relation to which we were unconsciously accustomed to place ourselves, which in disappearing had caused us to implode in this uncharacteristic fashion, clustered around the formica-topped table drinking coffee and eating sugar as the October light dwindled. We might have been mistaken for the gregarious denizens of some warm-weather culture where the women of the extended family were used to daily comings and goings beneath a single roof (though shouldn't we have babies playing around our feet?). It was almost cozy, somehow comforting. New Jersey mercifully receded.

After a while Uncle Bert came home, and then a tall bearded man in overalls with a pot belly and shiny bald crown was shuffling through the leaves in the driveway, and this was the famous Basil. He'd already won acceptance as Allison's current mate, I could see from the offhand way Aunt Geri greeted him. We took three cars and drove over to Gene and Judy's, where my uncles drank Scotch and defiantly so did I, though none of the other women had more than a light beer, and we ate roast beef and iceberg lettuce salad. Then Mother and Geri followed their hostess into the kitchen to help clean up (Basil offered assistance but was politely turned down), and before I knew it Aunt Les had vanished in there too, behind the cute Dutch doors. When I went to make a pot of decaf I found the Schlaghoffer sisters enveloped in a thick atmosphere all their own. There seemed to be one mood shared among the three, and it changed in quick pulses, veering from the "slap-happy" (their word) to the somber and reflective. When Aunt Geri cracked a glass it was

Mother who cried, and then together they retold the well-worn story of Grandma's serving platter.

When the coffee had dripped I took the pot in to Allison and the men, who were now in the living room. Uncle Bert reared up from his chair like a snake in the grass and bared his fangs at me. "We were just discussing what you'd call that grouping in there," he chuckled, "How about 'coven'? Would that be a good word?" I handed him his coffee, accompanied by a look I hoped would suggest the merited rebuke which I was too tired to deliver.

"Give it a rest, Dad," Allison said sharply, and amazingly, he did.

Later that night in the room we were sharing, I had my talk with Mother. I felt pressure to get the confession of failure over with. She was undressing when she gave me my opening, turning away from me to lift her white nylon slip quickly over her small grey head before unhooking her bra. "So how's the new job, Dale?" she inquired, reaching for her nightie, which I knew she would put on before removing her underpants. "How's Linda doing? We haven't heard much about her and Fiona lately. She still making out with that literary business?"

"The agency is fine. We're separating, though." I'd prepared the phrasing, and "we're separating" sounded calm to me, controlled. "Actually, I've rented an apartment in Manhattan. I wanted to wait to tell you until we had a little more time."

"Oh." A sigh, a wounded sound, I thought, escaped from beneath the nightgown, but when Mother's head emerged and she turned to look at me, she'd regained control. "I'm sorry to hear that. I did *like* Linda."

I realized it was probably true. It hadn't been the case with other lovers of mine, and I'd never thought about it very much, but it sounded plausible when she said it. And just my luck, at that.

She asked hesitantly, "Are you *sure* this is final?"

I felt the same despair I always felt. Why was it so impossible to communicate to her some approximate notion of my life's chaotic texture? I tried from time to time, but half-heartedly. Eventually I always gave up and substituted a version so schematic, so conventionalized, that it became a half-lie. I'd let her think of Linda and me as married, living quietly in the suburbs. Now I was paying for it.

I needed to cry, but couldn't in front of her. She'd have me then, I thought. I'd never get away.

"I tried," I said. "I stayed...as long as I possibly could."

"Well, of course I'd like to know anything you feel like telling me about it, but I'm not pressuring you."

Her tact was heartbreaking. I wished I could escape. At the same time, I wanted to stay. She still meant safety to me, at some impossibly primitive level. "I'd like to talk to you about it sometime, but right now I'm still trying to sort things out. I guess I'm not quite ready."

"If there's anything I can do...." She snapped off the light. "Even a loan or anything, while you're getting set up. I know this must be especially difficult with your career situation kind of up in the air. Why don't you think about coming out to see us for a couple of weeks when you can take the time off? It could be a break for you. Maybe it's silly, but I don't really like to think of you moving back to New York by yourself. Is it a safe neighborhood?"

There'd been a drug-related murder there the day I signed the lease. "Perfectly safe," I said.

As usual these days, it took me hours to fall asleep. Toward morning I woke sobbing silently, the pillowcase soaked. It was Prosperine Munkers I was mourning for, so beautiful and young and wrathful and despairing, who'd thrown herself into the coffin on top of Grandma and the roses.

I got up the next morning in a curious mood: dry, detached, bemused, I felt like a visitor to the family. Especially after that dream, the funeral was anticlimactic. Cruel Calvinism would have suited me, but all we got from either of the ministers was watery reassurance. Reverend Henry addressed a group of more than fifty at Grace Methodist, and about half of those continued on out to the suburban cemetery where Grandpa Eugene had been buried ten years before. Here Dr. Jerebold pronounced a few graveside platitudes, according to the clever compromise Aunt Geri had negotiated, and Reverend Henry offered another wimpy prayer. Then the coffin was quickly lowered into the narrow trench, at the head of which the grey stone marker already bore Grandma's name and date of birth beside Grandpa's name and dates; there was no epitaph. We straggled irresolutely back to the cars, leaving the rest to several young Black men in checked hunting caps who'd stood leaning on shovels on the sidelines, waiting for us to finish. It was another impeccable October day (all that week was clear and fine, in fact), Indian summer like a warm gold drapery subtly shot through with threads of ice and snow when the flat mother-of-pearl-tinted clouds winged across the sun.

My sharpest memory is of Amaryllis. It was the last time I saw her; she had a stroke in January, and died the following month. That day she carried herself very straight in a high-necked black dress, a quiet rebuke to the laxity of youngsters like me, who wore brown or navy blue. Her small black pillbox hat was hung with a strip of black veiling. I didn't speak to her, but I can still see her walking back to the black car, carefully picking her way across the turf in her patent high heels. Uncle Gene gripped her elbow like a Boy Scout, all solemn and double-chinned in a tight three-piece suit.

In the evening we had a family gathering back at Aunt Geri's (a "Methodist wake," Uncle Bert joked). Amaryllis called and excused herself, saying she had to rest, but most of the other relatives were present, along with a few friends my mother's age and slightly older who'd belonged to her church or had been neighbors of hers and Grandpa's. Phoebe was there too, the lone envoy from the Hill. Allison and Aunt Leslie had fixed some complicated foods which Aunt Geri supplemented with nacho chips and cold cuts. Allison and Basil, whose idea it was to have a sort of do-it-yourself memorial, had asked participants either to "share" some brief memory of Grandma, or else to read a poem or other short piece of writing expressive of their feelings. (It seemed to me that Basil was trying awfully hard—he'd barely known Grandma— but he explained that his own family had done something similar when his grandfather died, and they'd found it helpful in "working through their grief.") This part of the evening fell a bit flat, since most of the older people, the men especially, were reluctant and self-conscious. I ended up reading a section from Grandma's *Woman's Estate* piece, though in fact my morning detachment had congealed into a hard, dissenting mood in which it would have suited me better to have read the scalding letter in which Proppie bade farewell to her Rose.

In the end, Phoebe's contribution redeemed the awkward ceremony. To everyone's surprise she delivered a heartfelt, humbly eloquent little speech in which she evoked the brevity of human existence, even for someone with her friend's unusual span of years. "We don't live as we ought," she declared, "I'm sure none of us do. We ought to treasure every moment on this earth, and we waste so much time, and there's so much folly and unkindness! But Rose Schlaghoffer tried her best every day. In my book Rose was a far greater woman than most of those you read about, or see on TV. She did what she could."

At the end of the "sharing" I was dumbfounded when Aunt Geri came over and presented me with a small package tied with red ribbon. "I wrapped that up for you," she explained. "It's a present from Grandma. She spoke to me about wanting you to have it, one of the last times I saw her. Go ahead, open it."

Inside on a square of white cotton was the silver locket that had been a gift from Prosperine. It took me a minute to remember how the thing

217

opened, but finally I worked the tiny clasp, and there was my girl all right, surrounded by the finely braided wreath of light hair.

"Isn't that exquisite," Mother breathed. "Who can she be, all dolled up like that?"

"That's Mother's friend from Normal School, Prosperine What's-Her-Name," Aunt Geri explained. "Remember, Dale, how Grandma showed this to us on the day of the reading at the Hill? She told me where to find it in her room."

I wanted to know what Grandma had said, exactly.

"Let me think. I guess she mentioned appreciating your help with her book. I got the sense she wanted you to have something—well, like she gave to the other girls when they got married. You know. She said, 'I guess she isn't going to get married now,' or words to that effect." My aunt looked uncomfortable, and I wondered if more had been said. Certainly I remembered the much-publicized business of the symbolic dowry, which had rankled for quite a while though I always told myself I had no use for dark old furniture and femmy jewelry. Now, as I allowed Mother to hang the locket around my neck like a medal I'd earned in the family wars, I suddenly felt happy. It seemed to me that the gift was a good omen.

"Too bad," Aunt Geri was saying, evidently still uneasy, "that the girls that married soonest got the nicest heirlooms."

"But there's nothing I'd rather have had from her than this." I even felt good enough not to be disturbed by Uncle Bert, who popped out of his study just as I was on my way to the bathroom. He seemed to be out of sorts, his thin grey hair awry, malice tugging at the corners of his mouth. I remembered a snapshot, taken in my infancy, in which the family is gathered on a beach; he possesses the crewcut, predatory beauty of a young rocket scientist.

"Reminds me of Queen Victoria's funeral in there," he remarked.

"With stuffed mushrooms and corn chips? I don't see the parallel."

"End of an era," he shrugged. "Heads of state gathered. Twilight of the empire. All downhill from here."

"Let's just hope a major war doesn't break out."

" 'The worlds revolve like ancient women gathering fuel in vacant lots.' " He lobbed the quote like a grenade. "Care to join me for a drink? I noticed the other day you fancy my brand. Just so you don't betray me

218

to that howling mob of teetotalers in there."

He's had a few already, I thought. Well, I wanted one too, so I followed him into his lair. I enjoyed the sense that together we were subverting something, and didn't that much mind being a sounding board for his obliquely expressed grievances against Grandma, who'd dared to judge him, Bertram Ahrens, as she judged everyone and everything that touched her flesh and blood. (He'd measured up better than most, actually, but that wasn't quite the point.) We sat together for half an hour, flouting her rule of sobriety, until I said I thought I'd better rejoin the group.

After the Scotch I felt a little better, but I could tell that the lack of sleep and thoughts of what I faced at home were beginning to slow the momentum that had gotten me through the funeral. I returned to the living room and got a plate of food and stood on the sidelines watching my relatives and their guests, and what I saw was a party—a sedate, boring party, it's true, but a party nonetheless, a festival of the living—and it struck me as terribly peculiar that the guest of honor not only was absent, but in fact was out spending her first night alone under the topsoil of what probably used to be a cornfield or potato patch somewhere near Edina.

When Aunt Geri asked if I'd mind taking her car and driving Phoebe back to Fellowship Hill, I leaped at the chance to get out of the house. What a treat to breathe the chilly, unpeopled night air, to feel like a grownup for a change, zipping down the freeway behind the wheel of a Toyota Tercel with a mere ten thousand miles on it!

I told my passenger how much I'd liked the things she'd had to say about Grandma earlier in the evening. Then it seemed natural to mention what Grandma had said to me about the importance of their friendship. I hinted at her fears about Arnie Luckenbill's possible disruptive influence.

Phoebe, though shy, was surprisingly forthright. "Mr. L. and I spoke this afternoon. Matrimony was referred to once or twice. 'Course I told him it was way too soon to think of such a thing, with Rose scarcely buried. We'd have to do a lot of talking it over, anyway, first. But he does see something in me, that's a fact."

"And I take it you see something in him?"

"Well, you could say that." She was obviously pleased. "I won't pretend it isn't nice to be paid a little attention to, on the part of the opposite sex. It's not as if I've got to think about any of those practical things, like would he make a good father or provider. That's all over and done with.

"Of course I had my intuitions what was going through his mind, but I never would have let him bring up the subject while Rose was alive, knowing how she felt about it."

"Not even mention it?" I was amazed at such loyalty.

"Rose was the best friend I've had in thirty years," Phoebe declared passionately. "She had her likes and dislikes. You had to adjust to that. You get so lonely at that age, there's nobody left. I only showed her the same consideration I'd have wanted for myself. Oh, it will never be the same with Rose Schlaghoffer gone."

When we arrived at the Hill I parked the car and walked her slowly through the deserted corridors. Her expression was bleak, and I expected tears, but by the time we reached her door she'd perked up a little, and remarked with obvious satisfaction that she hadn't been out this late in she didn't know when. We'd just made it in before the ten o'clock curfew, after which you were supposed to call in and notify the staff of your whereabouts.

I kissed her and teasingly told her to be sure and send me a wedding invitation. As I hiked out to the silent parking lot, I remembered that I'd been intending to give Ruta a call. I'd try to manage that tomorrow, I decided—maybe even run over and see her—depending on how many details I still had to take care of following the discussion about the papers which I planned to have with Mother and Aunt Geri over breakfast.

I'd had quite a bit of Bert's Scotch, and was careful about my driving. When I reached the house, however, I somehow managed to overlook the erratic angle at which Basil's battered Valiant was parked in the driveway, and as I pulled in beside it, I scraped the side of Geri's car. I leaped out, bitterly cursing family and fate, to discover a nasty gash six or eight inches long.

The ensuing drama of recrimination and forgiveness—the former silent but palpable, the latter loud and unconvincing—took up the rest of the evening and extended into the following day, rather wrecking the atmosphere in which I'd planned to broach the subject of the Prosperine papers. At least I didn't feel I had to be so careful now. Almost surely I could have everything I wanted; the main question was how to get it as quickly as possible. How fortunate that it was all still in boxes and not in some collection!

While Mother and I were eating our Bran Flakes, and Aunt Geri, who'd breakfasted with Bert, was waiting for the repair shop to call back, I started out in a general way. "Grandma left so many papers, her own and other people's. Maybe we ought to talk about what to do with them."

"Goodness," my aunt interrupted, "that reminds me. There was something I've been meaning to tell you and Cele. It was the strangest thing, too. I can't believe I completely forgot about it, just like that. Maybe I'm losing my marbles." With a puzzled look on her face she got up to open the sliding glass door for the dog, who was signalling his desire to be admitted by running a large, sloppy tongue back and forth along the pane. "Darn that Lurch," she swore, "I'll have to get the Windex."

"Tell us what?" I prodded, in a rush to get on with it.

"Actually, Cele, I'd even sat down to write you a letter, but I never got it finished." She bent to get the Windex from beneath the kitchen sink, interrupting her narrative. "I wish somebody would invent some support services for families of old dogs. He's in and out of here thirty times a day. . . . At the time, you know, I thought of it simply as a whim, one of those ideas she'd been getting more and more strongly lately, that you couldn't argue with. Like people who keep changing their wills. You certainly couldn't say she didn't have a right to do what she wanted with her own things, though it bothered me at the time."

Suddenly I didn't like what I was hearing at all.

"What bothered you, Ger?" Mother urged, sensing my distress.

"Well, she wanted me to burn a bunch of papers."

"You didn't!"

Her guilty look answered me: the stricken expression of a conscientious child watching disaster emerge in the wake of some well-meaning action. "I really didn't see any way around it. You'd have to understand how she was about this, fixated almost. She just called me up one morning, and she wouldn't let me go until I'd promised to drive over there and pick her up with the things—well, some of them she had with her, anyway. Then she came back to the house with me and watched the whole time. She wouldn't take my word for it, no sir! We did it out back in the brick barbecue. She'd figured that out herself, that this was the best place, rather than the fireplace indoors, which I'd have suggested—it was a raw, blustery, nasty kind of afternoon, nothing like this week's weather. She sat out there in one of the lawn chairs, all muffled up. It was creepy.

"And I felt so peculiar, almost as though I was committing some crime, destroying evidence or something. Though she had every right."

"What *papers* did you burn?" But I knew. Oh, I knew.

"Lots of notebooks, diaries, what have you. Some were hard to get started, I had to use the charcoal lighter. Bert was unhappy about the mess I made—some of the diary-type volumes, the covers never did completely burn, and the ashes have a peculiar smell. From the glue, maybe, I don't know. Then there were some letters. Those of course were easier."

"Letters from your attic?"

"How did you know? She made me go up there with her and hunt through such a lot of boxes. She dragged herself up all those stairs, I couldn't stop her. Then a few days later when she was hospitalized, I thought maybe the strain of all that might have had something to do with it. But at the time I didn't see what else to do."

"How could you?" I stormed. "Of all the senseless waste—"

"Dale," Mother murmured uneasily.

"You didn't even ask her what they were, or why she was burning them? You just followed orders?"

"Believe me, it wasn't all that easy to question her just then. Cele, you'll know what I mean if I say she gave me something like what we kids used to call her 'eagle eye,' only ten times fiercer. It was really almost like she had some kind of supernatural strength—I guess she must have had to, to make an effort like that. I did sort of try to ask whether she didn't think they might have some value to somebody someday, and she only glared at me, or rather *through* me, as though I was obviously one of the bigger fools going, and said she guessed she'd been thinking it over long enough to know what she was doing, and there was such a thing as the right to privacy, even for an old woman living in an old folks' home. I never heard her like that about the Hill, either. 'Geraldine,' she said, 'I'll never ask another thing of you,' and that was awful somehow, it sounded like a threat. Come to think of it, I suppose it was about the last thing she did ask.

"You couldn't have budged her then. I guess I know her well enough.

"She said something else, just before we got started. I think she said, 'She'll understand,' or maybe it was, 'She'd understand'—I didn't hear clear enough to be sure which it was. And I asked who she meant, but she never did answer, only pointed to the lighter fluid so I'd get on with it—remember, Cele, how she'd do that when we were kids, just point to something she wanted you to do when you started to give her backtalk?"

"Do I ever! My, what a shame, though."

"You really didn't have any idea whose papers they were?" My tone said *you idiot*.

"Well, I knew they weren't family stuff—it wasn't her writing, or Dad's, and obviously nobody up on the farm would have gone to all that effort. I did remember you'd mentioned that gal you were interested in, that Prosperine. But I mean, the things *were* Mother's."

"They were not hers!" I cried in a dry fury. "They were Prosperine Munkers' life's work! She went to 'all that effort,' as you put it, because she had something to say and was bound to get it heard. Her writing belonged to all of us—anyone who could use it. Don't anybody tell me Grandma had the right!"

Clutching their toast, my companions stared, bodies stiffened against my tirade. I pitied them, faces grey and vulnerable without their ceremonial lipstick armor.

"Are we sure they were *all* destroyed?" Mother typically tried to soothe. "She might have overlooked something."

"After a bonfire like that? Don't kid yourself. You know how Grandma was; I'm sure she accomplished precisely what she set out to do."

"But why?" Mother pressed. "I'm not sure I see why she'd—"

"Do you really want to know?"

"Of course."

"Because Prosperine Munkers was a lesbian radical, a communist rabble rouser, and Grandma sold her farmer girl soul for a place in middle-class heaven. Because the two of them were lovers at one time—in a literal sense I think, though I can't be positive, but there was definitely a romance. And Grandma ditched her to marry Grandpa, and seventy years later still didn't want to think about what that did to Prosperine. And because it was the last control she had.

"If you ask me, she wanted to own the future. If she'd been a movie star or president, I don't suppose she could have given more thought to

223

her posthumous reputation. And deep down, she was a pessimist. Unlike Prosperine, she didn't believe we could use too much truth. Though you've got to hand it to her, she didn't just lie—I guess she actually tried to experience her life the way she wanted to present it to the world. What she couldn't fix that way, she tried to cover up."

"She was born in the nineteenth century," Mother pleaded.

"She had to know how badly I wanted those papers. Talk about handing out stones instead of bread!" With a short, sharp jerk I succeeded in ripping the locket on its slender chain from around my neck.

"Dale, she was ill."

"She wasn't herself."

I slammed the locket down on the table and headed for the stairs.

Up in the guest bedroom I began furiously stuffing my suitcase with the clothing that festooned my unmade bed. After a minute I went to listen at the half-open door. "I wouldn't go up there now," I heard from Mother. "Let things simmer down a bit." Then a sound of scraping chairs, the table being cleared, the dishwasher loaded. "It is a shame about those papers, though."

A muffled sound from my aunt, perhaps of protest or distress.

"I'm not saying you handled it badly, Ger. I certainly can't imagine what I'd have done, and how were you to know they might have been valuable?"

"She *had* to know how I felt," I repeated to myself, shutting the door and flopping down on the bed with the feeling that I never wanted to get up.

An hour later I of course apologized. Mother and Geri of course forgave me; all of us, they said, were liable to be easily upset at an upsetting time like this. Mother offered to have the locket chain repaired by a jeweler in Seattle who did that kind of work, and I didn't object. I called the airline and managed to get my reservation switched to an earlier flight, one that left around noon. Geri drove me to the airport in Bert's Volvo, while Mother followed in the scraped and dented Toyota, which they planned to leave in the shop on the way home.

By the time they dropped me off, I'd calmed down enough to feel sheepish about my outburst. I was glad to be getting away from the family atmosphere which so recently had come as a relief from the rest of my life, glad to be someplace where I could, without embarrassment, have a drink at this hour. I had only carry-on luggage, and with plenty of time before the plane I decided to call Ruta from the bar.

I reached her, all right, but she seemed preoccupied; I had to repeat my name three times before she sounded certain who I was. I knew I ought to say a quick goodbye, but couldn't resist telling her what had happened to the papers.

"A pity," she remarked objectively. "She must have been a remarkable woman, though. It took a lot of courage to do what she did."

I thought she meant Prosperine. "And then to have her work go up in smoke like that—"

"Actually, I meant your grandmother."

I felt rather indignant. "I doubt I can forgive her. That was history the rest of us could have *used*."

"Ah, history." Ruta's tone had an edge to it. "History, what was history to your grandmother? She'd outlived the history she felt at home in."

"And Prosperine? Doesn't she have any rights?"

"She's been dead a long time, Prosperine. She's broken down to her elements—up there on the Iron Range, is it, where she's supposed to be buried? Nothing lasts forever, Dale, not even words."

This wasn't what I needed to hear.

"Has it ever occurred to you your grandmother may have been fighting for her life?"

"I don't understand."

"At her age, and living in that place, what did she really have that she could call her own? Wasn't the past the only thing, really?

"But you'll have to excuse me. One of the dogs is sick, and somebody's coming to take us to the vet. I hope you'll get in touch next time you're in town."

If I ever am, I thought bitterly. I ordered a second drink. My reflections were not pleasant. What had just happened here was bad enough. What awaited in New Jersey looked completely unbearable: seeing Linda, settling details, explaining to Fiona, the drudgery of moving, starting a new life from scratch. But seeing Linda, that was the main thing. Not having done it for several days, I felt out of shape for the misery of it. I just wanted to disappear magically from that house and not have to deal with her, not have to negotiate, not even have to acknowledge her existence.

At some point shortly before my flight was due to board, I found myself remembering what Ruta had said about Prosperine "breaking down to her elements." That's it, I thought, the Iron Range. I'll change my flight. I can use a credit card. I'll rent a car and drive up there tonight.

"The leaves will be mostly gone that far north," the woman behind the car rental counter warned me when I asked for a tourist map that included the Iron Range. I told her it was okay, I was going to visit someone. And she was right: as I ploughed into the sweet blue weather, speedometer steady on sixty-five, the flat country quickly changed from gold to brown. I was seeing cattails in the ditches, corn stubble in the fields, dead woodchucks and raccoons bloody on the shoulder despite the dearth of traffic. After a while I came to a place of low small hills and bony stands of birch thickly sprinkled with pine and spruce.

Perhaps it had been just about this time of year that Prosperine had traveled south by train when she left the Range after the strike was called off. It was an empty territory in an emptying season, and gradually its influence began to unclog my thoughts. I wished I knew the name of the tree which looked like an evergreen, but had needles turning the bold deciduous yellow of maple leaves back in the Cities. I was locked in an odd split second of karmic intimacy with a grey fieldmouse that darted almost directly beneath my wheels, each detail of its small perfect body bared to my vision in the moment before it vanished to a fate I couldn't make out in my rear view mirror. I saw everything clearly in that clean, clement light: how the dreaming earth lay stripped for the coming ordeal, yet bore the prospect lightly, each lingering leaf and insect stretched in the temporary warmth.

Not that my own mood was mellow or forgiving. I was inclined to collect details and hold them against the country: the UNBORN CHILDREN ARE PEOPLE TOO—THINK PRO-LIFE billboard, the small-town water tower boasting BARNUM, HOME OF THE

227

BOMBERS. Even the perfectly innocent Lutefisk and Meatball Supper advertised by the ladies of Pilgrim Lutheran Church somehow struck me as emblematic of the failures of an empire. As did the patrons of the truckstop where I ate: the bent, bald horse of a fellow, pate sprinkled with age spots, who upended a salt shaker over his dish of iceberg lettuce; the wattle-throated woman with eyes the tint of pre-washed denim, stoically forking up her mashed potatoes and brown gravy. The bustling waitresses with their dimples and well-worn jokes, "gabbing" comfortably with the diners, were what my mother and aunts might have been if Grandma had married a farmer. What a stupid life, I thought savagely. I was sure they were the ones who'd plastered the place with orange and black crepe paper and cutouts of witches and pumpkins for Halloween.

I climbed into the car and drove. The shadows were taking over. Every so often a single tree still covered with pure gold leaves stood out in the drab woods. In the rear view mirror the sun was going down, a blurt of light behind the stripped birches. I could drive till I blasted into Canada, I thought; but by the time I pulled into Virginia in the dark, around me the looming shapes of great earth-heaps the mines had left behind, I was exhausted and checked into the first motel I found.

I had a drink around the corner, took a sleeping pill, and slept. When I woke I felt slightly better. I turned in my room key and went cruising around town, taking note of the red terraced hills, the ambitiously laid out streets, and the solidly built Socialist Opera House, all of which Prosperine would have been familiar with. It happened to be Sunday, and I slowed down when I came to a Methodist church with its sermon topic and admissions policy falteringly emblazoned on a readerboard out front: WHO IS A SI NER? EVE YONE WEL OME. Curious to see how the question would be answered, I parked and followed the stragglers who were hurrying inside. I was wearing jeans and sneakers, but they did say "everyone."

As I entered, an usher handed me a dingy mimeo sheet which gave the order of service. The pews, I noted, were thinly populated, predominantly by women. The choir was incompetent, the organ out of tune. Not that I objected to the flavor of genteel poverty; I actually found something comforting in the efforts of the mothers to keep their children quiet, the unadorned strains of the Doxology, the humble cadence of the Our Father, and the quarters and worn dollar bills trickling into the collection plate. But things went rapidly downhill when the energetic young minister with a cowlick began to read out his scriptural passage in a modernized translation. His rambling sermon never mentioned evil or redemption, and by the time it petered out with some advice on how to "dialogue with God," sin seemed trite and trivial: not the indelible spot which blights the soul, but a sort of spiritual ring around the collar.

The rest of that day I spent wandering through cemeteries in depressed half-empty towns with extravagantly beautiful names. I was looking for Prosperine, and I figured I might find her, if only because I surely deserved a break about now. She felt close, or at least I liked to think I could sense, when I gazed on the great, gouged countryside, something of how it had stirred her. After Virginia I drove on to Biwabik, where the Masonovich woman had been arrested with her baby in her arms. Wash blew in the yards of its wood frame houses crowded onto narrow lots. Here and there a TV satellite dish bloomed on a metal stalk like a strange rigid flower. Women stood talking together on street corners, purses dangling from the crooks of their folded arms, their mouths shaping the drawling, fully rounded "o's" heard in this part of the country. From Biwabik I drove to Aurora, where a miner named Greeni had started the '16 strike by walking off his job at the St. James pit. Now the pit was a lake with abrupt, injured edges, a complex of stucco two-story apartment buildings perched at one end.

I must have visited half a dozen cemeteries that afternoon, one or two of them romantically neglected, the rest martial with clipped turf and miniature flags and plastic flowers. Nowhere did I find the name Munkers, and by the time I reached my last planned stop in Eveleth, I had to admit the likelihood that Prosperine's mother would have taken her back to Bemidji for burial, even assuming the circumstances of her death—if possibly not the year—had been much as Grandma had claimed. Ruta's image of her moldering away, at one with the earth of the Range, was poetic but farfetched. With that admission, the sour realities of my own existence, which had stayed blessedly in the background since I left the airport, came back into focus. I continued on to Hibbing, where I planned to spend the night. From there I would drive to the Cities and fly home.

Hibbing, the metropolis of the Range, was full of bars called "lounges" and boasted a main drag of seedy department stores and pawnshops which probably hadn't changed appreciably since Great Aunt Iris's day. As the light grew colder and thinner I followed a series of markers that pointed the way to the city's major tourist attraction, the Hull-Rust Mine. A rough, deserted road led to a parking area flanked by a few coin-operated telescopes and large signs like those deployed in national parks as a gloss on natural wonders. Beyond was a manmade gap in the earth vastly deeper and wider than the other pits I'd seen; in fact, it looked geologic in scale. The terraced walls of this depression were red, with some black and grey layers. Far, far down was standing water. Birches had taken root on ledges halfway to the bottom, and on the slope opposite me a few tiny earth moving machines sat idle. I was gripped by the desolate vista, undeniably beautiful in blatant opposition to environmental precepts. As the sun set I stood looking, suppressing my ingrained Eastern nervousness at being alone near dusk in such a deserted spot.

Just as I was thinking I really ought to leave, a tall figure appeared from behind a little knoll and strode toward me through the dusk. I was ready to get out of there fast when I saw it was a woman in sweat pants, with blunt-cut salt and pepper hair. She flashed me a little smile of acknowledgement, and I knew I'd surprised her, too.

"Some view," I yelled, thinking she might even be a dyke.

"Yeah," she said, "biggest manmade crater this side of the Nevada bomb sites. I come up here to get some space sometimes."

We talked for a few minutes. Her family was Finnish, and had been active in union organizing in the area back in the Thirties. When I mentioned my interest in the 1916 strike, she suggest I visit the research center over in Chisholm; she'd been there to research her own family background, and said they had some unique written records on microfilm, along with early photographs.

The result was that I decided to spend another day on the Range. In the morning I called my school with a complicated story about family business that was keeping me in Minnesota, changed my flight one more time, and headed for Chisholm. It was there, in the small modern building on the lip of an abandoned pit, that I found Prosperine after all.

I spent the morning reading aimlessly. I started with microfilmed documents, copies of the Wobbly-produced strike bulletin with it hyperbolic references to the "Cossacks of Industry" and arch descriptions

230

of miners' wives pelting deputies with "ancient hen fruit." I also looked up some accounts of strike events in established papers like the Hibbing *Mesaba Ore* and even the rabidly pro-capital *Duluth News Tribune*, or "Duluth Spittoon" in the parlance of the strikers.

A librarian in a vest and floppy grey mustache evidently had some affection for my topic, and went out of his way to help me. He kept bringing me file folders full of newspaper clippings and bound masters' theses from twenty years back. Finally I asked to see some photographs. He sent a custodian to the basement, and fifteen minutes later the man returned with several boxes of eight by ten prints, in haphazard order and only sometimes identified as to subject and date by a pencil scrawl on the back.

The majority of the pictures, naturally, served to record the leisure moments and ceremonial occasions of the more fortunate classes of the Iron Range in the early period of its development. A shot of three portly men in buffalo robes was labeled "prominent citizens." There were pigeon-breasted ladies in the absurdly overblown hats of the 1890's, and cocky young men in shirtsleeves lounging against the counters of dry goods stores. There were dozens of pictures of mining company picnics from the late Teens and early Twenties, with spindly-legged kids eating pie and laughing pubescent girls shackled together for the three-legged races. There were shots of the open pits and endless shots of machinery, but one of the few photographs I came across which focused on mine workers was one that had somehow strayed from chronological order. It showed the last shift at the Vermilion workings before they shut down in the early Sixties: a group of grey-haired, thick-bodied men stood beneath a derrick clutching their lunch buckets, eyeing the camera mildly—an understated yet poignant image of extinction.

And then I quite suddenly came to the end of my search, for there on the pile before me stood Prosperine. I caught my breath as though it had been her ghost instead of an enlargement of one of the pictures I'd come across back in August when I looked through the papers at Grandma's. It was the unflattering one that showed her wearing bangs, surrounded by dour children, stars and stripes in the background. Eagerly I flipped it over. "White Lady Visitor at Vermilion Indian School," it said. Then the date, 1921, followed by a question mark.

Of course I tore madly through the rest of the photographs, but found nothing more. "This is all you're going to get," I whispered to myself. My excitement drained away. I was fed up with all this wasteful history, that thrashed and squirmed and struggled and chased its own tail and came out at nothing.

I gathered my things together. I didn't want to see another document, or face the librarian's sympathetic questions. At the last moment I slipped Prosperine inside my jacket. They hadn't heard of scholarly thievery up there, and had no security.

I drove like a bat out of hell for the Twin Cities, but arrived too late to get a flight that night, and ended up sleeping in the airport rather than paying for a room I'd only inhabit for five or six hours. Money was going to be tight, I suddenly remembered, as the facts of my new life pressed in on me again.

The next morning I flew out around seven. For the first time since my arrival in Minnesota, steely grey clouds blanketed the sky. I thought they looked almost like snow, and wished I could taste the air; cocooned in the terminal, I hadn't had the chance. As the checked pattern of the fields and silvery braidings of the river sank out of sight, I found myself mulling over the sermon I'd heard in Virginia, wondering what account of sin would have satisfied me.

My winter in the Hester Street walkup competes with the fall in Plainfield for the distinction of being the time in my life I remember least fondly. I walked around feeling flattened, though unaccountably functional, like one of those hapless characters in the Roadrunner cartoons who's had an encounter with a boulder dropped from a great height. I'd thought that moving to the city would make the transition easier, but discovered I was followed there by memories of Linda, and by all those cruel anticipations which the habit of companionship continues to generate even when the companion is gone. The objects I'd brought from the old life held lurking reminders as well, little time release capsules of pure poison, unpredictably activated. I hadn't realized how much my sense of belonging in the lesbian world had had to do with being in a recognized couple. Now it seemed there was no end to explanations. I kept running into someone who still hadn't heard, and when told was embarrassed and didn't know what to say.

At Thanksgiving I went to Chicago to visit Bonnie, who was newly in love but made an effort to play down her ecstasy out of consideration for me. Of course she didn't fool me for a minute. The week before Christmas, having recently decided that I ought to take advantage of my unattached state, I met a thirty-year-old film student with a nice body and an unnerving lack of affect, whom I discovered on our third date snorting heroin in the john. She assured me she never used needles, but I decided the whole thing was too heavy for me, and went alone to a New Year's Eve party I was pretty sure was safe, only to round a corner and almost stumble across Linda and Valerie making out in a darkened alcove. I was half smashed at the time, but retain an indelible picture

233

of Linda turning to me and baring her teeth in a nervous gesture meant to be a smile, stammering, "Happy New Year" with the traitorous tongue that she'd just removed from her new lover's mouth, and I in a moment of outrage dashing my drink in their faces. I'm told the hostess asked me to leave after that, that she called a cab for me. That's the part I don't remember.

Afterwards, I quit drinking. I didn't say to myself that I was an alcoholic, I didn't join any groups, and in fact it would be months before I'd go into individual therapy. I only told myself I needed to get control of my life, and this seemed like the way to do it. Recently I'd been increasingly uneasy at my sense that I couldn't do without a drink, frightened by occasional memory lapses, but more than anything I think my rage at Linda bolstered my resolve during the first two or three months. I couldn't stand to imagine her going around in the glow of her revolting idyll with Valerie, telling all her friends how sad it was about the shape I was in, subtly implying that any healthy woman would have felt she had to leave me.

I watched a lot of old movies on the VCR that winter, and gained more weight from all the ice cream and cheesecake I ingested. Toward the middle of February, in a further defiant gesture, I decided to start jogging; someday, I reasoned, I was going to start feeling halfway human again, and when it happened I wanted to be in better shape. Accordingly, I spent a few sessions slowly circling some wretched little park several blocks from my apartment, my Walkman headset clamped on underneath a ski mask to distract me from the pain. The result was that an incipient cold turned into a bad flu, and I spent a week in bed.

When I started feeling better and took a look at my accumulated mail, I noticed a package slip dated several days before, with my parents' zip filled in under "zip code of origin." A friend offered to go and pick it up for me, but I told her not to bother. I'd received my Christmas present from them on time, and figured this parcel probably contained nothing more interesting than a pair of fleece-lined gloves or long underwear, the sort of thing my mother occasionally purchases on sale and sends to me when she's heard too many news reports about a cold wave in the East.

In another few days, I was up and around. I struggled the nine icy blocks to my local post office, where the clerk scowled at me from behind

234

bulletproof plastic, then vanished for five minutes. When he reappeared he announced my package had been returned to sender two days previously. "Look at this," he barked, pointing to a scrawled date on the slip I'd handed him, "it says here pickup by the 25th. You been in Bermuda or somewheres?"

"I had pneumonia," I said with dignity. The number looked to me like the 28th, but I knew better than to buck the postal system. Besides, I didn't care much one way or the other about long underwear, if that's what it was; it just pissed me off to have made the trip for nothing.

A week later I got a call from Mother, who was concerned at not having heard from me recently. At the end of the conversation, she asked, "By the way, you got that notebook, didn't you?"

"What notebook?"

"I sent you a package about a month ago."

"Oh, they sent that back. I didn't pick it up on time. What do you mean, a notebook?"

It seemed that when Mother had been in Minnesota in December to help Aunt Geri sort through Grandma's things, she'd come across an item she thought would interest me. It was a small notebook containing a few journal entries that obviously weren't in Grandma's hand, though it had been buried in a box of her old diaries.

"Mother did make some notations at the end, which must be why the notebook ended up where it did. I didn't have time to read through the whole thing, and the part I did confused me, but I had a feeling the person who wrote it might have been that Prosperine you were interested in."

"Did you insure the package?" I demanded, appalled.

"Well, no, I didn't. I did think of it, but I wasn't sure what value to put down."

"That's okay," I said wearily. "It wouldn't be worth much to me anyway without the stuff Grandma burned. But thanks for trying, and let me know if it shows up. It probably will, sooner or later."

Ten days later, it still hadn't. I went down to the post office, waved my package slip around, and threw a fit the likes of which even those hard-boiled public servants probably didn't see more than once or twice a week. I was sure nothing whatever would come of the attempt, but two days later was rewarded by a call from an obviously chagrined postal

235

administrator. It seemed that my package had never left the station. It had been tossed into a mailbag with a few assorted items and left in a broom closet by "a temporary worker who is no longer with us." I could come in to collect it any time before five.

"What's the rush?" I said to myself. "You and Prosperine are finished." But I was out the door already.

I opened the package right there in the post office. The notebook had a flimsy green cardboard cover and yellowing lined pages. Perhaps it had been intended for a stenographer's use. I stood next to the clanking, hissing radiator and read the whole thing, tuning out the doomful mutterings of a homeless man who stood beside me warming himself.


*Chicago 6 Dec.*

*Arrived yesterday 6 a.m., completely fagged out, having sat up all night in the coach from the Cities. I couldn't eat my sandwiches and cake (Rose of course couldn't fathom my lack of appetite so I let her pack me a lunch)—the parcel now sits out on the window ledge and ought to be well frozen by morning, along with a pint of milk I bought and couldn't drink.*

*At least I'll have this nonsense over with soon. Mary scolded me and said I mustn't wait a week longer.*

*I waited in the station for it to get late enough then telephoned Maudie. A surly voice said she'd moved two months ago. Without much hope I went to the address I was given and found her in—not yet dressed in fact. I waited while she got ready and then we went out to a restaurant so we could talk. She looks slightly shopworn, with deepening creases in her plump white neck, but still with that exquisite way of holding her head, with one of her famous little hats way up top defying gravity somehow. Cheap shoes, but everything clean and well pressed, cunning thin gold rings on her little white fingers. She crooked her pinky to drink tea, and laughed when she heard my plight. Said it was nothing and gave me two names. Her flippancy hurt my feelings, I confess. We now treat each other in a superficial, bantering way. I asked about her plans. She claimed she's saving up to take a secretarial course in the spring, but I'm not sure I believe her. Clever as she is, she left school when she was 10. Her spelling is atrocious and she never reads much. Besides, I think*

236

*she would hate taking orders, arriving at work on time and all that sort of thing. I worry about her, if she keeps on like this for another five years or so and begins to lose her looks. I tell myself maybe I'll be in a position to help her someday, though it's hard to see how.*

*She offered me money. Naturally I refused. She did pay for the breakfast—I'd only had tea. I held her hand a moment when we parted, we kissed on the cheek. I doubt I'll see her again, this winter anyway. I'm like a sick old animal that has the instinct to crawl away into its burrow and hide from everybody.*

*Next I had to go around to the printshop where Frank is now working. He's switched jobs so many times since the paper closed down. He waggled his thick eyebrows at me and refrained from asking questions. (I did tell him what I wanted the loan for, in two sentences.) He's much greyer than I remembered from just a year ago, with frightful long hairs like tusks, three or four of them protruding from each nostril, and more purple veins broken on his nose. Poor Frank, he'll never make much of a splash now—no Big Bill Haywood he, nor even a Bill Foster. I actually heard him speak of "defending the workers' state," he'd got hold of some antediluvian flatbed press and was planning to print pamphlets exposing the "American Plan" and the open shop campaigns. . . .I conclude he is tired of defeat (who isn't?) and wants to believe in something, like a confirmed atheist who converts on his deathbed. Odd in Frank though, considering how he used to dismiss the "Bolsheviki boosters."*

*I felt bad asking him, as though I were trading on the past, because I know perfectly well he was in love with me once, though we never spoke of it. But what's worse is thinking I'm taking money away from Mary and the kids—of course I shall pay it back, but I've no idea when or how. He promised to have the sum for me by Thurs. morning, if I'd come by the shop. Mary is not to know.*

*So I dove back into the gale—I just had my small grip with me so I could manage that—and let the wind blow me about the inhospitable pavement till it blew me to the door of this rooming house. It is a place like a thousand others, which is to say hideous. The odd shaped room has green greasy curtains which a thousand greasy sets of fingers have, I imagine, plucked aside to look hopefully into the street—but there's only a narrow alley, a brick wall, and a window framing another desperate face. I have a lumpy sofa-bed, a warped bureau full of dead earwigs,* and an ancient oil stove in one corner on which I am forbidden to cook on pain of being ejected. As though I cared to look at food.

It's snowing "to beat the band," as Maudie would say. Possibly she's saying it right this very minute, with that silvery laugh of hers, to some gentleman with gravy stains on his shirt, in a room a cut above this one on the other side of the Loop. Of course I might have stayed with friends, but families dishearten me when I'm not feeling well. You always end up sleeping with the children, which means being prepared to wake cheerfully at dawn and pretend to enjoy all sorts of silly games. I prefer this mousehole, its chief drawback being that the toilet is about a million miles away down a twisting corridor. I must provide myself with a basin of some sort before the ordeal.

Am I much afraid? I try not to think about it. I've never been a hero about pain. Maude, whose mother used to hold the children's hands to the hot stove sometimes to punish them, says it's just like having a tooth extracted, only in the other place. Mary, when I visited her in the afternoon—without of course mentioning my interview with Frank—says she's never known anybody who died of it. "Direct action at the point of reproduction," she quipped, twisting up her mouth in the wry way she has. I was relieved she didn't ask where I had got the dough! She is sarcastic about Frank's new enthusiasm, still speaks of the "Soviet Onion" as we always used to do. She says now she thinks maybe the Anarchists had the right idea all along. Was very worked up about those Italian fellows, Sacco and somebody, who are being framed in Massachusetts. There is something splendid about her in her ruin—even now you can see how pretty she must have been—with her broken fingernails and scrubbing-brush. I could see she was worn out, and disillusioned with Frank. She hinted she might leave him if it weren't for the children. Was full of desperate money-making schemes.

She asked about Maude, which touched me. Last year before I left Chi. she offered to keep an eye on her for me. But Maudie didn't like her the one time they met—said she reminded her of a settlement house worker—not fair to Mary I thought.

My pantry on the window ledge is fast disappearing under a miniature snowdrift. The room faces north and my teeth are chattering though I'm sitting almost on top of the stove. Underneath it all I suppose I'm furious—why this now, on top of everything else—worse because it's

238

*my own idiotic fault. To be caught like that, like an ignorant country girl, and believe him when he promised to be careful. He seemed harmless I suppose because he was clean, clumsy, young (19 or 20 at the most), toting that Russian phrasebook everywhere. He wanted to go over and "build industry," but was too impatient to finish engineering school first. Mary hooted when I confessed how he wooed me—"Be a pal, Munkers," was his chief persuasive line—and how he murmured* Tovarishch *in my ear.*

*There actually was a week when I thought half seriously of going ahead with it. Other women I admire have done it after all. Though usually it is someone else who ends up rearing the child—in the case of Voltairine de Cleyre, the anarchist, for instance. Likewise with Gurley's boy, who lives in New York while she traipses around the country rabble-rousing. But no, I'm not willing to give in, not yet. Even after so many hopes have been dashed, I tell myself I'm only twenty-six years old. Probably in six months I could get some of my old optimism back, if only I could rest up, scrape together a little money—maybe get out of this wretched U.S.A. for a while.*

*"Wealth is now becoming the standard of success, to an extent perhaps unprecedented in the history of this Republic." So declares a prominent citizen in a newspaper I found on the streetcar this morning. Though perhaps not for the legless or one-armed veterans one still sees all over the streets. Rose, by the way, I thought reeked of the general prosperity and self-satisfaction. It was almost two years since we'd seen one another and she'd changed a good deal. (I am sure she thought the same of me.) She is now so stuck in that family of hers, like a fly in a spider web—not that it troubles her. Impossible to talk of anything without having her turn the conversation back to Eugene's job or Gene, Jr.'s exploits. She keeps the boy dressed up in little suits she sews herself, was eager to put him through his paces and let me see he knew his alphabet already. He had had the whooping cough recently, and though I gathered wasn't in any real danger, she hovered over him, making sure he ate every scrap of meat. We had some trivial dispute, over some remark I made that she thought wasn't proper for his ears. I doubt I have got that sort of mother-stuff in* me!

*I felt quite neutral toward Eugene. Peculiar, isn't it? It seems to me now as though Rose simply wanted to be married—and he was the occasion, like the grain of sand around which an oyster builds up a pearl.*

*Who can hold the grain of sand responsible?*

*She is really almost a complete reactionary. When I was telling about the Range I happened to mention Mrs. Avikainen and how she described the family's loyalty to the cause of labor despite the fact that her husband has been unable to get mine work for the past two and a half years. She said what fighters always say, that they're doing it for the children, they're thinking of the future generations. Rose looked up from her tatting and said quietly, "I would think she would do better to make certain that her children had the chance of a decent education."*

*I had thought I might tell her the truth of my situation, but after an hour in that bourgeois paradise I knew it was impossible. Especially with her stomach poking out so far, as though to emphasize her matronly respectability! When I lay in bed that night thinking back over our months in Chicago, I somehow felt a kind of consolation, as though it had to turn out the way it did in the end. I get the impression she is now quite remote from most of her own family. Not on* bad *terms, exactly, but she complained quite bitterly that Flora said she had a swelled head. I sympathize with Flora. Rose never would struggle down in the common heap with the rest of humanity. Evidently she's cultivating a doctor's wife or two, from whom she laps up little snobbish niceties having to do with entertaining and household decoration. She has her sister Amaryllis living there, helping out. I rather liked the girl, who has spirit—they got into a dispute over some dance tune that Amaryllis kept wanting to play over and over on the victrola, which Rose considered vulgar.*

*I ought to stop scribbling and try to get some sleep, but I'm going to roll a last cigarette before turning in. Tobacco and journal writing are my chief narcotics, like knitting or chewing gum for nice women. Now, tobacco is a common enough habit, if generally frowned on for the ladies. But why should I have this feeling I've somehow made a difference in things, just because I've* written something down? *As though words themselves could somehow hold at bay the forces of death and suffering. I want to write down, for instance, that colored woman I saw today, begging in the snow, wrapped up in a great shawl. She had a little girl by the hand, and as I passed them by she muttered they were hungry. I knew I should give her something, but then I wouldn't have enough carfare—what money I've got has to last till Thursday morning, I had to pay for the room in advance—and so I found myself making up excuses*

240

to justify my stinginess. I even told myself she might be a fraud, because she looked young and fairly healthy. Then I felt completely ashamed and turned back, and gave her twenty-five cents. She said God would bless me. I couldn't look her in the eye.

And suppose the world really can't get better, like a child with pleurisy that coughs too much at night and won't live to grow up? Hellish green curtains, oh how this room disgusts me suddenly, as though it's saturated with the secretions of all the ugliness that's slept here—as though people resolved to live in such squalor on purpose—not the poverty, of course that they can't help, but the absence of any smallest spark of beauty, imagination, hunger for truth....Capitalist papers yapping about a "partnership" between the owners and the workers. In '19 when the steel strike began we actually believed the Revolution was here! Only two years ago—two lifetimes, it seems.

But the Russian peasant has learned to read. Surely that means something, despite all the "tovarishch" nonsense.

8 Dec.

Felt better this morning, was able to eat eggs, and almost laughed at my fears of the other day. Even thought of organizing my notes from my stay on the Range into some sort of article for the rad. press, "Five Years After the Great Strike: The Mesaba Revisited" or something on that order. Not a cheerful story exactly but one that merits telling. Would probably include the stories of the Rukavalas, Mrs. Avikainen etc.; workings of the labor spy system; my visit to the Mine, Mill, and Smelter Workers local in Virginia; facts such as that following the Sept. wage reductions trammers are now getting 30¢ an hour, just about half of what they were getting at the peak of the boom.

And then the Indian School—could I work that in somehow? Probably not, as there really is no connection with the Range labor situation. The somber-looking children sitting quiet in their rows made such an impression on me—when one little boy grinned it was like a thunderclap. I remarked on the absence of laughter at the recess and the teacher said that Indians rarely laugh, but I couldn't help but wonder how they might behave if they were away from us, speaking their own language.

It is so strange, isn't it, how a particular moment feels, a time in a person's life, or the life of a workers' movement? That time always seems indelible, as though it would last or be remembered forever, but *then it passes and you are left unable even to remember what it felt like. Not only the events, those are easier to recall, but the thoughts and feelings that belonged to that time. . . . I thought of this because of something that happened when I went to Frank's office to get the money. He was out and I had to wait for half an hour. In a closet behind his desk he was keeping some things they'd cleared out of the* Stand *office. I found some old numbers of the paper, among them one from 1915 that had the account of Joe Hill's memorial at Thanksgiving time. (Actually this was just before I met Frank.) I hadn't thought about that day in years it seemed, and suddenly I had such a sharp recollection of walking in that crowd, the wreaths of flowers, and people in their thousands weeping openly. I thought the world* must *change after that! And then I was sad because Rose and I quarreled. . . .*

*"You were so* hungry *in those days," Mary said to me. That was just this evening, I'm just back from a meeting she dragged me to, to demand a new trial for the Italian Anarchists. Poor dried up Lucy Parsons was on the platform, ranting away as ever—imagine a life like that, the sublime indelible horror of Haymarket, and then to go on decade after decade shouting yourself hoarse in one cause after another. Still I felt a flash of the old fire. Good to stand at the end and sing with the rest.*

*I did return for* one *moment of weakness to the thought of having the child. Its life would be the end of my life—Mary convinced me of that. And this time tomorrow the thing will be settled. I do feel like a storekeepers's spoiled only daughter, though, stamping my foot and demanding a life of my own—after seeing the plodding grayness of existence on the Range, that goes on year after year for so many—worst of all for the women perhaps. I do so hanker for a change of scenery. If I drudge and save all winter and spring (at what?—heard of a proof-reading job, but the pay is wretched) perhaps I could pay Frank back and just manage the fare to Europe. Is there* any *chance I could survive there on my writing? Must try to form some new connections while in Chicago that could lead to this. It would have to be hack work though, certainly not those delicious experiments I secretly contemplate, and imagine would be "art."*

*Any article on the Range would have to include that bitter, defiant remark made to me by one of the Slovenian miners' wives, the one whose husband was a leader in '16 but now has an unsavory reputation due*

242

to his still having a good job, which clearly indicates an unhealthy degree of closeness to Oliver management—he might very well be a spy himself, the pits are crawling with them. When I asked this woman how she liked the current wages and working conditions, her black eyes were fierce. "I am an Americanist now," she rapped out in her strongly accented English. It was all I could get out of her, and what an eloquent answer!

And Rose, Maudie—old wounds, but they ache still. Am I never to be happy in my sex-feeling?

But for a while yet it must not be a matter of happiness, but simply of putting one foot solidly in front of the other, and so beating a path. Perhaps I will see my way more clearly as I go on. At least I know my own strength, a little.

This was the end of Prosperine's entry. The rest of the page and the succeeding one were blank; then in a darker ink Rose began, without noting the date:

I remember I took the night coach to Chicago, expecting Geraldine, and pretty far along, too. I followed Mrs. Munkers, who had called with the news on her way through, between trains. At first it seemed folly to drop everything and go, especially with Gene, Jr. so recently recovered from an illness, but Eugene urged me to do so, knowing what friends Proppie and I once were. Of course having seen her so recently only increased the shock. I did not know the cause at that time as Mrs. M. on her way through either had not known of it herself or had been unable to bring herself to speak of it. In the end I found out from the landlady in that cheap roominghouse, where the coffin was being kept in a back parlor she had closed off. A vulgar woman I did not like, but I will say this for her, she took charge of the details, though she kept hinting that such a scandal could be the ruin of her business. It was fortunate that she at least was capable, as Mrs. Munkers was completely helpless. Once I arrived I helped out where I could.

A little group of us went to the cemetery. Waldheim, I believe the name was, one of the city's best known. I thought they would have taken the body back to Bemidji, but Mrs. Munkers left all the arrangements to others and I believe the Stuberfields decided on that location. I don't remember who all attended but there was Frank and Mary and a few others

I recognized from the seedy Chicago crowd, including that fellow who always wore a red shirt and black tie and did so even for funerals evidently. I wasn't warm to any of them at first, but Mary who had a kindly disposition drew me aside and we talked a little. I didn't want to hear any more of the sort of thing I'd already gotten an earful of from that talkative landlady, who described coming in and finding her cold in bed, the sheet stiff with blood in the freezing cold room. I remember Mary saying, "She was crazy about you, Rose," and I almost broke down, but took myself in hand. I felt it wouldn't do to weaken in such a situation, especially with Mrs. Munkers requiring so much looking after. (She later had to be put under a doctor's care, and I accompanied her as far as St. Paul, where Mr. M. came down to meet her.)

"Why, Mary?" I asked when I felt a little steadier, and Mary naturally assumed I meant why would she try to get rid of it and said something about some women not being cut out for motherhood, but then she must have seen by my expression I meant why would Proppie of all people have gotten herself into such a fix in the first place? "She was just a woman like any of us," was Mary's explanation, and I found myself thinking of Flora, but Proppie wasn't a Flora after all! Then I thought I might have done something—if only she had told me. "Why, what could you have done?" Mary said, and the strange thought came to me that I could have raised the baby myself, that I would gladly have taken in a dozen extra babies so that Proppie might have lived.

It's all so long ago now, and of course so much has changed that I never imagined at the time. Everything looked promising then. Eugene had just been promoted and we had all sorts of plans. The Crash was years off. Of course I knew very well that Proppie was down on my marrying, but it is difficult even after all this time for me to read this and see how she reacted to our household, how she secretly sneered and judged us and felt superior. And I thought we had a pretty good visit! There were one or two little disagreements of course, but she seemed friendlier to Eugene than on previous occasions, and I was glad she could see how happy we were and how nicely Gene, Jr. was growing. I looked forward to showing her the new baby later on—I think I even mentioned the possibility of my coming down to Chicago to visit her in the summer, just for that purpose. I guess I hoped in time we might get back on something like the old footing—not the same of course, but to where we *could be comfortable and tell each other things, even though our lives were bound to be different.*

*Why should she think poorly of me that I took pleasure in making a comfortable home for my husband and son? Most people would find this an admirable occupation for a woman such as myself, but Proppie never could be like* most people. *There was such a restlessness and bitterness in her, that got worse as she got older it seems to me. I wonder, if she had lived would she have been happy now? I doubt it, reading these thoughts of hers from ten years ago. To insist on associating with persons such as this Maude she writes of, or that young Bolshevist!*

*Too, I don't think she would have been satisfied unless she had done something great, and how is greatness to be achieved by a little Bemidji girl with only a Normal School education? I wonder how well she would have fared in this Great Depression, with the need for thrift and practicality? These days people of modest means can't afford to go globe-trotting, with no thought for the future.*

*There was much about Prosperine I simply could not fathom. Why then I wonder is it that I have never felt so drawn to any other woman friend?*

*It was several weeks ago that we drove up to Bemidji, a few days before our return to St. Paul. We had been staying up on the farm with the folks for three weeks, longer than usual. The hot Aug. weather and Mother's ailments and Flora's "rubbering"—she spends about half her time hanging on the party line eavesdropping on other people's business—were getting on my nerves. Eugene suggested we pack a picnic and take a morning's drive, show the children where I attended Normal School and let them go swimming in Lake Bemidji. I didn't like to spend the gasoline money, but he talked me into it.*

*Naturally the thought occurred to me to look up Mrs. Munkers, though I had had no news of her in several years. The children were awfully cranky in the car and when we got to town Eugene suggested he might take them to the lake if I wanted to pay a call on Mrs. M. And that is what we did, she fortunately being home. She welcomed me and gave me root-beer, though she is now very feeble and seems even less capable of coping with the world than she was when I knew her. Her chin trembles so it is hard not to stare. Her housekeeping at least was always up to snuff, but now I noticed dustballs beneath sofa and piano,*

245

*and the windows were streaked as though they had been washed without being dried properly. Mr. M. passed away several years back and I suspect she would be very poorly off if it it wasn't for son Garrett whose taxi business seems to thrive even in these hard times. Most of her conversation centered around him and Mary Baker Eddy. (It seems she has converted to Christian Science.) She did ask about Eugene, and my parents, and the children—made an impertinent comment about the fact that with Cecilia nearly eight I am "in the family way."*

*I was very surprised when at the end of the visit, she insisted on my taking away with me a large box full of Prosperine's writings! We had spoken of P. very sparingly, and then mostly in connection with the Normal School days, nothing of course about that terrible time in Chicago. She made me follow her into a cluttered back room which I suddenly recognized as the one Proppie and I shared. I had to lift the heavy box for her. On top was this booklet, which she gave me to understand had been found with Proppie's things at the last. "I always meant to read it," she explained, "and once or twice I tried a page or two but I found it so depressing. Christian Science teaches us to think positive thoughts. But somebody ought to have it, and it's not in Garrett's line." Strange woman!*

*Of course once we arrived back home there were so many things to see to, that I have only now had a chance to dip in. The children started back to school on Monday, so now perhaps I can have half an hour each morning and get through it that way. I confess I am curious to see what Proppie wrote about me, in our schoolgirl "sweetheart" days—what funny ideas young girls sometimes get! It was a harmless enough attachment on my part, I am afraid however, she took it too seriously.*

*I thought that reading her old diaries might even inspire me to go back to some form of diary-keeping, or perhaps at least write down some early memories. But now I have gotten started (I began at the end, as I was afraid the thoughts of her death would make me sad, so preferred to have that over with) I feel blue and discouraged. I never remember being so tired out all the time in the eighth month before. I wonder if the baby is going to come early. I have been having trouble with enlarged veins, and some leg and ankle swelling. This heat doesn't help.*

*Must get busy and can tomatoes, I've got several bushels to do today. I wanted to get the slip-cover for the couch finished too, before the baby*

*comes, as afterwards I won't have time for much. The upholstery is
wearing through in places so I almost hate to have people over.*

*I thought of using the name Prosperine if I have another girl, but
Eugene feels that especially combined with Schlaghoffer, it might be too
unusual so we decided*

Grandma's entry broke off in mid-sentence. I closed the notebook
and replaced it in the cardboard box in which my cautious mother had
packed it before taping it up in several layers of heavy brown paper.
Around me rose the low, woeful murmur of New Yorkers attempting to
wrest a service from their public servants. Patrons on line muttered among
themselves at the mysterious delays. Babes in arms wailed and were
ignored or comforted. Tots in strollers whined and got their chubby hands
slapped. A man with a walker laboriously inched his way up to the
window, inquired about the cost of sending a parcel by air mail to the
Dominican Republic, and then was unable to understand the answer, which
the clerk kept shouting at him in English. At last he hobbled dejectedly
away. A mad beautiful brown young woman explained to the indifferent
room how she'd been cheated out of her comp. lit. degree by the registrar
at Columbia—or was it NYU? She declaimed Blake's poem "A Poison
Tree" in a convincing British accent, then uncannily switched gears:
"What do you know, the kind of city we be living in with King Koch
in Gracie Mansion, Bernhard Goetz might be among us right here in
this p.o. You make a false move, use any uppity body language, watch
out, blam, you're dead! *I* might be Bernhard Goetz! *I* might be Eleanor
Bumpurs. . . .What you staring at, Mister?" she added, staring at me.

I zipped my down jacket and fled into the world of snow, no hope
of charity in me but a serviceable fury, a vengeful resolution not to flinch
where *they* had not.

**R**ecently Womanpress, Inc. came through with its long-advertised, much-delayed reissue of Ruta Karlessen's *Mabel Hunneger*, and last weekend I drove out to Ruta's through combed-looking suburban cornfields to attend a combination book party and eighty-fourth birthday celebration organized by the author's friends. It was a Big Event. There must have been several hundred guests. The food and music were homemade, the beer (not that I drank it) dispensed from barrels. The muggy heat didn't seem to faze anyone, and an afternoon tornado watch served as a topic of relaxed conversation among the native Minnesotans. I'll admit that I, who've never quite recovered from *The Wizard of Oz* and family tales of storm cellars, did find myself glancing at the sky with increasing frequency, and it struck me at the time that, given the troubled pattern of Ruta's artistic development, it really wouldn't have been surprising if a natural disaster had descended on her triumph. However, not even a drop of rain marred the festivities, though later that evening I heard on the radio that a small twister had dipped down a few miles to the east in a Dairy Queen parking lot, spewing the contents of several dumpsters over a ten-block radius.

Ruta presided in her best imperial-radical manner. She was wearing a multicolored, flowing cotton tunic and was crowned with a twiggy wreath, doubtless meant to suggest laurel ("Is this my Crown of Thorns?" she quipped), presented by one of her fans. I'd assumed that her pleasure in the occasion wouldn't exactly be diminished by the fact that *Mabel* had just received complimentary if patronizing page five notice in the *Times Book Review*, and when I overheard her, champagne glass in turquoise-ringed hand, denouncing the control of that organ by what she termed "the gauleiters of the bourgeois literary establishment," I knew I'd guessed right. Of course most of the variegated crew of guests were non-literary locals, unaware of this development and its potential significance for the author's reputation—nor had they seen the sensitive *Nation* piece, nor the *Library Journal* rave. For them, Ruta was a success because they'd made her one, and required no validation beyond the fact that the *Pioneer Press* had sent a reporter and photographer to cover the party for the women's page.

Bonnie was visiting from Chicago that weekend, and came along with me. We stopped at the Hill to pick up Phoebe and Arnie Luckenbill. (Phoebe debated keeping her last name when they married, but decided, as she said, to "go all the way.") I'm now renting the St. Croix cabin for the third summer in a row, and I make a point of seeing them regularly. Or rather, it's Phoebe I make a point of seeing; it's just that ever since the Luckenbills moved into one of the highly coveted room-and-a-half suites which the Hill reserves for married couples, they've been hard to pry apart, so I put up with Arnie, who makes it difficult for his wife and her friends to get a word in edgewise.

Not that Phoebe could be said to be under his thumb. For instance, she continues her visits to the crafts room, and he's taken up yoga in order to have something to keep him busy in her absence. Recently I arrived at their room unannounced to find the door wide open and Arnie trying to stand on his head. She's satisfied that he's becoming more religious (her fond interpretation of the fact that he now attends church with her every so often), and the consensus among her peers, completely unironic, is that he "treats her like a Queen." The wedded state itself, being rare, confers a certain aura of distinction at the Hill, but the two of them enjoy added fame as the only current residents who actually tied the knot on the premises, and as such they figure prominently in newsletters and the glossy brochures sent out by Dr. Jerebold's office. All in all, Phoebe seems to relish the mild, late limelight, and I'm glad for her and glad that Grandma can't hear her call her spouse "Lucky."

Everyone got along very well in the car. Arnie sat in the back with Bonnie, who's only slightly toned down from her recent punk pitch, and they talked about baseball the whole way, which gave Phoebe a chance to fill me in on all the latest Hill news. When we drove up in front of Ruta's place—the pink trailer is now camouflaged, its front eclipsed by a neat brown wooden addition and screened porch which extend the living area—I noticed that something seemed to be missing. For a moment I couldn't think what it could be. Then, on the new-mown grass, beyond several rows of parked cars, I spotted the prone corpse of Ruta's she-elm, festooned like a felled Maypole with streamers and cut flowers. "Farout!" I exclaimed, "hand it to Evelyn!"

Evelyn is Ruta's new "friend." She's in her late sixties, wears ankle socks and a shoulder-length grey pageboy and cotton blouses with little round collars and peace symbol earrings. She's an old organizer, and highly organized. The first time I visited over there after she moved in, I was stunned by the household's unprecedented neatness. Since then she's persuaded her partner to give up most of the dog breeding business so she can concentrate on writing. She planned and supervised construction on the addition to the trailer, which involves a new study and three walls of floor-to-ceiling shelves to store Ruta's lifetime of notebooks.

At first I thought that the target of all these abrupt improvements might miss her old chaos, but she shows no signs of it. She's hard at work on the "Spanish" book, *Did We Count?*, for which she has a contract with a Bay Area radical press.

"I'm doing another draft," she explains, "trying to weave in the silences."

I've been summoned to her side quite often in recent weeks to explain the ins and outs of the word processing program she's using on the computer Evelyn got her to buy. Bonnie teases me that I've fallen into her orbit, but to me it feels like a version of friendship. At least we gesture at one another, across the generations.

Silence came up once again as the focus of Ruta's remarks at the birthday/book party. These she delivered sometime before the cake was cut and after the elm-tree-laying-to-rest-ceremony, in which twenty or thirty people sat in a semicircle around the felled tree, humming and swaying and visualizing its spirit enjoying a safe journey to wherever tree spirits go when their bodies are made into cord wood. There was an interlude of Nordic blues guitar, and then Roxanne Wingate, who's in women's studies at the University of Minnesota, got up and introduced Ruta. She first summarized the plot of *Mabel Hunneger* for those who hadn't read it, situating it in the context of Ruta's lifetime of courageous struggle for social justice. Ruta, she said, alongside such novelists as

Harriet Arnow, Tillie Olsen, Ann Petry, and Jo Sinclair, had pioneered in breaking silences about American working women.

Assisted to her feet by two young friends, Ruta quelled the cheering and stamping that greeted her. "Hmmmph," she grumbled, "nice work if you can get it—breaking silences. A darn sight easier than breaking prairie sod at any rate. I'm interested now in *mending* silences." Completely ignoring the novel, she launched into a wordy, opaque explanation of her theories regarding the relationship between the Life Force, silence, and what she termed "the horizontal qualities of female narrative," contrasted with "the vertical male."

"Say what?" whispered Bonnie in my ear. "I thought you told me she was writing about the Spanish Civil War."

"Picky, picky, picky," I whispered back. "Can't take you deconstructionists anywhere."

"I'm afraid that went right over my head," Phoebe appealed at my elbow when Ruta had sat down, besieged by well-wishers, many of them with the novel in hand. Evelyn, armed with a cash box and sporting a large button emblazoned MAKE MINE MABEL, was on duty behind a table on which copies were arrayed in an elaborate pyramid.

"My head, too," I answered. "I guess, though, she's trying to remind us that some experiences just have to be accepted on a nonverbal level."

"Taken on faith." Phoebe nodded approvingly.

"Or are just too tragic and profound, or maybe too intensely happy in some cases, to be put into words."

"Still, I thought the whole point of writing *was* to put things into words." She's shown a lot of interest in books and their uses lately. Aunt Geri and I have just finished editing a short manuscript of Grandma's which we're going to have printed, and Phoebe served as our consultant, explaining obscure references to farm procedures and old-fashioned technology. In an unguarded moment I mentioned to her that I might begin work on a book of my own, and now she asks about it every time I see her. I don't know whether it's the extraordinary level of literary activity to which she's been exposed or her satisfaction with married life, but something has overcome her old objections to trying her hand at the memoir business, and she tells me she now devotes an hour each morning to the years 1923-1927, though she hasn't yet revealed, and I haven't inquired, why she's singled that period out. She's even been talking about starting a writing workshop at the Hill, which she'd like me to teach for the remainder of the summer.

"Well, why don't you ask Ruta what she meant?" I prodded now.

"I hate to bother her. Just look at that throng!" But I knew Phoebe was dying to approach her heroine. Any time the two of them have met, she's been all agog for hours. Grandma, brooding on the advances of the noxious Luckenbill, had once complained to me that her friend was an "impressionable woman," and there's no doubt that in this case she's been highly impressed. "Ruta Karlessen makes me feel. . .she makes me feel. . .she makes me feel *tingly* all over," she confesses to me, fluttering her hands in an effort to convey the irresistible sensation. "That woman Evelyn is fortunate, don't you think? To share a home with her, and all?"

I suggested that we go sit in the shade and wait for the autograph seekers to thin out. I hoped we'd lose Arnie for a while, he having wandered off a few yards to reminisce about his experiences in the field of pesticide sales with a bald, dumpy fellow in jeans and a western shirt who'd been introduced to me earlier as Ruta's son Harry. I also preferred to move away from Sharon Decoteaux, who was standing behind us with a group of lesbians, several of whom I recognized. I'd seen her around Minneapolis a few times since our disastrous encounter at Grandma's reading two summers ago; once I realized she was a dyke, I knew that the discomfort of these chance meetings was something I might as well get used to. Lately she'd been working occasional evenings at the women's coffeehouse, where I'd gotten into the habit of going once or twice a week. (They've liberalized their no-chem policy, and now serve coffee and good desserts; I've also discovered that the clientele is quite a bit more varied than it seemed on my first visit.) I always said hello, and she acknowledged me, but I was in the uneasy position of being unsure whether she actually remembered how we'd met. Worse, I hypersensitively suspected that she remembered perfectly, and resented even the trivial interaction which required us to smile at one another when she handed me my change.

Phoebe and I found chairs in the shade, and after a comfortable period of leisurely conversation, never possible when Arnie's around, Ruta herself came strolling over, leaning on Bonnie's arm. They were drinking champagne, and Bonnie held the bottle as well as a shallow, long-stemmed glass.

"Let me sit down here with you folks and quit being famous-for-fifteen-minutes for fifteen minutes," Ruta grumbled charmingly, skillfully implying our inclusion in her circle of true intimates.

Phoebe had naturally forgotten all about literary theory by this time, but they discussed methods for keeping deer and gophers out of the garden, and that suited her just as well. I congratulated Ruta on the wonderful reception *Mabel* had had so far. I was thinking of the reviews, but Phoebe assumed I meant the party. "We'll have to have a lovely one like this when *your* book comes out," she exclaimed, squeezing my hand. "Lord willing, I'd be pleased to make a cake for it. You know I took that cake decorating class a while back and we learned all sorts of flowers and fancy scripts and things."

"What's this, what's this?" Ruta pounced, theatrical. I thought she'd had a lot of champagne, though with her it's sometimes hard to tell. "That's marvelous, Dale, you're working on a book? And *I* haven't heard of it?"

I felt annoyed. I'd wanted to be clearer in my own mind about what I hoped to do before talking to her or anyone else who, unlike Phoebe, would see just how hazy I still was on the crucial technical details. Now I had to explain that I'd been considering writing a book based on, or at any rate inspired by, the Prosperine material. I didn't think it would be fiction, but neither did I want to make it simply a conventional or documentary history. I wanted to express as a many-sided whole a number of parts that I knew were connected at the root, intrinsically juxtaposed in some older, more fundamental relation than that either of cause and effect or of chronology. The Wobblies would be at the center of it, their brash, doomed, muscular vision of One Big Union viewed from a woman's skeptical perspective. And the Sioux rising of 1862, a bloody shout from the wastes of history. And the miners' wives who'd pushed their baby buggies over the rutted roads of the Mesabi Range to call their men out after Joe Greeni's pay envelope came up short one payday too often. And Mrs. Masonovich, and Prosperine, and Grandma—Grandma belonged there too, in the essence of the thing, in spirit if not in literal detail.

"Maybe it'll be a sort of poetic history," I said. "That's what I hope, anyway. But then again, maybe that won't work and I'll end up doing a more conventional history of, say, women in the IWW, or women's organizing on the Range. Or maybe I'll come across some terrific primary sources, and what I do will be shaped by that. I'm not going to be sure

253

for quite a while yet. I need to spend some time on the Range, immerse myself in the materials up there, and probably do more research here and in Chicago as well."

Ruta said warmly that nowhere near enough had been written on the people's history of the Range, and of course she'd help in any way she could. I realized I should have known I'd have nothing to fear from someone of her expansive temperament, in her triumphal mood especially. Bonnie looked surprised, but didn't object. She's pretty much given up on saving my professional soul; besides, I think she's become slightly disaffected with academia herself recently, and occasionally observes that now that she's got tenure and is publishing regularly, she still isn't having more or better orgasms than when she was in grad school.

Loyally, she began thinking out loud about where I might apply for grants—though, as she said, it would be a "soft" proposal.

"That's okay," I told her. "I really don't want to get fancy about this. I just want to be free to fool around and see what I come up with and not have a funding source breathing down my neck. I *do* have a job, remember?"

Too late, I realized this sounded both sharp and defensive. I'm teaching at Borough of Manhattan Community College, not Bonnie's idea of appropriate work for me, but I'm actually getting a fair amount out of it. My students are single mothers who've been through drug rehab programs, pert teenagers with their names spelled out in gold around their necks and pink bows across their swelling bellies whose husbands are doing time in upstate prisons, youths with zigzag patterns grooved into their close-cropped hair, cynical and full of shifty hope, looking to computers to deliver them from the Bronx. I plan to stay there for as long as I have the energy and can make the money stretch. I might want to leave New York at some point—I've even thought of moving to Minnesota—but I'm not ready yet, for a variety of reasons.

"It *is* a shame about your losing those papers, the ones the Munkers woman left," Ruta observed—too offhandedly, I felt. Of course she didn't know what a harsh ache of loss still assailed me when she said it.

I only nodded.

"Did you ever figure out why your grandmother burned them?"

I felt that possibly this was a conversation we shouldn't be having in front of Phoebe, but when I glanced at her she looked her usual serene

254

self, sitting there with her stubby hands laced in her flowered lap and her legs so short that her feet barely touched the ground. I shook my head. "No more than I ever did, really. I've told you what I discovered about how Prosperine died, in that diary Mother sent me, and I guess you could think that has something to do with it. But I'm not sure it was anything so cut and dried, though maybe that's what prompted her to make up a whole different ending for Prosperine's life the way she did—I mean unconsciously, of course, because clearly she believed in it herself. Then there was the nature of their relationship. . . ." I was aware of speaking rapidly, in a kind of code, over Phoebe's head. "The strange thing is, I believe she accepted *me* in a way. Accepted my lifestyle. Anyway, that's how I choose to interpret the fact that she gave me the locket with Prosperine's picture."

With Grandma as with Linda, I've been over and over all the factors that could have made things go wrong, and keep coming back to alternative interpretations, new levels of motive, the difficulty of identifying a clear causal sequence. The ambiguities never save me from wondering: is there something I might have done differently, and averted disaster?

I wish I had been kinder to Grandma, gentler, less greedy. But that's a separate issue. I'm not convinced it would have saved the papers.

"Well, *I've* thought about this," Phoebe announced. "I believe Rose did what she did out of duty." We stared at her, surprised, as though she were a youngster who hadn't been expected to volunteer her own opinion. I'd only discussed the fate of the papers with her once, very briefly, at a point when my feelings were still too raw for me to want to go into detail. She'd known about what happened from Aunt Geri, and said she thought it was too bad, but hadn't suggested any insights into Grandma's motivation.

"Duty? To whom?"

"Well, not anyone, exactly. I only mean it was what she thought she ought to do."

"How do you know?"

"She told me so herself."

"You mean she actually *spoke* to you about burning the—?"

"No, not exactly. She didn't confide in me. But when I heard later what had happened, I remembered that afternoon when she'd gone over to your aunt's, just before she went into the hospital. I ran into her in

255

the hall, just when she was coming back. She was all bundled up, and seemed in a big hurry. I didn't like the looks of her, with her hair coming down and a smudge on her nose, and I asked her if she was feeling all right. She said, 'I've done my duty. I'm going in to rest.' I thought something was wrong, but I never did like to cross her when she spoke in that tone. I thought I'd just go over and check on her later.

"And then she turned to me, and I remember how she used a different voice, quiet and sad, and it made me shiver, because I wasn't even sure she knew it was me she was talking to. 'Why is it so *hard* to do my duty?' That's what she said."

I was touched, yet simultaneously tasted the old resentment. "But who *said* it was her duty? It's surely nothing to do with what Prosperine would have—"

Phoebe put up her hand to stem the flow of my rebellious reasoning. "Rose had a very strong sense of how things ought to be. In our day we were raised with the idea that certain parts of life ought to remain private. This is how it was.

"I couldn't tell you it was good or bad. I've never been able to keep up such high standards, myself. I guess that's why I've leaned on the Lord so much. I'm sure there were times when Rose herself would have liked to take an easier path, to bend a little and please others, but she had too much character. This is what people admired, you see. In *her* mind it was right, and that's what she followed."

"It seems you boast a quite remarkable lineage, Dale," Ruta remarked with a hint of irony that helped me to endure Phoebe's endless tolerance, as well as the reappearance of her husband in our midst. Arnie plunged like a friendly Labrador pup into the cold waters of a conversation in which he was out of his depth. Ruta, however, didn't hesitate to put him in his place when she thought he'd talked enough, and he soon persuaded Phoebe to accompany him to the refreshment tables, saying he needed her advice on what he could digest easily.

Bonnie and Ruta and I settled down to literary shoptalk, but to my dismay Ruta almost immediately spotted someone she thought I ought to meet.

"Dale McNab—Sharon Decoteaux. And this is Bonnie Schaefer. Sharon, Dale's just told me her new book is going to be dealing with some Native American themes, the Sioux rising and so on."

256

"Hi," said Sharon with a quick, tiny smile. "Actually, Dale and I sort of know each other."

I could only gulp and nod, wanting to wring Ruta's neck, frantic to correct the record somehow. Why, she'd made it sound as though my only subject was the very topic Sharon herself had introduced me to. Who could blame her if she thought me an incorrigible opportunist? But of course there was nothing I could say that wouldn't make matters worse, so there I sat, a miserable prisoner, while the two of them discussed a poetry reading that Sharon would be giving at a local arts center. She looked very cool and poised in a white linen shirt, with twists of silver in her ears and her dark hair cut short and feathery over the clean curve of her skull, tapering to a thin braid down her back.

Bonnie interrupted to pour Ruta more champagne; the bottle, she said, ought to be finished before it went completely flat. Ruta offered some to Sharon and me. We both refused, but she wouldn't let it rest.

"You know I don't drink anymore, Ruta," I had to remind her. Of course I'd told her that already on more than one occasion, but for some reason she never remembered, and frequently offered me beer or wine.

"But this is my *party*!" she insisted now, grinning like a jack-o'-lantern and waving the bottle over my glass, which had held Diet Pepsi. "This is champagne! Champagne in Minnesota! We're drinking to the Life Force!"

Her tipsy clowning exasperated me. "What's it to you?" I snapped. "You know, I sometimes wonder about people who can't enjoy themselves without insisting that everyone around them has to have a drink. What are you trying to prove?"

Ruta looked offended, but said no more. Half regretting my outburst, I excused myself to go to the bathroom. Later, when I was coming back from a stroll I'd taken out behind the vegetable garden to get away from the crowds for a while, Sharon came up to me and told me she'd appreciated my directness. "Maybe I should've just told her I'm in recovery, but I always feel like I just shouldn't have to do that, you know."

We got to talking. She told me about her lesbian AA group, and I explained that I'd never been to an AA meeting, that only recently, in a therapy group, had I felt ready to start exploring issues related to my drinking.

"Is that because you don't like the twelve step approach?"

257

"I mean, not exactly. I know it works, and I can't argue with that. I've just always been put off by the way some people seem to center their whole lives around dealing with addiction. I'd probably feel differently if I hadn't been lucky enough to quit when I did, before it got worse."

I was afraid she'd be offended, but she only said she knew what I meant ("there's always 'Born Agains' in any group"), but that in her experience it didn't have to be like that; you could get out of it pretty much what you wanted.

It was a short conversation, slightly awkward in places—once or twice I felt that I was trying too hard, and wondered if it showed—but when it was over I went away relieved, amazed that I'd allowed my guilt to complicate things so unnecessarily. I promised to come to her poetry reading, and she actually looked pleased.

Ruta apologized when she hugged me goodbye. Uncharacteristically, she blamed her forgetfulness about my having stopped drinking on her age, and though I was skeptical I didn't call her on it. "Now you be sure and bring your friend out to see Evelyn and me while she's here," she insisted. I promised I would, amused that now that Ruta has gotten all cozily coupled, she seems so anxious to marry off the rest of the world.

Drora's coming to visit in two weeks. She's a year older than I am, an economist, grew up on another continent, in a country where her parents settled as adults and never really learned the language. It's a place where they shave the top off a stick of butter or margarine, instead of slicing from the end, so that these days when I plumb the depths of my Manhattan refrigerator, I sometimes fail to recognize the peculiar, concave oblong that inhabits my butter dish. "You're so *American*," she complains frequently, an affectionate insult. She has residency problems, jokes that if I were a man she'd marry me tomorrow for her green card. We've been seeing each other for the past six months. We seem so separate sometimes, it unnerves me to think we're both women, and I have to make love with her again to know we inhabit the same planet. I feel joy with Drora, too, unpredictably: a sharp, scary jolt of happiness that at first I had trouble even recognizing, because I haven't felt it too often in my life before this.

Unavoidably, I still compare a lot, poking and probing my days to try to figure out how they're different from when I was with Linda. I think the biggest difference is that now my existence seems to lack a plan. Before there always was one, or at least I thought there was. My course was plotted weeks and years ahead. This way I feel freer, of course, but raw and wrong sometimes, ashamed to be unanchored at my age, wishing I had something to take cover behind—a drink or a career, if not a family.

The last time I saw Linda must have been eight or ten months ago at some sort of party. We chatted correctly for five minutes, and I left feeling dully angry, wondering why I'd bothered to be polite. Much more recently, just before I left town for the summer, I ran into Fiona in the Village. It was an eerie sensation to bump into her like that, as though a land mine of memory had detonated on a street full of strangers. We came face to face as she emerged from Barnes & Noble, so suddenly that there was no chance to avoid one another, presuming we'd wanted to. She was tall and tanned, wore very little makeup. She explained that she'd be going to U.C. Berkeley in the fall, and thought the freer atmosphere would suit her much better than "the Ivies." She asked what I was doing in a friendly, well-bred way, just as though I'd been some casual family friend and not her mother's ex-lover, someone who used to take her to the planetarium. She mentioned she'd be working in Boston for the summer; she'd been living up there with her father during the year, and was just down in Jersey for a visit. Though I'd seen Linda's photograph in *Publishers Weekly* in connection with some big contract, and had heard through the grapevine that she and Valerie had split up, this piece of news was completely new to me, and I tasted a moment of mean pleasure before the sadness set in.

Maybe I wanted to hear that Linda's efforts at conventional motherhood had been disappointed partly because it's so easy for me to feel that everyone but me knows how to live. The unmarked young surround me, woven bracelets on their wrists. Birth announcements reach me at frequent intervals. People are buying brownstones and co-ops, sinking their time and money into houses in the country. Even dykes are going in for formal marriages, called "commitment ceremonies." While I feather a nest of friends against the cold, while I dicker with switchblade joy.

In New York I'm busy; I don't think so much. But out at the cabin I have the time I need and sometimes fear. I feel as though I'm detoxifying from all those frantic years back East, unjamming the radio waves of my consciousness, mining my loneliness. Deep down I angle toward an impersonal bedrock core where a world of solitudes might join.

I keep mulling over this idea for a book, turning it around to catch the light from different angles, wondering how I'll manage to express what I see in the eyes of Prosperine and the Vermilion School students, who look steadily at me from out of the photograph that I hang above my desk everywhere I go. "We're so American," I say to them. Sometimes in the clear evening stillness, when birds swoop and dart all along the river bank, I feel an irremediable kinship with the dead, the lost of this continent. Then silence is an ocean, many-layered. Meanings swim up in it.